About the Author

Christine Merrill wanted to be a writer for as long as she c__ __mber. During a stint as a stay-at-home-mother, __ __ed it was time to 'write that book.' She could se__ __own hours and would never have to wear tights t__ __k! It was a slow start but she slogged onward and se__ __ years later, she got the thrill of seeing her first book h__ __e bookstores. Christine lives in Wisconsin with her __ly. Visit her website at: www.christine-merrill.com

Regency Scandals

Regency Scandal:

Dangerous Games

CHRISTINE MERRILL

MILLS & BOON

First Published in Great Britain 2020
By Mills & Boon, an imprint of HarperCollins*Publishers*
1 London Bridge Street, London, SE1 9GF

REGENCY SCANDAL: DANGEROUS GAMES
© 2020 Harlequin Books S.A.

Miss Winthorpe's Elopement © 2008 Christine Merrill
The Wedding Game © 2017 Christine Merrill

ISBN: 978-0-263-28214-6

MISS WINTHORPE'S ELOPEMENT

To Sean:
For doing his homework on the Greek classics.
Without you, honey, I'd have to do all my
own research.

Chapter One

In the quiet of the library, Penelope Winthorpe heard the front doorbell ring, and set her book carefully aside, pushing her glasses up the bridge of her nose. She smoothed her sensible, bombazine skirt. Then she stood and strolled toward the front hall.

There was no reason to rush since hurrying would not change the results of the trip. Her brother had accused her of being too prone to impulsive actions. Seeing her hare down the hall every time the front door opened would reinforce his view that too much education and too much solitude were affecting her nerves.

But her package was two days late, and it was difficult to contain her anticipation. She rose eagerly with every knock at the door, hoping each one to be the delivery she'd been expecting.

In her mind, she was already holding the package, hearing the rustle of crisp, brown paper, running her fingers along the string that held it in place. She would cut the twine with the scissors on the hall table, and the book would be in her hands at last. She imagined she could smell the fresh ink and the paper, caress the leather of the binding, and feel the gold-embossed title under her fingertips.

And then, the best part: she would take it back to the library and cut the pages open, spread them carefully, turning each one and catching glimpses of words without really reading, not wanting to spoil the surprise, even though she knew the story, almost by heart.

At last, she would ring for tea, settle into her favourite chair by the fire, and begin to read.

It would be heaven.

When she got to the hall, her brother was sorting through a stack of letters. The post had come, but there was no sign of a package from the book seller.

'Hector, did a delivery arrive for me? I had expected it by now, but I thought perhaps it might come with the post.'

'Another book?' He sighed.

'Yes. The latest printing of *The Odyssey*.'

Her brother waved a dismissive hand. 'It came yesterday. I sent it back to the shop.'

'You did what?' She stared at him, incredulous.

'Sent it back. You already have it. I did not deem it necessary.'

'I have translations,' she corrected. 'This was in the original Greek.'

'All the more reason to send it back. I dare say the translations will be much easier for you to read.'

She took a deep breath and tried counting to ten

before speaking, to control her rash tongue. She made it almost to five before blurting, 'I do not expect to have trouble with the Greek. I read it fluently. As a matter of fact, I am planning a translation of my own. And, since I cannot translate words that are already in English, the new book will most certainly be necessary.'

Hector was looking at her as though she had sprouted a second head. 'There are many adequate translations of Homer already available.'

'But none by a woman,' she responded. 'I suspect that there are insights and subtleties I might bring to the material that will be substantially different than those already available.'

'Inferior, perhaps,' countered her brother. 'The world is not clamouring for your opinion, Penny, in case you haven't noticed.'

For a moment, the truth of that statement weighed heavy on her, but she shook it off. 'Perhaps it is because they have not yet seen what I can accomplish. I will not know until I have tried. And for that, I will need the book I ordered. Which only cost a few pounds.'

'But think of the time you would spend wasted in reading.' Hector always considered such time wasted. She remembered his discomfort in the schoolroom, and his desire to escape from it as soon as possible, when their father was ready to leave the business in his hands. That a printer had such a low opinion of books never ceased to amaze her.

'For some of us, Hector, reading is not a waste of time, but one of life's great pleasures.'

'Life is not meant to be spent in pleasure, Penelope.

I am sure, if you put your mind to it, that you can find a better way to use your time.' He looked her up and down. 'While you needn't be so frivolous as some young girls who are hellbent on matrimony, you could devote your time to higher pursuits. Helping with the poor, or the sick, perhaps.'

Penelope gnashed her teeth and set to counting. It was not that she had a distaste for charity work. It was certainly necessary. But it only showed how awkward she was around people, both rich and poor. And it served as a continual reminder to all that she was properly on the shelf, with no hope of a husband or children of her own to tend to. It felt like giving up.

Although, perhaps it was time.

And yet, she reminded herself, if she meant to give up, she could do it just as successfully at home, in front of the fire, alone except for her Homer.

This time, she made it to eight before speaking. 'It is not as though I do not wish to contribute to society,' she argued. 'But I think that what I can do for the scholarly community is just as valuable as what I might accomplish tending the ill. And I do make regular donations to the church. The help that does not come by my hand can come from my purse instead. There have been no complaints.'

Her brother glared in disapproval. 'I believe there are complaints, Penelope, although you may think that it is possible to ignore them, since they come from me. But Father has left me in charge of you and your inheritance, and so you must listen to them.'

'Until such time as I marry,' she added.

He sighed. 'We both know the unlikelihood of that, Penny. I think it is time that we accept it.'

We meant *her*, she supposed.

'It is one thing to be a bluestocking for a time. But I had hoped that you would have put such nonsense behind you by now. I do not expect you to spend your whole day at the dressmakers, or in idle gossip. But to spend no time at all on your appearance and to fill your head with opinions? And now, Greek?' He shook his own head sadly. 'Someone must put a stop to this nonsense, if you will not. No more books, Penny. At least not until you can prove to me that you are ready to grow up and accept some responsibility.'

'No books?' She felt the air leaving the room. She supposed it was as some girls might feel if their strict older brothers had said, 'No gowns. No parties. No friends.' To be denied her books was to be left companionless and unprotected in a hostile world. 'You cannot speak to me thus.'

'I believe I can.'

'Father would never have allowed it.'

'Father expected you to have started a family by now. That is why he tied your inheritance to the condition of your marriage. You have not yet found a husband. And so control of you and your money belongs to me. I will not see you fritter away the fortune that Father left to you on paper and ink.'

'A few books are hardly likely to fritter away a fortune, Hector.'

'Only a few?' He pointed to the stack on the table next to the door. 'Here are "a few books", Penny. But there are more in the dining room, and the morning room and the parlour. And your room as well, I dare say. The library is full to overflowing.'

'As it was when Father was alive, Hector. He was a man of letters. What I have added to the collection hardly amounts—'

'What you have added to the collection is hardly necessary. There are books enough to last a lifetime already in your possession.'

Perhaps if she read as slowly as her brother did… But she held her tongue and began to count again.

'And now you are buying books that you already own. It must stop, Penny. It really must. If we are to share this house in peace, I will have no more of it.'

She lost count and her temper failed her. 'Then I do not wish to live with you a moment longer.'

'I fail to see what choice you have.'

'I will marry. Someone more agreeable than you. He will be sensible and understanding, and will not begrudge me a few pounds a month for my studies.'

Hector was looking at her with pity again, but his tone was sarcastic. 'And where will you find such a paragon, dear sister? Have you forgotten the disaster of your come-out Season? Even knowing of the substantial fortune attached to it, once you opened your mouth, no one would have you. None of them was good enough for you. You are too opinionated by half. Men want a woman who will follow where they lead, not one who questions her husband's wisdom and ignores the house and the servants because she is too busy reading.'

It had been four years, and the sting of embarrassment still rose to the surface at the mention of the utter failure that had been her Season. 'But surely there is a man who wishes an intelligent wife. Someone with whom he can converse.'

Hector sniffed in disapproval. 'At such time as you find him, you are welcome to marry. But I do not see you in pursuit of such a man, nor is he in pursuit of you. Since you show no inclination to leave your desk, unless he comes stumbling into the house by mistake, it is unlikely he will find you. And thus, I am left to make your decisions for you.

'I will not push you into society, for we both know that would be hopeless. But neither will I encourage you to further education, since what you have gathered so far has caused you nothing but trouble. Good day, sister. I suggest you find something to occupy your hands, and you will see no need to busy your mind.' And he went back to reading his mail.

She was dismissed. *One, two, three…* She retreated to the stairs before she could say something that would further solidify her brother's opinions.

He was right in one thing, at least. He was entitled to make monetary decisions for her, until she could find another man to take the responsibility from him.

Not that she needed any man to do so. She was quite smart enough on her own. Smarter, she suspected, than her brother was. His hand with the family business showed none of the mastery that her father had had.

Her father loved the books he printed and bound, loved everything about the papers, the inks, and the bindings. He turned the printing of even the simplest invitation or calling card into a statement of art. And to her father, a finished volume was a masterwork.

Four, five, six… To her brother, it would never be more than profit and loss. And so, there was more loss than profit. Given a lifetime, Penny expected to see her own part in the inheritance disappear, pound by pound, to cover the shortages that would occur from his mismanagement.

Of course, it was her mention of the fact at dinner the evening before that had caused her brother's sudden interest in bringing her to heel.

Seven, eight, nine… It was unbearable. She could not live out the rest of her life under Hector's thumb, sneaking books into the house on the sly and hoping that he did not notice. To live by his rules would be impossible.

Ten.

Which left her one choice in the matter: she must marry. Even the thought of her brother's edict and the lack of books made her throat tighten in panic.

She must marry quickly.

She walked to the corner of the room and tugged the bell pull three sharp times, then turned to her wardrobe for a valise, tossing in travelling clothes from the collection of half-mourning that she had never quite managed to leave behind, although her father had been gone for two years.

In a few moments, there was a discreet knock upon the door.

'Come in, Jem.'

The senior footman looked uncomfortable, as he always did when summoned to her rooms. He had often expressed a wish that she would find a ladies' maid, or some other confidant. She had reminded him that she would do so at such time as she needed her hair dressed or a ribbon ironed. But if she needed wise counsel, she would always call upon him.

'Miss?' He stood uneasily at the door, sensing a change in the air.

'I need you to hire a carriage and prepare for travel.'

'You are going out, miss?'

She gave him a fish eye. 'I would not need a carriage, else.'

'Are we going to the book seller's, miss?' He had overheard the conversation in the hall, she suspected. And balked at doing something in direct opposition to her brother's wishes.

'No, Jem. I am not permitted to do so.'

He sagged with relief.

'So I mean to limit myself to something my brother cannot possibly object to, since he has given me permission. He wishes me to be behave as other young ladies do.'

'Very good, Miss Penny.'

'And so we are going to go and find me a husband.'

'Lost with all hands…' Adam Felkirk, Seventh Duke of Bellston, stared at the paper in front of him and watched it shake with the trembling of his hands. He tried to remind himself that the loss of almost one hundred lives far outweighed the loss of the cargo. Had the wives and families of the ship's crew been in some way prepared for the possibility of this tragedy? Perhaps. But he had certainly been foolishly unready for the fact that his investment was a risky one.

A shipment of tobacco from the Americas had seemed like a sensible plan when he had put down the money for it. The spring lambing had not gone well, and his tenants' crops were not likely to thrive in the dry weather they had been having. But tobacco was almost guaranteed to bring in more money. It was a valuable commodity, if one could pay to have it brought to England. He could sell it for a healthy profit, and the money would tide him through this year and the next.

And now, the ship was sunk, and he was ruined.

He could not help but feel that it was his own fault. God was punishing him for the mistakes of the last year, and punishing those around him as well. The burns on his brother's arm were continual memories of his faithless actions and the fire he had caused by them.

Then summer had come and the crops had failed, and he was left with the decision to waive the annual rents or throw his tenants out into the street for non-payment. When they were already hungry, what good did it do to anyone to leave them homeless as well?

And now, one hundred innocent lives were lost because he had chosen what he thought was a sensible investment.

He must face facts and tell his brother that there was nothing left. Nothing at all of what their father had left them. The house was mortgaged to the rooftop and in need of repair. There would be no income this year, and he'd gambled what was left in the bank and lost all in a risky investment.

He was out of ideas, out of money, and afraid to take another step forwards, lest it bring disaster to some unsuspecting soul that might take his side.

He ordered another whiskey. If his calculations were correct, he had enough left in his purse to get stinking drunk. And not another penny, or a way to get one for at least a year. The innkeeper might allow him credit for the room, assuming by the cut of his coat that he was good for the debt. But soon the bill would come due, and he would have to stack it with the rest, unable to pay it.

Other than his father's watch, and the signet on the fob, he had only one thing of value. The insurance on his miserable life.

His hand stopped shaking as the inevitable solution occurred to him. He was an utter failure as a duke, and a man. He had brought shame and ruin to his family. He had betrayed a friend, and been well punished for it. The gentlemanly thing to do would be to write a letter of apology and blow his brains out. Let his brother, William, have the coronet. Perhaps he could do better with it.

Of course, it would leave Will with all the debts and the additional expense of burying Adam. And the cleaning of the study from the final mess he'd made with his suicide.

But what if the present duke should die by accident, while travelling on business? Then his brother would be left with the title and a tidy sum that might cover the debts until he could find a better source of income.

Adam thought again how unjust it was that the better brain of the family had found its way into the younger son. Will had inherited wisdom, forethought and an even temper. But all the stubborn impulsiveness and pigheaded unwillingness to take advice was lodged in his own thick skull.

And Will, God love him, had not an envious or covetous bone in his body. He worshipped his older brother, although heaven knew why. He was content to see Adam make as big a mess as possible of the whole thing, never offering a word of criticism.

But no more. His brother would make a fine duke. Let Will step up and do his part to keep the estate solvent, for Adam was more than sick of trying.

But it was up to Adam to step out of the way and allow his William to come forward and take his place.

Adam set down the newspaper. He was resolved. A simple accident would solve many problems, if he had the nerve to follow through. But how best to go about it?

He ordered another whisky. As he drank, he felt the glow in his head fogging rational thought, and numbing the pain of the failure. And realised he was well on the way to the first step in his plan. Raise enough Dutch courage to do the deed, and create the level of befuddlement in his body to convince anyone that cared to ask that this was an unfortunate accident, and not a deliberate act. He finished his drink and ordered another, staying the hand of the barman. 'Leave the bottle.'

The duke could hear the faint rumble of the coaches entering and leaving the busy courtyard. He imagined the slippery cobbles under his expensive boots, and how easy it might be to fall. And the great horses with their heavy hooves, and even heavier carriage wheels…

It would not be a pleasant death. But he doubted that any death was pleasant, when it came down to the fact.

This would at least be timely, and easy enough to arrange. He poured himself another stiff whisky. He might be thought drunken and careless. But many knew him to be that already. At least they would not think him a suicidal coward.

Very well, then.

He took one final drink. Stood and felt the world tipping under his feet. Very good, indeed. He doubted he could make too many steps. He dropped the last of his coin on the table, turned to the tavern keeper and offered an unsteady bow. 'Good evening to you, sir.'

And goodbye.

He worked his way toward the door, bumping several patrons along the way and apologising profusely, before he made it through the open door of the inn.

He could hear a carriage approaching, and deliberately looked in the opposite direction, into the sun. Now he was blind, as well as drunk. All the better, for his nerve could not fail if he could not see what was coming.

The sound was getting louder and louder and he waited until he could feel the faint trembling in the ground that told him the coach was near.

Then he started forward, ignoring the calls of the coachmen.

'Here, sir. Watch where you are going.'

'I say, look out!'

'Oh, dear God!'

And his foot slipped from under him, sending him face down in front of the approaching horses.

Chapter Two

~~~~~~~~

Penelope felt the steady rocking of the carriage, but the rhythm did nothing to lull the sense of dread growing in her. They had been travelling north at a steady pace toward Scotland, stopping at inns and taverns to dine or pass the night. And yet she was no nearer to her goal than when she had been sitting in front of the fire at home.

Jem's misgivings had eased only slightly, once he realised that he was not expected to be the groom. 'You cannot hire a husband as you would hire a coach, Miss Penny.'

'How hard can it be?' Penny announced, with an optimism that she hoped would carry her through the trip. 'I think disappointments in the past were the fault of expectations on the part of myself and the gentlemen involved. I wished a soulmate and they wished a biddable female. I shall never be biddable, and the fact was emphasised by the surrounding crowd of prettier, more agreeable young ladies. After the lack of success in London, I am willing to accept that there will not be a soulmate in the offing.'

The footman stared at her, as if to say it was no concern of his, one way or the other.

She continued. 'However, if I mean to hire a man to do a job of work? Times are hard, Jem. As we go further north, there will be many men seeking employment. I will find one and make my offer.'

Jem could hold his tongue no longer. 'I hardly think that marriage should be considered a chore, miss.'

'My brother assures me often enough that marriage to *me* is likely to be such. And that is just how I mean to phrase it to any worthy gentleman I might find. It will be the simplest of jobs, really. He has but to sign some papers, and spend a few weeks in my presence to pacify my brother. I will pay him amply for his time. And I will require nothing in the way of marital obligations. Not sobriety, or fidelity, or drastic change in lifestyle. He can do just as he pleases, as long as he is willing to marry.'

'A man is not likely to be so easily managed as that, miss.' His tone was warning, but the meaning was lost on her.

'I fail to see why not. It is doubtful that he will have any designs upon my person. Look at me, Jem, and tell me honestly that you expect me to be fighting off the forced affections of some man, if he has freedom and enough money for any woman he wishes.'

The footman looked doubtful.

'But I have brought you along to protect my honour, should my surmise be incorrect,' she assured him.

The elderly footman was not mollified. 'But when you marry, the money will no longer be in your control. It will belong to your husband.' Jem gestured to fill the empty air with scenarios, all of which foretold doom.

'I have no control of the money now,' Penny reminded him. 'If there is a chance that I can find a husband who is less resolute than my brother has become, then it is well worth the risk. I will need to act fast, and think faster. But I dare say I will find a way to take the reins of the relationship before my intended knows what I am about.'

He was not convinced. 'And if the choice proves disastrous?'

'We shall cross that bridge when we come to it.' She glanced out the window at the change in scenery. 'Will we be stopping soon? I fear we are getting near to Scotland, and I had hoped to find someone by now.'

Jem signalled the driver to stop at the next inn, and Penny crossed her fingers. 'It will help if I can find a man who is slow of wit and amiable in nature. If he is given to drink? All the better. Then I shall allow him his fill of it, and he will be too content to bother with me.'

Jem looked disapproving. 'You mean to keep the poor man drunk so that you may do as you will.'

She sniffed. 'I mean to offer him the opportunity to drink. It is hardly my fault if he is unable to resist.'

Jem rolled his eyes.

The carriage was slowing, and when she looked out the window, she could see that they were approaching an inn. She leaned back against her seat and offered a silent prayer that this stop would be the one where she met with success. The other places she had tried were either empty of custom or filled with the sort of rugged brawlers who looked no more willing to allow her freedom than her brother was. Her plan was a wild one, of course. But there were many miles to travel, and she only needed to find one likely candidate for it to prove successful.

And surely there was one man, between London and Gretna, who was in as desperate a state as she. She had but to find him.

Suddenly, the carriage jerked to a stop, and rattled and shook as the horses reared in front of it. She reached out and caught the leather strap at her side, clinging to it to keep her seat. The driver was swearing as he fought to control the beasts and shouting to someone in front of them as things began to settle to something akin to normal. She shot a worried look at Jem in the seat across from her.

He held up a warning hand, indicating that she keep her place, and opened the door, stepping out of the carriage and out of sight to check on the disturbance.

When he did not return, she could not resist, and left the carriage to see for herself.

They had stopped before the place she had expected, several yards short of the inn. But it was easy to understand the reason. There was a body, sprawled face down in the muck at the feet of the horses, which were still shying nervously. The driver held them steady, as Jem bent to examine the unconscious man in the road.

He appeared to be a gentleman, from what little she could see. The back of his coat was well cut, and stretched to cover broad shoulders. Although the buff of the breeches was stained with dirt from the road, she was sure that they had been new and clean earlier in the day.

Jem reached a hand to the man's shoulder and shook him gently, then with more force. When there was no response, he rolled the inert figure on to his back.

The dark hair was mussed, but stylish, the face clean shaven, and the long slender fingers of his hands showed none of the marks of hard work. Not a labourer or common ruffian. A gentleman, most certainly. She supposed it was too much to hope that he was a scholar. More likely a rake, so given over to dissolution that, left to his own devices, he was likely to drink himself to death before they reached the border.

She smiled. 'He is almost too perfect. Put him into the coach at once, Jem.'

Her servant looked at her as though she'd gone mad. She shrugged. 'I was trusting to fortune to make my decision for me. I hoped that she would throw a man in my path, and she has done just that. You must admit, it is very hard to doubt the symbolic nature of this meeting.'

Jem stared down at the man, and nudged his shoulder. 'Here, sir. Wake up.'

His eyes opened, and she could not help but notice the heavy fringe of lashes that hid the startlingly blue irises. The colour was returning to the high-boned, pale cheeks. He looked up into the blinding sun, and released a sigh. 'There was no pain. I had thought...' Then the man looked past Jem, and smiled up at her. 'Are you an angel?'

She snorted. 'Are you foxed?'

'It depends,' he muttered. 'If I am alive, then I am foxed. But if I am dead? Then I am euphoric. And you—' he pointed a long white finger '—are an angel.'

'Either way, I doubt you should lie here in the road, sir. Would you care to join me in my carriage? I am on a journey.'

'To heaven.' He smiled.

She thought of Gretna Green, which might be quite lovely, but fell far short of Elysium. 'We are all journeying towards heaven, are we not? But some of us are closer than others.'

He nodded, and struggled to his feet. 'Then I must stay close to you if the Lord has sent you to be my guide.'

Jem tossed the man a handkerchief, and he stared at it in confusion. Finally, the servant took it back, wiped the man's face and hands and brushed off his coat and breeches. He turned the man's head to get his attention and said slowly, 'You are drunk, sir. And you have fallen in a coach yard. Are you alone? Or are there friends to aid you in your predicament?'

The man laughed. 'I doubt any of my friends could help me find my way to heaven, for they have chosen a much darker path.' He gestured around him. 'None of them is here, in any case. I am very much alone.'

Jem looked disgusted. 'We cannot just leave you here. You might wander into the road again, if there is no one to stop you. And you seem harmless enough. Do you promise, if we take you along with us, not to bother the young mistress?'

'Take liberties with such a divine creature?' He

cocked his head to the side. 'I would not think of it, sir, on my immortal soul, and my honour as a gentleman.'

Jem threw his hands in the air and stared at Penelope. 'If you mean to have him, miss, I will not stop you. He appears to be a drunken idiot, but not particularly dangerous.'

The man nodded in enthusiastic agreement.

'Your brother will have my head if I'm wrong, of course.'

'My brother will not hear of it. He will not take you back, Jem, once he realises that you have helped me. You had best stay with me and hope for a favourable outcome. If we succeed, I will reward you well for your part in this.'

Jem helped her and the man back into the body of the coach, climbed in and shut the doors behind him. They set off again, and the man across from her looked surprised by the movement, before settling back into the squabs.

She smiled at him. 'I don't believe I asked your name, sir.'

'I don't believe you did.' He grinned at her. 'Adam Felkirk. And what am I to call you?

'Penelope Winthorpe.'

'I am not dead, then?' He seemed vaguely disappointed.

'No. Are you in some sort of trouble?'

He frowned. 'I most certainly am. Or will be, if I wake sober in the morning.' He smiled again. 'But for now, I am numb and free from care.'

'Suppose I could promise you enough brandy that you need never to be sober again?'

He grinned. 'At the moment, it is a most attractive proposition.'

'Brandy, Jem. I know you have some. Give it to Mr Felkirk.'

Jem looked horrified that his mistress would force him to acknowledge the flask in his pocket, and even worse, that she would require him to part with it. But he gave it over to the man in the seat next to him.

Felkirk nodded his thanks. 'If she is an angel, then you, sir, are a saint.' He raised the flask in salute and drank.

She examined him. He had an insubstantial quality. Harmless and friendly. She had feared that Jem spoke the truth when he had said that a real man might be more difficult to manage than the one she had imagined for her purpose. But Adam Felkirk seemed easy enough.

'Thank you for your kind words, Mr Felkirk. And if you wish more brandy, then do not hesitate to inform me.'

He smiled and drank again, then offered the flask to her.

She took it and considered it for a moment, before deciding that drink would not help her gain the courage to speak. 'But that is not all.' She tried a smile that was welcoming and friendly, since seduction seemed inappropriate for her purpose. 'You could have fine clothes as well. And a pretty mistress. Money always in your pocket, and a chance to do just as you please, in all things, at all times.'

He grinned at her, and she was taken aback by the whiteness of his smile. 'You truly are an angel, darling. And leading me to a heaven most suited for a man of my tastes. I had imagined something more pious.' He pulled a face. 'Downy clouds, flowing robes. Harps and whatnot. But heaven, as you describe it, sounds more like a fine evening in London.'

'If that is what you wish, you may have it. Whenever you want. I can relieve you of all cares. But first, you must do one thing for me.' She handed the flask back to him again.

He took it and drank deeply. 'As I suspected—it was far too pleasant to be heaven. And you are not an angel, but a demon, come for my soul.' He laughed. 'But I fear the devil might have that already, so what can I do?'

'Nothing so dire.' She smiled again, and told him her plan.

It was not at all clear that the truth was reaching him. He was smiling back at her, and nodding at the appropriate times. But with each sip of brandy, his eyes lost a little of their glitter. And, as often as not, he looked out the window rather than at her.

When she reached the word marriage, his eyes focused for a moment, and he opened his mouth. But it was as though he'd forgotten what it was he meant to say. He looked absently at her, then shrugged and took another drink, and his smile returned.

The carriage pulled to a stop, and Jem hopped down to open the door, announcing that they had arrived at Gretna Green. She stared at the man across from her, 'Do you agree to my terms, Mr Felkirk?'

'Call me Adam, my dear.' He was staring at her with increased intensity, and for a moment she feared that he meant a closer relationship than she intended. And then he said, 'I am sorry, but I seem to have forgotten your name. Oh, well. No matter. Why are we stopping?'

'We are in Gretna Green.'

'There was something you wanted me to do, wasn't there?'

'Sign a licence?' she prompted.

'Of course! Let us do that, then. And then we shall have some more brandy.' He seemed to think it was all jolly fun, and reached for the door handle, nearly losing his balance as Jem opened it in front of him. The servant caught his elbow and helped him down out of the coach, before reaching a hand up to help Penny.

When they were on the ground together, Adam offered his arm to her. She took it, and found herself leading him, steadying him, more than he ever could her. But he went along, docile as a lamb.

She led him to the blacksmith, and listened as Jem explained to the man what was required.

'Well, git on wi' it, then. I have horses ta shoe.' He looked critically at Penny. 'Da ya mean ta ha' him?'

'I do,' she said formally, as though it mattered.

'Yer sure? He's a drunkard. They cause no end a trouble.'

'I wish to marry him, all the same.'

'And you, sir. Will ya ha' the lady?'

'Marriage?' Adam grinned. 'Oh, I say. That is a lark, isn't it?' He looked down at her. 'I cannot remember quite why, but I must have intended it, or I wouldn't be in Scotland. Very well. Let us be married.'

'Done. Yer married. Na off with you. I ha' work ta do.' He turned back to his horses.

'That is all?' Penny asked in surprise. 'Is there a paper to be signed? Something that will prove what we have done?'

'If ya wanted a licence, ya coulda staid on yer own side o' the border, lass.'

'But I must have something to show to my brother, and the solicitors of course. Can you not provide for us, sir?'

'I canna write, so there is verra little I ca' do for ya, less ya need the carriage mended, or the horse shoed.'

'I will write it myself, then. Jem, run back to the carriage and find me some paper, and a pen and ink.'

The smith was looking at her as if she were daft, and Adam laughed, patted the man on the back and whispered something in his ear, offering him a drink from the brandy flask, which the Scot refused.

Penny stared down at the paper before her. What did she need to record? A marriage had taken place. The participants. The location. The date.

There was faint hammering in the background and the hiss of hot metal as it hit the water.

Their names, of course. She spelled Felkirk as she expected it to be, hoping that she was not showing her ignorance of her new husband by the misspelling of her new surname.

She glanced down at the paper. It looked official, in a sad sort of way. Better than returning with nothing to show her brother. She signed with a bold hand and indicated a spot where Jem could sign as witness.

Her new husband returned to her side from the forge, where he had been watching the smithy. He held a hand out to her. 'Now here, angel, is the trick if you want to be legal. Not married without a ring, are you?' He was holding something small and dark between the fingers of his hand. 'Give over.' He reached for her.

'I think your signature is all that is needed. And that of the smith, of course.' She smiled hopefully at the smith. 'You will be compensated, sir, for the trouble.'

At the mention of compensation, he took the pen and made his mark at the bottom of the paper.

'Here, here, sir.' Her husband took another drink, in the man's honour. 'And to my wife.' He drank again. 'Your Grace.'

She shook her head. 'Now, you are mistaking me for someone else, Adam. Perhaps it would be best to leave off the brandy for a time.'

'You said I could have all I wanted. And so I shall.' But there was no anger as he said it. 'Your hand, madam.' He took her left hand and slipped something on to the ring finger, then reached for the pen.

She glanced down. The smith had twisted a horse-shoe nail into a crude semblance of a ring, and her hand was heavily weighted with it. Further proof that she had truly been to Scotland, since the X of the smith held no real meaning.

Adam signed with a flourish, beside her own name. 'We need to seal it as well. Makes it look more official.' He snatched the candle from the table and dripped a clot of the grease at the bottom of the paper, and pulled out his watch fob, which held a heavy gold seal. 'There. As good as anything in Parliament.' He grinned down at the paper and tipped the flask up for another drink.

She stared at the elegant signature above the wax. 'Adam Felkirk, Duke of Bellston.'

'At your service, madam.' He bowed deeply, and the weight of his own head overbalanced him. Then he pitched forward, striking his head on the corner of the table, to fall unconscious at her feet.

Chapter Three

Adam regained consciousness, slowly. It was a mercy, judging by the way he felt when he moved his head. He remembered whisky. A lot of whisky. Followed by brandy, which was even more foolish. And his brain and body remembered it as well, and were punishing him for the consumption. His head throbbed, his mouth was dry as cotton, and his eyes felt full of sand.

He moved slightly. He could feel bruises on his body. He reached up and probed the knot forming on his temple. From a fall.

And there had been another fall. In the coach yard.

Damn it. He was alive.

He closed his eyes again. If he'd have thought it through, he'd have recognised his mistake. Carriages were slowing down when they reached the inn yard. The one he'd stepped in front of had been able to stop in time to avoid hitting him.

'Waking up, I see.'

Adam raised his head and squinted into the unfamiliar room at the man sitting beside the bed. 'Who the devil are you?'

The man was at least twenty years his senior, but unbent by age, and powerfully built. He was dressed as a servant, but showed no subservience, for he did not answer the question. 'How much do you remember of yesterday, your Grace?'

'I remember falling down in front of an inn.'

'I see.' The man said nothing more.

'Would you care to enlighten me? Or am I to play yes and no, until I can suss out the details?'

'The carriage you stepped in front of belonged to my mistress.'

'I apologise,' he said, not feeling the least bit sorry. 'I hope she was not unduly upset.'

'On the contrary. She considered it a most fortunate circumstance. And I assure you, you were conscious enough to agree to what she suggested, even if you do not remember it. We did not learn your identity until you'd signed the licence.'

'Licence?'

'You travelled north with us, your Grace. To Scotland.'

'Why the devil would I do that?' Adam lowered his voice, for the volume of his own words made the pounding in his skull more violent.

'You went to Gretna, to a blacksmith.'

He shook his head, and realised immediately that it had been a mistake to try such drastic movement. He remained perfectly still and attempted another answer.

'It sounds almost as if you are describing an elopement. Did I stand in witness for someone?'

The servant held the paper before him, and he could
see his shaky signature at the bottom, sealed with his
fob and a dab of what appeared to be candle wax. Adam
lunged for it, and the servant stepped out of the way.

His guts heaved at the sudden movement, leaving
him panting and sweating as he waited for the rocking
world to subside.

'Who?' he croaked.

'Is your wife?' completed the servant.

'Yes.'

'Penelope Winthorpe. She is a printer's daughter,
from London.'

'Annulment.'

'Before you suggest it to her, let me apprise you of
the facts. She is worth thirty thousand a year and has
much more in her bank. If I surmise correctly, you were
attempting to throw yourself under the horses when we
met you. If the problem that led you to such a rash act
was monetary, it was solved this morning.'

He fell back into the pillows and struggled to
remember any of the last day. There was nothing there.
Apparently, he had fallen face down in the street and
found himself an heiress to marry.

Married to the daughter of a tradesman. How could
he have been so foolish? His father would be horrified
to see the family brought to such.

Of course, his father had been dead for many years.
His opinions in the matter were hardly to be considered. And considering that the result of his own

careful planning was a sunk ship, near bankruptcy, and attempted suicide, a hasty marriage to some rich chit was not so great a disaster.

And if the girl were lovely and personable?

He relaxed. She must be, if he had been so quick to marry her. He must have been quite taken with her, although he did not remember the fact. There had to be a reason that he had offered for her, other than just the money, hadn't there?

It was best to speak with her, before deciding on a course of action. He gestured to the servant. 'I need a shave. And have someone draw water for a bath. Then I will see this mistress of yours, and we will discuss what is to become of her.'

An hour later, Penelope hesitated at the door to the duke's bedroom, afraid to enter and trying in vain to convince herself that she had any right to be as close to him as she was.

The illogic of her former actions rang in her ears. What had she been thinking? She must have been transported with rage to have come up with such a foolhardy plan. Now that she was calm enough to think with a clear head, she must gather her courage and try to undo the mess she'd made. Until the interview was over, the man was her husband. Why should she not visit him in his rooms?

But the rest of her brain screamed that this man was not her husband. This was the Duke of Bellston, peer of the realm and leading figure in Parliament, whose eloquent speeches she had been reading in *The Times* scant weeks ago. She had heartily applauded his opinions and looked each day for news about him, since he seemed, above all others, to offer wise and reasoned governance. As she'd scanned the papers for any mention of him, her brother had remarked it was most like a woman to romanticise a public figure.

But she had argued that she admired Bellston for his ideas. The man was a political genius, one of the great minds of the age, which her brother might have noticed, had he not been too mutton-headed to concern himself with current affairs. There was nothing at all romantic about it, for it was not the man itself she admired, but the positions he represented.

And it was not as if the papers had included a caricature of the duke that she was swooning over. She had no idea how he might look in person. So she had made his appearance up in her head out of whole cloth. By his words, she had assumed him to be an elder statesmen, with grey hair, piercing eyes and a fearsome intellect. Tall and lean, since he did not appear from his speeches to be given to excesses, in diet or spirit.

If she were to meet him, which of course she never would, she would wish only to engage him in discourse, and question him on his views, perhaps offering a few of her own. But it would never happen, for what would such a great man want with her and her opinions?

She would never in a million years have imagined him as a handsome young noble, or expected to find him stone drunk and face down in the street where he had very nearly met his end under her horse. And never in a hundred million years would she expect to find herself standing in front of his bedchamber.

She raised her hand to knock, but before she could make contact with the wood, she heard his voice from within. 'Enter, if you are going to, or return to your rooms. But please stop lurking in the hallway.'

She swallowed annoyance along with her fear, opened the door, and stepped into the room.

Adam Felkirk was sitting beside the bed, and made no effort to rise as she came closer. His seat might as well have been a throne as a common wooden chair, for he held his position with the confidence of a man who could buy and sell the inn and the people in it, and not think twice about the bills. He stared at her, unsmiling, and even though he looked up into her eyes it felt as though he were looking down upon her.

The man in front of her was obviously a peer. How could she have missed the fact yesterday?

Quite easily, she reminded herself. A day earlier he could manage none of the hauteur he was displaying now. Unlike some men, the excess of liquor made him amiable. Drunkenness had relaxed his resolute posture and softened his features.

Not that the softness had made them any more appealing. Somehow she had not noticed what a handsome man she had chosen, sober and clean, shaved and in fresh linen. She felt the irresistible pull the moment she looked at him. He was superb. High cheekbones and pale skin no longer flushed with whisky. Straight nose, thick dark hair. And eyes of the deepest blue, so clear that to look into them refreshed the soul. And knowing the mind that lay behind them, she grew quite weak. There was a hint of sensuality in the mouth, and she was carnally aware of the quirk of the lips when he looked at her, and the smile behind them.

And now he was waiting for her to speak. 'Your Grace…' she faltered.

'It is a day too late to be so formal, madam.' His voice, now that it was not slurred, held a tone of command that she could not resist.

She dropped a curtsy.

He sneered. 'Leave off with that, immediately. If it is meant to curry favour, it is not succeeding. Your servant explained some of what happened, while he was shaving me. It seems this marriage was all your idea, and none of mine?'

'I am sorry. I had no idea who you were.'

He examined her closely, as though she were a bug on a pin. 'You expect me to believe that you were unaware of my title when you waylaid me to Scotland?'

'Completely. I swear. You were injured in the street before my carriage. I was concerned for your safety.'

'And so you married me. Such a drastic rescue was not necessary.'

'I meant to marry someone. It was the intent of the trip.'

'And when you found a peer, lying helpless in the street—'

'As I told you before, I had no idea of your title. And I could hardly have left you alone. Suppose you had done harm to yourself?'

There was a sharp intake of breath from the man across the table from her and she hoped that she had not insulted him by the implication.

'I am sorry. But you seemed insensible. You were in a vulnerable state.'

'And you took advantage of it.'

She hung her head. 'I have no defence against that accusation.' She held out the mock licence to him. 'But I am prepared to offer you your freedom. No one knows what has occurred between us. Here is the only record of it. The smith that witnessed could not read the words upon it, and never inquired your name. I will not speak of it, nor will my servant. You have but to throw it on the fire and you are a free man.'

'As easy as that.' The sarcasm in his voice was plain. 'You will never trouble me again. You do not intend to reappear, when I choose to marry again, and wave a copy of this in my face. You will never announce to my bride that she has no legal right to wed me?'

'Why should I?' she pleaded. 'I hold no malice towards you. It is you that hold me in contempt, and I richly deserve it. Do I wish to extort money from you? Again, the answer would be no. I have ample enough fortune to supply my needs. I do not seek yours.'

He was looking at her as though he could not believe what he was hearing. 'You truly do not understand the gravity of what you have done. I cannot simply throw this on the fire and pretend nothing has happened. Perhaps you can. But I signed it, with my true name and title, and sealed it as well. Drunk or sober, for whatever reason, the result is the same. I am legally bound to you. If my name is to mean anything to me, I cannot ignore the paper in front of me.'

He stared at the licence, and his eyes looked bleak.

'You are right that no one need know if I destroy it. But I would know of it. If we had been in England, it would be a Fleet marriage and would mean nothing. But by the laws of Scotland, we are man and wife. To ignore this and marry again without a formal annulment would be bigamy. It matters not to me that I am the only one who knows the truth. I cannot behave thus and call myself a man of honour.'

She willed herself not to cry, for tears would do no good. They would make her look even more foolish than she already did. 'Then you shall have your annulment, your Grace. In any way that will suit you. I am sorry that scandal cannot be avoided, but I will take all the blame in the matter.'

'Your reputation will be in ruins.'

She shook her head. 'A spotless reputation has in no way balanced my shortcomings thus far. What harm can scandal do me?'

'Spotless?' He was eyeing her again. 'Most young girls with spotless reputations have no need to flee to Scotland for a hasty marriage to a complete stranger.'

'You thought I was…' Oh, dear lord. He thought she was with child, which made her behaviour seem even more sordid and conniving then it already was. 'No. That is not the problem. Not at all. My circumstances are…' she sought a word '…unusual.'

'Unusual circumstances?' He arched his eyebrows, leaned back and folded his arms. 'Tell me of them. If we have eliminated fortune hunting, blackmail and the need to find a father for your bastard, then I am out of explanations for your behaviour.'

He was staring at her, waiting. And she looked down into those very blue eyes, and, almost against her will, began to speak. She told him of her father. And her brother. The conditions of her inheritance. The foolishness over the book. 'And so, I decided that I must marry. It did not really matter to whom. If I could find someone on the way to Scotland… And then you fell in front of the carriage.'

He was looking at her most curiously. 'Surely you hoped for better than a total stranger.'

'Once, perhaps. But now I hope only for peace and quiet, and to be surrounded by my books.'

'But a girl with the fortune you claim…'

It was her turn to sneer at him. 'A plain face and disagreeable nature have managed to offset any financial advantages a marriage to me might offer. Only the most desperate would be willing to put up with me, for I can be most uncooperative when crossed.

'Since I know from experience that I will refuse to be led by my husband in all things, I sought someone I could control.' She looked at him and shook her head. 'And I failed, most dreadfully. In my defence, you were most biddable while intoxicated.'

He laughed, and it surprised her. 'Once you had found this biddable husband, what did you mean to do with him?'

'Gain control of my inheritance. Retire to my library and allow my husband to do as he chose in all things not pertaining to me.'

'In all things not pertaining to you.' He was staring at her again, and it occurred to her the things he might expect from a woman who was his wife. Suddenly, the room felt unaccountably warm.

She dropped her eyes from his. 'I did not wish for intimacy. But neither did I expect fidelity. Or sobriety. Or regular hours, or even attendance in the same house. I had hoped for civility, of course. But affection was not required. I did not wish to give over all of my funds, but I certainly do not need all of them for myself. If they remain with my brother, in time I will have nothing at all. I have thirty thousand a year. I should suspect that half would be more than enough for most gentlemen to entertain themselves.'

Again, there was an intake of breath from the man across from her. 'Suppose the gentleman needed more.'

'More?' She blinked back at him.

'One hundred and fifty thousand, as soon as possible.'

One hundred and fifty thousand. The number was mind-boggling, but she considered it, doing the maths in her head. 'I should not think it would be a problem. I have savings. And I do not need much to live on. While it will reduce my annual income considerably, it will leave more than enough for my needs.'

He studied her even more intently, got up and walked slowly around her, considering her from several angles. Then he returned to his chair. 'If I go to your brother and present myself as your husband, which indeed I am, then you would give me one hundred and fifty thousand pounds and the freedom to do as I wish with it?'

'It is only money. But it is my money, and I can do as I will.' She looked back into his eyes, searching for anything that might give her a clue as to his true nature, and hoping that it aligned in some small way with the man who had written such wonderful speeches. 'I should as soon see you have it as my brother, for I am most angry with him. You may have as much money as you need. If you agree to my other conditions, of course.'

He met her gaze without flinching. 'Why would I have to do that? Now that I am your husband, I can do as I please with all the money. You are a woman, and lost all say in the matter when you were foolish enough to wed a stranger.'

'There was the flaw in my plan,' she admitted. 'I expected to find a man slower in wit than the one I seem to have married. A drunken fool would be easy enough to gull. I could distract him with pleasures of the flesh. By the time he sobered enough to realise the extent of his good fortune, I meant to have the majority of my assets converted to cash and secured against him.'

She looked as closely at him as he had at her. 'But you are likely to know better. And I have given you the licence that proves your right to control my money, should you choose to exercise it. In truth, I am as much at your mercy now as you were at mine yesterday.'

There was a flicker of something in his eyes that she could not understand.

She said, 'You say you are a man of honour. And so I must appeal to your better nature. If you wish it, you may destroy the paper in front of you or we can go to London and seek a formal annulment.

'Or we can go directly to my bankers, and you can

take control of the fortune, which is your right as my husband. If so, I beg you to allow me some measure of freedom, and the time and money necessary to pursue my studies. The choice is yours.'

She thought to dip her head in submission, and decided against it. She waited in silence, watching for some sign of what he might say next. And the look in his eyes changed gradually from one of suspicion, to speculation, to calculation and eventually to something she thought might be avarice. He was thinking of the money. And what he might do with it, God help her.

It was a day too late to inquire what that might be. She had found the man, drunk as a lord in a public place. Who knew what vices he might be capable of? If she had not cared to discover this yesterday, it did no good to care now. And if his lechery and drunkenness were strong enough to run through the whole of her money, then it would prove to her brother just how foolish she was.

At last, he spoke. 'When you found me, I was near the end of my rope. An investment that should have returned enough to tide me and my estate through the coming year had failed, utterly. I have responsibilities. People are depending on me for their welfare. And I am destitute.

'Or was, until you appeared and offered me this opportunity. What I need to do may take a larger portion of your money than you had hoped to part with. But I hope it will be a temporary loss. My land is fertile most years, and returns more than enough to live in luxury. Had I not gambled with the profits, hoping for an increase, I would not be in need of your help.'

Gambling? Although it did not please her, it made perfect sense. Many men of considerable wealth lost all over a green baize table. She could but hope that she might hide some of the money from him, or perhaps, through sound advice, she might prevent him from making a similar mistake in the future.

He was waiting for some response on her part, and she gave him a faint nod of understanding.

He continued. 'In exchange, you shall be a duchess, which will make it possible to do largely as you please in all things. No one will dare to question your actions or your spending, least of all me. If you do not have cash in hand, no one will deny you credit. The bills will come to me, to be paid at such time as we have the funds for them.'

Doing business on credit went against her nature. But the prospect of freedom beckoned, and hope flared in her. 'And my studies?'

'If you do not wish to question my diversions, then what right would I have to question yours?'

As her husband? He would have every right in the world. But he was being most reasonable about things, so she held her tongue on the literalities. 'I doubt we would have much in common—in the matter of diversions, I mean.'

He nodded. 'Quite possibly not. We might live comfortably as strangers, although in the same house.' There was no sense of remorse as he said it. 'But I see no reason that we cannot succeed at it. As long as we have no intention of impeding each other's pleasure, we might manage well together. Certainly better than some couples I know who seem bent on ensuring their spouse's misery.'

It seemed so cold, when stated thus. But her new husband seemed content with it. He did not care that she wished to be alone with her books. And looking at his full lips and the seductive light in his blue eyes, she suspected the less she knew about his activities when he was not in Parliament, the happier she would be.

She ventured, 'It sounds most pleasant when you describe it thus.' Which was not precisely true. 'And very much what I was hoping for.' Which was. It was exactly what she had hoped for, and she must not forget the fact.

He smiled in return, although there was a frozen quality to his face that made her unsure. 'Very well, then.' He reached out a hand to her, and she stared at it for a moment before offering him her own. He took it and shook. 'We are in agreement. Let us hope that this union will prove mutually beneficial.'

'Will you be ready to start for London today?'

He started at the impertinence of her request. He was not accustomed to having another set his schedule.

She hesitated. 'I admit to being most eager to bring the news of my marriage to my brother. And my bankers, of course.'

He remembered the money, and his resistance to her suggestion evaporated. 'Today would suit me nicely. Have your footman prepare the carriage.' He nodded in such a way that she knew the interview was at an end and she was dismissed.

Adam watched his new wife exit the room and sank back into his chair, exhausted. What in God's name had he just agreed to? He'd sunk so low as to marry a cit's daughter, just to get her money.

And a cool voice at the back of his head reminded him that it was better than his first plan, if it meant that he could be alive to correct his mistake and rebuild his fortune. He had been given a second chance and would make the most of it. There would be money in the bank before his creditors noticed that there had been an absence. And by next year, the drought would be over, the coffers refilling and the present state of penury no more than a bad dream.

And he would be a married man. What was he to do with—he struggled to remember her name— Penelope Winthorpe?

He shook his head. She was Penelope Felkirk now. And there was nothing to be done, according to her. She wished to be left alone.

He was more than willing to grant her wish. He could not very well parade her in front of his friends as the new duchess. He'd be a laughing stock.

He immediately felt guilty for his pride. He'd be a laughing stock in any case, knowing his circle, who often found the humour in the misfortunes of others. Let them laugh. It would not matter, if he managed to save the estate.

But it pained him that they might laugh at her, as well, with her unfashionable clothes, her spectacles and outlandish ideas. To what purpose did the world need another translation of Homer? The majority had had more than enough of that story, by the time they'd left the schoolroom. And yet she was still worrying over it.

But he could find no indication that she meant him harm, by picking him up out of the street. In truth, she had saved his life. And her money would save his land as well.

What would people think of it? She was most obviously not his sort, in temperament or in birth. She was nothing like the ladies of the *ton* that he usually chose as companions. The world expected him to marry someone more like Clarissa Colton: beautiful, worldly, and with wit that cut like a razor. He shuddered.

Perhaps it told him something of his true mental state that he had married Clare's opposite. Penelope Winthorpe's clothes were without style, and her manner was bookish and hesitant. And her looks?

He shook his head. She'd called herself plain, but it was not truly accurate a definition. Plainness implied a commonality with the norm. A face unmemorable. And that did not describe his new wife.

Her looks…were disturbing. Her hair was too pale, almost white. Her skin as well, from too much time spent indoors with her books. And her spectacles hid eyes that were bright and far too observant. He wanted to know what she saw when she looked at him, for she had been studying him most intently. It was like being pierced to the soul, when her eye had held his. A gimlet, not a razor.

The intelligence in that gaze was daunting. And in her words as well. He'd have expected it from another man, but to hear such reasonable behaviour from a woman? There had been no nonsense. No tears behind the lashes. No attempt to appeal to him with her frailty. Their interview had been a frank meeting of intellectual equals.

Her presence had been both calming and stimulating. The combination made him uneasy. It was far too much to take before one had had one's morning tea.

But it shouldn't matter, he reminded himself. He needed nothing more from her than her money, and she needed nothing from him but his name. There would be scant little time staring into those disquieting eyes over breakfast. If she did not care for his title, then she need not concern herself with society, after the briefest introduction. And he would be spared the expenses of time or money that were involved in the keeping of a wife in the height of fashion.

And it dawned on him that there were other responsibilities in the taking of a wife that had nothing to do with the purchase of jewels and the redecoration of the manor.

There should be children.

He thought of her eyes again, and imagined a brood of little eyes following him with that same direct stare: dangerously clever children with insatiable curiosity. The prospect intrigued him, but it was not something he was likely to experience, if their current plan went forwards.

It came as somewhat of a relief to know that the title could follow another branch of the family tree. He had his brother as heir. That had been a fine plan yesterday. And if not William, then perhaps William would marry and have sons of his own. Good-tempered and intelligent children, just like their father. Any of those might do for the next duke.

Very well, then. He would take her back to London, or let her take him. And if what she said was true, he would sort out the money, right enough. And once she and her books were safely stowed at Bellston, then he could return to his comfortable old life. They would live, happily ever after, as was told in folk tales.

Just not with each other.

Chapter Four

The carriage ride to London was nothing like the one to Gretna. The trip outbound had been more excitement than misgiving, since she was convinced of the soundness of her plan and the immediate improvement it would bring to her life.

But now that she had succeeded, she found it most disquieting. Jem had been relegated to a seat beside the driver, leaving her alone with her new husband with a morose shake of the head that showed no confidence in a brighter future.

The man seated across from her was not the drunkard she had rescued on the way to Scotland. That man had been relaxed and friendly. His posture was familiar, as was his speech.

But when sober, the duke continued to behave as a duke. She hoped he was still feeling the effects of the liquor, for his expression was most forbidding, and she hoped it was not she that had put the look of disgust on his face. Or, worse yet, that his foul mood was habitual. Perhaps it was only the strain of travel, for they had been almost two full days on the road.

For whatever reason, her new husband sat rigidly in his seat across from her, showing no desire to close the distance between them.

And in response, she felt repelled from him.

It was foolish to care on that account. Jem's original fears were quite the contrary to the truth. He had imagined her wrestling a brute for her virtue in the back of a moving carriage. But this man no more desired the physical contact of his spouse than she did herself.

The chatty voyage to Gretna had been replaced with an uninterested silence that she suspected could stretch the length of the trip and far into the future.

And it was all right with her, she reminded herself. Once they were settled, she would return to her books and would appreciate a husband who was not likely to interrupt her work with demands for her attention.

Still, there were things that must be decided before they arrived in London. And that would be impossible without some communication.

She cleared her throat, hesitating to speak.

He looked up at her expectantly.

'I was wondering if you had considered what we might do once we reach London.'

'Do?'

'Well, yes. I wish to go to my bank, of course. And make my father's solicitors aware of my change in status.'

He nodded.

'But once that is done? Well, we cannot very well

live with my brother. There is room, of course, but I doubt that it would be in any way comfortable…'

He was staring at her and she fell into embarrassed silence. He spoke. 'When we arrive in the city, we will be going directly to my townhouse, and can make the financial arrangements after that.'

'Your townhouse.'

'Of course.'

She readied an objection, but paused before speaking. He was her husband, after all. And a man used to being obeyed. Insisting on her own way in this was liable to meet with objections. She said, 'Wherever we reside, I will need room for my collection of books, which is quite substantial. And a quiet place to study. A London townhouse might not be the best choice…'

He sighed, quite out of patience with her. 'Perhaps not the ones you have seen. But I assure you, the Bellston property in London is more than sufficient. We will not be staying there for long, since no one of any fashion is in London at this time. We will adjourn to the manor, once you have settled your business.'

'Manor?'

He was still looking at her as though she were an idiot. 'My home. I have a hunting lodge near Scotland, as well. I was visiting there when you found me. But there is no reason for you to see it at this time or ever, if you have no interest.'

'A manor,' she repeated.

His expression had grown somewhat bemused. 'And where did you think I lived, madam? Under a bridge?'

'I did not think on it. At all.' And now she looked

foolish. It annoyed her even more that she probably was. She had acted in a fit of temper, without considering the consequences.

'So you truly gave no thought to my title.' There was still a touch of amazement in the statement, as though he found the fact hard to comprehend, even after two days' trying. 'The peerage has both responsibilities as well as advantages. A title such as mine comes with a reward of land. In many years, it is a gift, but in some, it is a burden. In either case, I cannot simply walk away from it to indulge a whim.'

'A burden?'

'A recent fire has left portions of the manor house unlivable. Repairs are in effect, even as we speak. Expensive repairs,' he added significantly.

She nodded, understanding his most specific request for funds.

'Most of the house is livable, but I have business to complete in town. And so we will remain for a time in London, and reside in the townhouse. You will find space ample for your needs, I assure you.'

'That is good to know.' She was not at all sure that it was, but there was little she could do to change it.

'We will go to your bank as soon as you wish. You will introduce me as your new husband, and I shall need to make it clear to my solicitors that I have taken a wife. I doubt we can escape without the marriage becoming an *on dit,* for it is rather irregular.'

And there was another thing to worry about. She had not taken into account that his social life would be disrupted by the sudden marriage. No wonder he seemed cross. For her part, the idea was more than a little disturbing.

He continued. 'As soon as is possible, we shall retire to the country. We will take your books, of course. Have no fear of that. I doubt anyone shall wonder very much about us, once we are out of the public eye. I will need to return for Parliament, next session. But whether you choose to accompany me is your own affair.'

She searched his plan for flaws and found none. After the initial shock of it wore off, of course. She had expected to choose her own dwelling, and that her circumstances might diminish after leaving her brother's home. Why did she need a large house when a smaller one would suit her needs? But a manor…

'Did you have a better solution?' There was a touch of acid in the tone, but it was said mildly enough, considering.

He had taken pains to assure her that she would not lose her books. The least she could do was attempt to be co-operative. 'No. No. That is most satisfactory.'

'Satisfactory.' His mouth quirked. 'My holdings are not so rich as some, but I assure you that you will find them much more than satisfactory, once the improvements have been made.'

'Of course.'

Silence fell again. She looked down at her hands and out at the passing countryside, trying to appear comfortable. So, she was to be lady of a manor in the country. What part of the country? She had forgotten to ask. It would make her appear even more ignorant, if she waited until they were packed and driving toward it, to inquire.

Of course, once she was back in London, it would be easy enough to find the information, without having to ask her husband.

Unless her failure to ask made her appear uninterested in her new spouse…

It was all becoming very confusing.

He cleared his throat. 'This brother of yours. Is he a printer as well?' There was a pause. 'Because the servant mentioned that your father had been. And I thought, perhaps, family business…' He trailed off, displaying none of the eloquence that she had expected from him. Apparently, he was as uncomfortable in his ignorance as she was with hers.

She smiled and looked back at him. 'Yes. It is a family business. My father loved it dearly, and the books as well. And reading them, of course. He and Mother named us from the classics. My brother's name is Hector. Father always said that education was a great equaliser.'

'It is fortunate that a lack of education does not work in the same way. I was sent down from Oxford. It has had little effect on my status.'

They fell silent, again. She longed to ask why he had been forced to leave Oxford, but did not wish to seem impertinent. Was he like her brother had been, unimpressed by her desire for scholarship?

If so, he was biding his time before making the fact known. He'd had ample opportunity in the last few days to point out her foolishness over the translation. But he had said nothing yet.

'Marriage is also a great equaliser,' he said, to no one in particular.

Did he mean to refer to her sudden rise in society? If so, it was most unfair of him. She looked at him sharply. 'Apparently so. For once we reach the bank, your fortune shall be the equal of mine.'

She noted the flash of surprise in his eyes, as though she had struck him. And she waited with some trepidation for the response.

Then his face cleared, and he laughed. And suddenly she was sharing the carriage with the man she thought she had married. '*Touché.* I expect I will hear similar sentiments once my friends get wind of our happy union, but I had not expected to hear them from my own wife. I recommend, madam, that you save some of that sharp tongue to respond to those that wish to offer you false compliments on your most fortunate marriage.'

People would talk.

Well, of course they would. Why had she not realised the fact? And they would talk in a way that they never would have had she married the drunken nobody she was seeking. She was a duchess.

She would be noticed. And people would laugh.

A hand touched her, and she jumped, and realised that she had forgotten she was not alone in the carriage. She looked up into the face of her new husband, and read the concern on his face.

'Are you all right?' He said it very deliberately, as though he expected her to misunderstand. 'For a moment, you looked quite ill.'

'It is nothing. We have been travelling for some time, and the trip…' She let her words drift away, allowing him to make what he would of them.

'Shall I tell the driver to stop?'

'No, really. I will be fine.'

'Perhaps if we switch seats—a change of direction might help.' He took her hands and pulled her up off her bench, rising and pivoting gracefully in the tight space of the rocking carriage, to take her place and give her his. Then he pulled the shade on the window so that the moving scenery did not addle her gaze.

'Thank you.' She did still feel somewhat faint at the realisation of what she had done by marrying, and the impact it might have on the rest of her life. The distant and strange idea occurred to her that her husband was being most helpful and understanding about the whole thing. And that it might be nice to sit beside him, and rest her head against his shoulder for a time, until the world stopped spinning around her.

Which was a ludicrous idea. He was solicitous, but he had done nothing to make her think she was welcome to climb into his coat pocket. She looked at him again, even more beautiful in his concern for her, and closed her eyes against the realisation that they were a ridiculous study in contrast. A casual observer could not help but comment on it.

If he noticed the clamminess of her hand, which he still held, he did not comment, but reached out with his other hand as well, to rub some warmth back into the fingers. 'We will be in the city soon. You will feel much better, I am sure, once we have had some refreshment and a change of clothes.'

She certainly hoped so, for she doubted that she could feel any worse.

Chapter Five

When she opened her eyes a while later, the carriage was pulling up in front of a row of fine houses, and he tapped on the door, waiting for the servants to open it and put down the step. Then he descended and offered his hand to her. 'My dear?'

She reached out nervously to take it, while her mind raced to argue that she was in no way dear to him. The endearment was both inaccurate and unnecessary.

He saw the look in her eyes, and said, before she could speak, 'It might go easier with the servants if we maintain a pretence of familiarity. They will obey you, in any case. They would be foolish not to. But all the same…'

She nodded. 'Thank you, Adam.' There. She had said his name.

A footman opened the door before them, and she entered on the arm of the duke, who greeted the butler with a curt, 'Assemble the staff. Immediately.'

The man disappeared. He reappeared a short time later, accompanied by what Penny assumed must be the cook and the housekeeper, and, as she watched, an assortment of maids and footmen appeared from various entrances, lining up in an orderly row behind them.

She counted them. It must be a great house, as he had said, to need a staff so large. The home she had managed for her brother had made do with a staff of four. She reminded herself with some firmness that they were only servants and it did not do to show her fear of them.

The duke looked out over the small crowd assembled. 'I have called you all out from below stairs for an announcement. On my recent trip north, things did not go quite as expected.' He paused. 'Actually, they went much better than I expected. I married.'

There was an audible gasp from the room, before the servants managed to regain control of their emotions.

'May I present her Grace, the Duchess of Bellston—'

Before she could stop herself, she felt her knees begin to curtsy to the non-existent duchess, and her husband's hand came out to lift her back to her feet.

'—formerly, Miss Penelope Winthorpe. In celebration of this fact, you may all take the rest of the day off, to do as you will.'

There was an unexpected moment of tension.

'With pay, of course,' he added, and she could feel the staff relax again. 'We will be dining out. You need do nothing on our behalf until breakfast.'

The gasp had turned to a murmur of excitement, as the staff realised their good fortune.

'Three cheers for his Grace and the new lady of the

house.' The butler made an offer of 'huzzah' sound subdued and polite, but she accepted it with pleasure, as did her husband. 'Thank you. And now, you are dismissed. Enjoy the rest of your day.'

As quickly as they had gathered, the staff evaporated.

She looked at him, waiting for some indication of what was to be done next.

He glanced around him, seeking inspiration. 'Perhaps, a tour of the rooms would be in order. And then we will refresh ourselves, before a trip to your bankers.'

She nodded. 'An excellent plan. Please, your Grace, lead the way.'

He flinched. 'Remember, I am to be Adam to you. And you shall be?' He cocked his head to the side. 'Do you prefer Penelope, or are you a Penny?'

'Penny.'

'Then Penny it shall be, and whatever small endearments I can muster. Come, Penny.' There was a hesitation, as though he was struggling with a foreign language. 'Let me show you your home in London.' He led her down a short corridor, to doors that led to a parlour, which was grand; and a dining room, grander still, with room to seat twenty people. At the back of the house were a study, and a morning room.

'And this shall be yours.' He gestured into the sitting room, hesitating in the doorway as though he were afraid to enter.

She could understand why. Whoever had decorated the room had been the most ladylike of ladies. The furniture was gilt and satin, with legs so delicately turned that she was almost afraid to sit on it. If she chose a second sandwich at tea, the settee might collapse from the additional weight. And the desk, which would need to hold her books and writing materials, looked as though it might faint dead away, if expected to hold anything more serious than social correspondence. The other tables in the room were too small for anything larger than a rosebud, which would have to be candy pink to match the horrible silk upon the walls. The total was so sweet it made her teeth ache to look at it.

She looked in disgust at the ormolu clock on the mantel, which was supported by tiny gold goats and overflown with cherubs.

In response to her glare, the clock chimed the quarter hour, if such a stubbornly unobtrusive bell could be considered a chime.

She looked to her husband and struggled to speak. The correct response should have been 'thank you'. But it was quite beyond her. Eventually she said, 'It is very—pretty.'

He nodded in apology. 'We can find you furniture more suitable for work, and install additional shelves.' He pointed to a rather foolish collection of porcelain shepherds that graced a corner of the room. 'The bric-a-brac and nonsense can be dispensed with, if you wish.'

She looked dubiously around her.

'The room itself is large enough, is it not?'

She tried to ignore the design, and focus on the dimensions. It was larger than the one she had been using. She nodded.

'Very good, then. Redo it to suit yourself. I expected nothing less than that, from whatever woman I married. The rest of the house as well. If you see something that does not suit your tastes, it is well in your power to change it.' He paused. 'Except for my rooms, if you please. I would prefer that my bedroom and study remain as they are now.'

'I think that is not an issue. For I have seen nothing so far that needs alteration, and have no desire to change everything for change's sake.' She neglected to point out that, since any cosmetic changes to the house were to be made with her money, it hardly seemed like a sensible use of the funds. 'But this—' she gestured into her new work room '—must go.'

'Thank you.' He seemed relieved as well. There had a been tension in his back that eased as she said the words, and she suspected the first marital hurdle had been jumped with ease. He made no effort to open the door to his study, and she suspected that he wished some areas of his life to remain unviewed as well as untouched.

Fair enough.

'Let us go upstairs, then, and see the bedrooms.' He led her up the wide marble staircase and turned to the left, opening a door for her. 'These will be your rooms. There is a bedroom, a dressing room and a small room for your maid.'

None of which had been aired, she noted. The fireplace was cold and empty, and there was an uncomfortable chill in the unused room.

He noticed it as well, and wrinkled his nose. 'Well. Hmm. It seems I spoke too soon, when sending the staff away for a day of celebration. I have left no one to light you a fire.' He stepped across the room and opened a connecting door to his suite. There was a nervous pause. 'And I see the servants have brought your things to my room. They assumed…' He looked back at her, helplessly. 'This is not as it appears.'

What upset him more? she wondered—that she might think he wished to bed her, or that the servants had assumed that he would? 'It is all right. We will work things out between us, somehow.'

He nodded. 'Do you wish to change? You are welcome to use my room. There is a basin of fresh water. And clean towels. I could send for a maid to help you… Oh, damn. If you need help, I suppose, I…'

She imagined the feel of his hands at her back, undoing buttons. 'No. Thank you. I have become most adept at managing for myself, if there is no one to help me. If you will give me but a few minutes?'

He nodded and stepped aside, allowing her access to his room.

As the door shut behind her, she went hurriedly to the portmanteau on the floor and chose a fresh gown, struggling briefly with the closures at her back and slipping out of the travelling dress. Then she splashed some water from the basin on to her face, slipped into the new gown and used her brush to arrange her hair as best as was possible.

She could not help it, but glanced in the mirror behind her, examining the room. The man they had rescued from the street was obviously wealthy, but had seemed to have little care for health, his own cleanliness or welfare.

But the room behind her was orderly and immaculate. A sign of good housekeeping, perhaps. But there was more to it than that. The items in the room were expensive but well used and well cared for. The style and arrangement were elegant but simple. The whole suggested a well-ordered mind in repose. It gave her some level of comfort, knowing that her new husband's private rooms looked as they did. This was what she had expected from the Duke of Bellston.

She opened the door to the wardrobe and examined the line of coats and neatly hung breeches and trousers, and the row of brightly polished boots. Expensive, but not gaudy. The man was well tailored, but not a dandy. If he had sunk his fortune because he was prone to excess, there was no indication of it here.

From behind her, he cleared his throat.

She whirled, shutting the wardrobe door behind her.

'I am sorry. I knocked, but obviously you did not hear. Is there something you needed?'

That would cause her to snoop in his closet? He did not finish the sentence, allowing her a scrap of pride to hide her embarrassment. 'No. I am quite finished, thank you.'

'Then I would like to use my room as well, if you do not mind…' There was a hint of challenge there, but his face showed bland inquiry.

'I'll just wait downstairs. In the sitting room?'

'Thank you.'

She turned and exited the room before he could see the blush on her cheek, retracing her steps to her room on the first floor.

Adam waited for the click of the door latch before struggling out of his coat. It would be easier to call for his valet and admit that he had spoken in haste when releasing the staff. But he could manage to do for himself, if his wife had done so. And a day of leisure for the servants would unite them in support of the new mistress, and quell fears of upheaval and negative gossip. The minor inconvenience would be worth the gains in goodwill. He untied his cravat and tossed it aside, washing his face in the basin. Then he chose fresh linen, managing a sloppy knot that he hoped looked more Byronic than inept. He glanced behind him at the open door of the wardrobe.

She'd been searching his room. The thought should have annoyed him, but instead it made him smile. His new bride had a more-than-healthy curiosity. He walked over and pulled a coat off its hanger to replace his travelling clothes. Then she'd likely have been disappointed. There was nothing to see here. No skeletons. And not, fortunately, the bodies of any previous wives. Perhaps he should reassure her, lest she think him some sort of Bluebeard.

He glanced at her portmanteau on the floor beside the bed. Two could play at that game. Although what he expected to find, he was not sure.

He laid his hand on a spare gown, a clean chemise, a night rail, trimmed with embroidery and lace. It was all to be expected. Neatly folded and cared for, even though his wife travelled without a maidservant. The case was large and very heavy for only a few days' travel. But that was very like a woman, was it not? To pack more than was absolutely necessary. His hand stopped short of the bottom of the bag.

Books. Homer. Ovid. A book of poetry, with a ribbon tucked between the pages so that the reader would not lose her place. Not the readings of a mind given to foolish fancy.

He replaced things carefully, the way he had found them, and turned to go to meet her in the sitting room. She was as studious as she claimed, if she could not manage a few days without some sort of reading material. And it was well that she had brought her own to his house. There were many books he fully intended to read, when he had leisure. But for the life of him, he could not think what they would be, and he certainly did not have anything to read in the London house that held any enjoyment. It probably made him look a bit odd, to be without a library but well stocked in Meissen shepherds. But there was little he could do to change that now.

He approached her room in trepidation. The door was closed. Should he knock or enter freely? It was one of many decisions they would have to make together. If they did not mean to live as most married couples, then boundaries of privacy would have to be strictly observed.

At last, he settled on doing both: he knocked and then opened the door, announcing himself and thinking it damn odd that he should need to do it in his own house.

His wife looked up from a book.

'You have found something to read?' he said, and wished he did not sound so surprised at the fact.

'There were a stack of books on the shelf, here. Minerva novels. And Anne Radcliff, of course.' She glanced around her. 'Overblown and romanticised. They are most suited to the décor.'

'They are not mine,' he said, alarmed that such things even existed on the premises.

'That is a great comfort. For I would wish to rethink our bargain were they yours.' There was a twinkle in her eye as she said it. 'But if you favour melodrama, I suspect that this afternoon's meetings will be quite entertaining.'

And she was correct in what she said, for the trip to his wife's bank was most diverting. He was not familiar with the location, which was far from Bond Street, nor did the men working there know him. But it was obvious that they knew his wife and held her in respect. She was ushered into a private office before she even needed to speak her request.

When her bankers entered the room, she wasted no time on introductions, but straight away announced that she had married, and that all business matters must be turned over, post haste, to her new husband.

He could not help but enjoy the look of shock on the faces of the bankers. There was a moment of stunned silence, before the men sought to resist, arguing that the union had been most impulsive and possibly unwise. They eyed him suspiciously, and hinted at the danger of fortune hunters where such a large sum was involved. Was she sure that she was making the correct decision? Had she consulted her brother in the matter?

Adam watched as his new wife grew very still, listening in what appeared to be respectful silence. Although there were no outward signs, he suspected the look of patience she radiated was a sham. And at last, when they enquired if she had obtained her brother's permission to wed, her cool exterior evaporated.

'Gentlemen, I am of age, and would not have needed my brother's permission if the decision to take a husband had taken a year instead of a day. In any case, it is too late now, for I cannot very well send the man away, explaining that our marriage was just a passing fancy on my part. Nor do I wish to.

'May I introduce my husband, and manager of all my finances from here on, Adam Felkirk, Duke of Bellston.'

He did his best to maintain an unaffected visage, although the desire was strong to laugh aloud at the sight of the two men, near to apoplexy, bowing and calling him 'your Grace', and offering tea, whisky or anything he might desire, hoping to erase the words 'fortune hunter' from the previous conversation.

'No, thank you. I merely wish to see the account book that holds the recent transactions on my wife's inheritance.'

The men looked terrified now, but the account book appeared, along with a cup of tea.

Adam glanced down the row of figures, shock mingling with relief. His financial problems were solved, for there was more than enough to effect repairs on the house, and tide the property over until a more favourable season. He was equally glad that he had known nothing of the numbers involved when he had wed the girl. Considering his financial condition, he feared he'd have lost all shame, fallen at her feet, and begged her to wed him, based on what he saw before him.

He looked at the line of monthly withdrawals, increasing in amount as time passed. 'Do you have any regular expenses that need to be met, my dear?'

'Not really. My brother allows me a small allowance, and I take care not to exceed it. I doubt I'll need more than twenty or thirty pounds a month.'

Which was far less than the expenditures on the account. He tapped the paper with his fingertip and glanced up at the bankers. Where was the money going? To the only man with access to the account.

Until now, that is.

Hector had not touched the principal, as of yet. But Penny had been correct in her fears. If measures were not taken, there would be no fortune left to hunt.

He smiled, as condescending and patronising as he could manage. 'You gentlemen were wise to be concerned with the prudence of my wife's decision. But you need concern yourself no longer. Please prepare a draft, in this amount…' he scribbled a number in the book '…and send it to my bankers. I will give you the direction. The rest can remain here, as long as the investments continue to be as profitable as they have been. But under no circumstances is anyone to have access to the account other than myself.' He glanced at Penelope. 'Or my wife, of course. She has my permission to do as she pleases in the matter. Should she send any bills to you, please honour them immediately.'

He shot a sidelong glance at Penelope, and watched her eyes go bright and her mouth make a tiny 'O' of surprise.

He smiled. 'Is that to your satisfaction, dear?'

'Very much so.' The smile on her face was softer than it had been, with none of the hesitance that he had seen in her from the first day. Her body relaxed enough so that her arm brushed the sleeve of his jacket.

She trusted him. At least, for now.

And it cleared the doubts in his own heart, that he had married her for her money. Her fortune could stay separate from his, and he would leave her the control of it. With the look she was giving him, he felt almost heroic.

He was quite enjoying it.

After the success at the bankers, Penny had hoped to feel more confidence when confronting her brother. But as she entered the house, she could feel all the old fears reforming in her. Living here had felt a prison, as much as a haven. And her brother's continual reminders that this was all she would ever know, since no one would want her, had reinforced the iron bars around her.

And now, after only a few days away, the house felt strange. It was as though she were visiting a friend and not returning to her home. She had not realised how thoroughly she had put it behind her, once she made her decision. But it was comforting to think that there would be no foolish longing for the past, now that she was settling into her new life. Once she had her clothing and her things, there was no reason to return again.

She rang for servants, signifying that a maid should be sent to her room to pack her belongings, and sent Jem and another footman to the library with instructions for the crating and removal of her books and papers.

In the midst of her orders, her brother hurried into

the room and seized her by the arm. 'Penny! You have returned, at last. When I realised that you were gone I was near frantic. Do you not realise the risk to your reputation by travelling alone? Especially when you gave me no indication of where you were going. I absolutely forbid such actions in the future. I cannot believe…' Hector appeared ready to continue in his speech without ceasing, and showed no indication that he had recognised the presence of another in the room.

It annoyed her to think that he cared more about her disobedience than he did her safety. She pulled away from him, and turned to gesture to the man in the corner. 'Hector, may I present my husband, the Duke of Bellston. Adam, this is my brother, Hector.' She hoped she had not hesitated too much on the word Adam. She did not wish to appear unfamiliar with the name.

Hector ran out of air, mid-sentence, taking in a great gasp before managing, 'Husband?'

'Yes,' she replied as mildly as possible. 'When last we spoke, I indicated to you that I intended to marry, to settle the question of who should control my inheritance. And so I have married.'

'But you cannot.'

'Of course I can. I am of age, after all.'

'You cannot expect me to take a stranger into our home, on the basis of such a brief introduction.'

Her husband stood the rebuke mildly.

'Of course I do not. I have come for my possessions and will be moving them to my new home as soon as is possible.'

'Your new home.' Apparently, her brother was having some problem following the speed of events.

'Yes, Hector. I will be living with my husband, now that I am married.'

'You will do nothing of the kind. I have had more than enough of your nonsense. This is what comes of too much learning. Ideas. And telling jokes that are in no way funny. You will go to your room, and I will apologise to this gentleman, whoever he may be. And tomorrow, we will all go to the solicitors and straighten out the mess you have created.'

This time, she did not even bother to count. 'I will go to my room, Hector. To gather my clothing. From there, I mean to go to the library and the study, and empty them as well. And then I will be gone from this house and your presence. You have no power over me to stop it. And that, Hector, is what comes of not enough reading.'

His face was growing red, and he was readying a response.

And from behind her, she heard her husband, quietly clearing his throat. His voice was mildness and reason itself. 'Perhaps, Penny, it would be best if you saw to your packing, while I speak to your brother.'

She had the most curious feeling that he had issued a command, although it showed in neither his face nor his voice.

She opened her mouth to object, and then remembered how effectively he had dealt with the bankers. If he wished her to leave the room, then perhaps there was a reason for it. It would serve no purpose, challenging him in front of her brother. That would only prove Hector's point: that she had been foolish to marry in the first place. She blinked at Adam for a moment, then shrugged her shoulders and said, 'Very well.' And then she left the room, shutting the doors almost completely behind her.

Then she turned back and put her ear to the crack.

Her husband waited for a moment, giving her enough time to get to her room, she suspected. And then he waited even longer.

When the silence became oppressive, Hector blurted, 'Now see here, sir—'

Adam responded, 'The correct form of address when speaking to me is "your Grace". Perhaps you did not know it, since you obviously have little acquaintance with the peerage. But since we are family now...' disdain dripped from the last words '...you may call me Adam.'

Hector snorted. 'You cannot expect me to believe that Penny has been gone from the house less than a week, and has returned not only a married woman, but a duchess.'

Adam said, 'Your belief is not a requirement, Mr Winthorpe. The marriage exists. The bankers have been informed of it, and I have taken control of my wife's inheritance.'

This last seemed to give her brother pause, for he took a moment before letting out a weak laugh. 'But you cannot wish to be married to my sister. She is a nothing. A nobody.' There was another pause, and his tone changed. 'Albeit, a very wealthy nobody. And that could not possibly have influenced your decision when seeking such a humble bride—'

'Stop right there.' Adam did not shout, but the command in the tone was no longer an implication. 'I recommend that you pause to think before speaking further.' His voice dropped to just above a whisper. 'Here are the facts, and you would do well to remember them. Penelope is neither a nothing, nor a nobody. She is her Grace, the Duchess of Bellston. It will do you no good to hint that I am after her fortune, since she has gained as much, if not more, than I have by the union.'

There was another long pause, to allow the facts to sink into the thick skull of her brother. And then Adam said, 'But you have lost by her marriage, have you not? I've seen the books at the bank, and the withdrawals you have been making to keep your business afloat.'

Hector sputtered, 'I've done nothing of the kind. Those monies were for Penelope's expenses.'

'Then it shall not matter to you in the least that I am willing to take the management of the monies out of your hands. I can take care of my wife's bills without your help. You need trouble yourself no further with the management of her funds, but devote the whole of your time to business.' Her husband's tone clearly said, 'Dismissed.'

Penny covered her mouth to stifle a laugh.

But her brother refused to yield all. His voice rose to near a shout. 'All right, then. Very well. She has married and you have taken her money, and her as well. I wish you luck, your Grace, for you will find her fractious nature, her impulsive temper and her unending stubbornness to be more curse than blessing. She may pack her clothes and leave immediately, if she is so eager to do it. But she shall leave the books where they are. I have no intention of allowing her to put the contents of the family library into trunks and carry them from the house.'

Her husband seemed to consider on it, and then replied, with a neutral, 'If she wishes it, then it shall be so.'

Her brother shouted back, 'But it will leave the shelves empty!'

Adam responded quietly, 'That should not present much of a problem. You are a book printer, are you not? Bring home something from work to fill the shelves. I doubt it matters much what the titles may be, if one has no intention of reading them.'

If her brother recognised the insult to his intelligence, he let it pass without comment. 'This has nothing to do with whether I wish to read the books in question.'

'I thought not.'

'It is the value of the things. Do you know how many pounds has been spent to furnish that room?'

'Quite a few, I should think. She purchased many of those books herself, did she not?'

'When I could not manage to stop her.'

Adam's voice was cool reason. 'Then I see no reason that she need purchase them twice to stock the library in her new home. It is not as if she will be returning here to study.'

And still her brother would not give up. 'See here, you. You cannot think to take her from her family.'

'That is generally what happens when one marries,' Adam said, in a bored drawl. 'There is something in the

Bible about it, although I cannot say I remember the words. She is cleaving unto me, now. You have nothing to say in the matter of her future.'

Penny could almost imagine the wave of his hand, as he dismissed her brother's argument.

'Only because you have stolen her from me,' Hector snapped.

'Stolen her?' The duke laughed out loud. 'How long have you known your sister, sir? Is there some chance that you are adopted, or that she is some changeling, recently added to your family? I have limited acquaintance with her, I'll admit. But in that time I have learned enough to know that it would be exceptionally difficult to steal her from a place she wished to be, or to dissuade her from a path she had chosen for herself.'

'But that does not mean that I will allow her to behave foolishly.'

She was angry before she could even remember to count, and grabbed the door handle, ready to push her way back into the room and tell her brother that, after all that had been said and done, he had no right on earth to control her.

But Adam cut in before she could move. 'You have no authority over my wife. Penelope shall arrange for the transport of the library and the rest of her things to my townhouse. She shall do so at her own pace and in her own way. If I hear of any interference from you in the matter, if you place even the slightest obstruction in her way, I will take whatever action is necessary to thwart you, and it shall be my goal, henceforth, to see that you regret the impertinence. Are we in agreement?'

His voice held a cold fury that she had never heard before, and he was every bit the man she had imagined from *The Times*, so powerful that he could move the country with a few words.

Hector appeared to have been struck dumb, and so Adam answered for him. 'Very good. Our interview is at an end. I will be waiting in the carriage, should Penelope need me for anything. Which, for your sake, Mr Winthorpe, I sincerely hope she does not.'

Which meant he would be coming out into the hall in a moment, and he would realise that she was so lost to all manners as to listen at keyholes on private conversations. And, even worse, he might see the effect his speech had upon her, for her heart was fluttering so that she could hardly breathe.

She turned and sprinted towards the library, ducking into the open door, only to collide with Jem, knocking a case of books from his arms. The sound of the crash mingled with his bark of objection at people charging around the house and not watching where they were going.

Which in no way covered the faint chuckle she heard from the hall as her husband passed by on his way to the exit.

Chapter Six

Her heart was lighter, now that she had faced her brother at last. But empty as well. Hector was furious, and she'd cut herself off from the only home she'd ever known. It would have happened eventually, she supposed. Just as it should have happened four years before. But she had been prepared then. Now, the sudden marriage and all that came with it made her feel more alone than she had been, even though she had a life's companion to share it with.

And what a strange companion she had chosen. It had been much fun to watch him in action against her adversaries. And she hoped that her current feelings for him were not too apparent, for the afternoon's appointments and the masterful way he had handled things had left her breathless and not quite herself. She had half a mind to throw herself upon him, in a display of affection that would be most inappropriate towards a man who was nearly a stranger to her. And she feared that, if she spoke, she was liable to ramble on and sound as foolish as a schoolroom miss.

Her husband was seated opposite her in the hired carriage with a faint smile on his face, showing no effects of the day's changes. When she said nothing, he spoke. 'We have done a good day's work, I think. Your money is taken care of. Your things will be brought to the house tomorrow. I recommend that we send your manservant on his way, and attend to our supper, for we have missed tea, and I am feeling quite hungry. I can recommend several restaurants…'

Eating in public. She had always found it difficult to relax when in a crowd, and sitting down to a meal surrounded by strangers seemed to amplify those feelings. Suppose she were to order the wrong thing, use the wrong utensil when eating or break some other rule that would make her appear gauche to the duke or the people around them? If she took a simple meal in her rooms at the townhouse, she need have no worries of mistake. She would beg off, and save her husband the embarrassment of being seen with her. She said, 'I am accustomed to eat at home of an evening.'

'And I am not,' he said, with finality. 'I belong to several clubs— Boodle's, White's, Brooks's—and frequent them most evenings when I am in town. Of course, I cannot very well take you there. No ladies.' He stopped to consider his options.

So many clubs. It gave her a good idea where his wealth might have run to. And why he had needed so much of hers. 'It is more economical to dine at home,' she offered.

He raised an eyebrow and said, 'I imagine it is on such nights as the servants are engaged. My kitchen is most fine. You will know that soon enough. But remember, I have released the staff for the evening. You may go back, if you wish, and explain to them that economy requires they return to work.'

She gave a small shake of her head.

'I thought not. In the future, you may dine at home, as you wish. But do not be terribly surprised if I do not join you there, for I prefer society to peace and quiet. And tonight, we will dine out to celebrate the nuptials. That is only natural, is it not?'

She nodded hesitantly.

'I thought you would agree.' He smiled again, knowing that he was once more without opposition and gave directions to the driver.

On entering the restaurant, they were led by the head waiter to a prominent spot with the faintest murmur of 'your Grace'. Penny was conscious of the eyes of the strangers around them, tracking them to their table.

Her husband's head dipped in her direction. 'They are wondering who you are.'

'Oh, no.' She could feel the blood draining from her face and a lightness in her head as the weight of all the eyes settled upon her.

'My dear, you look quite faint.' He seemed genuinely concerned. 'Wine will restore you. And food and rest.' He signalled the waiter. 'Champagne, please. And a dinner fit for celebration. But nothing too heavy.' When his glass was filled, he raised it in toast to her. 'To my bride.'

The waiter took in the faintest breath of surprise, as did a woman at a nearby table, who had overheard the remark.

'Shh,' Penny cautioned. 'People are taking notice.'

'Let them,' Adam said, taking a sip. 'While you packed, I arranged for an announcement in tomorrow's *Times*. It is not as if it is to be a secret.'

'I never thought...'

'That you would tell anyone besides the bank that you had wed?'

'That anyone would care,' she said.

'I have no idea what people might think of your marriage,' he responded. 'But if I marry, all of London will care.'

She took a gulp of her own wine. 'That is most conceited of you, sir.'

'But no less true.'

'But there must be a better way to make the world aware than sitting in the middle of a public place and allowing the world to gawk at us,' she whispered.

He smiled. 'I am sorry. Have I done something to shame you, Penelope?'

'Of course not. We barely know—'

He cut her off before she could finish the sentence. 'Are you embarrassed to be seen with me?'

'Don't be ridiculous. You are the Duke of Bellston. Why would I be embarrassed?'

'Then I fail to understand why we should not be seen dining together, in a public place. It is not as if I do not wish my wife at my side.'

She was readying the argument that, of course, he

would not wish to dine with her. He was a duke, and she was a nobody. And he was every bit as beautiful as she was plain. And if he meant to embarrass her by showing the world the fact…

And then she looked at the way he was smiling at her. It was a kind smile, not full of passion, but containing no malice. And she imagined what it would be like, if he had dropped her at the townhouse, and gone on his merry way. Perhaps he would mention casually to some man at a club that he had wed. And there would be a small announcement in the papers.

People would wonder. And then, someone would see her, and nod, and whisper to others that it was obvious why the duke chose to leave his wife alone. When the most attractive feature was a woman's purse, you hardly need bring her along to enjoy the benefit.

Or, they could be seen in public for a time, and people might remark on the difference between them. But they would not think that the eventual separation of the two was a sign that he had packed her off to the country out of shame.

He watched as the knowledge came home to her. 'People will talk, Penny. No matter what we do. But there are ways to see that they speak aloud, and then lose interest. It is far less annoying, I assure you, than the continual whispering of those who are afraid to give voice to their suspicions.'

The plates arrived, and he offered her a bite of lobster on the end of his fork. 'Relax. Enjoy your dinner. And then we will go home.'

She took it obediently and chewed, numb with

shock. *Home. Together. With him.* The thoughts that flitted across her mind were madness. After the rough start in Scotland, her new husband was proving to be almost too perfect. In the space of a few hours, he had gained for her everything she could have wished. And now, if he would only let her go home and seclude herself in that horrible pink room before she said something foolish... If he insisted on staring at her as he had been with those marvellous blue eyes, and feeding her from his own plate as though she were a baby bird, who could blame her if she forgot that the need for familiarity was a sham, and began to think that deeper emotions were engaged.

There was a very subdued commotion at the entrance to the room, and Adam looked up. 'Aha. I knew news would travel quickly. But I had wondered how long it would take.'

A man strode rapidly toward them, weaving between the tables to where they sat. He noticed the space, set for two, and turned to the nearest empty table, seizing a chair and pulling it forward to them, seating himself between Penny and the duke. Then he looked at Adam and said, without preamble, 'When did you mean to inform me? Do you have any idea how embarrassing it is to be at one's club, enjoying a whisky and minding one's own business, only to have the man holding the book demanding that I pay my wagers on the date of your marriage? Of course I insisted that it was nonsense, for there was no way that such a thing would have occurred without my knowledge.'

Adam laughed. 'Ah, yes. I had forgotten the wagers.'

He looked sheepishly at Penny. 'I stand to lose a fair sum of money on that as well. I had bet against myself marrying within the year.'

Gambling, again. And losing. Another confirmation of her suspicions. 'You bet against yourself?'

He shrugged. 'I needed the money, and thought it must be a sure thing. But when I found you, darling, I quite forgot—'

'Darling?' the man next to her snapped. 'So it's true, then? You ran off to Scotland to get a wife, and told me nothing?'

'It did not occur to me until after,' Adam answered. 'Penny, may I present your brother-in-law, Lord William Felkirk. William, Penelope, my wife, the new duchess of Bellston.'

William stared at her, reached for his brother's wine glass and drained it.

William was a younger version of her husband. Not so handsome, perhaps, but he had a pleasant face, which would have been even more pleasant had it not been frozen in shock by the sight of her. Penny attempted a smile and murmured, 'How do you do?'

Will continued to stare at her in silence.

Adam smiled in her direction with enough warmth for both of them, and then looked back to his brother. 'Manners, Will. Say hello to the girl.'

'How do you do?' Will said without emotion.

'Penny is the heiress to a printer, here in London. We met when I was travelling.'

She could see the alarm in his eyes at the word printer, followed by a wariness. He examined her closely, and glanced from her to his brother. 'You were not long in the north, Adam. The trip lasted less than a week. Your marriage was most unexpected.'

'To us as well.'

He stared back at Penny, daring her to confirm the story. 'My brother never spoke of you.'

Her gaze dropped to her plate. 'We did not know each other for long before we married.'

'How fortunate for you to find a duke when you chose to wed. You must be enjoying your new title.' He had cut to the quick with no fuss.

'Frankly, I do not give it much thought.'

'Really.' He did not believe her.

Adam took a sip of wine. 'William, Penny's feelings on the matter of her sudden elevation to duchess are none of your concern. Now, join us in our celebration, for I wish you to be as happy as I am.' His voice held a veiled command.

Adam signalled for the waiter to bring another glass and plate, and they finished the meal in near silence, and William made no more attempts to question them.

Adam rubbed his temples and did his best to ignore the dull pain behind his eyes. It had been the longest meal of his life. First, he had needed to calm Penelope, who was clearly unaccustomed to the attention of the other diners. But he had done a fair job charming her back to good spirits. It had been going well, until Will had come and set things back on edge.

He'd had a good mind to tell his brother that the middle of a public dining room was no place to air the family laundry. If he could not manage to be a civil dinner companion, then he should take himself back to whatever foul cave he'd crawled from, and let them enjoy their food in peace.

When it was time to leave, William offered his carriage, and when they arrived at the townhouse, he followed them in, without invitation.

Adam should have refused him entrance, after his reprehensible behaviour in the restaurant. But if Will had anything to say on the subject of his brother's marriage, it might as well be said now and be over with, when the servants were away.

They were barely over the threshold before Will said, 'We must speak.' He glanced toward the study, then to Adam, totally ignoring the other person in the room.

Penny was aware of the slight. How could she not be, for Will made no effort to be subtle? She said, with false cheer, 'I will leave you two alone, then. Thank you for a most pleasant evening.'

Liar. But at least she was making an effort, which was more than he could say for his own family.

Penelope was barely clear of the room before William muttered, 'I will send for the solicitors immediately and we will put an end to this farce before anyone else learns of it.'

'The study, William,' he snapped, all patience gone.

They walked down the corridor, and he gestured Will into the room, slamming the door behind them.

Will paced the floor, not bothering to look in his direction. 'It has been only a few days, has it not? And most of that time, spent on the road. No one of importance has seen, I am sure. I will consult the lawyers, and begin the annulment proceedings. You will spend the night at your club, safely away from this woman.'

'I will do no such thing. I have no intention of leaving this house, and there will be no more talk of annulments.' Adam stalked past him, and threw himself into the chair behind the desk.

'You've lain with her already, have you?'

'That is none of your business, little brother.'

William nodded. 'I thought not. It is not a true marriage, but you have too much pride to admit the mistake.'

'This has nothing to do with pride.'

'Neither does it have to do with a sudden affection.'

Adam laughed. 'Affection? You expect me to marry for love, then?'

Will ceased his pacing and leaned over the desk, his fists planted on the wood. 'I think it is reasonable that there be at least a fondness between the two people involved. And it is plain that none exists between the two of you. You sat there at dinner with a false smile, pretending nothing was wrong, and she could barely look up from her plate.'

'We have an understanding.'

'That is rich.' Will snapped. 'She married you for your title, and you married her for her money. We can all claim the same understanding, for the fact is perfectly obvious to everyone who cares to look.'

'It is more complicated than that.'

'Do you mean to enlighten me as to how?'

Adam thought of the condition he'd been in when he'd made the decision to marry. And the condition just before, when he'd meant to end his life. 'No, I do not. That is something between my wife and myself.'

'Your wife.' Will snorted.

Adams hands tightened on the arms of his chair until he was sure that his fingers must leave marks in the wood. 'My wife, William. And I will thank you not to take that tone when referring to her. Despite what it may appear, I did not marry her for her money, any more than she sought to be a duchess. That we are both so blessed is a most fortunate occurrence, and I have no intention to annul. Lord knows, the estate needs the money she brings with her, and she has no objections to my using it.'

'So you will tie yourself to a woman that you do not love, just to keep the estate going.'

Adam stared at him, hardly understanding. 'Of course I would. If it meant that I could rebuild the house and protect the tenants until the next harvest time. Her money will mean the difference between success and failure this year.'

'What are the tenants to you, Adam? It is not as though they are family. And the manor is only a house.'

'It is my birthright,' Adam said. 'And I will do what is necessary to protect it. If it were you, would you not?'

William stared back at him, equally confused. 'I thank God every day that your title did not come to me. I have no desire to possess your lands, Adam.'

'But if it were to fall to you?' he pressed.

'Do not say that. For that would mean that you were dead. You are not ill, are you? Your line of questioning disturbs me.'

Adam waved his hand. 'No, no, I am not ill. It is only a rhetorical question. Do not read so much into it.'

'Then I will answer truthfully. No, I would not marry just for the sake of the title. Do not think you can marry for money to a woman you cannot bring yourself to bed, and then force me to be Bellston when you die without an heir. I would as soon see it all revert to the crown than become a slave to the land, as you are.'

Slavery? It was an honour. How could Will not understand? 'Search your heart and answer again. For it is quite possible that the whole thing will come to you, at any rate.'

Will waved the suggestion away. 'Not for long. If you mean to escape your responsibility with a hypothetical and untimely death, then two of us can play the game. I would rather die than inherit.'

Adam paused to thank God for the timely intervention of Penelope and her wild scheme. His death would have served no purpose if it had forced Will to take such action as he threatened. And he would not have wanted the heir he saw before him now. Will had always seemed so strong. Why had he never noticed that he was selfish as well?

Will continued. 'I suggest again that you seek an annulment if you do not wish for a legitimate heir from this poor woman. It is not fair to her, nor to me, for you to play with our fates in such a way, so that you can buy slate for your roof.'

Adam tried one last time. 'But if it falls to you…'

'I will take whatever measures are necessary to see that it does not.'

Damn it to hell. Here was another thing that he would have to contend with. Until now, he had assumed that there would be no problem with the succession. He had thought no further than the immediate crisis, just as he had thought no further when attempting suicide.

He must learn to play a longer game if he wished to succeed.

He looked to his brother again. 'I do not mean to abandon this life just yet, so you need not fear an inheritance. I had no idea that you felt so strongly about it.'

'I do.'

'Very well, then. No matter what may occur, you will not be the next duke. But neither do I intend to abandon my current plan just yet. The heir situation will sort itself out eventually, I suspect.'

'Do you, now?' His brother laughed. 'If you think it can sort itself out without some intervention on your part, then you are as cloth-headed as I've come to suspect. You wife is waiting in your bed, Adam. Let the sorting begin.'

Chapter Seven

Penny tried to put the mess downstairs behind her as she climbed the stairs to her room. William Felkirk had made little effort to disguise his distaste for her and was no doubt pouring poison in his brother's ears on the subject of marriage to upstart title hunters.

There was little she could do about it if Adam chose to listen. An acquaintance of several days and a trumped-up marriage were not equal to a bond of blood. She could only wait to see if he came to her room to explain that it had been a mistake, that he was terribly sorry, and that they would be undoing today's work in the morning.

She looked at her bedchamber and sighed, nearly overcome with exhaustion. No matter the outcome, she needed a warm bed and a good night's sleep. But the room in front of her was as cold and dark as it had been earlier in the day. If there was fuel available, she could manage to lay her own fire, but she could see by the light of her candle that the hearth and grate were empty. Not an ash remained.

She looked in trepidation at the connecting door to her husband's room. If she could borrow some coal and a Lucifer from his fire, and perhaps a little water from the basin, she could manage until the servants came back in the morning.

She knocked once; when there was no answer she pushed the door open and entered.

The bed had been turned down and a fire laid, despite the servants' day off. It was warm and cheerful, ready for occupation, and nothing like the room she had just left. There was a crystal bowl on the night table filled with red roses, and stray petals sprinkled the counterpane. Their fragrance scented the room.

Her portmanteau was nowhere to be seen, but her nightrail lay on the bed, spread out in welcome.

The door to the hall opened, and she looked back at her husband, leaning against the frame.

'My room is not prepared,' she said, to explain her presence.

He ran a hand through his hair in boyish embarrassment. 'The servants assume…'

She nodded.

He shrugged. 'You can hardly expect otherwise.'

'And what are we to do to correct the assumption?'

He stared at her. 'Why would we need to do that? That a man and a wife, newly married, might wish to share a bed is hardly cause for comment. But that a man and a woman, just wed, do not? That is most unusual. More gossip will arise from that than the other.'

She looked doubtful. 'I wondered if that might not matter to you so much now you have spoken to your brother.'

'Whatever do you mean?'

'That perhaps, now that you are back in your own home, you might wish to call a halt to our marriage. It is not too late, I think, to have second thoughts in the matter. And I would not fault you for it.'

'Because my brother does not approve?' He made no attempt to hide the truth from her. Although it hurt to hear it, his honesty was admirable.

He stepped into the room and closed the door behind him. 'What business is this of Will's? When he takes a wife, he will not wish me to trail along, giving offense and offering advice where none was requested. I recommend that you ignore Will as I intend to.' He moved across the room to a chair, sat down and set to work removing his boots.

Very well, then. There had been no change in her status. But what was to happen now? Did he mean to change in front of her? She was torn between embarrassment and a growing curiosity. How far did he mean to take their marriage? They had discussed nothing like this on the road from Scotland.

Then he stood up and walked across the room in his stockinged feet, locked the door and dragged the heavy comforter from the bed across the room to his chair. 'It shall not be the finest bed in London, but I have had worse.' He gestured to the rose-strewn mattress on the other side of the room. 'Be my guest.'

She sat on the edge of the bed and watched him as

he divested himself of coat and waistcoat, untied his cravat and undid his cuffs. He sat down again, slouching into the chair, long legs stretched out before him, wrapped the comforter around his body, and offered her a sketch of a salute, before closing his eyes.

She blew out her candle, placed her spectacles on the night table beside the bed, removed her slippers and stretched out on top of the sheets, arms folded over her chest.

From across the room, her husband's voice came as a low rumble. 'Is that how you mean to sleep? It cannot be comfortable.'

'For you either,' she said.

'But at least I am not fully dressed. Shall I call someone to help you out of your gown?'

'I can manage the gown myself, for I am most limber and can reach the hooks. But that would leave the corset, and I fear the lacing is too much for me. If we do not wish the servants to gossip, then I think not.'

He sighed and got out of his chair. 'I shall help you, then.'

'That would be most improper.'

He laughed. 'For better or worse, madam, I am your husband. It is the most proper thing in the world.'

She hesitated.

'It will look much stranger to have the maid undo the laces tomorrow than to let me do it tonight. Here, slide to the edge of the bed, and turn your back to me.'

She sat up and crawled to where he could reach her, turning her back to him. She could feel his touch, businesslike, undoing the hooks of the bodice and pushing it open wide until it drooped down her shoulders. She tensed.

'You needn't worry, you know. I will not hurt you or damage the gown.' He laughed softly. 'I have some small experience with these things. In fact, I can do it with my eyes closed if that makes you feel more comfortable.'

It would be ludicrous to describe the sensations she was experiencing as comfort. It would have been comforting to have the efficient, easily ignored hands of a maid to do the work. She would have climbed into bed and not thought twice about it.

But a man was undressing her. And since he had closed his eyes, it seemed he needed to work more slowly to do the job. He had placed his hand on her shoulders and squeezed the muscles there in his large palms before sliding slowly over the bare skin of her upper back and down the length of the corset to the knot at the bottom. He reached out to span her waist, and she drew a sharp breath as he undid the tie of her petticoat and pushed it out of the way. Then he leaned her forward slightly, and his fingers returned to the corset to work the knot free.

She could feel it loosen, and tried to assure him that she could manage the rest herself, but no breath would come to form the words.

He was moving slowly upwards, fingers beneath the corset, pulling the string free of the eyelets, one set at a time. She could feel the warmth of his hands through the fabric of her chemise, working their way up her body until the corset was completely open.

There was a pause that seemed like for ever as his hands rested on her body, only the thin cotton between his touch and her skin. And then he moved and the corset slipped free. She folded her arms tight to her chest, trying to maintain some modesty before it fell away to leave her nearly bare.

'Can you manage the rest?' His voice was annoyingly clear and untroubled.

She swallowed. 'I think so. Yes.'

'Very well, then. Goodnight, Penelope.'

And she heard him returning to his chair.

She squinted at him from across the room, until she was reasonably sure that his eyes were closed and he would see nothing. She hurried to remove her clothing, throwing it all to the floor and diving into her nightgown and under the sheets, safely out of sight.

She settled back on to the bed, pulling the linens up over her and waiting for sleep that did not come. The fire was dying, and the chill was seeping into the corners, though her skin still tingled with the heat from his touch.

It probably meant nothing to him. He was familiar with women's garments and the removing of them. He had done what he had done many times before, albeit with different results.

Her unwilling mind flashed to what it would have been like, if she was anyone other than who she was. His hands would be as slow and gentle as they had been while undoing her dress. Only, when the laces of the stays were undone, he would not stop touching her. Instead, he would lean forwards, and his lips would come down upon her skin.

She stared at the canopy of the bed, eyes wide, unable to stop the pictures playing in her mind and the phantom feeling of his hands and his mouth. Her body gave an uncontrollable shudder in response.

Across the room from her, her husband stirred in his chair, and rose, moving through the darkness towards her.

Without warning, the comforter dropped upon her body, and his hands smoothed it over her, tucking it close about her. Warmth flooded her, the warmth of his own body, left in the quilt. She sighed happily.

He returned to his chair, stretched out and slept.

Chapter Eight

When she awoke, light was seeping through the cracks in the bed curtains, which had been drawn at some point during the night. She could hear movement, and hushed voices from the other side. She sat up and placed her ear to the crack, so that she could listen.

Her husband. Talking to a servant, who must be his valet. Arranging for someone in the staff who would serve as a lady's maid, temporarily, at least. Perhaps permanently, since he was unsure if her Grace had servants of her own whom she wished to bring to the household. He had not discussed the matter with her.

The valet hurried away, and the door closed. She could hear her husband approaching the bed, and she pulled back from the curtain.

'Penny?' He said it softly, so as not to startle a sleeper.

'Yes?'

'May I open the curtains?'

'Yes.' Her voice was breathless with excitement, and she cleared her throat to cover the fact. As the light streamed in and hit her, she rubbed her eyes and yawned, trying to appear as though she had just awakened.

Adam was wrapped in a dressing gown, and she could see flashes of bare leg when she looked down. She must remember not to look down, then, for the thought that he was bare beneath his robe made her feel quite giddy.

'Did you sleep well?' He was solicitous.

'Very. Thank you. Your bed is very comfortable.' She glanced in the direction of the chair. 'I am sorry that you did not have the same luxury.'

Which might make it sound like she had wanted him there. She fell silent.

He ignored the implication. 'I slept better than I have in a long time, knowing that the financial future of my property is secure. Thank you.' The last words were heartfelt, and the intimacy of them shocked her.

'You're welcome.' She was in the bed of an incredibly handsome man, and he was thanking her. 'And thank you. For yesterday. For everything.'

He smiled, which was almost as blinding as the sunlight. Why must he be so beautiful, even in the morning? A night sleeping upright in a chair had not diminished the grace of his movements or dented his good humour. And his hair looked as fine tousled by sleep as it did when carefully combed.

She dreaded to think how she must appear: pale and groggy, hair every which way, and squinting at him without her glasses. She reached for them, knocking them off the night table, and he snatched them out of the air before they hit the floor and handed them to her, then offered the other hand to help her from bed.

She dodged it, and climbed unaided to the floor, pulling on her glasses.

'It will be all right, I think,' he said, ignoring her slight. 'We have survived our first day in London as man and wife. It will be easier from now on.'

Perhaps he was right. She went through the door to her own room to find it bustling with activity. Her clothing had arrived, and an overly cheerful girl named Molly was arranging a day dress for her, and had a breakfast tray warming by the fire. When she went downstairs, the first crates of books had arrived and were waiting for her in the sitting room. She had marked the ones that she expected to be the most important, opened those, and left the others lined up against a wall to obscure the decorating. The rest she could arrange on the shelves that had held the china figurines. She handed them, one piece at a time, to a horrified Jem to carry to storage, until his arms were quite full of tiny blushing courtiers, buxom maid servants and shepherds who seemed more interested in china milkmaids than in china sheep.

Jem appeared torn, unable to decide if he was more horrified by the overt femininity of the things or the possibility that he might loose his grip and smash several hundred pounds' worth of antique porcelain.

She waved him away, insisting that it mattered not, as long as they were gone from the room and she could have the shelves empty.

She gestured with the grouping in her hand, only to glance at the thing and set it down again on the table, rather than handing it to the overloaded servant. The statue was of a young couple in court clothes from the previous century. The man was leaning against a carefully wrought birdcage, and had caught his lover around the waist, drawing her near. She was leaning into him, bosom pressed to his shoulder, her hand cupping his face, clearly on the verge of planting a kiss on to his upturned lips.

And Penny's mind flashed back to the previous evening, and the feel of her husband's hands as they had touched her back. What would have happened if she had turned and pressed her body to his?

Jem shifted from foot to foot in the doorway, and she heard the gentle clink of porcelain.

'Never mind,' she said. 'You have more than enough to carry. I will keep this last one for now. Perhaps it can serve as a bookend.' She placed it back on the shelf, pushing it to the side to support a stack of books. *The Maid of Hamlet. The Orphan of the Rhine.* She'd kept the Minerva novels. Her lust-crazed Germans were supporting a shelf full of fainting virgins.

She sank back on to a chair, defeated by rampant romance.

There was a commotion in the hall, breaking through the silence of the room, and coming closer as she listened, as though a door had opened and a dinner party had overflowed its bounds. She could hear laughter, both male and female, and her husband by turns laughing and attempting to quiet the others.

At last there was a knock on the closed door of her room before Adam opened it and said with amused exasperation, 'Penelope, my friends wish to meet you.'

She did not know how she imagined the nobility might behave, but it had never been like this. The crowd pushed past the duke and into the room without waiting for permission to enter. The women giggled and pulled faces at the great piles of books, and one man leaned against a pile of open crates, nearly upending them on to the floor. Only the last to enter offered her anything in way of apology: he gave an embarrassed shrug that seemed to encompass the bad manners of his friends while saying that there was little he could do about it one way or the other.

'So this is where you've been keeping her, trapped in the sitting room with all these dusty books.' A pretty blonde woman in an ornate, flowered bonnet ran a critical finger over her library.

'Really, Barbara—' the laugh in Adam's response sounded false '—you make it sound as though I have her locked in her room. I am not *keeping* her anywhere.'

'She is keeping you, more like.' An attractive redhead made the comment, and Penny stiffened.

The woman clarified. 'I imagine the bonds of new love are too strong to break away, Adam. I wonder if you will manage to leave your house.'

Penny returned her cold smile. That had not been what she'd meant at all. It had been a slight on her wealth, followed by sarcasm. She was sure of it.

But Adam ignored it, smiling as if nothing had been said, and Penny vowed to follow his example.

Her husband gestured to his friends. 'Penelope, may I present Lord John and Lady Barbara Minton, Sir James and Lady Catherine Preston and my oldest, and dearest, friend, Lord Timothy Colton, and his wife, the Lady Clarissa.' He gestured to the cruel redhead and the man who had acknowledged Penny earlier. Adam smiled proudly at the man, and then looked to Penny. 'You will get along well with Tim, I think, for he is also a scholar. Botany. Horticulture. Plants and such. No idea what he's doing half the time. Quite beyond me. But I am sure it is very important.' Adam waved his hand dismissively, and Tim laughed.

Penny didn't understand the reason for her husband's pretended ignorance or the meaning of the joke. But clearly it was an old one, for the others found it most amusing. The room dissolved in mirth. It was like finding herself in a foreign land, where everyone spoke a language that she could not comprehend.

When their laughter had subsided, Clarissa spoke again. 'And what shall we call you?' The woman reached out to her, and took both her hands in what seemed to be a welcoming grip. Her fingers were ice cold.

'I know,' said Lady Barbara. 'We could call you Pen. For Adam says you like to write. And you were a book printer's daughter.'

Lady Catherine rolled her eyes. 'You write on paper, Bunny. Not in books.'

Clarissa looked down at Penny with a venomous smile. 'Surely not "Penny", for you are not so bright as all that.' There was a dangerous pause. 'Your hair, silly. It is I who should be called Penny.' She released Penny's hands and touched a coppery curl, smiling past her to look at Adam.

Penny watched, with a kind of distant fascination. Clarissa's gesture had been blatant flirtation, and she seemed not to care who noticed it. Yet her husband, Timothy, paid it no attention. He seemed more interested in the books on the table before him than his wife's behaviour to another man.

Adam ignored it as well, avoiding Clarissa's gaze while answering, 'But it is not your name, is it, Clare? Penny was named for the loyal wife of Odysseus. And she is worth far more than copper.'

There was an awkward pause.

Clarissa responded, 'So we assumed. We can hope that you are worth your weight in gold, Pen, for you will need to be to equal your husband's spending.'

And then they all laughed.

One, two, three... Penny felt shame colouring her skin compounded by anger at Clarissa and her own husband, and the pack of jackals that he had allowed into her study to torment her. She wanted nothing more than to run from the room, but it would only have made the situation worse. So she forced a laugh as well.

Her response would not have mattered, for now that she had wounded, Clarissa ignored her again and returned her attention to the duke. 'Darling Adam, it is so good to see you back amongst us. It is never the same when you are not here. London is frightfully boring without you, is it not, Timothy?'

Her own husband was looking at her with a sardonic twist to his smile. 'Would that you found such pleasure in my company as you do in Adam's, my darling.' He turned to Adam. 'But I missed you as well, old friend. Without you, times have been sober, as have I. We must put an end to that sorry condition as soon as possible. White's? Boodle's? Name your poison, as they say.'

'White's, I think. This evening?'

'Of course.'

Clarissa stamped her foot. 'You will do nothing of the kind. I expect you to dine in this evening. With us.' She made little effort to include her husband in her invitation. And none to include Penny, literally turning away to shut her out from the group.

Adam eluded her gaze again, speaking to the room rather than the woman before him. 'We would, but I believe my wife has other plans.' There was the subtlest emphasis on 'we', to remind Clarissa of the change in status. And then he glanced at Penny, waiting for her to confirm what he had said.

She tried to imagine herself responding as Clarissa had. She would say something clever, about how divine it would be to spend an evening at table with a woman who her husband held so dear. And there would be the same ironic tone that the others were using, to indicate an undercurrent of flirtation, and proof that she knew what was what. It would anger Adam, but he would admire her fearlessness. And it would enrage Clarissa. Which would be strangely pleasing, for Penny found herself taking an instant dislike to the woman.

Instead, she replied haltingly, 'Yes, I fear I am most busy. With my studies. And will be unable to get away.'

'You cannot leave your books.' Clarissa turned and

glanced down at her, then looked back at the others as if Penny's social ineptitude had been more than confirmed. 'But you do not mind if Adam comes without you, of course.' The woman dared her to respond in the negative.

And here was where she must admit defeat, ceding the field with the battle barely begun. Although why she would feel the need to fight for this, she had no idea.

Before she could answer, Adam spoke for her. 'My darling wife would have my best interests at heart, no matter what she might say, for she wishes to see me happy. And since I have already expressed a desire to go to White's with Tim, she would not think to drag me into mixed society, no matter how pleasant it might be for her.' He glanced back to his friend. 'Eight o'clock, then?'

If Tim was relieved, he did not show it, only smiling in acknowledgement of the plan. And then he smiled at Penny with unexpected warmth. 'Do not worry, my dear. No gels allowed at White's. I will keep your new husband on the straight and narrow. As long as you have no objection to cards and whisky.'

Penny searched again for a clever reply that would not come. 'Of course, not. Whatever Adam wishes…'

Clarissa was clearly piqued. 'It does not do, Penelope, to give a man latitude in these things. It leads them to take one too much for granted.'

Adam snapped back at her, 'On the contrary, Clarissa, a man is more likely to give his affection to one who can manage, on occasion, to put the needs of others before her own selfish desires.' Adam was looking straight into the woman's eyes for once, and

Penny realised, with sickening clarity, why he had been avoiding the contact.

They were lovers. They had been, or soon would be—it mattered not which. While Adam might smile at the wives of the other men in the room and laugh at their foolishness, he dared not acknowledge Clarissa, for when he looked at her, the guilt was plain in his eyes for all who cared to see.

After the brief lapse, he looked away from her again, and proceeded to act as though she were not in the room with them.

Penny looked to the others, watching the silent messages flash between them. Those who were positioned to see Adam's expression passed the truth to those who could not, with furtive glances and hungry smiles. Only Timothy appeared oblivious to what had happened, his attention absorbed by a volume of Aristotle.

And then the moment passed, and Adam stepped around Clarissa to stand behind his own wife. 'I am lucky to have married such a gracious woman, and hope never to take the fact for granted.'

Penny felt the mortification rising in her, forming a barrier between her and the outside. Was she expected to put her needs so far to the side that she must condone his adultery?

And then her husband put his hand upon her shoulder, as a gesture of affection and solidarity, and she jumped, as though she had been burned.

There were more sidelong glances and more wicked smiles. Suddenly Lord Timothy cut through the silence, shutting his book with a snap. 'Yes, Adam. We must offer you congratulations on your amazing luck. And it is good that you recognise it, for a man is truly blessed when he has the love and respect of such an intelligent woman.' He turned to the others in his party. 'And now, ladies and gentleman, we should be going, for we are quite destroying the peace of the household and keeping her Grace from her studies.'

'Let me show you out.' Adam took the lead, and the others fell obediently in behind him. Clarissa made as if to stay behind, but her husband held the door for her, making it impossible for her to linger.

When she was gone, Lord Timothy turned back into the room, and favoured Penny with another brief, encouraging smile. 'Good day to you, Penelope. And good fortune as well.' And then he was gone, shutting the door behind him.

She sank back on to the settee, weak with confusion. Adam had seemed so kind. He was good to her. Affectionate, in a distant sort of way. And in a short time it had become easy to imagine the affection blossoming into something warmer. Never passion. She could not hope for something so ridiculous. But love, in the classical sense. A respect for each other that might lead to a mutually satisfying relationship.

But how could she ever trust a man that would betray his best friend? And what did he mean for her, in any case? They had talked in Scotland about living as amiable strangers. And then he had paraded his lover under her nose, allowed her to be the butt of his friends' jokes, then glossed it over with fine and empty words about mutual respect.

If this was how fashionable society behaved, then she had been right in her decision to turn her back on it. But what was she to do if society hunted her out and continued to harass her?

She could hear her husband's step in the hall, and prayed that, for once, he would abide by his earlier promises, go to his study, and leave her in peace.

But instead he opened her door without preamble and shut it tightly behind him, then glared at her. He was angry. She could see it flashing in his eyes, and noted the stiffness of his back, as though his movements were containing some sudden physical outburst. His tone was curt. 'I wish to speak of what just happened here.'

'Nothing happened, as far as I noticed.'

'Exactly.' He frowned. 'And those around us took note of the nothing. It will be quite the talk of the town.'

'They took note of so many things, I am at a loss as to which one you refer to. Could it have been when you informed them of my monetary worth to you?'

'I misspoke. I had intended to praise your virtues, and the words went wrong.'

'Perhaps because I have so few virtues to extol. Since you cannot discuss my birth or my beauty, I should thank you on the compliment to my purse.'

'Believe me, Penny, I do not wish to call further attention to your wealth. It is not a point of pride that my friends suspect I married beneath me to get to your money.'

'Beneath you?' she snapped. 'When I discovered you, you were face down in a stable yard and under the horses. To marry beneath yourself, you would have to look quite a bit further than the daughter of a cit. There was not much lower you could have sunk.'

He flinched. 'I will avoid fulsome praise of you in the future, for I have no talent for flattery. In any case, it is wasted on one who makes no attempt to hide her distaste of me.'

'*I* have a distaste of you? Whatever do you mean?'

He glared at her. 'I might have been face down in the muck when you found me, but in marrying me, you got control of your inheritance and bagged a title. You understand, do you not, that many men would not be nearly so tractable as I have been towards you? We get on quite well, considering. And I did not mean to insult you in any way, nor do I plan to in the future. But I expect the same in return.

'It is one thing, madam, to refuse my affection, when we are alone. You avoided my hand this morning, but I thought, "Perhaps she is shy. I must give her time to trust me." But it is quite another thing to shrink from my merest touch when we are in public.'

'I did nothing of the kind.'

He reached to touch her hand, and she pulled away from him.

He smiled, coldly. 'Of course not, my dear. You are just as welcoming now as you were before. I touched your shoulder, and you looked to all the world as if I had struck you.'

'I thought it was agreed—'

'When I agreed to a marriage in name only, I did not realise that you found me so utterly repugnant that you would deny me all physical contact. Nor did I expect that you would make the fact known to my friends.'

'You do not repel me.' No matter how much she might wish he did.

'Oh, really? Then you had best prove it to me. Take my hand and assure me.'

She stared at the hand he held out to her, the long fingers curled to beckon, but she made no move to take it.

He nodded. 'I see. Most comforting.'

'I do not see why it is so important to you.' *You have her attention. Why must you have mine as well?*

He stared back at her until she met his eyes. 'I am a proud man. I do not deny it. It does not reflect well on either of us to have the full details of our relationship as public gossip. We are married, and I hope to remain so. The time will pass more easily for both of us if you can bring yourself to be at ease in my company, at least when we are in public. I will not bother you at home any more than is necessary.'

There was frustration and anger in his eyes, but they were still the same compelling blue, and just as hard to resist as they had been when she had trusted his motives. 'How can I do this?' she asked herself, as much as she did him.

His shoulders relaxed a little. 'You could, on occasion, smile while in public. I would not expect unceasing mirth. Merely as pleasant a face as you wear when we are alone. And if my hand should happen to brush yours, you need not flinch from it.' He raised his hand in oath. 'I promise to treat you with the care and respect due my wife and my duchess.' And then he offered it to her again.

She closed her eyes, knowing in her heart what his respect for his wife was worth, if he could not respect the marriage of another. Then she reached tentatively out to put her hand in his.

She heard him sigh, and his fingers closed over hers, stroking briefly before pushing her hand back until they were palm to palm and he could link fingers with her. He squeezed. 'There. Feel? There is nothing to be afraid of. I mean you no harm.' His other hand came to her face, and the fingertips brushed lightly against her cheek. 'I only wish for you to leave others with the impression that there is some warm feeling between us. Nothing more. That perhaps we might share something other than an interest in your money. Help me undo my foolish words.' His hand touched her hair and stroked to the back of her neck, and he moved close enough so she could feel his breath on her skin, and the change in the air against her lips as he spoke.

'This is much better, is it not?' His voice was low and husky, as she had never heard it before, barely more than a whisper.

She opened her eyes. He was right. When he was this close and looking at her, it ceased to matter how he looked at other women. She could feel the magnetic pull to be even closer. She had but to lean in a few inches, and his lips would be upon hers.

Which was madness. She had to resist yet another urge to jump away from him in alarm, and watched as his pupils shrank, and the soft smile on his face returned to its normal, more businesslike form. He withdrew slowly, with easy, unruffled grace. 'Very good. That is much more what I had hoped for. I do not expect you to fall passionately into my arms as a false display for visitors. But if we could at least give the appearance that we are on friendly terms, I would be most grateful.' His fingers untwined and his hand slipped away from hers.

'Most certainly. For I do wish to be on friendly terms with you in more than appearance.' She sighed, and hoped it sounded like a longing for her books, and not for renewed contact. 'And now, if you will excuse me? I must return to work.'

'Of course.'

Adam left the room, closing the door behind him, and moved quickly down the hall. Hell and damnation, it had been an unbearable morning. First, the invasion of his friends, before he'd had a chance to explain to Penny how things were likely to be. Although she probably suspected, what with the way Clarissa had been making a fool of herself, with no care for the fact that Tim was in the room with them.

Penny must think him a complete fraud. She had looked around the room, at his friends and at Clarissa, and had seen it all. She'd read his character in a glance and must regret her decision.

And he, who had always been so sure of his words, even when nothing else would go right for him, had stumbled so egregiously as to let it appear that he had married her for money. If possible, it was even worse than the truth to say such a thing. He had allowed her no dignity at all. And he had seen the mocking light in the eyes of his friends when she had flinched from his touch.

He had been foolishly angry, at himself and at Clarissa, and had taken it out on Penny for not offering affection that he had not earned. But what had he been about, just now? Had he been trying to teach her some kind of lesson? Hopefully, it had been lost on her, if he had. He should have come back to her and taken her hand in a most friendly fashion, and tried to mend the breach he had caused. He should have assured her that although he had been guilty of grave transgressions, it was all in the past, and that he meant to be a better man.

Instead, he had touched her hair and forgotten all. What sense was it to talk when there were soft lips so close, waiting to be kissed? And she had closed her eyes so sweetly, allowing him to observe the fine lashes and the smooth cheek and the sweetness of her breath as it mingled with his. It was a matter of inches, a bare nod of the head to bring them into contact with his own, and to slip his tongue into her mouth and kiss her until she reacted to his touch with the eagerness he expected in a wife.

He shook his head again. Had he forgotten whom he was speaking of? If he needed to persuade his own wife to let him hold her hand, then passion-drugged nights were not likely to be in the offing.

Not while he remained at home, at any rate. Perhaps it had been too long since last he visited his mistress. A man had urges, after all. And he was neglecting his if his own wife began to tempt him more than someone else's. An afternoon relaxing in the arms of his paramour would clear his mind, which was clouded with misdirected lust, and make it easier to decide what to do about the impossible relationship with Clarissa and the unwelcome attraction to Penelope.

He called for a carriage and set out to regain control of his emotions.

As he passed out the door, he saw Penny's manservant, who stood at the entrance to the house, wearing the Bellston livery as though it were as great an honour as a night in the stocks. He looked at Adam and bowed with as much respect as the other servants, while conveying the impression that the lady of the house was worth two dukes.

Adam glared back at him. 'Jem, isn't it?'

'Yes, your Grace.' And another bow.

Damn the man. Adam fished in his pocket and came up with a handful of banknotes and forced them into the servant's hand. 'I have an errand for you. Go to the bookseller's. And buy my wife that damned copy of Homer.'

Chapter Nine

In the two years they had been together, Adam's mistress, Felicity, had been a most accommodating and entertaining companion. But now, as he looked at her, he could not seem to remember why. She was beautiful, of course. There was little reason to have her otherwise. While she might not be the most enchanting conversationalist, he employed her to listen, not to talk. And so it mattered little.

She greeted him as she always had, with a passionate kiss. Her perfect hands reached out to stroke him and to smooth his brow.

And to search his pockets, as well. 'What did you being me, Adam?' Her smile was as satisfied as a cat's.

He smiled back. 'And why must I have brought you anything?' Although, of course, he had.

'Because you always do, my darling. I have come to expect it. And there is the little matter of your recent marriage.' She experimented with a pout, but her heart was not in it. 'You could at least have told me your plans. Even though it does not change what we share, it is not pleasant to be surprised when reading *The Times.*'

He nodded. 'I am sorry. I never intended for my situation to change so suddenly, or I would have fore-warned you.'

She nodded. 'It was love at first sight, then.' Clearly, she did not believe it any more than he did, but it was sweet of her to give him the benefit of the doubt.

'Rather. Yes.'

'Then, let us celebrate.' She kissed him again with an ardour guaranteed to arouse.

But the irony of the situation washed over him, and it was as though he were watching the kiss from a distance, rather than being an active participant in it. To be celebrating one's wedding in the arms of a Cyprian was probably sin enough for God to strike him dead on the spot. When their lips parted, he laid his against her ear and murmured, 'Then you no longer wish to see your gift?'

'I wish to see it, if you wish to show it to me,' she said, the most co-operative woman in his life.

He guided her fingers to the breast pocket of his jacket, to the package he had purchased on the way to her flat.

She was immediately distracted and withdrew the bracelet from the jewel box in his pocket. 'Adam, it is magnificent. The size of the diamonds. And the clarity.' She examined it with the eye of a professional. 'Th-thank you. It is quite the nicest thing you have ever brought me.'

He must have chosen well, if he had made a whore stammer. 'I am glad you appreciate it.'

For it cost me more than all your other gifts put together. Now that I can borrow from my wife's purse, money does not matter. And she will not care that I am here, for I have bought her a book. The truth sickened him, even as he thought it. And again, it was as though he was viewing the scene from a distance.

His mind might be shamed by what he had done, but his body cared not, and awaited the reward forthcoming after a gift.

And his mouth agreed with neither of them. As though he had no control over it, it announced, 'Yes. Of course. I thought, under the circumstances, an extra expenditure was called for. For you see…'

And his mouth proceeded, unbidden, to explain that now that he was married, their relationship had indeed changed. Since it was unlikely that he would be able to spend much time in her presence, it was hardly fair to keep her. The lavish gift was meant as a parting token. The apartment would be available for her use until such time…

His body howled in disappointment, and called him all kinds of fool, but still the words would not stop. And with each one, his conscience felt lighter.

His mistress was taking the whole thing annoyingly well.

She shrugged. 'I suspected as much. When a man gets it into his head to marry, his priorities change. And we have been together for quite some time, have we not?'

He started. She sounded bored with his attentions. The fact that she bored him as well was small consolation.

'And you have always been most considerate of me, and very generous of spirit. Should you need similar companionship in the future, I would not hesitate to recommend you as a protector.'

It sounded almost as if she was giving him references. 'And I, you.' He stuttered. 'Recommend, I mean. Should you need…'

He returned to his townhouse, numb with shock. The day was not turning out as planned. His old friends annoyed him. He'd just denied himself an afternoon of pleasure for no logical reason. And he still had no idea how to deal with his new wife. He returned home, because he could think of nowhere else to go. There was no joy in lunching alone, but his clubs would be too full of people, asking questions he did not desire to answer. At least in his own house he could have the consolation of solitude.

He was over the threshold before he remembered that he no longer lived alone. He had handed his hat and stick to the servant, and was halfway down the hall when he heard the rattle of tea things from the sitting room. Her door was open.

Too late, then, to take back his hat and back out of the door. Perhaps she would not notice if he quietly went to his rooms.

And then his wife peered into the hall. 'I was just sitting down to tea. Would you care to join me?'

'Thank you.' Once again, his mouth had said something that came as a surprise to him.

'I will have the butler bring another cup. You look in

need of refreshment. Come. Sit down.' And she graciously welcomed him to sit in his own home.

Her home as well, he reminded himself. She had every right to be taking tea in the room he had promised was solely for her use. And she was performing her duty as wife to see that he was provided with his. What right did he have to complain?

He sat down on the sofa next to her and waited in silence, while she pulled a tiny table closer to him and prepared his cup as she'd seen him take it. 'Biscuit?'

He stared at the unfamiliar thing in front of him.

She responded without his asking, 'I am accustomed to take sweets in the afternoon. These are a favourite of mine. I find the lemon zest in them most refreshing, so I have given the recipe to Cook. But if you would prefer something more substantial…'

'No. This is fine. Thank you.'

She was staring at him now. And he raised his eyes from his cup, to stare back at her.

'I am sorry for suggesting it,' she remarked, 'but is something the matter? You seem rather out of sorts.'

'What business is it of yours?' he snapped. And immediately regretted his outburst.

She was unfazed. 'Only that, earlier in the day, you said you wished to be friends.'

'I said I wished to appear to be friends. That is an entirely different matter.'

Again, she was unfazed, but answered thoughtfully, 'As you wish. Although it is sometimes easier to keep up the appearance, if an actual friendship exists.' There was no tartness in her voice. Merely a statement of fact.

He rubbed his brow with his hand. 'I apologise. Of course, you are right. I had no call to snap at you.'

'As you wish. I was not offended by it. It is I who should apologise to you for intruding on your peace. I merely wished to thank you for sending Jem to get my book. It was nice that you remembered.' She fell silent and allowed him to enjoy his tea.

But the silence was almost more discomforting than the noise, for it allowed him to feel the guilt again, although he could not imagine what it was that pained him.

'You are not disturbing my peace, Penny. But I fear I disturbed yours. I think—it may be possible that I am not comfortable when at peace. I must always be doing something to keep back the quiet. Thus, I released my ill-behaved friends on you this morning.'

She chuckled. 'We are an unsuitable pair, are we not?'

'Opposites attract.' But he could not manage to sound as sure as he wished.

'But at least our political views agree. It would be most difficult to respect you if—'

'Our politics?' It was his turn to laugh. 'To what purpose does a woman have political views?'

'To no purpose, other than that I live in this country, and am concerned with how it progresses. While I am not allowed to vote, there is nothing to prevent me from reading the speeches and governmental proceedings in *The Times*. That I cannot do anything to forward my views is no fault of mine.' She cast her eyes downwards, and then favoured him with a sidelong glance through her lashes. 'As a weak woman, I must pray that the country is in good hands.'

He felt the small thrill along his spine that he always got when a woman was trying to capture his attention. Could it be? He looked at her again. There was a faint smile on her face, and an even fainter flush on her pale skin.

His wife was flirting with him. Over the proceedings of the House of Lords.

It was an unusual approach, and unlikely to be successful. It would be easy enough to prove that she knew nothing of the subject with a few simple questions. And then, if she truly wished to flatter him, she could return to safer subjects favoured by other women of his female acquaintance: the colour of his eyes, or the cut of his coat and how well it favoured his shoulders. 'So you agree with my politics, do you?'

'Most definitely. Your grasp of economy is most erudite.'

'And you feel that the country is competently governed? For having seen the political process up close, I sometimes have my doubts.'

'Well, as far as I can tell, Lord Beaverton is a fool,' she said. 'He has little understanding of domestic trade, and even less of international issues. And he seems to disagree most vehemently with you on the subject of cotton imports.'

'Because he has interests in India,' Adam supplied. 'He is feathering his own nest.'

'Well, your interchange with him sounded most spirited. Although, if you could clarify a certain point…'

He had wondered when she would allow him to

speak, for she seemed to have no understanding of the conversational gambit that encouraged a woman to listen more than she spoke. Her first question was followed by another, and then another. And some were of a level of complexity that he was required to refer to a gazetteer in his study, and other references as well.

And soon it seemed easier just to move the tea things and conversation to his desk. He ceded her the chair, for he sometimes found it easier to think while on his feet, and she peppered him with questions while he paced the room.

There was a discreet knock at the door, and the butler entered. 'Your Grace? You have guests.'

A head appeared around the back of the servant. Tim was there, and he could see other friends crowding behind him in the hall. 'Have you forgotten, Adam? Dinner at the club?'

He glanced at the clock on the mantel. How had it got to be so late? 'It will be the work of a moment, and I will be ready to go.' He glanced down at Penny. 'Of course, if you wish, I will cancel.'

She shook her head. 'That is all right. I prefer to remain at home.' He thought he detected a trace of wistfulness in her answer.

'If you are sure?'

She nodded again, gathering her tea things from his desk. 'I should be going back to my room, after all. I meant to accomplish more today.'

'I am sorry if I distracted you. Until tomorrow, then.' And before he knew what he was doing, he'd bent and kissed her on the cheek.

She turned as pink as the walls of her sitting room, but she did not flinch from him. In fact, the smile he received in reward was quite charming, before she remembered that there were others present, and hurried across the hall and into her study, closing the door.

In retrospect, he'd have been better to have remained at home, for that seemed to be where his mind resided. The strange day only served to accent the commonness of the evening. The boring conversation and stale jokes of his friends were punctuated with exclamations of 'Adam, why must you be so glum?'

The constant reminder that he was not himself only served to make his mood darker.

When they were at cards, and Minton had presented some outlandish political position, Adam had snapped, 'Really, John, if I wished to talk politics, I'd have stayed home with my wife. She, at least, has some idea of what she is talking about.'

There was an amused murmur in the crowd around him, as though he had confirmed to the men around him that his sudden marriage had addled his mind. Only Tim looked at him and nodded with approval.

Soon after, a servant arrived, bearing a note on a salver for Tim. His friend unfolded the paper, grew pale, and asked a servant for his hat and gloves. 'I must make my apologies. I am called home. There is an emergency.'

'Nothing serious, I hope,' Adam said.

'I suspect it is little Sophie. She has been sick again. And I am a little worried.' Judging by Tim's agitation, minor worry did not describe his true state of mind.

Adam stood up. 'I will go with you. We will take my carriage to save time, and I will return home once your mind is at rest.'

But on arrival at the Colton home, they discovered the true nature of the emergency. All the lights were blazing, and from the salon came the sound of voices, laughter, and a soprano warbling along with the piano-forte.

Tim swore softly and with vehemence threw his hat into a corner and stalked into the room with Adam following in his wake.

His wife seized him by the arm, forcing a drink into his hand and announced to the gathering, 'Here they are! As I told you, they were detained.'

Adam was close enough to hear Tim murmur to his wife, 'You knew my intentions, and yet you brought me home to play host to a gathering that is none of my making.'

She responded through clenched teeth. 'And you knew my intentions. I wished for you and your friend to dine at home this evening. Do not cross me again, or you shall live to regret it.'

'More so than I do our marriage?' Tim laughed loud enough for the guests to hear, although they could not make out his words. 'That would be an impressive feat, madam.'

'You know how creative I can be.' She turned away from Tim, and reached for Adam, linking her arm in his and pulling him forwards. 'Come along, Adam. Do not think you can escape so easily. Have a drink with us before you go.' She was pressing against him in a way that must be obvious to her husband, and smiling up at him too brightly.

He eased free of her grasp, stomach churning, unable to look his friend in the eye. 'A glass of wine, then. Only one. And then I must be going home.'

Clarissa said, loud enough for all to hear, 'Ah yes. Hurrying home to your bride, Adam. Just when will she be making an appearance in society? People are beginning to think that the woman is a product of your over-heated imagination.'

'You know full well, Clare, that she wished to remain at home, for you spoke to her this morning.'

'But, Adam, everyone is dying to meet her. I have told them so much about her. They are aflame with curiosity. Penelope is the daughter of a cit,' she informed the group gathered around them. 'And from what I've been told, she is very rich. But she will not mix with us, I'm afraid. She is far too busy to be bothered. Adam's wife is a bluestocking.' The last was said with enough pity to make the other revelations pale in comparison.

He was expected to say something at this point, but was at a loss as to what. Most of what Clarissa had said was perfectly true, although it sounded far worse coming from her mouth. And she had probably used his absence to embroider what facts she had with as many scurrilous fictions as she could invent. So he seized upon the one thing he could safely refute. 'Really, Clarissa. You make her sound so exclusionist that she should be a patroness at Almack's. She is at home tonight, reading *The Odyssey* in the original Greek. I bought her the book this afternoon as a wedding gift. But she'll mix with society soon enough.'

And then, he could not help himself—he added a fabrication of his own. 'We are planning a ball, and I suspect most of you will be invited to it. Then you can meet her and see for yourself.'

The crowd nodded, mollified, and there was an undercurrent of curiosity in the gossip that stole the thunder from Clarissa's tales. Bellston rarely entertained. The new duchess might be an eccentric, but no one would dare comment on the fact if it meant losing the duke's favour and missing a chance to attend an event that would be eagerly anticipated by everyone of importance in London.

Everyone except the Duchess of Bellston.

Penny sat at the vanity in her bedroom, which she had transformed, with the help of a strong lamp, into a makeshift writing desk. The work had seemed to fly this evening, with words flowing out of her mind and on to paper as easily as if the text were already in English and she was only copying down what she saw. Perhaps it had been the gift of the book that had inspired her. Adam could be so effortlessly kind that she scolded herself for thinking ill of him earlier in the day.

Or perhaps the intellectual stimulation of strong tea and good conversation had freed her thoughts.

That was all it had been, of course. Any stimulation she might have felt, beyond her intellect, was girlish fancy. She had always admired the Duke of Bellston. To see the actual man in front of her, moved by his subject matter until he'd all but forgotten her existence, was more invigorating than she'd imagined. He'd invited her into his study, allowing her past a barrier of intimacy that she had not expected to cross, and for a time she'd felt she was very much in his confidence.

And then he had kissed her. Thank the Lord that their conversation had been at an end, for she doubted that she would have been able to string two thoughts together after that buss on the cheek.

She had gone back to her sitting room and curled up on the sofa and opened the book, ready to enjoy his gift, only to have her eyes drawn, again and again, to the kissing couple on the bookshelf. She must have looked as dazed and eager as that when he'd left her.

And it had not stopped him from going out, she reminded herself, returning to cool logic. Not that there was anything wrong with being apart in the evenings. How would she get any work done if he forced her to accompany him everywhere, like a dog on a leash? She enjoyed her work.

And she had been quite satisfied with her progress once she left the sitting room, which seemed to attract foolish fantasy like a normal library attracted cobwebs. She could work without fear of interruption in her bedroom.

Certainly without fear of interruption by her husband. If he preferred to be elsewhere, in the company of others than herself? That had been their plan, had it not? She could hardly blame him for it. An evening of cards at an all-male club was hardly cause for jealousy on her part.

And if she was not mistaken, he was arriving home; through the open window she heard the sound of a carriage stopping in front of the house, and the faint sound of her husband's voice as the footman greeted him at the front door. She glanced at the clock. Barely eleven.

She had not expected him so soon. It had been later than this when they'd returned to the house on the previous evening, and he'd proclaimed it early. Was tonight's behaviour unusual?

Not that she should care. She hardly knew the man, and his schedule was his own affair.

But he had come home. Not to her, precisely. But he was home, all the same. Perhaps it would not be too forward to go downstairs in search of a cup of tea, and pass by the door to his study to see if he remained up. She got out of her chair, reached to tighten the belt of her dressing gown, and, without thinking, straightened her hair. Then she laughed at herself for the vanity of it.

With her hand on the doorknob, she stopped and listened. But, no. There was no need to seek him. He was climbing the stairs, for she could hear him on the landing, and then he was coming down the hall carpet toward his room. She waited for the sound of his bedroom door, opening and closing.

It did not come. He had walked past his room, for she had been unconsciously counting the steps and imagining him as he walked.

And then he stopped, just on the other side of her door. She waited for the knock, but none came. Perhaps he would call out to her, to see if she was asleep, though he must know she was not, for the light of her lamp would be visible under the door.

If she were a brave woman, she would simply open the door and go after the cup of tea she had been imagining. Then she could pretend to be surprised to see him, and inquire what it was that he wanted. She might even step into the hall, and collide with his body, allowing him to reach out a hand to steady her. Perhaps he would laugh, and she would neglect to step away, and she would know if he merely wished to continue their discussion, or if there was some other purpose for his visit.

But she was not a brave woman, and she was foolish to think such things, since they made no sense at all. There was a perfectly logical explanation for his being there, which he would no doubt tell her in the morning at breakfast. If she waited, she could save herself the embarrassment of making too big a thing out of something so small.

But all the same, she kissed the palm of her hand, and then silently pressed it to the panel of the door, holding it very near where the cheek of a tall man might be.

Then she heard his body shift, and his steps retreating down the hall, and the opening and closing of the bedroom door beside her own.

Chapter Ten

When she woke the next morning, she found herself listening for sounds from the next room and hoping for a knock on the connecting door. Surely Adam would come to her as soon as he was awake, and explain his behaviour the previous evening?

But she heard only silence. Perhaps he was a late sleeper, or simply did not wish to be disturbed.

When she could stand to wait no longer, she called for her maid. She would go downstairs and wait for him at breakfast. But when she arrived in the breakfast room, she was told that his Grace had been up for hours, had had a light meal and gone riding in the park.

Very well, then. If he had wished to speak to her, it had been nothing of importance. Or perhaps she had only imagined it, for things often sounded different through a closed door. Whatever the case, she would go on with her day as if nothing had happened.

She gathered her papers from her bedroom and

returned them to the sitting room, where the morning light made working easier. And in daylight, with her husband nowhere about, there seemed to be fewer romantic fantasies clouding her mind. But to avoid temptation, she turned the figurine of the lovers to face the wall.

She had barely opened her books before there was a quiet knock on the door, and a servant announced a visitor, offering a card on a tray.

Lady Clarissa Colton.

The card lay there on the tray before her, like a dead snake. What was she to do about it? 'Tell the lady that Adam is not at home.'

The servant looked pained. 'She wished specifically for you, your Grace.'

'Then tell her I am not—'

'Hello.' Clarissa was calling to her from the hall. She laughed. 'You must forgive me, darling. I have viewed this as a second home for so long that I quite forget my manners.'

'I see.' Penny had hoped to load those words with censure. But instead they sounded like understanding and permission to enter, for Clarissa pushed past the servant and came into the sitting room.

She sat down next to Penny, as though they were confidants. 'Adam and I are old friends. Particularly close. But I'm sure he must have told you.' Clarissa was smiling sweetly again, but her eyes were hard and cold. She reached out to take Penny's hands, giving them a painful squeeze. 'And when I heard the good news, I simply could not stay away.'

'News?'

'Yes. He told us last night, at the party. Everyone was most excited.'

'Party?' Obviously, there was much Adam had not told her. And now, she was left to parrot monosyllables back to Clarissa, until the horrible woman made the truth clear.

'Ooo, that is right. You did not know of it.' Clarissa made a face that was supposed to represent sympathy, but looked more like concealed glee. 'Adam came to our house last night after dinner. Not for the whole evening, as I had hoped. But he could not bear to disappoint me. The man is beyond kind.'

Far beyond it, as far as Penny was concerned.

'We knew you would not mind, of course, for you did not wish to come. In any case, he told us about the ball.'

'Ball?' She had done it again. Why in heaven could she not find her tongue?

'That you will be hosting, to celebrate your marriage. I am sure it will be the most divine affair. Your ballroom is magnificent, is it not? And Adam uses it far too seldom…'

Obviously, for she was not even sure of its location since her husband had neglected to show it to her. She nodded mutely, along with the flow of Clarissa's words.

'It is more than large enough to hold the cream of London society. We will begin the guest list this morning, and the menu, of course. And in the afternoon, we can see about your gown.' She glanced down at Penny's sombre grey day dress. 'I do not know what fashion was like where you came from—'

'I came from London,' Penny interjected.

'But these clothes will hardly do. We must fit you with a new wardrobe, gloves, perhaps a turban for evening. With an ostrich feather. You will adore it, I am sure.'

Penny was quite sure that she would look ridiculous with her hair dressed in plumes. And that was probably the point of the suggestion.

'We will go to my modiste, together. And I will instruct her on just how you must look, to display your true self to the world.'

There could not be a more horrifying prospect than that. Must she be polite to this woman, for the sake of her husband? Or could she say what she thought, and risk making a powerful enemy?

'Penelope. So sorry to intrude, I had no idea you were entertaining.' Adam stood in the doorway, still in his riding clothes, expression unreadable.

'That is all right, dear. You are not interrupting anything of importance. Only discussion of our ball.'

Discussion had been a charitable way to describe it. 'Clarissa says that you announced it at her home last evening. It was most unwise of you to give the secret away before we set a date.' *Or before telling your wife*.

He seemed to pale ever so slightly at being caught out. Then he regained his smile and said, 'So sorry, darling. I could not help myself.'

'Really?' They would see about that. 'No matter. Clarissa has come to offer her help in the matter, if I need it.'

Adam smiled again. 'How kind of her. But I am sure you have the matter well in hand, so she needn't have bothered.'

Clarissa laughed. 'Don't be ridiculous, Adam. She will have no experience in handling a gathering of this sort. She knows nothing of our set, or what will be expected of her. And you have thrown her into it, assuming that she will not embarrass herself. It will be a disaster.'

Penny hardly dared breathe, for fear that Clarissa would notice how close to the truth she had come.

But Adam waved his hand and shrugged. 'I doubt it is so hard as all of that, and Penny is a most enterprising and intelligent woman. No need for you to bother about it. But thank you for your concern. Let me show you out, and we will leave my wife to her work.'

'I could not think to leave the poor creature in the state she's in.' Clarissa spoke as if Penny was not in the room. 'At least convince her to leave her books long enough to go shopping, like a normal female.'

'You were going shopping, eh? Well, I know how much you enjoy that, and we mustn't keep you from it. Perhaps, some day, when Penny is finished with her book, you may come back for her. But for now…' Adam reached out a hand to her.

Clarissa weighed, just for a moment, continuing the argument against the chance to be nearer to Adam, if only for the short walk to the door. Then she smiled up at him and said, 'Very well, then. There is nothing for it—if you wish me to go, I must go.' She rose, and linked her arm with his. 'And perhaps you can be persuaded to tell me what I must purchase, so that I look my finest when I return for the ball. I do wish to look my best when in your presence.'

She watched them leave the room, Clarissa smiling brightly and leaning on Adam as if she could not manage to walk the few steps to the door without his support.

Penny did not realise that she was still clutching a pencil in her hand until the thing snapped under the pressure of her fingers. The gall of the woman. The infernal nerve. To come into her house, to point out her flaws and to rub her face in her husband's perfidy. The rage simmered in her, as she waited for Adam to return.

Before he was near enough to speak, she met him in the hall, and demanded, 'What is going on?'

'Penny. The servants.' He said it as though the lack of privacy should be sufficient to contain her temper.

But she was having none of it. 'The servants might also want to know the amount of extra work you have brought to this house, for you have certainly set us all a task. We are to have a ball, are we? Do we even have a ballroom? Clarissa seems to think so, but I do not know, myself.'

His ears turned slightly red, which might indicate embarrassment, but nothing showed in his voice. 'It is on the third floor. We have not had time for a whole tour—'

'Because we have been married less than a week. I have lived in this house for only two days, and at no time do I remember any discussion of our hosting an entertainment.'

He backed her into the sitting room, and shut the door behind them. 'The subject came up yesterday evening.'

'When you were at Clarissa's party. Another thing you made no mention of.'

'And *I* do not remember, in any of our discussions, the need to inform you of my whereabouts at all times. In fact, I specifically remember our agreeing that our social lives would remain separate.'

'An agreement which you chose to violate when you invited all of London to our house and neglected to inform me. While I can hardly complain over your choice of *entertainments* last evening, it embarrasses me when your *hostess* chooses to come to my house and make me aware of them.'

She glared at him, and watched the guilty anger rise in his face. 'I do not like what you are implying.'

'I did not think you would. But that is hardly a denial, is it?' She waited, praying that he would tell her she was wrong, and dishonoured them both by thinking such horrible things.

Instead he said coldly, 'It does not suit you to be jealous over something that was over before we even met.'

The admission, and the easy dismissal of her feelings, made her almost too sick to speak. 'I am not jealous, Adam. What cause would I have? You know that our relationship is not likely to be close enough to merit jealousy. But I am disappointed, and more than a little disgusted. I had thought you a better person than that. And to carry on in such an obvious fashion, under the very nose of a man you claim as friend...'

'Perhaps, if I had married a woman who wished to be at my side, then there would be no cause to wonder at my relationship with another man's wife.'

She laughed in amazement. 'It is all my fault, then?

That you choose to make a fool of yourself over a married woman?'

'I am not attempting to make a fool of myself. I am endeavouring, as best I can, to make our marriage seem as normal as possible to the rest of the world. But apparently I am failing—already there has been talk about you.'

'Only because Clarissa spreads it, I am sure. Better that they should talk about me than the two of you.'

He made no effort to correct her. 'If we do not appear together in public, and supremely happy, everyone will say that I am keeping you out of sight because you are an embarrassment to me.'

'What do I care what people think of me?'

'Apparently nothing, or you would not look as you do.'

One, two, three… She closed her eyes, to stop any chance of tears, and continued her counting. She had known he would say something about her looks eventually. How could he not? But she had hoped, when the time came, it would be as a casual statement of the obvious. Then she would be better prepared, and could agree and laugh the pain away. But he had been so good about not commenting. To have it thrown back in the heat of anger had taken the breath from her and her argument with it.

She made it all the way to nine and then blurted, 'If you had a problem with my looks, then you should have thrown the licence on to the fire when we were in Scotland. There is nothing I can do to my appearance to make it a match for yours. No amount of money will turn a sow's ear into a silk purse.'

He waited until she was through with her outburst, and then said, 'Do not turn soft on me, now that I need you to be strong.' There was no kindness in his voice, but neither did he seem angry. 'Our initial plan will not work. At least, not while we are in London. And so I am making another, and I expect you to obey me in it. If you do not wish to follow my advice, I will allow Clarissa to return and badger you into your new role as duchess. She is better qualified to teach you how to navigate in society than any other woman I know. But she can be amazingly stubborn and surpassingly cruel. Do you understand?'

She bit her lip and nodded.

'First, you will not, nor will I allow you in future to, refer to yourself as a sow's ear, a lost cause, wasted effort, nothing, nobody, or any of the other terms of scorn. Self-pity is your least attractive feature, and not one I wish to see displayed in my home for the duration of our marriage.'

When she was sure her eyes were dry, she opened them and glared at him.

'Very good. You look quite like a duchess when you are angry with me.'

She could not tell if he meant to be amusing, but she had no desire to laugh.

He stared down her body. 'Is all your clothing like this?'

She nodded. 'Practical. Easy to care for.'

'Dull. Ugly. Drab.'

'I put foolish things aside when my father died.'

'And how long ago was that?'

'Two years.'

'Two years,' he repeated. 'And you are still dressed in mourning. You are a bride, Penny. And to see you dressed so is an insult to me. It is as though I pulled you from weeping on a grave, and forced you to marry.'

'Very well,' she said. 'I will wear my old things. I have more than enough gowns in storage, hardly used since my come-out.'

'But they must be…' he added quickly on his fingers '…at least five years old.'

'They are not worn, so I have not needed to replace them.'

'But hardly the first stare of fashion.'

She laughed bitterly. 'As if that would matter.'

He let out a growl of exasperation. 'You listened to nothing of what I just said. Very well, then. My patience is at an end.' He seized her by the wrist and threw open the door.

She pulled her hand away. 'What do you think you are doing?'

'What someone should have done a long time ago. You are coming with me this instant, Penelope, and you will remedy the sad state of your wardrobe.'

'There is nothing wrong with the clothing I have. It is clean and serviceable.'

'And totally unfitting for the Duchess of Bellston.'

'I never asked to be the Duchess of Bellston, and I fail to see why I should be forced to conform to her needs.'

It was Adam's turn to laugh. 'You are the duchess, whether you planned it or no. When you decided to pull a stranger from the street and marry him, it never occurred to you that there might be complications?'

She sneered. 'Of course. I suspected if I was not careful that I would have a husband eager to waste my money on foolishness. I was willing to allow it to such a degree as it did not interfere with my comfort or my studies. And I was right to be concerned, for you have breached both boundaries with this request.'

As she watched, her husband became the duke to her again, drawing in his power in a way that was both intriguing and intimidating. His voice dropped to a barely audible murmur. 'Well, then. I am glad I have fulfilled your worst fears. We must set something straight, if we are to live in harmony.'

He meant to dictate to her? Reason fled her mind, and was replaced with white-hot rage. He had no right to do this, no right to tell her who she must be, if she was to be his wife at all. *One, two, three…*

'The wardrobe I am suggesting is in no way wasteful. Think of it as a uniform, nothing more. You wish to be left in peace? Then you will find it easier to deflect notice if you can play the part of a duchess with reasonable facility. The clothing I am suggesting will make this easier and not more difficult.'

Four, five, six…

'It will be expensive, but I have seen the statements from your bank, and you can most certainly afford it. If it helps, think of it as no different than you would allow me to purchase for my mistress. You had allotted an expense of this amount, hoping to keep me occupied so that you could work. Think for a moment the level of stubbornness and bullheadedness that you must project if you allow me to spend the money, but will only berate me for it if I wish to spend it on you.'

Seven, eight, nine…

'I take your silence for assent.' He rang for a servant and ordered the carriage brought round. 'I will deposit you at a modiste, and you can work out, between you, what is best done. I care not for the details, as long as the project is completed.'

Ten. And still she could not find a hole in his argument.

'And if you balk or resort to tantrums, I will throw you over my shoulder and carry you there, for you are behaving as a spoiled child over something that any other woman in the world would enjoy.'

The nerve of the man. Very well, then. She would go to the dressmaker, get a few simple gowns in the same vein as those she owned, and escape the ridiculous display that he intended for her.

She rode in silence with him, still irritated by his insistence on controlling a thing that he could know nothing about. Before her come-out, she had had more than her share of pushy dressmakers, shoe sellers and haberdashers, all eager to force her to look a way that did not make her the least bit comfortable. She had lacked the nerve to stand up to them, and had felt no different than a trained pony at the end of it, paraded about to attract a buyer.

And it had all come to naught.

The carriage pulled to a stop in front of an unassuming shop in a side street, far away from the hustle of Bond Street. Adam stepped down and held out his hand for her, but she would not take it. Unlike some women she could name, she could manage to walk without the assistance of Adam Felkirk.

The horses chose that moment to shy, and she almost fell into the street.

But her husband caught her easily, and pulled her into his arms, and safely to the ground. Then he had the gall to smile at her. 'This is what happens when you try to resist me. There is no point in it. I suggest you surrender, now.'

She glared at the shop in front of her. 'And do you come here often to purchase clothes for women? Or is this the store that Clarissa was threatening me with?'

'I have never been here before, and I have no idea where Clarissa would have had you go. This shop was frequented by my mother.' His smile turned to an evil grin. 'She decorated the sitting room that you enjoy so well. Since it does not matter to you what you wear, the fact should not bother you at all.'

She had a momentary vision of herself, clothed in bright pink organza, and could not control her grimace.

Adam nodded. 'I will leave you to it, madam, for you know best what to do. But do not think you can return home without purchases, for I am taking the carriage and the driver will not return for you for several hours.' He looked at her servant, hanging on the back of the carriage. 'I will leave Jem with you.' He tossed the man a sovereign. 'When the carriage comes back, if you can carry the purchases in one trip, she has not bought enough. Tell the driver to leave and return in another hour.'

And her own servant, who she should have been able to trust, pocketed the coin and bowed to his new master.

Adam looked to her again. 'When you are home, we will discuss the ball. Do not worry yourself about it. My mother had menus and guest lists as well. I am sure they will serve, and we can pull the whole thing together with a minimum of bother.'

Chapter Eleven

Penny watched the carriage roll away from her. Damn the man. He knew nothing about anything if he meant to pull a ball together with the help of a woman who, she suspected, had been dead far longer than her own father. Clarissa was right: it was a disaster in the making.

And what was she to do for the rest of the afternoon, trapped here? If she had known his intent was to abandon her, she'd have brought something to read. She stepped off the street and into the shop.

A girl dropped the copy of *Le Beau Monde* that she had been paging through and sprang to her feet behind a small gold desk. She said, with a thick French accent, 'May I be of assistance, your ladyship?'

The girl sounded so hopeful, that Penny found it almost pleasurable to introduce herself with her new title. It made the girl's eyes go round for a moment, and then her face fell.

'Your Grace? I believe there has been a misunderstanding. You husband the duke must have been seeking my predecessor in this shop.'

'There is no Madame Giselle, as it says on the door?'

The woman laughed. 'Unfortunately, no. Until her death, she was my employer. She had been in this location for many years.'

'And before she died, you were…'

'A seamstress, your Grace. Madame died suddenly. There was no family to take the shop, and many orders still to fill. It made sense to step out from the back room and become Madame Giselle, in her absence.' The French accent had disappeared to reveal the Londoner underneath. Apparently, she'd taken more than the shop when she'd come out from the back room.

The girl took her silence as hesitation. 'We are not as fashionable as we once were, I'm afraid. I will understand, of course, that you prefer to go elsewhere. I can recommend several excellent modistes who are frequented by the ladies of your class.'

If she was not careful, she'd get her chance to shop with Clarissa. Penny's eyebrows arched in surprise. 'No wonder you are not as busy as you should be. For when one is in trade, one should never turn down commerce, especially an order as large as the one I am likely to make.' When she had come into the shop, she had had no intention of spending money. But suddenly, it seemed the most natural thing in the world.

'A large order?' the dressmaker repeated, dumbly.

'Yes. Day dresses, travelling clothes, outerwear and ball gowns. I need everything.'

'Do you wish to look at swatches?'

She gritted her teeth. 'It does not matter. Choose whatever you wish. And styles as well. I do not have any idea how to proceed.' And then she prepared for the worst.

The girl ran her through her paces, draping her in fabrics, and experimenting with laces and trims. And Penny had to admit that it was not as bad as it could have been, for the girl made no attempt to force her into gowns that did not flatter, but chose clothes that would suit her, rather than poking and pinching to get her to fit the fashion.

The choice of shops had been most fortunate, although Adam could not have known it. Now if she could find a way around the inconvenience of dinner and dancing for a hundred or so of her husband's friends… The man was cracked if he thought he could use his mother's guest lists. The names on it were likely to be as dead as her modiste.

Penny glanced down at the girl, who was crouched at her feet, setting a hem in the peach muslin gown Penny was modelling. 'Giselle?'

'My real name is Sarah, your Grace,' she said, around a mouthful of pins. 'Not as grand as it should be. But there is no point in hiding the truth.'

'Sarah, then. Do you have family in service?'

'My mother is housekeeper at Lord Broxton's house.'

One of her husband's adversaries in Parliament, but closely matched in society. It would do to go on with. 'It seems, Sarah, that I am to throw a ball. But I am no more born to be a duchess than you were born a French-woman. If I had guest lists and menus from a similar party, it would help me immensely. No one need know, of course. And I would be willing to pay, handsomely.'

Jem was summoned from the street and given a note from Sarah, and directions to the Broxtons' kitchen door.

He was back in a little more than an hour, with a tightly folded packet of papers containing names and addresses of the cream of London society, and the menus for a variety of events.

Penny sat comfortably on a stool in the back room and smiled at Sarah, who was throwing a hem into another sample gown. 'This is turning out to be a surprisingly productive trip, and not the total waste of time I had suspected. If I am careful, and can avoid any more of my husband's outlandish plans for me, I might still manage an hour or two of work.'

Adam would no doubt be irate when he saw the clothing that that woman was making for her. It did not in any way remind her of the dresses worn by the ladies of his circle. The colours for evening were pale, and the sprigged muslins she had chosen for day dresses hardly seemed the thing for a duchess.

Although just what duchesses wore during the day, Penny was unsure. Whatever they liked, most likely.

She gritted her teeth again. Or whatever their husband insisted they wear. But Sarah had seemed to know her business, despite the lack of customers. She had loaded Penny up with such things as were ready, more than enough petticoats, bonnets, and a few day dresses that had been made for samples, but fit so well they might have been tailored for her.

She inquired of the total, not daring to imagine how much she might have spent.

She saw the wistful look in the girl's eye as she said, 'The bills will be sent to your husband, of course. You needn't worry about anything, your Grace.'

Of course not. For nobility did not have to concern themselves with a thing so mundane as money. But she had taken much of the poor girl's sample stock, and there would be silks to buy, and lace, and ribbon to complete the order.

And since she was the Duchess of Bellston, it could all be had on credit while the false Madame Giselle found a way to pay her creditors with aristocratic air. Her husband, who had been so eager for this wardrobe, would send the girl some money in his own good time. She must manage as she could until then.

Penny reached into her reticule, and removed a pack of folded bank notes, counting out a thick stack. 'Here, my dear. This should go a fair way in covering the materials you will need. You may send the balance directly to my bank for immediate payment. Do not hesitate to contact me, should you need more. If I must do this at all, I would that it be done right and wish you to spare no expense.'

She saw the visible sag of relief, and the broadening of the smile on the face of the modiste.

When the carriage returned, and Jem saw the pile of boxes, he looked at her with suspicion, and gestured to an underfootman to throw them on to the carriage and tie them down. 'I'm to spend all my time, now that you're a "her Grace" two steps back and carrying your ribbons?'

'If it makes you feel better, Jem, think of it as charity work, just as my brother always wanted me to do. Or perhaps as economic investment in a small business.'

Jem stared sceptically at the boxes. 'I'm thinking, at least ladies' dresses are lighter than books.'

'Well, then. You have nothing to complain about.'

She had chosen to wear one of her new dresses home, a simple thing in pale pink muslin, with a rose-coloured spencer. The matching bonnet was a work of extreme foolishness, with a shirred back and a cascade of ribbons, but it seemed to suit the dress and she did not mind it overmuch. When she walked up the steps to the townhouse, it was a moment before the man at the door recognised her, and smiled before bowing deep.

Very well. The transformation must be startling. Adam would be pleased. She was certain of it. And he would admire the way she had managed the ball with a minimum of effort.

And then she remembered it did not matter at all to her what Adam thought. The whole of this production was an attempt to fool society into believing in their sham marriage, and put up a united front for his spurned lover, Clarissa.

If she was truly spurned. It was quite possible that Penny had wandered on to the scene in the middle of a contretemps and things would be returning to their despicable normal state at any time. If she allowed herself to care too much about her husband's good opinion, she would feel the pain of his indifference when he was through with her.

She hardened her heart, and walked down the hall to her husband's study, pushing open the door without knocking.

He was not alone. Lord Timothy was there as well. They had been deep in discussion over something, but it came to a halt, as she entered. 'I have returned. As Madame Giselle would say, *"C'est fini".*' The men stared at her as she pulled the bonnet from her head and dropped it on to her husband's desk. She reached into her reticule and removed the papers. 'Here is the list of guests for your ball. Add any names I have missed to the bottom of the list. Dinner will be buffet, but there will be no oysters, because it is too late in the season. You have but to choose a date. You know your social schedule better than I. For my part, I mean to be studying every night, for the foreseeable future. Which means any night you choose for this ball is equally inconvenient.

'Once you have decided, send the cursed guest list to the printer yourself. If you do not know where I wish you to take it, I will tell you, in no uncertain terms.' She looked down her nose at her husband, in what she hoped was a creditable imitation of a *ton* lady. 'Is that satisfactory, your Grace?'

Her husband stared at her in shocked silence. Lord Timothy grinned at her in frank admiration and supplied, 'Oh, yes. I should think so.'

'Very well, then. I shall retire, in my mildly pink dress, to my incredibly pink sitting room, put my feet on a cushion and read Gothic novels. I do not wish to be disturbed.' She turned to cross the hall, only to have Tim bound ahead of her to open the door.

Before it shut behind her, she heard a noise from the study that sounded suspiciously like a growl.

Chapter Twelve

Adam stared through the open door of his study at the closed door across the hall. The silence emanating from the room was like a wall, laid across the threshold to bar his entrance. She spoke to him no more than was necessary, ate in her rooms and politely refused all visitors. She had succeeded in achieving the marital state that they had agreed on, allowing herself total solitude, and deeding complete freedom to him. He could do as he wanted in all things. His life was largely unchanged from the one he had before the marriage, with the exception of a near-unlimited supply of funds.

Why did he find it so vexing?

Perhaps because he had grown tired of that life, and had been quite ready to end it by any means available. Sick to death of playing, by turns, the wit, the lover or the buffoon for a series of false friends. Bone weary of dodging the insistent affections of Clarissa, who refused to believe that he looked back on their affair with regret and self-disgust.

And Tim, still at his side as a true friend and adviser. He chose to play the absentminded academic, more interested in his books and his conservatory than in the people around him. He pretended no knowledge of what had occurred between Adam and his wife, until such moments as he let slip an idle comment or odd turn of phrase to prove he knew exactly what had occurred, and was disappointed, but not particularly surprised.

Adam had hoped that the introduction of Penelope to his life might lead to a lasting change. She had qualities most unlike the other women of his set: sweetness, sincerity and a mind inquisitive for things deeper than the latest fashion. And she had seemed, for a time, to hold him in respect. He must present a much different picture in *The Times* than he did in reality. For though she claimed to respect Bellston, the politician, it had taken her a week to become as disgusted with Bellston, the man, as he was himself.

A servant entered, offering him a calling card on a silver tray.

Hector Winthorpe.

It was some consolation to see that the card was impeccably done, for Adam had sent the invitations for the ball to the Winthorpe shop. And he had grudgingly added Hector's name to the bottom of the guest list, as a good faith gesture. The man would not fit, but what could be done? Hector was family and they must both get used to it. But what the devil was he doing, coming to the house now?

Adam gave his permission to the servant and in a moment, Hector entered the room without making a bow, then stood too close to the desk, making every effort to tower over him.

Adam responded with his most frosty expression and said, 'If you are searching for your sister, she is across the hall. But it is pointless to try, for she refuses visitors when she is at work.'

'You have had no better luck with her than I did, I see, if she is shut up alone in a library. But I did not come for her. I wish to speak to you.'

'State your business, then.'

'It is about this, your Grace.' There was no respect or subservience in the title, as the man slapped the invitation to the ball on the desk in front of him.

'A written response of regrets would have been sufficient.'

'Regrets? It is you, sir, who should have regrets.'

Adam stared back, angry, but curious. 'And what precisely should I regret, Hector? Marrying your sister? For I find I have surprisingly few regrets where she is concerned.'

Hector sniffed in disapproval. 'Because she has given you your way in all things, I suppose. And because you care naught for her happiness, you have no guilt of the fact. If you felt anything at all for her, you would know better than this.'

Adam stared down at the invitation, truly baffled now. 'I fail to see what is so unusual about a small gathering to celebrate our nuptials.'

'Small?' Hector shook his head. 'For you, perhaps.

But for my sister, any gathering over two is a substantial crowd.'

'That is ridiculous. I have noticed no problems.' Which was a lie, but he could not give the man the upper hand so easily.

Hector let out a disgusted snort. 'If you noticed no problems with my sister, it is because she is a proud woman, and does not wish to admit to them. Did you not think it strange that she wanted nothing more from you than a chance to lock herself in her study and read?'

'Not overly,' he lied again, thinking of his first suspicions of her.

'Or that an argument over something so simple as a book would drive her to such extreme action as marrying a total stranger?'

There was nothing he could say that would cover the situation, and he certainly could not tell the whole truth, which reflected badly on the man's sister as well as himself. 'It has not proved a problem thus far.' He turned the argument back upon its sender. 'Do you think she chose unwisely?' And then he waited for the apology that must surely come.

'Yes, I do, if you mean to trot her out before your friends as some sort of vulgar joke.'

'How dare you, sir!'

Hector continued to be unabashed by the situation. 'It was too late, by the time she brought you to our home, to insist that you answer this question. But what are your intentions toward my sister, if not to make her the butt of your jokes?'

Adam smiled bitterly. 'I do not mean to fritter away

her fortune, as you were doing. You were keeping her unmarried and under your control so that you could pour her money into your business.'

The shot hit home, and he saw rage in Hector's eyes. 'I am not proud of the fact that the business is in trouble, sir. And I did, indeed, borrow the money from her trust without inquiring of her first. It was wrong of me, for certain. But I did not need to keep her unmarried to plunder her fortune. She did quite a fine job of scaring away any potential mates when she had her come-out. Her subsequent isolation was all her own doing. As of late, it had become quite out of hand. When I attempted to correct her on this, she lost her temper and went to Scotland. Apparently, she was looking for any fool that would have her. And she found you.' Hector said the word as though his sister had crossed the border and picked up not a husband, but some exotic disease.

Adam refused to rise to the bait. 'She can be rash, of course. But I fail to see what is so serious in her behaviour that would cause you to censure her or deny her simple purchases. It was wrong of you, just as was the theft of her money.'

'What do you know of her social life before you married her?'

Adam tried to think of anything he could say that would make him sound like he was an active participant in his own marriage, who had taken the time to get to know his wife, either before of after the ceremony. At last he said, 'Nothing. Other than her reasons for wishing to marry, and that she was interested in translating the classics, she has told me nothing at all.'

'Did you not think it odd that she has had no visits from friends, congratulating her on her marriage?'

He had not questioned it. But of course, there should have been guests to the house. If it had been any other woman, her friends would have beaten a path to the door, eager to meet the peer and bask in the reflected glow of Penny's rise in stature. 'I thought perhaps she had cast them off as unworthy. Now that she is a duchess…'

He could not manage to finish the sentence. He had thought no such thing. It was impossible to imagine Penny, who had little interest in her title or anyone else's, being capable of such cruelty to her friends.

Hector was silent, letting the truth sink in. And then he confirmed Adam's new suspicions. 'She has received no visitors because there is no one who has missed her. No one has expressed concern at her absence, or will wish her well on her good fortune. She has no friends, sir. None.'

'That is strange.' He could not help but say it, for it was. 'There is nothing about her that would indicate the fact. She does not complain of loneliness. Nor is there any reason that people might shun her society.'

'That is because she has been most effective at shunning the society of others. Her behaviour in public is, at best, outlandish, and at worst disturbing. When Father tried to give her a come-out, she made such a fool of herself that before the Season was complete, she had taken to her bed and was unwilling even to come down for tea. We hoped, with time, she would calm herself. But by the next year she was even more set in her ways than she had been. Small gatherings made her nervous, and large groups left her almost paralysed with fear.'

Hector looked at Adam with suspicion. 'And so it went, until she went off to Scotland in a huff, and came back with you. You will find, once you get to know her, that no fortune will make up for deficiencies of the mind.' His smile twisted with cruelty. 'Or do you claim some sudden deep affection for the girl that caused you to sweep her from her feet?'

Once again, Adam was trapped between the truth and the appearance of the thing. 'I can say in all honesty that I did not know of her fortune when I married her. And as far as my deep and abiding affection for her…' the words stuck in his throat '…you will never hear me claim otherwise, in public or private.'

Hector smiled and nodded. 'Spoken like a politician. It is not a lie, but it tells me nothing of what really happened.'

Adam stared at him without answering.

'Very well.' Hector tapped the invitation on the desk. 'You will not explain. But as a politician, you must be conscious of how her behaviour will reflect on you. It might be best to cut your losses, before she exposes herself, as she is most sure to do, and brings scandal down upon you.'

Adam drew in a breath. 'Cut my losses. And how, exactly, do you propose I do that?'

Hector smiled. 'You may think it is too late to seek an annulment. But you can hardly be expected to remain married, if there is any question as to the mental soundness of one of the parties involved. Think of the children, after all.'

'And if I cast her off?'

'I would take her back, and make sure she had the care she needed.'

When hell freezes. 'And you will take her money as well, I suppose.' Adam made a gesture, as if washing his hands. 'You are right, Winthorpe. I am growing worried about what a child of this union may be like. Suppose my heir should take after you? If that is not reason to remain childless, I cannot think of a better one. And as for any balls or entertainments we might choose to have? Such things are between myself and my wife and none of your affair.' But he felt less confident than he had before.

Hector threw his hands in the air. 'Very well, then. On your head be it if the poor girl drops on the dance floor in a fit of nervous prostration. Do not say you were not warned. The wilfulness of marrying was her doing. But you, sir, must take credit for the damage from now on.' And with that, he collected his hat and left the house.

Adam stared across the hall and felt a wave of protectiveness for the woman behind the closed door. Her brother was even more repellent than Adam had imagined, and he understood why she might have been willing to risk a stranger over another moment with Hector.

His accusation was a ploy to regain control of her fortune, of course. But suppose his wife was as frightened of society as her brother claimed? It explained much of Penny's behaviour, since they had been married. She was obviously happier alone with her books. It would be terribly unfair of him to expect her to stand before his friends as hostess.

Unfair, but necessary. People would talk, of course. There was no stopping it when Clarissa was egging them on. The longer his wife hid behind her studies, the louder the voices would become, and the crueller the speculations. A single evening's entertainment would do much to settle wagging tongues.

But the sight of her, frozen in terror in front of a hundred guests, would do nothing to help and much to hurt. Hector was right in that, at least. He must avoid that, at all costs.

He rose, crossed the hall and knocked upon her door, opening it before she could deny him.

She was seated in a chair at the tiny writing desk in the corner, attired in a pale blue gown that must have been one of the purchases he had forced upon her. He doubted it would win favour to tell her that the colour and style suited her well, although, in truth, they did. She looked quite lovely in the morning sunlight, surrounded by books.

She set down the volume she had been reading, pushed her glasses up her nose and looked up at him with cool uninterest. 'Is there something that I can help you with?'

How best to broach the question? 'I was wondering—are preparations for the ball progressing well?'

She nodded, and he felt the tension in the air as she stiffened. 'As well as can be expected. The invitations have been sent, and replies are returning. The hall is cleaned, the food is ordered.'

'I thought…perhaps we could cancel the plans, if it is being too much trouble.'

She was looking at him as though he had lost his

mind. 'After all the trouble of choosing the food, decorating the hall, and sending the invitations, you now wish
me to spend even more time in sending retractions?'

'No. Really, I—'

'Because if you think, at this date, it is possible to
stop what you wished to set in progress, you are quite
mad.'

He closed his eyes and took a deep breath, vowing
to remain calm in the face of her temper, no matter
what might occur. 'I do not wish to make more work
for you, or to take you from your studies. I swear, that
was never my goal. My decision to hold the ball was
made in haste, and without any thought to your feelings
or needs. It pains me greatly that you heard of it from
someone other than myself, for it further displayed my
carelessness in not coming to you immediately to
explain.'

'Apology accepted.' She turned back to her books,
as though to dismiss him.

'Your brother was here. In my study, just now.'

That had her attention. She looked up at him in
surprise. 'Whatever did he want?'

'He came to throw my invitation back in my face and
tell me that you were unfit to attend such an event,
much less be the hostess. And that I was a brute for
forcing you into it.'

She laughed with little confidence and no mirth. 'It
is a pity I was not there to thank him, his faith in my
emotional stability has always meant so much to me.'

'What happened when you had your Season to give
him such ideas?'

'It was nothing, really.'

'I do not believe you.'

She shook her head. 'I was a foolish girl…'

He stepped farther into the room, moving toward her without thinking. 'You might have been impetuous. But I cannot imagine you a fool. Tell me the story, and we will never speak of it again.'

'Very well.' She sighed. 'The truth about my come-out—and then you will see what a ninny you have married. I have always been awkward in crowds, more comfortable with books than with people. But my father admired my studiousness and did nothing to encourage me to mix with others my age. It was not until I was seventeen, and he sought to give me a Season, that the problems of this strategy became apparent.'

Adam pulled a chair close to hers, sat down beside her, and nodded encouragingly.

'Mother was long past, and there was little my father or brother could do to help me prepare for my entrance into society. Father engaged a companion for the sake of propriety, but the woman was a fifty-year-old spinster. She knew little of fashion and nothing of the ways of young ladies, other than that they needed to be prevented from them. I was more than a little frightened of her. I suspect she increased the problems, rather than diminishing them.'

She paused and he wondered if she meant to leave the story at that. He said, 'So you had your come-out, and no one offered. Or were you unable to find someone to suit yourself?'

She shook her head. 'Neither is the case, I'm afraid.

Any young girl with a dowry the size of mine could not help but draw interest. Father dispensed with the fortune hunters, and encouraged the rest. And at the end of the summer, there was a young man who seemed to suit. He was a lord of no particular fortune, but he seemed genuine in his affection for me.' She looked up at him, puzzled. 'It was so easy, when I was with him, to behave as the other girls did. The crowds were not so daunting. I grew to look to the parties and balls with anticipation, not dread. And I did quite enjoy the dancing...' Her voice trailed away again.

She had been in love. Adam felt a bolt of longing at the idea that his wife had known happiness, before she had known him.

She came back into the present and smiled at him, bright and false. 'And then I overheard my beloved explaining to a girl I thought a friend that, while he loved this other girl above all things, he would marry me for my money, and that was that.

'A sensible girl might have ignored the fact and continued with what would have been a perfectly acceptable union. Or broken it off quietly and returned to try again the next Season. But not I. I returned to the room and told the couple, and all within earshot, that I thought them as two-faced as Janus for denying their hearts with their actions, and that I would rather die than yoke myself to a man that only pretended to love me for the sake of my money. Then I turned on my heel, left the assembly rooms and refused all further invitations. My mortification at what I had done was beyond bearing. I had not wanted to draw attention to myself. I only hoped to find someone who would want me for who I was. Was it so much to ask? But my brother assured me that I had shamed the family. No one would have me, now I'd made such a cake of myself.' She smiled, wistfully. 'The last thing I should have done, to achieve my ends, was behave in a way that, I'm sorry to say, is very much in my character.'

Adam felt the rage boiling in his heart and wished that he could find the man who had been so callous to her, and give him what he deserved. Then he would pay a visit to her brother, and give Hector a dose of the same.

She swallowed and lifted her chin. 'Of course, you can see that I have learned my lesson. I expected no such foolishness when I married you. If we must hold a ball and make nice in front of your friends, so be it. As long as there is no pretence between us that the event means something more than it truly does.' She lowered her eyes and he thought for a moment he could see tears shining in them, although it might have been the reflection of the afternoon light on her spectacles.

And he reached out spontaneously and seized her hand, squeezing the fingers in his until she looked up at him. 'I would take it all back if I could. Throw the invitations on the fire before they could be sent. You must know that I have no desire to force you into behaviours that will only bring back unpleasant memories. It was never my intention to make you uncomfortable or unhappy. And if there is anything I can do to help…'

Perhaps he sounded too earnest, and she doubted his sincerity. For when she looked at him, her face was blank and guarded. 'Really, Adam. You have done more than enough. Let it be.'

But damn it all, he did not want to let it be. He wanted to fix it. 'The ball will go on. There is no stopping it, I suppose. But in exchange, I will do something for you.'

She was staring at him as though the only thing she wished was that he leave her alone. What could he possibly do? It was not as if he could promise her a trip to the shops. She had made it clear enough what she thought of them, when he had forced her to go the first time. And if her mind had changed and she wished such things, she could afford to purchase them for herself.

And then, the idea struck him. 'At the ball, we will announce that it is our farewell from society, for a time. We will be repairing to our country home. There, you will have all the solitude you could wish for. It is Wales, for heaven's sake. Beautiful country, and the place where my heart resides, but very much out of the way of London society. Your books can be sent on ahead, to greet you in the library when we arrive. Between the house and the grounds, there is so much space that you can go for days without seeing a soul. Dead silence and no company but your books, for as long as you like.'

Her eyes sparkled at the sound of the word 'library'. And she seemed to relax a bit. 'This will be our only party, then?'

'For quite some time. I will make no more rash pronouncements in public without consulting you first.'

'And we may go the very next day?' She seemed far more excited by the prospect of rustication, than she did by the impending ball.

'If you wish it.' He smiled. 'And we will see if you prefer it to London. But I warn you, it is frightfully dull at Felkirk. Nothing to do but sit at home of an evening, reading before the fire.'

She was smiling in earnest now. And at him. 'Nothing to do but read. Really, your Grace. You are doing it far too brown.'

'You would not be so eager if I told you about the holes in the roof. The repairs are not complete, as of yet. But the library is safe and dry,' he assured her. 'And the bedrooms.'

And suddenly, her cheeks turned a shade of pink that, while very fetching, clashed with the silk on the walls. To hide her confusion, she muttered, 'That is good to know. The damage was confined, then, to some unimportant part of the house?'

And it was his turn to feel awkward. 'Actually, it was to the ballroom. When I left, it was quite unusable.'

And her blush dissolved into a fit of suppressed giggles. 'It devastates me to hear it, your Grace.'

'I thought it might. I will leave you to your work, then. But if you need help in the matter of the upcoming event, you will call upon me?'

She smiled again. 'Of course.'

'Because I am just across the hall.' He pointed.

'I know.' She had forgiven him. At least for now. He turned to leave her, and glanced with puzzlement at a lone remaining Meissen figurine, turned face to the wall and occupying valuable space on his wife's bookshelf. He shook his head at the carelessness of the servants, and turned it around, so that it faced properly into the room. 'I will send someone to have this removed, if it annoys you.'

She shook her head. 'Do not bother. I have grown quite used to it.'

Chapter Thirteen

The night of the ball had finally arrived, and Adam hoped that his wife was not too overwrought by the prospect. He had nerves enough for both of them.

Clarissa would be there, of course. He combed his hair with more force than was necessary. Another meeting with her was unavoidable. He could not hold a party and invite his friend, only to exclude his wife. There was very little to do about Clarissa without cutting Tim out of his social circle entirely. And he could hardly do that. They had been friends since childhood. Tim's unfortunate marriage to the shrew, and Adam's regrettable behaviour over her, had done nothing to change it, although Adam almost wished it had. It would have been so much easier had Tim called him out and shamed him in public, or at least cut him dead. But the veneer of civility, when they were together at a social gathering, was a torture much harder to endure.

He hoped that the presence of Penny, and success of the evening, would cool the look in Clarissa's eye.

There was a change in the light that fell upon the table, and a discreet clearing of a throat.

He looked up into the mirror to see his wife standing in the connecting doorway behind him.

He didn't realise he had been holding his breath until he felt it expel from his lungs in a long, slow sigh. It was his wife, most certainly. But transformed. The gown was a pale green, and with her light hair and fair skin, she seemed almost transparent. As she came towards him, he imagined he was seeing a spirit, a ghost that belonged to the house, that had been there long before he had come.

And then the light from his lamp touched the gown and the sarsenet fabric shifted in colour from silver to green again, and the silver sequins sparkled on the drape of netting that fell from her shoulder to the floor.

Even her glasses, which had seemed so inappropriate and unfeminine when he first met her, completed the image as the lenses caught the light and threw it back at him, making her eyes shimmer.

His friends would not call her a beauty, certainly. She was most unlike all the other women who were lauded as such. But suddenly it did not matter what his friends might say. It only mattered what he knew in his heart to be true—she looked as she was meant to look. And now that he had removed her from whatever magic realm she had inhabited, he was overcome with the desire to protect her from the coarse harshness of the world around them.

She had reached his side, and tipped her head quizzically to the side. 'Is it all right?'

He nodded and smiled. 'Very much so. You are lovely.'

'And you are a liar.' But he could see the faint blush on her cheek as she said it.

'You're welcome. It is a most unusual gown. Vaguely Greek, I think, and reminiscent of the Penelope of legend. And therefore, most suitable for you. Are you ready to greet our guests?'

'Yes.' But he saw the look in her eyes.

'And now you are the one who is lying.'

'I am as ready as I am ever likely to be.'

'Not quite. There is something missing. I meant to deal with it earlier, but I quite forgot.'

He removed the jewel box from where he had left it in the drawer of his dresser. 'It seems, in the hurry to marry, that we forgot something. You have no ring.'

'It is hardly necessary.'

'I beg to differ. A marriage is not a marriage without a ring. Although the solicitors and banks did not comment, my friends must have noticed.'

She sighed. 'You do not remember, do you? You gave me a ring, when we were in Gretna. I carry it with me sometimes. For luck.' She pulled a bent horse nail from her fine silk skirts and slipped it on to her finger. 'Although perhaps I need the whole shoe for it to be truly lucky. I do not know.'

He stared down at it in horror. 'Take that from your finger, immediately.'

'I had not planned to wear it, if that is your concern. It is uncomfortably heavy, and hardly practical.'

He held out his hand. 'Give it here, this instant. I will dispose of it.'

She closed her hand possessively over it. 'You will do nothing of the kind.'

'It is dross.' He shook his head. 'No, worse than that. Dross would be better. That is a thing. An object. An abomination.'

'It is a gift,' she responded. 'And, more so, it is mine. You cannot give it me, and then take it back.'

'I had no idea what I was doing. I was too drunk to think clearly. If I had been sober, I would never have allowed you to take it.'

'That is not the point,' she argued. 'It was a symbol. Of our…' She was hunting for the right word to describe what had happened in Scotland. 'Our compact. Our agreement.'

'But I have no desire for my friends to think I would seal a sacrament with a bent nail. Now that we are in London, I can give you the ring that you by rights deserve.'

She sighed. 'It is not necessary.'

'I believe that it is.'

'Very well, then. Let us get on with it.'

Another proof that his wife was unlike any other woman in London. In his experience, a normal woman would have been eager for him to open the jewel case on his desk, and beside herself with rapture as he removed the ring. The band was wide, wrought gold, heavy with sapphires, set round with diamonds. 'Give me your hand.'

She held it out to him, and he slipped it on to her finger.

It looked ridiculous, sitting on her thin white fingers,

as though it had wandered from the hand of another and settled in the only place it felt at home. She flexed her hand.

She shook her head. 'I retract what I said before. In comparison, the horse nail is light. This does not suit.'

'We can go to the jewellers tomorrow, and get it sized to you.'

'You do not understand. It fits well enough, but it does not suit me.'

'It was my mother's,' he said. 'And my grand-mother's before her.'

'Well, perhaps it would suit, if I were your mother,' she snapped. 'But I am your wife. And it does not suit me.'

'You are my wife, but you are also Duchess of Bellston. And the Duchess wears the ring, in the family colours of sapphire and gold.'

'*My* mother was happy with a simple gold band,' she challenged.

'*Your* mother was not a duchess.'

'When your mother worked, did she remove the ring, or leave it on? For I would hate to damage it.'

'Work?'

'Work,' she repeated firmly.

'My mother did not work.'

'But, if you remember our agreement, I do.' She slipped the ring off her finger and handed it back to him. 'My efforts here are hardly strenuous, but a large ring will snag in the papers and could get soiled, should I spill ink. It is not a very practical choice.'

'Practicality has never been an issue,' he admitted.

'It is to me. For I am a very practical person.'

'I am aware of that.'

She looked at the box on the table, which was large enough to hold much more than a single ring. 'Is there not another choice available that might serve as compromise?'

He re-opened the box, and turned it to her. 'This is a selection of such jewellry as is at the London address. I dare say there is more, in the lock rooms at Bellston.'

She rejected the simple gold band she saw as being a trifle too plain for even the most practical of duchesses, and chose a moonstone, set in silver. It was easily the least worthy piece in the box, and he wondered why his mother had owned it, for it was unlike any of her other jewellry. His wife ran the tip of her finger lightly along the stone: a cabochon, undecorated, but also unlikely to get in the way of her work. 'I choose this.'

'Silver.' He said it as though it were inferior, but then, at one time, he might have said the same of her, had he not been forced to recognise her. And he would have been proved wrong.

'At least I will not feel strongly, should I damage it. And for formal engagements, I will wear your mother's ring. But not tonight.' She slipped the moonstone on to her hand, and it glittered eerily.

'It suits you,' he conceded.

'I suspected it would. And it is better, is it not, than if I wore the horse nail?' She admired the ring on her hand and smiled.

He smiled as well. 'I feared, for a moment, that you might do it, out of spite.'

'I am not usually given to act out of spite,' she said. He laughed.

'Well, perhaps, occasionally.' Then she laughed as well, and surrendered. 'All right. Frequently. But I shall be most co-operative tonight, if you shall take me to Wales tomorrow.'

'A bargain, madam.' He reached out and took her hand. 'Let us climb the stairs and await our guests.'

Whoever had selected the top floor of the house for a ballroom had not made the most practical of choices, but Adam had to admit that the tall windows, front and back, provided a splendid view of London below, and the night sky above. He felt Penny tense as the first guests arrived, and thought to offer her a last chance to return to her room and avoid the evening. But he saw the determined look in her eyes and thought better of it. She meant to hang on, no matter what, although the bows and curtsies of the guests and polite murmurs of 'your Grace' were obviously making her uncomfortable.

He reached out and laid a hand on her back, hoping to convey some of his strength to her. She was able to suppress the brief flinch of surprise he could feel, when his fingers touched the bare skin above her gown. And then he felt her slowly relaxing back against his hand, and step ever so slightly closer to him, letting him support and protect her.

He smiled, because it felt good to know that, whatever else she might feel, she trusted him. And it felt good as well, to feel her skin beneath his hand. He shifted and his hand slid along her back, and it was smooth and cool and wonderful to touch. The flesh warmed beneath his hand as the blood flowed to it.

And he found himself wondering, would the rest of her feel the same? If he allowed his fingers to slip under the neckline of her gown, would she pull away in shock, or move closer to him, allowing him to take even greater liberties?

'Adam? Adam?'

He came back to himself to find his wife staring up at him in confusion. Her eyes shifted slightly, to indicate the presence of guests.

'Tim and Clarissa, so good to see you.' He smiled a welcome to his friend and nodded to the woman beside him. 'Forgive me. My mind was elsewhere.' He could feel Penny's nervousness under his hand and drew her closer to him.

And as the introductions droned on, his mind returned to where it had been. It might have been easier to concentrate, if he did not have the brief memory of her, changing clothes in his bed. She had been very like a surprised nymph in some classic painting. Beautiful in her nakedness, and unaware of the gaze of another. And he had allowed himself to watch her, for even though she was his wife, he had not expected to see that particular sight again.

And now, of all times, he could not get the picture from his head. While the object of the evening was to prove to his social circle that he admired and respected his new wife, it would not do to be panting after her like a lovesick dog. A few dances, a glass of champagne, and he would retire to the card room, to steady his mind with whisky and the dull conversation of his male friends.

* * *

It was going well, she reminded herself, over and over again. She had survived the receiving line, and, except for a moment where Adam behaved quite strangely, it had been without incident. Clarissa had been quite incensed that Adam had not paid her a compliment. But he had barely seemed to notice the woman. It gave her hope that perhaps the worst was over, and that she need see no more of Clarissa after tonight.

She looked around her, at the throng of people enjoying the refreshments, and at the simple buffet, which was anything but. There was enough food for an army, if an army wished to subsist on lobster, ice-cream sculptures and liberal amounts of champagne. The orchestra was tuning, and soon dancing would begin.

Adam was surveying the room from her side. 'You have done well.'

'Thank you.'

He hesitated. 'I understand that this was difficult for you.'

'It was not so bad,' she lied.

He smiled sympathetically and whispered, 'It will be over soon, in any case. The sooner we begin the dancing, the sooner they will leave.'

'We must dance?' What fresh hell was this?

'Of course. It is our ball. If we do not dance, they will not.'

'Oh.' She had been so convinced that she would embarrass herself with the preparations for the party, or disgrace herself in the receiving line, that she had forgotten there would be other opportunities for error.

He took her hand in his and put his other hand to her waist. 'I know it goes against your nature,' he said. 'But let me lead.'

She remembered not to jump as he touched her, for it would be even more embarrassing to demonstrate again that she was not familiar with the feel of his hands on her body. He seemed unperturbed as he led her out on to the floor. 'You have nothing to fear, you know. Even if you stumble, no one will dare comment. I certainly shall not.'

She nodded, to reassure herself.

'Have you waltzed before?'

She could only manage a frantic glance up into his face.

'It does not matter. The music is lovely, and the step is easy to learn. Relax and enjoy it. One two three, one two three. See. It is not a difficult.'

He was right. It was simple enough, when one had so commanding a partner. In this, at least, she could trust him to lead her right, and so she yielded. And he turned her around the dance floor, smiling as though he enjoyed it.

She tried to match his expression. Perhaps that was the trick of it. She had but to act like she was having a pleasant evening, and people would trouble her no further.

'You are a very good dancer,' he remarked. 'Although not much of a conversationalist. I cannot keep you quiet when we are alone together. Why will you not speak now?'

'All these people…' she whispered helplessly.

'Our guests,' he answered.

'Your guests, perhaps, but they are strangers to me.'

'You met them all in the receiving line just now. And yet they frighten you?'

She managed the barest nod.

He laughed, but squeezed her hand. 'You are quite fearless in your dealings with me. Perhaps it will help you to remember that I am the most important person here.'

'And the most modest.' She could not help herself.

He laughed again, ignoring the gibe. 'At any rate, they all must yield to me. And since I intend to yield to you, you have nothing to be afraid of.'

'You yield to me?'

'If you wish, we will cancel the evening's entertainment, and I will send the guests home immediately.'

'For the last time: no. It would be even more embarrassing to do that than to stand in front of them as I do now, looking like a goose.'

He nodded. 'At least you are speaking to me again. Even if you are lying. Your obedient silence just now was most disconcerting. And you do not look like a goose. Do not concern yourself.'

'We are the centre of attention.'

He glanced around. 'So we are. But it cannot be very interesting for them, to stare at us and do nothing. Soon they will find other diversions. See? The floor is beginning to fill with couples. And others are returning to the buffet. Crisis averted. They no longer care about us. As long as the music is good and the wine holds out, they will entertain themselves and we are free to enjoy ourselves for the rest of the evening in peace.'

It was true. The worst was over. She could pretend that she was a guest at her own party, if she wished, and allow the servants to handle the details.

And as he spun her around the room, she relaxed at the sight of smiling faces and happy people.

And there was Clarissa, staring at her with death in her eyes.

He turned her away, so that she could no longer see, and they were on the other side of the room by the time the music stopped. When they parted, he brought her hand to his lips, and she could feel the look of pleasure on her face when he'd kissed the knuckles. And then he turned to part from her.

'You are leaving me alone?' She could not hide the panic in her voice.

He nodded. 'Our job as host and hostess is to entertain the guests, not each other. There is nothing to be afraid of, I assure you. Continue to smile, nod and say "thank you for coming". Much of your work is done.' He smiled again. 'And I swear, once you have done this thing for me, I am yours to command.'

She squared her shoulders and lifted her chin, prepared to meet the horde that had infested her home.

He nodded. 'Very good. If you need me, I will be in the card room, hiding with the other married men. Madam, the room is yours.'

She fought the feeling of disorientation as she watched him go, as if she was being spun by the elements, with no safe place to stand. But she admired the way her husband moved easily through the crowd, stopping to chat as he made his way to the door. Smiling and nodding. Listening more than he spoke. He was an excellent example to her.

What had she to fear from her guests? It was not as it had been, during her come-out, when all the women were in competition, and the men were prizes. The race was over. And, without trying, she had won first place.

She thought how miserable she had been at those balls, and how awkward, and how good it had felt to find a friendly face or hear a hostess's word of welcome or encouragement.

And then she scanned the crowd. There was the daughter of an earl, barely sixteen, excited by her first invitation, but terrified that it was not going well.

Penny made her way to the girl's side. 'Are you enjoying your evening?'

The conversation was unlike anything she'd ever experienced. The girl was in awe of her. The conversation was peppered with so many 'your Grace's' and curtsies, that Penny had to resist the urge to assure the girl that it was not necessary. She was a nobody who had stumbled into a title.

She smiled to herself. The less said on that subject, the better. She had the ear of the most important man in the room. She could do as she pleased. And it pleased her that people like the girl in front of her should be happy. They talked a bit, before she gently encouraged the girl to a group of young people near to her age, and made a few simple introductions. When she left, the girl was on her way to the dance floor with a young man who seemed quite smitten.

After her initial success, Penny threw herself into the

role of hostess as though she were playing a chess game, with her guests as the pieces. Penelope Winthorpe had been an excellent player, and loved the sense of control she got when moving her army around the board. This was no different. Tonight she could move actual knights, and the ladies accompanying them, urging weaker pieces to the positions that most benefited them. While her husband was able to engage people more closely, she enjoyed the gambits she could arrange in a detached fashion. It made for a harmonious whole.

Perhaps that had been her problem all along. She had never been a successful guest. But that did not mean she could not be a hostess.

'Your Grace, may I have a dance?'

She turned, surprised to see her brother-in-law. 'Of course, Will.' She stammered on the familiarity, and felt her confidence begin to fade.

He smiled, and she searched his face for some shred of duplicity or contempt. 'Penelope?' He gestured to the floor. Since she was rooted to the spot, he took her hand, leading her to the head of the set.

She watched him as they danced, comparing him to his older brother. He was not unattractive, certainly, and moved with grace and confidence. But he lacked his brother's easy sense of command. When they reached the bottom of the set and had to stand out, he leaned closer and spoke into her ear. 'I owe you an apology.'

She looked at him without speaking.

'When I found that my brother had married in haste, I told him to get an annulment. I was convinced that you would both regret the decision.'

'I had no idea,' she replied blandly.

He smiled. 'I suspected you had, for I saw the look in your eyes when you left us that night. I am sorry I caused you pain. Or that I meddled in something that was none of my affair to begin with. It is just that…' he shook his head '…Adam has always had an excellent head for politics, and I cannot fault him for his dedication to responsibilities as Bellston. But in his personal life, he has always been somewhat reckless. He thinks last of what would be best for himself in the distant future, and seems to see only what is directly in front of him.'

She shrugged. 'I cannot fault him for that. I, too, have been known to act in haste.'

'Well, perhaps your tendencies have cancelled each other. You appear to be a most successful match.'

She looked sharply at her new brother. 'We do?'

'You are just what my brother needs: a stable source of good advice. He speaks well of you, and he appears happier than I have seen him in a long time.'

'He does?' She tried to hide her surprise.

'Indeed. He is at peace. Not something I am accustomed to seeing, in one so full of motion as Adam is. But his activity in society brings him near to people that are not as good as they could be. Compared to the foolish women that normally flock to his side, you are a great relief to a worried brother. And I can assure you, and your family, if they are concerned, that in my brother you have found a loyal protector and a true friend. I am glad of your union, and wish you well in it.'

'Thank you. That is good to know.' Impulsively, she

reached out and clasped Will's hand, and he returned the grip with a smile.

Her eyes sought her husband on the other side of the room, and she smiled at him as well.

He returned a look that indicated none of the affection that Will had described. Perhaps her new brother was mistaken.

The music ended. 'I will leave you to your other guests, then. I suspect we will have ample time in the future to speak.' And Will took his leave of her.

Another guest asked her to dance. And then another. At last she excused herself from the floor to check on the refreshments. And found Clarissa, standing in her way.

'Penelope, darling. What a charming party.'

There was no way to cut the woman, no matter how much she deserved it. Penny pasted a false smile on her face and responded, 'Thank you,' then went to step around her.

Clarissa reached out to her, in what no doubt appeared to the room as a sisterly gesture of warmth, catching both hands in hers. Then she pulled her close, to whisper what would look to observers like a girlish confidence. 'But if you think it makes any difference to your standing in society, you are wrong.'

Penny summoned her newfound bravery. 'My position in society is secure. I am Duchess of Bellston.'

'In name, perhaps. But in reality, you are a trumped-up shop girl. People know the truth, and they can talk of little else this evening.'

She had heard nothing, and she had been to every corner of the room. It must be a lie, intended to wound her.

But there was no way to be sure.

Then she thought of what Will had said, and tossed her head in her best imitation of someone who did not give a jot for what people 'said'. 'Let them talk, then. They are most unaccountably rude to be doing so in my home while drinking my wine and eating my food.'

'They are saying nothing more than what your husband has said.'

It was her worst fear, was it not? That he felt she was beneath him. And she feared it because it was based in truth. Clarissa must have guessed as much or she would not speak so.

But there was nothing she could do about it now. So she favoured Clarissa with her coldest look, and said nothing.

'He is taking you to Wales, is he? Very good. I heartily approve. You must go home and complete your work which is, no doubt, noble and of much scholarly import.' The last words were sarcastic, as though Penny's life goal was so much nonsense.

'But no matter what you mean to do, I doubt that Adam means to stay with you in isolation, if there are other more entertaining opportunities open to him. He will come back to London, or find a reason to go to Bath, or somewhere else.

'And the minute he does, you will know that he is coming to me. He was happy enough before you arrived on the scene. And he is even happier, now that he has your money. He has told us as much. He simply needs to get you out of the way, so that he may spend it in peace.'

Penny controlled the flinch, for the last words struck as hard as any blow.

Clarissa continued, 'Adam is happy. And I am happy with Adam. You have promised to be happy with your books. You have nothing further to add to the discussion, other than regular infusions of gold.'

Penny struggled to speak. 'And is Timothy happy?'

'Timothy?' Clarissa laughed again.

'Yes. Timothy. Your husband.'

'He is glad to see Adam back, for they are great friends.'

'And it must be very handy for you to share such affection for Adam. They are good comrades, are they not? And if you seek to be unfaithful, how handy that it be with your husband's best friend.'

Clarissa was unaffected. 'Why, yes. It is most convenient.'

'Until you get caught at it. And then there will be the devil to pay, Clarissa. The scandal will be enormous.'

'Caught? Caught by whom exactly? Dear me, Penelope. You make it sound as though we are likely to be run down with a pack of hounds. How diverting.'

'Your husband,' Penelope hissed. 'You must be mad to think that you can carry on in front of him and remain undiscovered. And if you believe, for one minute, that I will allow you to drag my name, and the name of my husband, through the muck with this public display, you are even more mad. This is my first and final warning to you, Clarissa. Stay away from Adam. Or I will tell Timothy what is going on, and he will put an end to it.'

Clarissa laughed, and it was no delicate silvery peal

of ladylike mirth, but a belly-deep whoop of joy. 'You mean to tell my husband? About me and Adam? Oh, my dear. My sweet, young innocent. You do not understand at all, do you? My husband already knows.'

Penny felt her stomach drop and thought with horror that she was likely to be sick on the floor of her own ballroom. What a ludicrous scene that would be. Clarissa, or any of the other ladies of her husband's acquaintance, would have managed a genteel faint.

'Clarissa, we must dance. You have monopolised our hostess long enough.' Lord Timothy was standing behind her, and she prayed that he had not heard what his wife had been murmuring, for the situation was quite mortifying enough.

'But I was having such a lovely chat with Penny.' Clarissa's voice was honey sweet.

'I can see that.' Tim's was ice and steel. 'She bears the look of one who has experienced one of your chats, darling. Drained of blood, and faint of heart. Remove your claws from her and accompany me.' He laid a hand on Clarissa's wrist and squeezed. 'Or I will pry them loose for you.'

Clarissa laughed and released her, then turned to the dance floor. 'Very well, Timothy. Let us dance. So long as it is not a waltz. I am saving the waltzes for someone special.' Then she walked away as though nothing had happened.

Penny stood frozen in place, watching her, and felt Tim's hand upon her shoulder. 'Are you all right?' His face was so close to her that his cheek brushed her hair.

'I will see to it that my wife goes home early. And then we will speak. Until then, do not trouble yourself.'

She nodded without speaking.

He eased away from her, passing by to follow his wife. In a tone loud enough to be heard by people passing, he said, 'Lovely party, your Grace. I never fail to find entertainment on a visit to Bellston.'

Chapter Fourteen

Penny closed her eyes, and focused on the sound of the room, rather than the faces of the people in it. She had thought things were going so well. But now, it was impossible to tell friends from enemies. When she was seventeen, the falsehoods and sly derision had come as a surprise. But she knew better now. When she looked closely at those around her, she could see from the strained expressions on the faces of her husband's friends that she did not fit in.

And the looks of suspicion, jealousy and disdain seemed to follow, wherever Clarissa had been. The woman could spread discord like a bee spreads pollen.

Damn them all. She would send the guests away, just as Adam had told her she could. And never, ever, would she submit to such torture again. In time, Adam would forget about her, since it was obvious that he wished to be elsewhere. If it mattered so much to him that there be entertainment in his house, he would have been at her side when she was all but attacked by his mistress.

She steadied her breathing. To call a sudden halt to the proceedings would be even more embarrassing than to continue with them. If there were any left in the room that were not talking about her, they soon would be, once she drove them from her house and slammed the doors.

She would retire herself, then. It was embarrassing for a hostess to abandon her guests. But she found herself— suddenly indisposed. Too ill to continue, no doubt due to the stress of the event. People would understand. Some would know the cause of the indisposition, but not all. She might still save some small portion of pride.

She had but to find her husband, and tell him that it behoved him, as host, to rise from the card table, and attend to his guests, for she could not hold up another instant.

She exited the hall and was almost in the card room before she knew what she was about. The sound of male laughter echoed into the hallway.

It would be embarrassing to invade the privacy of the men, but it could not be helped. It was her house, after all. Even if she might need to continually remind herself of the fact.

She paused in front of the partially open door, standing behind it, and taking in a deep breath, scented with the tobacco smoke escaping from the room. And without intending to, she heard the conversation, escaping from the room as well.

'Of course, now that Adam is an old married man, he will not be interested in cards or horses. I dare say your new bride does not approve of your track losses, Bellston.'

There was general laughter.

'She has not yet had the chance to approve or disapprove of them, Mark. We have been married a short time, and even I cannot lose money so fast as that, despite my dashed bad luck. When one is throwing one's money away, it takes time to pick a horse that can do the job properly.'

'You took little enough care in the finding of a wife, Adam.'

So she was no different than choosing a jade. Anger mingled with shame at the hearing of it.

'Indeed. You were alone when you left London. Wherever did you find her?' It was her husband's friend, John.

'She found me, more like. I was not even looking.' Her husband's voice.

She drew back from the door. Her father had often told her that people who listened at keyholes deserved what they heard. She should retreat immediately if she did not want Clarissa's stories confirmed.

'She must have a fat purse, then, for you to marry so quickly.'

She could feel her cheeks reddening. *One, two, three…*

'Her father was a cit?' Another voice, edged with curiosity.

Four, five, six.

'In printing, I believe,' her husband answered. 'Books and such. My wife is a great reader. Probably through his influence.'

Someone laughed. 'What does a woman need with reading?'

Idiot. Her fists balled.

'I wouldn't know, myself. But she seems to value it.' There was the faintest trace of sarcasm in her husband's voice. And she relaxed her fists. 'I imagine it proves useful, if one does not wish to appear as foolish as you.'

'But it must take her time away from other, more important things,' John responded. 'Her appearance, for example. She is a bit of a quiz.'

Her husband, and his damned friends, sniping and backbiting, as she had seen them on the first day. She would not cry, she reminded herself. She was a grown woman, in her own house, and she would suffer these fools no longer, but go into the room and remind her husband who had paid for the party.

And then she noticed the silence emanating from the room. John's comment had been followed by a mutter of assent, and some nervous laughter, that had faded quickly to nothing.

Her husband spoke. 'I find her appearance to be singular. Her eyes, especially, are most compelling. Not to everyone's taste, perhaps, but very much to mine. You might wish to remember that, in future, if you wish to visit my home.' The warning in his voice was clear, and she imagined him the way he had been when he stood up to her brother. Quiet, but quite frightening.

Her jaw dropped.

There was more muttering in the room, and a hurried apology from John.

Her husband spoke again. 'If any are curious on the matter of how I came to be married so quickly after my recent financial misfortunes, and to one so wealthy as my wife, let me clarify the situation, that you may explain it to them. It was a chance meeting of kindred souls. The decision on both our parts was very sudden, and on my part, it had very little to do with the size of her inheritance. I consider myself most fortunate to have found so intelligent and understanding a woman, and must regret that circumstances imply an ulterior motive. Would anyone else care to comment on it?'

There were hurried denials from his friends.

'I thought not. Furthermore, I do not expect to hear more on the subject of my wife's family. Her brother is in trade, and our backgrounds are most different. But I wished the woman I married to be worthy of the title, and with sufficient character to bring pride to my name. I am more than happy with my choice. Would that you are all as lucky as I have been.'

Nervous silence followed, and someone cleared his throat.

Then, when tension had reached a near-unbearable point, she heard the sound of shuffling cards, and her husband drawled, 'Another hand, gentleman?'

She could feel the tension release, as the men rushed to offer assent.

She leaned her back to the wall, and let the plaster support her as the room began to spin. The Duke of Bellston found her 'singular'. Whatever did that mean? If another had said it, she'd have thought it was faint praise, and that the speaker had been too kind to say 'odd'.

But from Adam's lips? It had sounded like 'rare'. As though she was something to be sought for and kept safe.

She could not help the ridiculous glow she felt at the knowledge. The most important man in the room thought she did credit to his name. And there had been no false note when he had said he was happy.

She walked slowly down the short hall, toward the ballroom. At the doorway, the butler came to her with a question about the wine, and she answered absently, but with confidence. She could not help smiling, as she went back to her guests, and even managed to stand up for another dance when her husband's brother offered.

The evening was drawing to a close, the crowd already thinning, and it did not really matter if the guests liked her or not. They were leaving soon, and she would be alone with a man who, she smiled to herself, thought she was 'singular'. She looked up to see her husband returning to the main room to seek her out. He took her hand to lead her to the floor for a final dance, but paused, with his head tipped to the side, staring at her.

'Your Grace?' she responded, and smiled back at him.

He shook his head. 'Something is different. What has occurred?'

'I do not know what you mean.'

'You have changed.'

She glanced down at her gown, spreading the skirt with her hand, and shrugged back at him. 'I assure you, I am no different than when we left our rooms earlier today.'

He smiled. 'Perhaps I should have chosen my words more carefully. You are transfigured. I was gone from the room for a short time, and I return to find I've missed a metamorphosis.'

She laughed then, and looked away, remembering his words from earlier. And she could feel the heat in her cheeks as she answered, 'Is this transfiguration a good thing? For not all of them are, you know.'

'I hope so. For you are looking most…well… hmm… I assume you had a pleasant evening.'

'Well enough. But better, now that it is over.' She saw Lord Timothy, staring significantly at her, from across the room. 'If you will excuse me. I think your friend wishes to speak to me.'

'Very well.'

Adam watched her back as she walked away from him and toward the stairs. There was definitely something different about her. A sway in her hips, perhaps? Or a toss of her head as she turned. And her colouring was better. Where she had been deathly pale at the beginning of the evening, to the extent that he feared she might faint in his arms, now there were roses in her cheeks, and a sparkle in her eye. She was smiling as she walked away from him, and he heard her laugh in response to something that Tim had said to her.

The whole impression was most fetching, if a bit disconcerting. As he looked at her, he found himself comparing her with the few ladies remaining in the room. He found the others wanting. She would never be known as a great beauty, but she was certainly handsome. Tonight, she was displaying a strength of character and a confidence that had been lacking in the early days of their marriage. She glanced back at him from her spot beside Tim, and her smile was spontaneous and infectious.

And he had got the distinct impression, when she'd greeted him just now, that she had been flirting with him.

He scanned what was left of the crowd to see if any had noticed, or if there might be some explanation for the change in behaviour. His eye caught his brother, and he signalled him with a nod of his head.

Will crossed the room to his side, smiling and relaxed. It appeared he had also enjoyed the party. 'The evening went well.'

'That is good to know.' Adam indicated his retreating wife with an inclination of his head. 'Penelope did well, I think.'

Will smiled after her. 'So it seems. She is looking most fine this evening.'

Adam nodded agreement. 'What put such colour in her cheeks, I wonder? I spent much of the evening in the card room, and too little time with her.' That his absence might have contributed to her good mood was more than a little irritating.

'Perhaps it was the dancing. I had opportunity to stand up with her on several occasions. She is most adept for one who spends so much time amongst her books. And an intelligent conversationalist, once she overcomes her shyness. It was why I was so opposed to your match. You are a gad, not much for sitting home of an evening, while she would like nothing better. It is not the recipe for a happy union, when two partners are so dissimilar.'

'As you know, with your vast experience as a married man.'

His brother ignored the gibe. 'But I rescind my former feelings on the subject. She seems to be warming to her job as hostess. And once she began to open up to me, I found her views on scholarship to be most refreshing.'

'She opened up to you.'

'Yes. As the evening wore on, she was most chatty. We had several opportunities to speak, as we danced.'

'Oh.' He remembered seeing her, clasping his brother's hand, and the look she had given him, as though she wished him to see. Did she mean to make him jealous? She had succeeded.

Will continued. 'It is good that you plan to allow her to continue with her work. She is correct: her views have value. I most look forward to reading her translation when she completes it.'

Adam searched his heart for a desire to read Homer, in any form, and found it wanting. He could still remember the sting of the ruler on the back of his hand, for all the times he had neglected his studies to go riding, or attempted them, only to miss a conjugation. And now, Will would be there to appreciate the work, once Penny had completed it.

Damn him. But that was ridiculous. He had nothing to fear from his brother. Will would rather die than come between him and his new wife. He should be happy that Penny would have someone to talk to.

Then why did he feel so irritated that she was talking to him tonight? Adam had left her alone to fend for herself. And she had done it, admirably. By the end of the evening, he'd heard murmurs about what a fine hostess she had been, and the people wishing him well had sounded sincere and not sarcastic. The evening had been a success.

And now, his brother could not stop prattling on about his wife's finer qualities, as though they were any business of his. '…and a lot in common with Tim as well. Perhaps when you go home, she will have opportunity to see his research, for I think she would find it fascinating. He was a dab hand at languages when you were in school, was he not?'

'Tim.' *Oh, dear God. Not him as well.*

'Yes. They went off together, just now, while we were speaking? Probably looking for a quiet corner where they can conjugate verbs together.' Will laughed.

'Not if I can help it.' And Adam left his brother to search out his wife.

Chapter Fifteen

'Fair Penelope.' Lord Timothy was being most effusive in his praise, and she wondered if he were the worse for drink. 'I have sent my wife home, and she will bother you no further.'

'You wished to speak to me?'

He caught her hand, and slipped it through the crook of his arm, then led her away from the ballroom. 'In your sitting room, if that is all right. Somewhere we can be alone.'

'What do you wish to say that requires privacy?'

'Things I do not wish others to hear.' He led her past her husband, who was deep in conversation with his brother, and hardly aware of his surroundings. 'Perhaps I wish to be the first man of the *ton* to attempt a flirtation with you. I expect there shall be many, and do not wish to lose my chance, for lack of courage.'

She tried a laugh, and failed. 'If that was meant as a joke, I fear it was not very funny. I do not wish you to flirt with me, now or ever, if that is truly your intent.'

'A pity.' He sighed. 'We would likely do well together, just as our spouses suit each other. For we are studious and bookish, and not at ease in society. Just as they are mercurial and charismatic.'

'It was true what she said, then. You know about them.' Then Penny stopped to look around, afraid that a guest might have heard her speak.

Tim hurried down the last flight of steps and pulled her down the hall and into her own room, shutting the door behind them. 'I am many things, Penelope, but I am neither blind, nor foolish. I was well aware of what happened. Clarissa made certain of it.'

'It does not bother you that your wife is so flagrant in her attentions to other men?'

He sighed. 'Many of the couples in my set have such agreements. We married for reasons other than love. She was rich, as well as beautiful. I have been able to finance my studies.' He grimaced. 'Although she makes me pay dearly for them.'

'And you all look politely the other way when there is something you do not wish to see?'

'Precisely.'

'But if I make the slightest social *faux pas*?'

'Then you will be the talk of the town. You are already notorious for aspiring to a better class than you were born to. People like Clarissa wish to see you fail, to prove that you do not belong. Then they may continue to feel superior.'

'Timothy, this is grossly unfair.'

He nodded. 'But do not believe what she told you. You did well tonight.'

She ignored the compliment. 'It is not particularly moral of you all to allow such chaos and infidelity in your midst.'

'You must have a very limited understanding of society to think so, my dear.'

'I never claimed to have one. Not your idea of society, at least. In the circles I moved in, people did not work so at playing false. My mother loved my father, and my father loved her. They were a most happy couple, until she died. And I would swear they were faithful; even after she was gone, my father did not seek the company of women, or wish to remarry. He threw himself wholeheartedly into his work.'

Timothy laughed. 'Perhaps that is the problem, for we have no work to throw ourselves into. Idle hands, as they say, my dear. Clarissa is proof of that, for she has never done a moment's real labour, but is the devil's handmaiden if there is mischief to be made.'

Penny did not wish to speak ill of the man's wife, and attempted, 'I am sure that she has many qualities that I will consider admirable, once I know her better.'

'And I came here to warn you not to bother. You will never get from her other than you got tonight. Backbiting, sly innuendoes, threats and tricks. If you show weakness, she will use it against you. Once she finds a chink in your armour, she will strike there, to bring you all the pain she can. That is the only reason that she wants Adam back, now that he has finally come to his senses. It amuses her to drive a wedge between me and my oldest friend.'

Penny seized on the only hopeful note in the speech. 'So they are no longer together?'

'Not for some time. But she is persistent, and I feared he would weaken. When he returned from Scotland with you, I was much relieved.'

Penny shook her head. 'It is no love match. Do not expect him to choose me, should there be a choice to be made.'

'And yet, he says he did not marry for money, and I believe him.'

She weighed the truth, and the burden of keeping the secret from one who could help her understand. At last she said, 'We are married because I tricked him. I needed a husband to gain control of my fortune. When I found him, he was face down in a coach yard. It appeared he had tried to throw himself beneath the carriage and make an end of it. He said something about gambling and bad debts when he was sober enough to talk. But he was far too drunk to know what was happening at the time of the actual marriage.'

'It was not binding, if he was too drunk to agree.'

'That was what I thought. I offered to let him go. But he felt an obligation. I needed a husband, and he needed money. And since we were already married, we struck a bargain and came back to London.' She looked sadly at Timothy. 'I am sorry to disappoint you, if you were expecting a grand romantic tale. But that's the truth of it.'

'Nonsense. He is yours if you want him, and Clarissa has no hope. I know him better than I know myself. And I have seen the way he looks at you.'

She laughed. 'What way is that?'

'Like a man in love. You are good for him, Penelope. No matter how things appear, you must not lose heart, for Clarissa is no threat to you.' Tim caught her hand and held it in his.

She laughed. 'You are mad.'

'Adam may be too big a fool to tell you, just yet. But not so big a fool as to pass you by for that harridan I am shackled to. What happened pains him greatly, and I am sick to death of seeing the guilt in his eyes when he looks at me. Make him forget, and you will help us both.'

'But why do you bother, Tim? I am sure he would not blame you if you could not forgive him.'

Tim smiled. 'I know how much of the blame lies with my wife. Clare angled after him for years before she finally trapped him. It was a wonder he held out as long as he did.'

'But she was not the only one at fault,' Penny said.

'True enough. And try as I might, I cannot help but forgive him. I'm sure you have noticed by now that he is a most likeable fellow, especially when you wish to be angry with him. Very persuasive. Has he told you what happened, to get him sent down when we were at school together?'

'No.' She tried to hide her curiosity.

'It was all my doing.' Tim shook his head. 'I was a heavy drinker in those days. And one night, while deep in my cups, we got to brawling with each other in a public house, like common ruffians. That was over a woman as well, for it is the only reason we ever argue. Missed curfew. And gave him the worst of it. Blacked his eye and nearly broke that handsome face of his. It was all around the school that I assaulted Bellston's heir. Added to my lack of academic attention, I deserved a one-way ticket home. But somehow, Adam managed to convince the deans that it was all his fault. Took the whole blame. Issued the apologies, paid the bills, put some ice on his black eyes and allowed himself to be sent home in disgrace to face his father. Told me, if I loved science so much, I had best get about proving it, for with no title and no money, I would need an education to secure my future. But since he was to be duke, he could be as big a fool as he liked and no harm would come of it.'

Tim smiled and shook his head. 'Couldn't well be angry with him after that. You will see what he is like, if you haven't already. When he tries, let him charm you. You will not regret it, I promise you.'

There was a rather loud sound of someone clearing his throat in the hallway, and then the door opened and her husband walked into the room.

Adam glanced at them, as though not noticing anything unusual, and said, 'I was looking for a book, for the trip tomorrow.' He looked at her. 'Perhaps you could recommend something?' And to his friend, 'Or you, Tim. For I assume that is why you are secluded with my wife. So that you may talk books, without boring the rest of us.' There was a touch of menace in her husband's voice that she had never heard before.

'Of course,' Tim answered innocently. 'For what other reason would one choose to be alone with such a lovely woman? Not making you jealous, am I?'

'Do I have reason to be?'

'I think I might have reason to be jealous of you. But that is between you and your wife. Good luck, old friend, as if you need any more. And goodnight.' Tim let go of her hand, and rose to leave.

Adam watched him with suspicion. 'Close the door behind you, please.'

He waited until his friend had gone down the hall and was out of earshot. And then he said without warning, 'I will not let you cuckold me in my own home.'

'Would you prefer that I do it elsewhere?' She had almost laughed at the ridiculousness of it before she realised he was serious.

He did not raise his voice, but she could tell that his temper was barely contained. 'You know what I meant. I would prefer not to have to kill a man over you. Especially not that one.'

'Kill Tim? Adam, listen to yourself. Have you gone mad?'

She could hardly recognise the man before her, for his eyes were dark and his face more grim than she had ever seen it. 'Do not be flip with me. If you do not set that young puppy straight, I will be forced to deal with him on the field of honour, the next time I wander in on the two of you.'

'For holding my hand? That is rich, after what he has suffered from you.'

'Which is another reason I do not wish to hurt him. He has not, as yet, done anything I cannot overlook. But I suspect it is only a matter of time before I will have reason to act. I beg you to stop it, to prevent me from having to do so.'

She rolled her eyes. 'As if it would matter to you. From what I gather, in talking to your friends, the nobles of your acquaintance have the morals of cats in an alley. Not one wife amongst them is faithful, and all the husbands have mistresses.'

'That is different,' he answered.

'I fail to see how. It is not as if we married for love, unless that is a mandatory precursor to the level of infidelity I have seen. Ours was a purely financial arrangement, and I thought we were of an understanding on the subject of sexual attachments. I told you it did not matter to me.'

'And do you remember my saying, in response to you, that what you did would not matter to me? Because I did not. I was under the impression that while you intended for me to find a mistress to deal with my personal needs, you meant to stay home alone with a good book.'

'So the situation is agreeable, so long as it benefits you and not me?' she said.

'I fail to see how it does, since I have not yet taken advantage of the liberties you seem so eager to allow me.'

She grew even more confused. 'You have no mistress?'

'Not at this time.'

'Nor any other…'

'No.'

'Since we married, you have not—'

'I said, no,' he snapped.

'I do not understand.'

'Nor do I,' he responded. 'But that doesn't mean I

wish for you to take a lover after less than a month of marriage. You cannot expect me to sit idly by and do nothing about it.'

Her argument ran out of fuel, and her anger cooled. But his argument became no clearer. And so she said, 'Your friends do not seem overly bothered by their wives' conduct.'

'My friends all have several children. Any inheritances or titles have been assured. Their wives have performed the duties, which you have expressed no interest in. They have earned latitude.'

'And is that the only problem? You think that I encourage Timothy too soon?'

'People will say that turnabout is fair play, and I am getting a taste of what I deserve. And they will question the legitimacy of my heir, should there be one, even if I do not.'

She smiled at the nonsense of it. 'But I have no intention of getting myself with child.'

He shook his head. 'You are wise in many things, but there is much you do not know. Let me try to explain. First, you understand that you do not get yourself with child, it is a collaborative effort.'

'I do not plan to collaborate.'

He sighed. 'If you have feelings for Timothy, or any one else, for that matter, these feelings could lead you to a place where collaboration is inevitable.'

'I am not so easily led, Adam,' she said.

He shook his head. 'At one time, I thought I was as wise as you think you are now. A private conversation, a shared joke, the touch of a hand in friendship, or a waltz or two in public would lead to nothing. It was all innocent flirtation that I could stop before it got out of control. But considering our histories, you should sympathise with how easy it can be to respond poorly in the heat of the moment. And there is much heat in a forbidden kiss.'

He sank down on the couch, his head in his hands. 'The next morning, I realised what I had done, and could not bring myself to look in the mirror. I was too ashamed. And that wasn't the last time. I could not seem to stop it until I had driven myself near to ruin and hurt family and friends with the indiscretion.

'And I am not as noble as my good friend Timothy, to be all understanding and forgiveness. Should he try to do to me what I did to him, I am more like to put a ball through him in the heat of anger than look quietly aside. I do not wish it to end thus.' He looked up at her, in desperation. 'If you truly prefer him to me, tell me now, and I will request the annulment that you once offered. Then you will be free to do as you like.'

'I would make you pay back the money you have used,' she countered.

'You would have no right to do so. An annulment will make it as if you have never been married. Control of your estate would revert to your brother. I think he would consider the debts I incurred to be money well spent. The man would be more likely to kiss me than you would.' He put his hand on hers. 'I do not like Hector, and have no desire to aid him in controlling you, but neither will I allow you to shame me in public or destroy an already fragile friendship.'

She shook her head in amazement. She could not

decide which was stranger: her husband's jealous raving, or the twisted logic of the upper class. 'So if any man speaks to me, you will be convinced that I am unfaithful, like all the other wives. And then you will corner me to rant, as you have tonight, although you have no reason.'

He gave her a sad smile, and nodded.

She continued. 'And although in time you are likely to stray from me, I will be allowed no indiscretions at all, for you do not wish people to think that your heirs are illegitimate. You understand that there is no point in suspecting the legitimacy of your children until you have some?'

And now, he was looking at her with speculation. The silence drew out long between them.

'But if you did, that would mean…' Her pulse quickened in response. 'Oh, no.'

'We could remain unfortunately childless, I suppose. And celibate. And hope that my brother marries and produces. But that is a lot to assume. If there is any hint of infidelity on your part, annulment will continue to be an option.'

'You mean to hold that over my head for the rest of our lives?'

'If necessary.' The intensity of his gaze grew. 'Or we could try another way.'

Her pulse was racing now, as it began to occur to her that he was serious in what he was suggesting. 'That was most definitely not part of the original bargain.'

'When you planned to marry, you must have considered the possibility.'

Strangely, she had not. She had assumed it would be hard enough to get a man to the altar, and that any so doing would not be the least interested in sexual congress with her, if other opportunities presented themselves. But the need for succession had not been part of her plans. And now, Adam was looking at her in quite a different way than he did after political discussions in the study. He was looking at her as a woman, and she remembered what Tim had said to her.

She sat down beside him, afraid to meet his gaze lest he see how she felt about him. 'I'd never have married a duke had I known it would become so complicated.'

'I am sorry to have inconvenienced you,' he said, not the least bit contrite. 'But I will need an heir. Once one has married, it makes sense to look at the obvious solution to the problem.'

'And you would…with me…and we…'

He nodded. 'Two male children are preferable, but one might be sufficient. If it was a boy, and healthy. If the first is a daughter, then…'

'But that would mean…we would…more than once…'

'Most certainly. Repeatedly. For several years at least.'

Repeatedly. She sat there, eyes round, mouth open, mind boggled. Unable to speak at all.

He continued. 'When you think of it, a sacrifice of a year or two, against the rest of your life, is not so long a time. You are rich enough to have nannies and governesses to care for any offspring. It would in no way interfere with your studies, for it must not be too hard to keep up on reading while in your months of confinement. What else would you have to do?'

'And once you have an heir…'

'Or two,' he prompted.

'Then I am free to do as I like?'

'We both will be. The marital obligations are fulfilled. Gossip is silenced. We can go our separate ways, as planned, even while remaining under the same roof.'

'Like everyone else.'

'If we wish.'

He was right, which made it all the more maddening. After the initial display of temper, he had presented his case most rationally. He was not asking more than an average husband would expect. She had been the one to make the unreasonable request. But he was quite upfront about his willingness to return to her plan, once the niceties were performed. Other than the absolute terror she felt, when she thought of what they would do together, she could find no flaw in his logic.

She stared at him. 'And you are willing to…with me.'

'Of course.' He said it as though the fact somehow answered her question.

'But when we married…there was no plan to… I never expected that you would want…'

He smiled. 'If I had found the idea repellent, I would never have agreed to continue with the marriage. And I will admit, as we have grown familiar with each other, I have been giving the matter some thought. I have no wish to force you, of course. But neither can I stand idly by while you take a lover.'

If he was to be believed, he had been faithful to her,

despite opportunity and temptation, for the brief duration of their marriage. And it must be true, for he would gain nothing by lying, since she did not care.

But if she did not care, then why was the idea so flattering? As was the idea that he was seriously considering… She looked at him, sitting beside her, with the candlelight in his eyes, and the beginnings of a beard shadow on his pale cheek. He was the most beautiful man she had ever seen. She could not help an uncontrollable attraction. It was why she had learned to look at him as little as possible, much as one learned not to stare directly into the sun.

'Are you planning to answer today?' he asked. 'Because you have been quiet for a very long time, and I find it unnerving. If you wish more time to consider, I will understand.'

'No. No, really I am fine.' Tim had said she should let him charm her. And he was only asking her to do what she had secretly wanted for quite some time.

'And?' He made a gesture, as if to coax more words out of her.

'Oh. Yes. And… Well… Although I did not expect it, I do not see anything unreasonable about your request. You are right. I will inform Tim, if he should flirt with me again, that his attentions are inappropriate. And I will…'

He raised his eyebrows, and gestured again.

'Accede to your request for…' she searched for a word that was not too embarrassing '…collaboration.'

He smiled. 'Thank you. Shall we begin?'

'Now?' She slid down the couch to be as far away from him as possible.

'I fail to see why not.' He slid after her to be near to her again, and covered her hands with his. 'I do not mean to take you here, if that is what frightens you. Now that I have your consent, it is not as if we need to rush.'

'Oh.' Her heart was hammering as his hands stoked up her arms, to touch her shoulders.

'But I do find you quite fetching this evening. Which gave rise to the jealousy of a few moments ago. I feared that other men had noticed what I was seeing in you. For how could they not? Can you forgive me?'

She blinked.

'It was foolish of me. You should not have to bear the brunt of my mercurial temper.'

She blinked again, and took a shaky breath.

'I am afraid I have an overly passionate nature. But as such, it would be most out of character for me if I did not try to steal a kiss or two, to celebrate our last night in London and your successful entrance into society.'

'A kiss.' The words came out of her mouth on a sigh. And she nodded.

'Or two.' He reached behind her, to undo the hooks of her gown.

'Then why…?' She started forward, which only brought her closer to his body, and his hands worked to loosen her stays, proving again his knowledge of lady's underthings.

'I have been told that, although they are lovely, ball-gowns tend to be rather constricting. It will be easier for you to relax if we undo your lacing.'

'Oh.' Perhaps he was right, for it was becoming difficult to catch her breath, especially when he held her the way he was doing now.

He felt her trembling, and rubbed his cheek against hers and whispered, 'You have not been kissed before?'

'You did, once. When we first came to London.'

He reached out, and took the glasses off the bridge of her nose, folding them up and setting them aside. 'This will be very different, then.' As his lips moved from her temple down to her mouth, she quite forgot to breathe. And her sudden gasp for air pulled his tongue into her open mouth, which, judging by the way he was using it, seemed to be his object, all along.

He pushed her back into the cushions of the couch, and the kiss became harder, and he sucked, to bring her tongue to him, urging her to stroke and lick in return. This was no ordinary kiss, for there was no sweetness in it, just raw desire. And she opened herself to it, loving the feel of him, wanting her and claiming her for his own.

And suddenly she realised the true reason he had opened her gown, for in her movements under him, her breasts had slipped out of the low bodice, and he was massaging them with his hands, and teasing the tips with his fingers, until she squirmed under him. Then his kiss travelled from her chin, to her neck, to her bare shoulder, before his hands cupped her breasts to bring the nipples, one by one, into his mouth. He settled his head against her, and began to suckle at them, the stubble on his chin rough against them, and the hair of his head, so very soft in contrast. His mouth pulled hard upon them, until she was arching her back, and moaning in pleasure. And then she felt the feeling rush through her body until it left her trembling in his arms.

As he looked up and smiled at her, the clock on the mantel struck three. 'That is enough for tonight, I think.'

She tried to ask him what he meant, in stopping, but the words that came out of her were unintelligible.

'Technically, I think I have fulfilled my promise.' He was still smiling. 'For that was one kiss. Two at most. I don't recall stopping at any point in the last hour. Do you?'

An hour? Had it been so long? She shook her head.

'I could go longer, but it is late, and we are travelling tomorrow, as I promised. But your initial response was most favourable. I think it bodes well for our future together.'

Their future? If tonight had been an indication of things to come, then she hoped the future was not distant. 'When?'

His smile broadened. 'I am not sure. There is an art to these things. I would not want to hurry, but neither am I willing to wait too long. Some time after we have gone home, and can lie in our own bed for as long as we like, taking pleasure in each other.' His hand dipped to her skirt, and he raised the hem. 'You may let me know when you are ready.' His fingers trailed up her leg, until they were above her knee and had searched out the top of her stocking. He ran his fingertips lightly along the bare skin above the silk, before untying her garter. The stocking slipped, and he pressed the pad of his thumb against the naked flesh of her inner thigh.

She felt her legs trembling at the touch, and moaned in response.

'Not that way, although it is music to hear, darling.' He pulled the ribbon down her leg and waved it in front of her. 'You will be ready when you are brave enough to take this back from me.' And he tucked it into his coat pocket, and offered her his hand. 'Now sit up, so that I may put your clothing back together, and we will go upstairs to let the maid take it apart again.'

Chapter Sixteen

The next day he sat across from her in the carriage, watching as she watched the road. She was not the uneasy traveller that had returned with him from Gretna. As the city passed away to be replaced by villages and open road, he watched her taking in the changing landscape, returning to her book time and again, only to gaze back out the window. She was as happy in leaving London as a normal woman would be to go there.

He shook his head and smiled to himself. Last night's conversation had been more than strange. If it had been any other woman in the world, the solution would have been easy. The merest suggestion on his part, and an assignation would have been guaranteed. That he should have to explain the obvious, quietly and politely to his own wife, and then wait for her assent, was an idea beyond comprehension.

But he had not realised, until last night, that their plan

to remain apart was a disaster in the making. It had never occurred to him that his wife might have favourites, just as his friends' wives did. That he had no right to expect her fidelity nor method to encourage it had struck him like a thunderclap.

And to see his best friend at her side, so far from the ballroom, had churned up all the feelings of guilt that he had been trying to hide. If only Tim had told him not to be an idiot when he'd questioned him. But he had laughed it off, and given him a knowing look that said, 'It would serve you right.'

Adam must nip it in the bud immediately. He was not without charm. He had been told he was surpassingly handsome. And he was a duke, damn it all, which should be more than sufficient for even the most selective of wives. He would bring the sum total of his experience to bear on the problem and the inexperienced printer's daughter would melt in his hands like butter.

Was already melting, come to that. He'd felt her kisses the previous night, and seen the stricken look she had given him when he'd stopped.

This morning, she sat there, her lips swollen and chapped from his kiss, and watched him when she did not think he would notice. This was much more of what he expected. She had not noticed him before, and he had not realised how it had annoyed him.

Now she was aware. Sexually aware of him. Watching his hands and thinking that they had touched her. Watching his mouth and knowing that it would kiss her again. And wondering about the garter that lay coiled in his pocket, and what she might be willing to do to get it.

He had wondered about that himself. He had imagined her response would be stiff and awkward, and perhaps a little cold. But the image of warm butter was more apt. Hot and delicious.

He licked his lips, and she followed the movement of his tongue with fascination, before looking away and feigning interest in her book.

It would not be too very long before she was as eager to give herself to him as he was to take her. He would do as he willed with her for as long as he liked— for a lifetime, if necessary—and there would be no more of this nonsense about taking lovers and leading separate lives.

And it all would be settled before the first snows fell, and his wife realised that her main sources of entertainment for the long winter months would be visits from his brother Will, and their good neighbour, Tim. He would have no peace in his own home if he could not trust the woman he had married when she was out of his sight. And while he wished, in many things, he could emulate the fine character of his friend, he had no wish to marry for wealth, only to have the woman put horns on him and make him the laughing stock of London.

They pulled into an inn yard for the evening, and he helped his wife from the carriage and told Jem to arrange food for them, a private sitting room, and a single bedroom.

The servant could not hide his brief look of surprise, and followed it with an insolent glare before doing as he was bid. Later, after Penny was safely inside, he caught up with his wife's servant, slouching the baggage toward the rooms. 'Here, fellow. I wish a word with you.'

Jem turned and set the bags on the floor and then straightened. For the first time, Adam noticed the bulk of the man, who stood several inches taller than he did, and was broad and strong of back, despite his advancing age. The servant glared down at him, too close for a bow in the enclosed space of the hallway, and touched his forelock. 'Your Grace?'

'Just now, in the courtyard. I did not like the look you gave me when I gave you instruction.'

'So sorry, your Grace. I will endeavour to improve myself in the future.' But the man was still looking at him as though concluding that one good slap would be all it might take to send the title to Will.

Adam straightened as well, putting on the air of command that served him so well in the House of Lords. 'It is no business of yours where your mistress sleeps. Or if we might choose to put aside the ridiculous arrangement created by Penny in favour of something closer to sanity. From this point forward, we will be acting as other couples do, and not as two strangers pretending to be married.'

Jem's eyes narrowed, and he said, 'Very good, your Grace. Because all intelligent people aspire to a union that is the current mode of the day: full of luxury, casual carnality and pretence, but devoid of any sincere feeling between the parties involved. Unless one is to count the contempt you seem to have for one another. My mistress has never wanted more than her parents had: a true meeting of the minds and a deep and abiding affection, strong enough to transcend the bonds of life itself. When her father died, your Grace, it held no fear for him, for he was convinced that his wife waited for him on the other side. That is what my mistress expected. When she found she could not have it, then she wanted to be left alone, and in peace.'

The servant looked down upon him again, as if he were still face down in the muck of the inn yard. 'And in the end, she will have to settle for you.' He picked up the bags that he had dropped, balanced them easily on his shoulders, and started down the hall. 'This way to your room, your Grace.'

She was waiting for him, there, in the tiny sitting room that connected to the room where they would sleep. A supper had been laid for them on the low table: cold meat pies, cakes, ale for him and tea for the lady.

And as he came to her, she hastily set down the mug of ale, and wiped some foam from her lips. She looked down, embarrassed. 'I'm sorry. You must think me frightfully common.'

He smiled. 'For doing something that you enjoy?'

When she looked back at him, there was fear in her eyes. A desperation to please him that hadn't been there before the party. She hadn't given a damn for what he thought of her then. But things had changed. 'I suspect the wives of your friends do not steal ale from their husband's mug when he is not looking.'

He sat down next to her. 'They do things far worse.' He tasted the ale. 'And this is quite good. We can share it, if you like.' He set the mug between them, and reached for his plate. His sleeve brushed against her arm; instead of shying from him, as she once might have done, she leaned to be closer.

And when she did it, his heart gave a funny little leap in his chest. He covered the feeling by taking another sip of ale. Not knowing how to proceed, he said, 'I spoke to my brother last night as the guests were leaving. Apparently, you told him how your work was progressing.'

She gave a little shake of her head. 'I am afraid I am not very good at small talk. I'm too little in public to have the knack of it.'

'No,' he corrected quickly. 'It was all right. More than all right. He was most impressed by you, and told me so. Still a little surprised, of course, that I found a woman with a brain who would have me.'

She laughed. 'What an idea, that the Duke of Bellston could not attract a woman of intelligence. I used to read the papers, and imagine what it would be like to meet you. I was sure that your wife would need her wits about her at all times if she were to speak to you at all.'

'Then you must have been sorely disappointed to find so little challenge...' He stopped. 'You used to imagine *me*?'

She put her hand to her temple, to hide her embarrassment. 'There. The truth is out. I sat at home reading Greek, and shunning society, spinning girlish fancies over a man who I would never meet. I assumed, by the wisdom of his speeches, he must be long married, and perhaps already a grandfather. I would never dare speak to him. But perhaps, if I could ever find the nerve, I would write to him with a question concerning his position on something or other, perhaps pretending to be my brother, or some other male, and he might deign to answer me.'

'And then you found me drunk in the street, and I hauled you to London and ignored you, and then forced you to dress in ribbons and dance with my friends, while I sat in another room, playing cards.' He laughed until tears came to his eyes, and when he noticed she was still pink with mortification, he pulled her close, and hugged her to him until he felt her laugh as well.

Then he buried his face against her neck, and murmured, 'I hope we are close enough now that, if you have any questions, you will not feel the need to submit them in writing.'

She said, 'I…think whatever I meant to ask you has gone quite out of my head.'

'Speak of something you know, then. For I do love the sound of your voice.' He breathed deeply, taking in the scent of her hair.

'Do you want me to ask for my garter, now?' It was the barest whisper, fearful, but full of hope as well.

And it tugged at his heart, to know how hard she had been trying to be what he wished, and how little he had done to make it easy for her. 'No games tonight.' He put his arms around her. 'Come. Sit in my lap. Tell me about your work. What is it about this Odysseus fellow that makes him worth the attentions of my Penelope?'

She hesitated at first, and then did as he said, wrapping her arms around his neck and whispering the story to him. He relaxed into the cushions of the divan, and thought what a great fool Odysseus must have been to get himself so cursed that he couldn't find his way back, and to waste time with Calypso or Circe when everything he needed was waiting at home.

When she finished, it was late. The fire was low and the candles were guttering. She lay still against him for a moment, and then said, 'I have talked too long.'

He stroked her head, and pulled a pin from her hair. 'Never. But it is time for bed. Let me help you.' He pulled more pins from her hair, uncoiling braids and combing them out with his fingers. He had never seen it down before, and the softness surprised him. He ran his fingers through the length of it, and closed his own eyes. 'Silk. I have never felt anything so soft.'

'It is too fine,' she argued. 'If I do not keep it tied, it tangles.'

He brought the strands to his face, breathing the scent of it and letting it cascade through his fingers. 'I will braid it for you again. Later.'

She reached out to him, and caught the end of his cravat, and undid the knot, letting it slide through her fingers to the floor. The gesture was carelessly erotic, although she seemed to have no idea of the fact. Then she slid from his lap and stood up, starting toward the bedroom and looking back over her shoulder at him.

He rose as well, stripping off his coat and waistcoat, and undoing his shirt. Then he went to stand behind her, and she held her long hair out of the way as he undid her clothing. She was very still as he worked, loosening hooks and lacings, pushing her gown off her shoulders and to the floor, kissing the back of her neck. Then he went to sit on the end of the bed, pulling off his boots and stockings, and undoing the buttons on his trousers.

He looked up at her, still standing where he had left her, the firelight outlining her body through the lawn of her chemise. She was watching him. Her eyes travelled slowly over his body. He could feel her gaze, like the touch of fingers, on his shoulders, his chest, his stomach and lower. Then she removed her glasses, holding them tightly in her hand, and closed her eyes.

He stood up and took them from her. 'Would you like me to put out the lights?'

'Please.'

He set them on the table beside the bed and blew out the candles, one by one, until the room was lit only by the fire. 'There. Now we are both a bit blind, and there is nothing to be afraid of. Remove your shift, and climb into bed.' He removed his trousers, hung them over a nearby chair, then threw back the covers and climbed in himself.

She waited until he was settled, and then quickly stripped off the last of her clothing, draping it over the end of the bed and going around to her side. Her movements were slow and sure, for she had believed him when he said he was near blind. But he could see her well enough: the hair, pale as moonlight, trying and failing to hide her full breasts, slim waist and soft, round hips.

She climbed into the bed, and he threw the covers back over her and pulled her close to bring her forehead to his lips. She trembled a little and so he said, 'Do not worry. I will do nothing tonight that will alarm you. We can wait until we are home to be more intimate. But I wish very much to touch you.'

'And kiss me again?'

'Once or twice.'

'I would like that. Very much.' And she turned her open mouth to his.

He kept his movements slow and gentle. His tongue stroked hers and traced the edge of her teeth, and his hands massaged her neck and her shoulders, making her muscles relax and her body melt into his. He let his hands slide lower down her back, and cupped her to him as he thrust his tongue into her mouth.

Instinctively, she parted her thighs and tried to get closer still, until he had to stop for a moment, to remind himself that he meant to go slowly, and not take what she was offering.

He pushed away from her, rolling her on to her back, and she moaned, reaching to bring him close to her again. He pulled himself up to kneel between her parted legs, and let the covers fall away so that he could watch her as he played with her breasts. If she had been shy of him before, she had forgotten it, and looked up at him with love-drugged eyes as he stroked her, catching her lip between her teeth as he teased her nipples, and stroking her own hands up the sides of her body to squeeze his hands on her, encouraging him to be less gentle.

He took her permission and kneaded and pinched, until she was writhing on the bed, her hips bucking as her body begged to be loved. The sight was making him dizzy with lust and painfully hard.

He fell upon her then, pushing her body back on to the bed, and burying his face against her breasts, letting his teeth do what his fingers had, and sliding his hands between her legs to stroke her, gripping her thighs and spreading them wider, sliding his thumbs up to part the hair and find her most sensitive places. He could feel her heart, beating under his cheek, and waited until he was sure that it must be near bursting it was so loud. And he lifted his face from her breast and swore to her that it would be ever like this between them, if she would trust him and let him love her as she deserved. Then he thrust, filling her with his fingers.

She was hot and tight, and he imagined the feeling of sliding into her body, night after night, and waking to her sweet smile, day after day, knowing that she would always belong to him. And he heard her cry out and collapse against his hand, sated.

He released her and slipped up her body to kiss her upon the mouth again, and she gasped and laughed. 'That was magnificent.'

He rolled off her, and said, 'That was just the beginning. Here, turn over and let me do up your hair.'

'My hair?'

'To give me something else to do with you.' He reached out and pulled the length into a messy braid. Then he wrapped it around her to tease her breasts with the end. 'For if I do the things I am thinking of, we will get no sleep at all, and you will have a most uncomfortable ride tomorrow.'

She yawned. 'That sounds very wicked.' And then she settled back into him, grinding her hips against him, and driving him one step closer to insanity. 'But I am very tired. Perhaps you may show me tomorrow.' She yawned again. 'I think I shall very much want to reclaim my garter.'

'I sincerely hope so.' And he lay back against the pillows and cradled his wife's body to him for a night of delicious agony.

Chapter Seventeen

The next day, Penny watched her husband dozing on the other side of the carriage. He said he had not slept well, but he did not seem overly bothered by the fact.

She, on the other hand, had had an excellent night's sleep. Her body could remember every kiss and every touch from the previous evening, and it woke hungry for more. The feeling was aggravated by the gentle rocking of the carriage. She was excited enough by the prospect of the new home that her husband had described to her. But the nearness of him, and the promise that they would be alone together from now on, left her nearly overcome.

Adam started awake, and looked out of the window, smiling and pointing to a marker that he said indicated the edge of his property.

He leaned his head out of the window of the carriage, closed his eyes, and inhaled deeply. Then he looked sheepishly back at her. 'You will find it embarrassingly sentimental of me, I'm sure. But I find that the air smells sweeter in Wales than anywhere in England. And is not the quality of the sunshine brighter than that in the city?'

She thought to comment on the coal burning in London, and the noise of the traffic, which were impediments to the climate and perfectly rational explanations for the changes he described. If the Welsh air smelled of anything, she suspected it was sheep, for there were flocks in many of the pastures they were passing. She smiled at him. 'Black sheep?'

He grinned at her and nodded. 'Perhaps it is symbolic.' He looked critically at the flocks. 'But there are not as many as there should be. It was a hard winter, with a late spring and a dry summer.' He shook his head.

She looked out the window at the land they were passing. The year had obviously been difficult. The fields and gardens were not as green as she expected them to be, nor the crops as large. But the tenants appeared happy; as the carriage passed, people in the fields looked up and smiled. They dropped curtsies, removed caps and offered occasional shy waves.

And Adam smiled back and surveyed the land with a critical eye and a touch of possessiveness. He had missed it. And no matter how at ease he had seemed in London, he belonged here.

The carriage slowed as it came up the long curved drive and pulled abreast of the house, and he leaned forward in his seat as though his body strained to be even closer to home. When the footman opened the carriage door, he stepped out, forgetting her. He was immediately surrounded by a pack of dogs, barking, wagging and nudging him with wet noses for his attention. He patted and stroked, calling them by name and reaching absently into a coat pocket for treats that he was not carrying.

She watched him from the door of the carriage as he was drawn like a lodestone to the open front door. And even the butler, whose kind were not known for their exuberant displays of emotion, was smiling to see the return of the master of the house.

Adam took a step forwards, and then froze and turned back to her, embarrassment colouring his face. He strode back to the carriage and reached up to offer her his hand to help her down, making a vague gesture that seemed to encompass his brief abandonment of her. Then he laughed at himself and kicked the step out of the way, held both hands out to her and said, 'Jump.'

She stared at him in amazement. 'Why ever for?'

'Trust me. I will catch you.'

She shook her head. 'This is nonsense.'

'Perhaps. But the sooner you do it, the sooner it will be done. Now, do as I say.'

He showed no sign of relenting, and at last she closed her eyes, and stepped from the carriage into open air.

He caught her easily under the arms, and let her slide down his body until her slippered feet were standing on his boots. The closeness of their bodies was shocking, and she meant to pull away, but he was smiling down at her with such ease that a part of her did not wish to move ever again.

He said softly, 'There are customs about brides and

thresholds, are there not? You must not stumble, or it would be bad luck to us both.'

She pointed to the house. 'I see no reason to hold to superstition. There is nothing wrong with my legs, and the way is not strewn with disaster. I think I can manage.' But it felt good to be held so close to him.

'You have been very lucky for me, up 'til now. It is better to be safe than sorry. Perhaps it were best if I were to see you safely into the house.' And before she could object, he scooped an arm beneath her knees and had lifted her into his arms.

She surprised herself by squealing in delight. She should have demanded that he let her down immediately, and that it was all highly undignified. But instead, she wrapped her arms around his neck, tipped back her head and laughed into the Welsh sunshine. The crowd of dogs still milling about them had to jump to nudge and sniff her as well. And even as he took care to guide her through the pack, she could feel the strain of his body, wanting to go faster and take the last few steps at a run to be inside his house again.

As they passed the butler, the man bowed to her as well as her husband, and murmured, 'Your Grace, welcome home. And welcome to you as well, your Grace. May I offer my congratulations?'

Adam nodded, as though his heart were too full to speak, and held her even closer, before taking the last step that brought them both into the house. Then he set her down and took her by the hand to lead her into the entry, where the servants were assembled.

The introduction was easier than it had been on the

first day in the townhouse, and she hoped that this was a sign that she was adjusting to her new role as well. Although it might have had something to do with the change in the man beside her, who was neither as distant nor as superior. When he smiled with pride as he spoke to the staff, she had a hard time distinguishing whether it was happiness with them, or his eagerness for them to meet her. And she could not help but smile as well.

At last, he held out his hand in a broad gesture and said, 'Your new home,' as though the manor were a person and the introduction would result in a response.

She looked up at the high ceilings, and the wide marble steps that led to the second floor of rooms and a portrait gallery above them.

She could feel his hesitation next to her. He wanted her to like it. And how could she not? It was the grandest house she'd ever seen. Although the idea that it was to be her home was faintly ridiculous.

'The roof needs new slate,' he said in apology. 'But that is the way it is with all old homes. Something is always in need of repair. And nothing has been done in decoration for many years. But the part that is undamaged by the fire is warm and clean, and I find it most comfortable.'

Comfortable? She looked at him. If one found museums to be a comforting place, perhaps. But museums were not so different really than… 'May I see the library?' she asked hopefully.

'Certainly. I believe your books have already arrived.' He led her down the hall and opened a door before them.

She poked her head into the room. Books. Floor to ceiling. Some shelves were so high that a set of brass steps was necessary to reach them. But there was plenty of space for the contents of the crates that stood stacked by the door. A fire had been laid in the grate, and the warmth of it extended to the oak table at the middle of the room. There was space for her papers, ample lamps to light the words. Comfortable chairs by the fireside where she could read for pleasure when she was not working. And the heavy rug beneath her feet was so soft and welcoming that she was tempted to abandon the furniture and curl up upon it.

'Will there be sufficient room for your collection, or shall we need to add extra shelves?'

Without thinking, she had been counting the empty places, and reordering the works. 'There is ample room, I am sure.'

'And here.' He walked to a shelf by the window, and pulled down a battered volume. 'You will not need it, for I think you are well stocked in this. It is left over from my own school days.' He looked at it sadly. 'Which means it has seen very little use.' He handed her a schoolboy's edition of Homer, in the Greek.

She stared down at the book in her hand, and then up to the man who had given it to her. When he was at home, he was a very different person. No less handsome, certainly. The light from the windows made his hair shine, and his eyes were as blue as they had been. But the cynical light in them had disappeared. He seemed younger. Or perhaps it was that he did not seem as arrogant and unapproachable after the previous night.

'It is all right, then? Do you think you can be happy here?'

Happy? It was a paradise. She hardly dared speak.

'Of course, there is more. I haven't shown you your rooms yet.' He led the way out of the library and down the corridor.

She peered in the next room as they passed.

'My study,' he answered. And this time, he opened the door wide so that she could see the desk within. 'It connects to the library. As does the morning room on the other side. I had thought, perhaps you might wish to use it as well, should the library not prove to have sufficient space.' He backtracked down the hall and opened another door. 'It is rather…' He waved a hand at the decoration, which was rococo with gilt and flowers, and a ceiling painted with cherubs and clouds. 'My mother, again.' He looked at her. 'And there are more of the damn china shepherds.'

She reached out to touch a grouping that was very similar to the one she had left in London, a court couple, locked for ever in passionate embrace. She ran a finger along it and felt the heat of the kiss in her body. 'That is all right. I think I am growing used to them.'

He gestured her out of the room and led her down more halls to a music room, separate rooms for dining and breakfast, another parlour, and a formal receiving room. Then he took her up the stairs past the portraits of his family to a long row of bedrooms and opened a door near the end. 'This is to be your room. If you wish.'

It was beautifully appointed, and larger than the one

in the townhouse, but of a similar layout. She looked for the connecting door that should link her room to his. 'And where do you sleep?'

He looked away. 'I am not particularly sure. I had used this room, for a while. But I could choose another. Here, let me show you.' He took her into the hall and opened the door to what must have been the master suite. A strong smell of smoke crept out into the hallway.

He sniffed. 'Better than it was, I'm afraid. The real damage is farther down the hall. But your room is not affected. Let me show you the worst of it.' He seemed to steel himself, gathering courage, then led her down the corridor to the left, and as they walked the odour of smoke got stronger. The line of tension in her husband's back increased. He quickened his pace as they reached the end of the corridor, and threw open the heavy double doors at the end.

He caught her, before she could attempt entrance, for there was little floor to step on. The hall seemed to end in open air before him. She was looking down into what must have been the ballroom before the fire. The light in the room had a strange, greasy quality as it filtered through what was left of the floor-to-ceiling windows on the back of the house. Some of the panes were missing, leaving spots of brightness on the floor and walls. Some were boarded shut, and some merely smoke-stained and dirty. At the second-floor level, there were bits of floor and gallery still clinging to the outer walls. From a place near the roof, an interloping bird sang.

'Oh, my.'

'It was beautiful once,' Adam remarked, bitterness in his voice. 'The retiring rooms were off this hall, card rooms and galleries for musicians. A staircase led up from there.' He pointed to a blank space opposite them.

'How did it happen?'

'There was an accident. After a ball. One of the candleholders was overbalanced, and the flames touched the draperies.' He stopped and swallowed, then started again. 'The truth. You should hear it all, before we go further. It was I who caused it. The party was over, and most of the guests had gone. And I followed Clarissa to the second floor, so that we could be alone. My room is just down the hall and I thought…' He could not look at her, as he spoke. 'But she chose the musicians' gallery. I had too much wine that night, and was thinking too slowly to realise that the acoustics would be excellent. Tim was searching for her, to take her home. He must have heard it all. She made no effort to be quiet that night. And when I cautioned her, she laughed and asked what did I think she'd meant to happen.

'I pushed her away from me, and she overturned the candles. I pulled her clear of the fire, but the flames spread quickly. Fortunately, the walls on this side of the house are old and stone. The damage was limited to this room, and the rooms above and below. And smoke damage to my bedroom, of course. Divine justice.'

'Was anyone hurt?'

Adam seemed to flinch at the thought. 'Will has a burn on the back of his arm, gained from fighting the fire. A beam fell upon him.'

She looked up at the roof, and the badly patched holes, and piles of new lumber on the floor below. 'And this is why you needed the money?'

'Not a thing has gone right since the night of the fire. It was as if I was cursed. I invested. Badly, as it turns out. In tobacco. The ship sank, and my hopes with it. The profits should have been enough to repair the house and account for the failure of this year's crop.' He reached out and took her hand. 'And then I met you. Before that, I had no idea how to go on.'

She looked at him, and at the wreckage before them. 'And you swear, this is over.'

He smiled sadly. 'Nothing brings you to the knowledge that you are behaving like a fool quite so fast as burning your house half to the ground, and seeing your brother nursing injuries that were a result of your stupidity in chasing after another man's wife. And I saw the look on Tim's face that night. Yet he insists on forgiving me, which is the worst punishment of all.'

She tugged at his sleeve. 'Close the doors on this mess, then. Let us go downstairs and find supper.'

Chapter Eighteen

He took her to the formal dining room, which was set for two. And she watched as the servants went through their paces, attempting to impress their new mistress with speed of service and excellence of presentation.

She wondered what Jem thought of it all, and if they had managed to force some work out of him, or had he found a warm corner somewhere to sleep. Perhaps she could find a post for him, something that involved short hours and long naps.

And while her husband might think of them as being totally alone in Wales, she found the room crowded with servants. There were footmen behind each chair and a regular influx of courses arriving and departing. She watched Adam, who was staring at the contents of his plate, but doing very little with it. He must think himself alone, for he seemed to have forgotten her entirely. Instead, he cast furtive glances in the direction of the damaged wing, as though he could sense it through the walls.

By the look in his eyes, he had been wrong. He might think that things were over, and managed to keep them at bay when he was in London and could keep busy enough to ignore them. But his good spirits had begun to evaporate the moment he had opened the door to the ballroom. She wondered how many rooms of the house held bad memories for him. She imagined Clarissa, as Tim had described her, attempting to trap Adam in an indiscretion. The music gallery had been an excellent choice, if she wished discovery.

But had it been the first attempt? Or had she taken every opportunity she could to embarrass her husband and create talk? Penny might be forced to see her own husband starting at ghosts of memory in every room of their home.

Why must the woman have been so beautiful and so audacious? So without shame as to be unforgettable? How was she expected to compete? When they were together, in the inn, Penny had felt like the only woman in the world to him. And in scant hours, he had forgotten her.

The idea angered her, and she prepared to count, when it occurred to her that, in fighting this battle, a measured and thoughtful response would not win the day. If she thought at all, she would never have the nerve to act.

She looked back at Adam, who was staring into his dessert in confusion, as though wondering where the earlier courses had got to. She slid her chair closer to his, so that they might not be overheard. 'Adam. Darling. I was wondering if you had given thought as to where we would sleep?'

'Oh.'

His response to what she had said sounded quite like a moan, and she smiled in triumph. She looked again, as she felt him shuddering under her hand as she stroked him. 'Shall we play hot and cold?'

'Very hot,' he murmured, and tore at the knot on his cravat.

'I am still looking for the garter, silly. I do not think you have it hidden here at all.'

With one hand, he yanked at the buttons on his waistcoat, and the other cupped the back of her head, dragging her mouth to his for a desperate kiss. When his chest was bare, he pulled her empty hand to his heart, and she stroked the hair on his chest, and the nipples hidden in it. He broke the kiss and guided her mouth down to them, letting her bite and suck as he had done for her, while he fumbled at the closures on her gown, swearing as he fought to dispense with her clothes.

Had she unbalanced him to that degree? A feeling of power rushed through her, along with desire, and she could feel her body readying itself for what was to come. Her breasts ached to be touched, and as she stroked him she could feel the heat building inside her, where he would soon be.

She stopped what she was doing and enjoyed the moment, and then looked at her husband. She'd thought him a master of seduction. But tonight the tables were turned, and he could not undo the simple knot that held her stays in place. 'Really, Adam. If you cannot manage, perhaps I shall go to my room and send for the maid.'

'You will do no such thing.' He grabbed her hands and placed them firmly on his knees, bending her over the arm of his chair. 'Do not move.' And then he seized a knife from the table in front of them, and slit the lacings of her corset from bottom to top.

She sat up and took a deep breath, which he stole with another kiss and then pulled the thing free of her, and threw it on to the floor. She stood up and let the gown follow it, and then he grabbed her by the waist and lifted her to sit on the table, kissing her face, her throat and her breasts. Between the kisses he undid the last button on his trousers. Pushing them out of the way, he panted, 'Sorry, darling. Most undignified. And not as gentle as I should be. I cannot help myself.'

He could not help himself. And he was talking to her. She took a breath to calm her nerves, and then pulled up her chemise and spread her legs, leaning back to tip her hips up. 'Stop talking and take me.'

'Say that you love me,' he whispered. 'I want to hear you say the words.'

And it was surprisingly easy to tell him the truth. 'I love you,' she whispered back.

This time, he was the one to groan, 'Soon.' And he kissed her again, rough and insistent. So she reached out and put her hand to him again, and mimicked the strength of his kiss. She could feel herself losing the boundary between what she was feeling, and what he must be feeling as he found her with his fingers and thrust.

She rocked her hips against his hand, and let him fill her, as the feelings grew inside of her, and his sex grew slippery in her palm.

'Very soon,' he whispered. His hips thrust toward hers until the head of his sex rested against her, and she writhed against it, stroking so that it rubbed her body where it felt most right. She was trembling with excitement, balancing on the edge of something wonderful. He removed his fingers from her, clutching her hip with his hand to steady her, and bring her closer to him.

The emptiness frustrated her, and she stroked harder, feeling him tremble, and rubbed herself with him until his sex slipped against the opening to her body, making her gasp.

And he said, 'Now,' and drove into her.

There was a shock of pain, and he kissed her until it hardly mattered, and the tension grew in her again. He pushed her back to brace her hands on the table so that her hips stayed steady, put his hands on her breasts and thrust, over and over again, staring into her eyes.

She leaned back and wrapped her legs around him so that the friction of their bodies changed, driving her wild with touches that were never long enough. But they brought her close again, so very close. And when he shuddered against her and stopped, she moaned in protest until he stroked her with his thumb and took her over the edge.

When she came back to herself, they had moved very little. She held him inside her, her legs wrapped around his waist, and he was leaning over her on the table, staring down into her face.

He dropped a kiss on her lips, and glanced around the shambles they had made of dinner. What clothing they had managed to remove was scattered around them, chairs were tipped, and goblets were knocked over on the table. He reached beside her, and fed her a candied apricot from the dessert tray, watching her mouth with interest as she ate. 'In case you are wondering,' he said, 'I had intended something a bit more sedate for our first evening together.'

'Oh, really?' she touched her tongue to her lips, and waited as he offered her a bit of cake.

He furrowed his brow. 'I believe my original plan was to seduce you at my leisure, and render you docile and agreeable through lust.'

'And my garter?'

'Is tied around my shirt sleeve, for I thought, perhaps, you would summon the nerve to help me off with my jacket.'

'And what do you think of your plan now?' She shifted her legs to grip him tighter.

He sighed and smiled. 'It is an utter failure. You control me body and soul. Command me.' And he looked supremely happy to have lost.

She released him, and offered her hand to him, so that he could help her down from the table. 'Take me to our bedroom.'

His smile broadened and he scooped up her dress and tossed it over her head. Laughing and whispering, they collected the rest of the discarded clothing and a plate of cakes. Then he opened the door, checked the hall to make sure it was empty and they ran from the room together, not stopping until they were safely behind the closed bedroom door.

Chapter Nineteen

Adam came down to the breakfast room and took his usual seat. His coffee was already poured, the mail was stacked beside the plate, and his wife was seated at his side. Life was as close to perfect as any man had a right to expect.

Penny was as happy in Wales as he had known she would be, even more so now that they had each other. For a month, they had awoken every morning, tangled in the sheets and each other, breakfasted together, and then he went to his study, and she to the library. He could read his paper, ride out to inspect the property, or argue with the workmen who had begun renovations on the ballroom, knowing that when he came back, his steadfast Penelope would be waiting for him.

They had not yet made love in the library, perhaps because he had spent so little time there, before Penny had come to the house. She had learned the measure of him, on that first night. And now, if she felt he was growing morose, or attempting to dwell in the past, she had but to lock the door and show him a flash of garter, and he was lost to the world.

But any suggestions made in the library would be of his own doing. He looked up into her face, startled by the thought, and smiled as he caught her looking at him.

'Excuse me?'

'What?'

'Was there something…?'

They spoke in unison, to cover their mutual confusion, and fell silent at the same time.

'The eggs,' he lied. 'I bit down on a piece of shell.'

'I will speak to Cook.'

'Do not worry, it is nothing.'

She nodded and looked down into her plate.

'They are very good eggs today,' he supplied. 'The best I have ever tasted, I think.'

'You say that every morning.' She went back to her breakfast. But she was blushing.

At some point, he would have to return to London, or share her with the world. But not just yet. For now, they were the only two people on earth, and it was enough. He opened the first letter on the stack, and a folded sheet dropped on to his plate.

> …torment me no longer. For I cannot live without the perfection of your body, the taste of your kiss, the sound of your voice as you call my name…

He recognised his own hand, and remembered the letter well. It had been drunken folly to have written it.

He should have thrown it on the fire rather than sent it. And it was hardly the most damning thing he put to paper in the months before the fire.

It was accompanied by another sheet, with a single line.

Come to me at Colton, or I shall go to her.
Clare

She had followed them to Wales.

'Something interesting in the mail?' Penny did not look up from her tea.

'Nothing important.' Perhaps he had grown better at concealing his feelings from her, for she did not seem to notice that the room had gone cold, or that his mouth had filled with smoke and ashes.

'Then I will leave you to it, and return to work.' She raised her eyebrows. 'Ithaca calls.'

'With its rosy fingers of dawn?'

'There must be a better way to say that,' she said, and wandered down the hall, lost in thought.

He stared back at the letter in front of him, and then threw it into the fireplace, watching the edges curl and the words disappear. He poked at the bits of ash until there could be nothing left of them to read.

Then he went to the stables to saddle a horse.

The Colton property abutted his, and as he rode toward it, he could feel the tightening in his chest. He should have spoken the truth to Penny, and got it over with. Soon she would be seeing Clarissa again, and that it would be impossible to avoid contact, if the Coltons had returned to Wales.

But it was very unlike them to be here in the summer. Clare much preferred Bath. He had not been prepared for the letter, and he had no response at hand. Perhaps the situation was not as bad as it seemed. He could assess, and return to Penny by lunch, with an explanation.

Tim's house seemed as it always did, preternaturally quiet. There was nothing to indicate that the family was in residence, although what he expected to find, he was not sure. Tim must be out riding in the hills. Probably trying to avoid his wife.

The servant allowed him entrance and took him to the sitting room without introduction.

Clare was waiting for him, lounging on a divan in dishabille, her dressing gown artfully arranged to display a length of bare leg, the globe of a breast, and the barest hint of nipple, peeking from the ruffles of lace. 'Adam. At last.'

Her voice raised the hairs on the back of his neck, just as it always did, and he wondered how he could have mistaken the feeling for passion. 'Clarissa. Why have you come here?'

'Because it is my home.'

'It is Tim's home. And you loathe it. You have told us often enough.'

'Then I will be honest. I came because I missed you.' She pulled a pretty pout, which made her look more like a spoiled child than a seductress. 'It has been so long.'

'Barely a month.'

'Why did you leave London?'

'You should know that. I sought to be where my wife would be happiest.' *And to be where you were not.*

'Timothy would not let us travel home to be near you. He insists on staying in the city, although it is unbearably hot, and everyone of fashion is leaving.'

'Go to Bath, then. Somewhere that suits you.'

She sighed. 'I did not want Bath. I longed for the comforts of home. If he does not wish to follow, I cannot very well force him. He may stay in the city with the children for all I care.'

'You left your husband and your children as well.' Adam shook his head in disgust.

She shifted, allowing her robe to fall open, so that there could be no mistake of her plans for the next hour. 'I am totally alone, if you still fear discovery. My servants know better than to talk. And your wife spends most days poring over her books, does she not? No one will be the wiser.'

'I thought I made it clear that there would be nothing more between us.'

'On the contrary. You think that by saying nothing, and running away from me, you can end what we had together. If you truly wanted to end it, you would have told me so, outright. But I think you are afraid to speak to me. You are still not sure what you will say to me, Adam, when we are alone. And I have your letters, you know. I read them often. I know the contents of your heart.'

He felt a wave of humiliation, remembering the things he had written to her. Words he wished he'd have saved for the woman who deserved them. 'That is all in the past, Clare. If you must hear me speak the truth plainly, before you believe it, then listen now. Anything that there was between us is at an end. I will not come crawling back to you like a whipped dog. I have a wife now.'

'Why should it matter? I have always had a husband, and it did not seem to bother you.'

The mention of Tim cut at his heart. 'It bothered me a great deal, Clarissa. He is my friend.'

'And I am your lover.'

'Do not dignify what we did by calling it love. There was no higher feeling involved than lust. I disgusted myself with my behaviour.'

She laughed. 'You did not seem so disgusted at the time, as I remember it.'

'I betrayed Tim. That was why you were so eager to snare me, was it not? You enjoyed our liaisons all the more, for knowing how it would hurt your husband.'

'I viewed it as a challenge,' she admitted. 'To see if my charms were strong enough to break your fragile sense of honour. And it snapped like a twig. Now you think silence, distance and a hasty marriage is all it will take to gain your freedom.

'Do you not remember trying this trick before with me? The cold silence. You lasted for six months. And when you came back, I made you beg before I would let you share my bed.' She tipped her head to the side and smiled in remembrance. 'It was really quite amusing. I wonder what I shall make you do this time, once you grow bored with your shop clerk and you want me again.'

He heard the words and, for the first time in months, everything came clear. Suddenly, as if a bond had been cut, he felt truly free of her. And it was his turn to laugh. 'You trapped me well, with your sly affections and your subtle advances. You came to me when I was most vulnerable, when I was troubled, or lonely, or too drunk to care what I was doing. You used my weaknesses against me and took what you wanted. And afterwards, you left me broken. Cursed by my actions, ashamed of what I had become.

'But when Penny found me in that state, she gave herself to me until I was healed. She has made me, in a few short weeks, into the man I wished I was. I can never give her what she truly deserves, for nothing I have is equal to her casual generosity towards me.

'I love her, Clarissa. And I never loved you.'

She laughed back at him. Long and hard and unladylike. 'Never mind, then. For she appears to have made you into the very thing I abhor. The virtuous prig that you never were, before you met her. Your head is full of romantic nonsense. What you mistake for sincerity is emotional claptrap. I wash my hands of you.'

He felt a flood of relief. And then he saw her smile, which was sly and catlike, and knew that there was no chance in the world that he would escape so easily.

She continued. 'Since your love for her is true, I assume that you have her heart as well. So she will stand by you, head held high, while I reveal the particulars of our relationship to the world. You detailed in writing what we had done, and what you wished to do. I could send the letters to your wife, as a belated wedding gift. Or shall I leave them for Timothy some morning, mixed up with the mail? Or I could take them to our friends in London, to read aloud. Everyone will find it most diverting, I am sure.'

The idea of it turned his stomach. There was so much shame to be had in his past behaviour. Heaps of disgrace for all concerned. Timothy would no longer be able to feign ignorance, and must be moved to act. He would meet his best friend at dawn with a weapon in his hand, and attempt to defend himself for an indefensible action.

Will would shake his head in pity, as he had at the news of the marriage, and at all the other stupid things Adam had done in his life. Perhaps Adam was destined to be an eternal source of disappointment, and a terrible example to his brother.

But Penny. If Penny found out, it would be worst of all. Would she be more hurt by a full revelation from Clare, or would the *ton* throw the information back in her face some night, when she least expected it? Either way, it did not seem likely that she would wish to make love to him in the library, once she knew all the sordid details of his affair. She might return to her study and never venture forth again.

And the worst of it was that the truth could leave him relatively untouched. What did it matter what people said of him? For no matter how shocked the world might be, he was Bellston until he died.

But it would wound the people most dear to his heart.

What were the alternatives? He could return to Clarissa, to buy her silence for a time, and hope that she would grow bored enough to let him go. It would hurt the same people just as much, if not more. For how could he claim that his infidelity was meant to lessen the damage? There was no easy answer. But the choice between right and wrong was clear. Better to bear the agony, lance the wound, and allow the poison to drain, than to leave things as they were, dying from within.

He opened his eyes and stared at Clarissa. 'Do your worst, then. I should have expected no less from you, for you are wicked to the bone. Bring down the ruin upon my head. It is just as I have deserved, and I have known for a long time that there was no preventing it. What will happen will happen. But do not think that you can control me any longer with the fear of revelation. Whatever may occur, I am through with you, Clarissa.'

And he turned and left the room, feeling lighter than he had, despite the sense of impending doom.

Chapter Twenty

Penny sat in the library, watching the blur of sunlight through the leaded windows, as she cleaned her glasses with her handkerchief. Her husband had been right: the air was sweeter here, and the sunshine more bright than any place else on earth.

And then a shadow fell upon her table. Timothy Colton stood, blocking the light from the door.

She smiled and stood, reaching out for his hand. 'Timothy. Whatever are you doing in Wales?'

He was leaning against the door frame, and as her vision cleared, she took note of his appearance. He was the worse for both drink and travel. His hair was wind-blown, his coat dirty, and he smelled of whisky, though it was not yet noon. 'I live here, as does Clarissa. We are near enough to walk the distance on a clear day.' He smiled mirthlessly. 'Did your husband not tell you of the fact?'

She racked her brain, hoping that there had been a revelation, and that she had forgotten. 'No.'

'Now, why do you suppose he would forget to mention it?'

There had to be a reason. He had said that Tim was a childhood friend. And she knew that Clarissa had been there, the night of the fire. But had he told her they would be neighbours? He must have assumed she would know. 'I am sure it was a harmless omission.'

'Really. Then he did not tell you, this morning, that he has gone to my home, to be with my wife.'

'He would not,' she said.

'I was there, and saw them together myself.'

'You lie.'

'When have I ever lied to you, Penelope, that you would distrust me now?' His voice was colder than she'd ever heard it, but he did not avoid her gaze, as her husband had that morning at breakfast. 'She left me in London several days ago. When I realised where she would go, I shut up the house and came after her. It is not so easy when you have children. You cannot simply hare off to Wales, and abandon them to be with your lover. Not that my wife would care.'

'But Adam has not been with her, I would swear it.'

'His horse is in my stables now. And as I approached the house, I could see them clearly through the windows of the sitting room.'

She shook her head. 'I'm sure there is an innocent explanation for it.'

'She was lying bare before him, Penny. There was nothing innocent about the scene I witnessed.'

'Then I will ask Adam about it, when he returns.' She would do nothing of the kind. She would do her best to pretend that it did not matter to her. Perhaps Adam had eyes only for her because she was the only one near enough to see. But she had convinced herself that there would be no worries in the future. It would always be just as it had been for the last month. Now Timothy meant to spoil it all.

'And now I wish you to leave.'

He stepped around her, and shut the door. 'I am not through speaking.'

'I have nothing to say to you. If you wish to talk to anyone, it should be Adam or your wife.'

Timothy laughed. 'And now you will pretend that your husband's affairs do not hurt you. I think this matters more than you care to admit.'

'What business is it of yours?' she snapped.

'If your husband does not wish to be faithful to you? It can be very lonely, knowing that one's chosen mate has little interest. Now that you have had a taste of what marriage might mean, you will find it is very difficult to content yourself with solitude.'

'On the contrary, I much prefer to be alone.'

'If that is true, you are likely to get your wish. But Adam likes company. He is not alone this morning, any more than my wife is. Perhaps it does not matter to you, as a woman, to see your vows tossed back in your face. But I am tired of standing alone while my friend makes me a cuckold again.'

It amazed her, after all they had said to each other, after all they had done, that her husband could be so cruel. 'Challenge him, if you care so much.'

'Do you want us to duel?'

'No.'

Timothy sagged against the wall. 'Strangely, neither do I. Our friendship is over, of course. But I have pretended for so long that I did not care, that it seems foolish now to reach for a sword.' He was staring at her with a strange light in his eyes, as he had the night of the ball.

'Do you mean to reach for me, instead?' she asked.

He sighed. 'There is nothing we can do to stop them, should they wish to be together. But there is no reason for us to be alone.'

'We will be alone,' she responded. 'If we feel anything for them, we will be alone.'

'But we could be together, in shared misery.'

She shook her head. 'I am sorry. I cannot…'

He smiled, and removed a flask from his pocket, taking a deep drink. 'I thought not. And it is truly a shame, Penelope. For I feel I could grow most fond of you, should I allow myself to.' His voice was low and welcoming. 'You are a lovely woman with a quick wit and a sweet nature. You are too good for Adam, my dear. He has many admirable qualities, and has been a true friend in many things. But he is proving to have no more sense than he ever did, when it comes to women. I thought that you brought a change in him.'

'I hoped…' She choked on the words. 'I did not mean to, you know. It was all to be so easy. We both had what we wanted. And then I fell in love with him.'

'There, now.' He reached for her and drew her into an embrace that was more brotherly than passionate. 'Do not cry over him. He is not worth your tears.'

'Oh, really?' Her husband's voice from the doorway was cold.

She sprang back from Timothy's grasp, and hastily wiped at her face with her sleeve.

'It was nothing, Adam,' Penny murmured.

'Other than that you are making this poor woman miserable with your careless philanderings,' Timothy supplied.

'Hush.' Penny cringed at the description of her feelings, hauled out into the light for all to see. 'I was overwrought. It was nothing.'

'Nothing?' Adam stared at her. 'When I find you in the arms of another man, it is not "nothing", madam.'

'She was crying over you,' Tim goaded. 'I could not very well leave her, could I? Although you seemed to have no problem with it.'

'And I suppose, when it comes to comforting my wife, you are worth two of me?' Adam glared at his friend.

'Much as you are, when it comes to my wife.' Timothy glared back. 'Of course, you would have to be as good as two men, for you seem intent on keeping both women. It is hardly fair, old man.' Timothy grinned, but the smile was cold and mirthless.

'I do not want your wife.'

'That was not how it appeared this morning, Adam. After you swore that it was over and you would not be alone with her again.'

Adam made to speak, but hesitated.

Timothy nodded. 'You cannot look me in the eye and deny it, can you?'

'I was with her,' Adam admitted grudgingly. 'But it was nothing. I swear it, Tim.'

The tears rose in her throat as her husband declared his innocence to his friend. But not to her. Never to her, for she did not deserve it. She had sold the rights to his fidelity for a pile of books.

'Do you take me for a fool? I saw you plain, through the window. She was naked before you, in broad daylight.'

'It was not as it appears.'

'It never is,' Timothy responded drily. 'I believe you said that the night of the fire, as well. And I heard the whole thing clearly, although I did not see. Can you not, for once, favour me with the truth? I will at least admit that, given a little more time and the co-operation of your wife, the scene you witnessed, which was truly nothing, would have been exactly what it appeared.'

'How dare you.' Adam's fury was cold. He appeared ready to strike and Penny rushed to his side to take his arm.

'Adam, nothing happened. And no one knows of any of this. Please.'

Tim laughed, 'So what are we to do, then? Do you wish to challenge me, or should I challenge you?' And then he muttered something in Welsh that she did not understand, and spat upon the floor.

She might not have understood the words, but Adam clearly had, for he broke free of her and struck his friend, knocking him to the ground. Tim staggered to his feet with blood in his eye, ready to fight.

And at last, Penny snapped. 'You may do as you please, the both of you. And Clarissa as well. But whatever you do, you can do it without my help.'

'Penny, go to your room.' Adam barely looked at her.

'That is how it is to be, is it? You will be brother and guardian to me, and banish me to my quarters, so that you can do as you please? Take my money, then. I offered it to you freely, in exchange for peace and freedom. And I have scant little of either. But the money was not enough for you. You wanted my affection when it suited you, so that I did not embarrass you in public. And then, you needed my body to be a mother to your children. And now you expect my loyalty, while you lie with another man's wife.

'I want none of it, Adam. No more than I ever did. I want to be alone. And I would sooner see my children raised by jackals than by you or your twisted friends. I am leaving you.'

'You cannot. I will not permit it.' Her husband had turned away from his friend, no longer caring for the fight before him.

'And you cannot stop me. The bargain between us is irretrievably broken. If you thwart me today, I will try again tomorrow. Sooner or later, I will succeed in escaping you. If you wish, you may drag me back to your home by the hair, and lock me in my room. The Duke of Bellston, charming, handsome, lecherous and debauched, will need to keep his wife, and her fortune, by force. And then we will see what people say of you and your precious reputation.'

And she swept from the room.

Chapter Twenty-One

Adam thought, all things considered, that he should feel much worse. But he felt nothing. She had left the room, and taken his anger with her.

He had turned back to Tim, who must have been more than a little drunk, for he had collapsed back on to the floor, and absently offered him a hand.

Tim had ignored it and struggled to his feet, wiping blood from his mouth and on to his shirt cuff. 'There. Are you satisfied now?'

He stared back at Tim. 'Are you?'

'I think I am. For you finally look the way I feel. All these months you have spent, wallowing in ecstasy, or lust or guilt.' Tim made a bitter face. 'Never content unless you were torn by some emotion or other, and convinced that no one felt more deeply than you. Now, she will go. And you are all hollowed out.'

Adam nodded. He could feel the growing emptiness as she withdrew from him. A space that needed filling.

Tim smiled. 'Now imagine her with someone else.'

The pain of the thought was exquisite, for there was nothing to dull it. It was untouchable, like the phantom pains that soldiers claimed, in a limb that was no longer there. 'And this is how you feel?'

Tim nodded. 'Clarissa knows it, and she works all the harder to make me hurt. And yet I cannot leave her. She says, if I do, she will take the children, even though she cares little for them. They are innocents. They do not deserve such a mother.'

'She does not deserve to live. And if I cannot find a way to mend this?' Adam smiled. 'Then I will send her back to hell from whence she came.'

He offered his hand to his friend again, and Tim pushed it aside. 'It is a bit late for that, I think. I am going home, to my loving wife. You will understand, I trust, if the door is shut to you, should you attempt to visit.'

Adam nodded. 'As my door is now shut to you. But a word of warning. It all may get worse before it gets better. Your wife is none too happy with me. I refused her this morning. If you find letters to her, in my hand? They are old. Burn them without looking. For both our sakes.'

Tim nodded. 'Goodbye, then.' And he left him alone.

One, two, three… She'd had to start over on several occasions, for she was so angry that she kept losing her count. Penny stormed into her library and rang the bell for Jem. *Twenty-seven, twenty-eight*… And why did she even bother with it? For what good did it do to keep your temper, and be agreeable in all things, if someone you thought you could trust used your even nature against you?

Jem entered and looked at her suspiciously.

She waved an arm at the walls. 'Pack them up again.'

He squinted. 'Your Grace?'

'My books. Bring back the crates. Take them down and box them up.'

'Where will I be taking them, once I'm done?'

'I have no idea. Box them.'

'Are we going back to London, or the Scotland property that everyone talks of? Or is there somewhere…?'

'Away. I am going away, and not coming back. You were right all along. My idea was foolish, and now I am punished for it. So stop arguing with me and box these cursed books.'

'No.'

'I beg your pardon?'

He raised his voice. 'I said no, Miss Penny. I have put up with more than my share of nonsense from you over the years. But today it stops. I have carried these books halfway across England for you. You may not have noticed the fact, since you lift them one at a time. But as a group, they are heavy. And they are not moving another inch.'

'They are not remaining here,' she shouted, 'and neither am I.'

To this, Jem said nothing, merely fixed her with a long, hard look and stood, blocking the door.

'You refuse to pack the books? So be it. I'd probably

have a hard time sorting them from the ones that were already here. It is amazing how quickly one's things can get tangled with another's… But never mind that. Go to my room. I will send the maid for my dresses. They are unquestionably mine. Although I never wanted the cursed things in the first place.'

Jem showed no sign of obeying this order, either.

'What are you waiting for? Go!' She sounded shrill, even to her own ears.

Jem folded his arms.

'Look at me.' She pointed down at her clothes. 'How long has it been since I met him? A scant two months. And I no longer know myself. I dress differently. I act differently. I do not even live in the same city. I was totally content to spend days by myself. And now, if he leaves me for more than an hour or two, I miss him.

'Little by little, he has made me into exactly the thing that he wants, and now he is bored with me.'

'And for this reason, I must pack your things and carry them to you-do-not-know-where.' He remained unmoved.

'He does not love me.'

'I did not think you wished him to. When you dragged me to Scotland—'

'I was wrong.'

'And so you wish to compound the first bad decision by making another.' Jem shook his head in pity. 'I will admit, I had my doubts about the man at first. But given time, he will love you beyond reason, if he is does not already. It is hardly worth the strain on my back to bring your things down from your room, only to carry them back up again. If you insist on going, you may carry your own damn bags. Your Grace.' He added her title as an afterthought and left the room.

Chapter Twenty-Two

Penny glanced around the room, painfully aware of the silence. When had it become such a burden to be alone? It was what she had always thought she wanted.

She had been in the library for almost a week, leaving only when she was sure that the corridor was empty, to creep to her room to wash or to sleep.

But it had become harder and harder to avoid the inevitable confrontation. Most times, she could hear her husband prowling outside the library door like some kind of wild beast. On the first day, he had pounded on the oak panels, demanding that she open for him, and hear what he had to say. She feared he would shake the thing off its hinges with the force of the blows, but had put her fists to her ears, and shut her lips tight to avoid the temptation of answering him. For she knew if she saw him again, she would forget everything that had happened, and remember only how it felt to be in his arms. She would believe anything he told her, and trust any promise, no matter how false, if only he would lie with her again.

But after a day of thundering, his temper had passed like a summer storm, and the knocking had become quieter, more civilised. His shouts had turned to normal requests, 'Penny, open this door. We must speak. We cannot go on like this.'

And at last, it had come to her as a whisper. 'Penny, please…'

And now, for several days, there had been no sound at all. Just the ceaseless rustling of his footsteps on the carpet outside.

It was all foolishness. If he wanted to enter, there was nothing to stop him. He must have the key, for this was his house, not hers. If it was not in his possession, he had but to ask the servants, and they would open for him in an instant. He was the duke. He had proved often enough that he could do as he pleased.

But he did not. He respected their bargain. She had wanted privacy. And he had given this space to her. He would not cross the threshold without her permission. It was maddening. She had gotten exactly what she wanted: a library full of books and all the time in the world to enjoy them.

And yet she could not stop crying. The sight of her own books was torture, for she could not seem to concentrate long enough to read more than a few words. And those she managed all seemed to remind her of her own fate: unfaithful Odysseus and his myriad of excuses, weak will and false guilt. And Penelope, waiting for him, perpetually alone.

Why did it have to bother her so, that her husband had visited his lover? Nowhere in their original agreement, or in any of the bargaining that had occurred since, had there been any mention of his fidelity. She had not asked it of him, nor had he promised. She had held her own against the woman, for a time. But she had always known that the moment would come when she would lose. And she felt dead inside, knowing that when the mood had struck him, he would leave her to her books, as though she meant nothing to him.

And now, he thought that he could wait outside her door until her mood softened, and worm his way back into her good graces. He wanted the best of both worlds: a co-operative wife when it suited him, and his freedom all the rest of the time.

Out of the coldness in her heart rose an ember of burning rage. He had been the first to break the agreement. If he had but let her alone, she could have stayed in her study, and never have known or cared. If he had not insisted on coming to her bed, she would not be feeling jealousy over a thing that she had never wanted. If he had remained indifferent, or neglectful or at least absent, she would have viewed this liaison as just another example of his uninterest in her.

But he had treated her with kindness and respect, almost from the first. He had guarded her from ridicule and shepherded her through the maze of society, then he had touched her, and brought her more pleasure than she could have imagined possible.

And then he had taken it away. Given the chance, he would do so again. She must hold that thought foremost, and make sure it would not happen. The longer she stayed in this house, the more likely her heart would soften, and she would forget how it had felt to see Tim and her husband fighting for the attention of another. She would begin making excuses for it, and then all hope was lost.

She must leave while the anger was still fresh and she had the strength. With just the clothes on her back, if necessary. There was nothing holding her here but the fear of confronting him. Once it was done, she would be free. If he tried to stop her in the hall, she would push past without speaking. Let him follow her to her rooms. She would ignore him. She would slam the door in his face again, pack a valise and leave immediately.

She threw open the door, ready to cut him and walk by, but she almost stumbled. For he was not standing before her, but right there in the doorway, sitting on the rug with his legs drawn up to his chest, his back leaning against the frame.

She caught her hand against the wood to steady herself, and before she could stop, she had looked down into his beautiful blue eyes and felt the fight going out of her, as she feared it would. 'What on earth are you doing down there?'

He blinked up at her, surprised by her sudden appearance. 'Waiting for you to open this door. I assume you must go to your rooms at some point, but I have not been able to catch you, so I resolved to remain until you came out. I grew tired of pacing. It has been days, you know.' There was a faint accusation in his voice, as though it were somehow her fault that he was weary.

'I know exactly how long it has been.' She could feel each minute since last she had seen him. 'I would not still be here if I had managed to get my own servant to obey me. He is loyal to you, now, and will not help me move my things.'

'You really do mean to leave me, then?' At least he did not waste time in apologies that she would not have believed anyway.

'Yes.'

'I cannot say I blame you.' He looked away for a moment, sucked in a small breath and stood up. When he turned back to face her, he had become the distant, rather polite stranger she had known in London. He gestured to the library. 'May I at least come into the room? I'd prefer not to discuss this in the hall.'

As though there was a servant left in the house who was not aware of their difficulties. Perhaps he had forgotten how little effort he had made to hide them, when he had been shouting the details through the closed door. She almost smiled, before remembering how serious the situation was. She gestured through the open door and preceded him into the room.

He came through and shut it behind him. Then he turned to face her. His hands were folded behind his back like a penitent schoolboy. His mouth worked for a bit before he could find more words. 'Have you given thought as to where you will go? Not to your brother, I hope.'

It would be the logical choice. Hector would take her back. But he would never let her forget the mistake she had made in leaving. 'I do not think so.'

He nodded, obviously relieved. 'I am concerned for

your welfare, although I might not seem so. You understand that there may be a child involved as well?'

She had not thought of this fresh complication to her future. 'I will know soon enough.'

'And wherever you go, you will need space enough for your books.'

She looked at the shelves around her, and where she had seen friends before, now all she saw was dead weight. 'I doubt I will be taking them. Suddenly, it seems an awful lot of bother. And without knowing what the future holds for me…'

'No.' There was a wild light in his eyes, and he dropped his attempt at calm. The words rushed out of him. 'I can understand if you cannot abide my presence after what has happened, but do not tell me that you are abandoning your work because of me. There is a dower house on the grounds. You could stay there. The books could stay here. And you could visit as often as you liked.'

She considered how painful it would be to see him, and forced herself to look away. 'I would hardly have succeeded in escaping your influence if I were visiting this house as a guest for the majority of my days.'

'I could go from you, then.' His voice was bleak. 'You would have the books, and the space and quiet for your studies. I could go to London. I would not set foot upon the grounds without your permission. And I would be here no more than was necessary to run the estate.'

She stared at him. 'Does Clarissa approve of this plan? I imagine she would like to spend more time in London.'

'I do not know. Or care,' he added. 'It is a bit late to

tell you now. But I only went to her to say goodbye. If it troubles you still, the thought that we might meet in secret, I could travel abroad, or stay at the property in Scotland. It is farther away.'

'And you would leave the estate to me?'

'I would be honoured if you would accept it.'

She was confused. 'You love this house.'

He nodded.

'You are different, when you are here. It is where you belong.'

'You, as well. And if it can only be one of us in residence?' He smiled sadly. 'Then I wish it to be you. Without you, there would be no estate. And it is wrong that you should be banished from it for my misdeeds, or to suffer any discomfort because of my behaviour. It is my wish that you accept it from me, and anything else you might need. You are my wife. All that I have is yours.'

'That is ridiculous,' she responded. 'I never wanted all that you had. I have need of a quiet place to study. That is all.'

'And I thought I wanted nothing more than your money.'

'And a position in society. And an heir…'

He stared at the ground. 'Things have changed since the first day, have they not?'

'Yes.' She smiled sadly at the floor as well. 'Perhaps we could go back to the way we first planned.'

'I don't think that will work,' he replied.

She nodded. 'Too many things have changed.' She'd felt like a fool for even suggesting it, especially after banishing him from her life just a few days before. But when she was near to him, she remembered. And it was so hard to give him up.

'It would work fine, for a time,' he hedged. 'But I am afraid I cannot control my impulses sufficiently to keep our lives as separate as we had planned.'

Impulses? Even the thought made her temper start to rise.

One, two, three…

'Knowing I could not have you? The sight of you with other men, any other man, even if it was quite innocent, or you were very discreet, would drive me mad with jealousy.'

Four, five… 'What?'

He continued, ignoring the interruption. 'Before we came to Wales, I thought if I could keep you all to myself, then you would forget anyone but me. I am sorry.'

'And you did not tell me that we were neighbors to the Coltons?'

'Because I did not want you to see them. Especially not Tim, for I did not think I could trust him, given all that has happened. If the world were different, and we were all free, you would have done better to choose him, for his temperament would suit you.'

Adam's face darkened and his lips twisted in a bitter smile. 'But I find that I do not care, when you are near, what is best for you or that you deserve better. You are mine, and I want to keep you all to myself.' His smile softened as he remembered. 'It was so good, being alone with you. And you seemed content with just me for company.'

'But what about Clarissa?' She held her breath.

'The day I went to her, she sent me a letter, saying that if I would not come to her, she would come here. It would have ruined everything.' He looked up, and his face was blank. 'It wouldn't have mattered. Things are ruined, in any case. There will be less bother, now that Tim and I are quits. I will not need to pretend civility with her. She is angry, and promises to make a scandal. There are letters that I wrote to her.'

He rubbed his hand over his eyes, as though to blot out the memory. 'They are very detailed. And I would ask you, as a last favour, to destroy them without reading them should they come your way. The words are no longer true, but to read them might cause you pain.

'But if she does not send them to you, then she will circulate them freely in London next Season. You may be more comfortable if you remain here, far from the gossip of the *ton*. I am sorry, but whatever might happen, you should know and prepare yourself. Perhaps it will not matter and she will be quiet, now that she sees we are…apart.' The last word seemed to come difficult to him.

'It will not matter to your position, of course. You are Duchess of Bellston for as long as you wish to be. Nothing anyone says will change that. But people will talk. I am afraid you will find it embarrassing.' He said it as gently as possible, and his face was full of remorse.

The idea of talk, which would have appalled her a few weeks before, seemed distant and unimportant. What did it matter what people said? Nothing could hurt as bad as being without Adam. 'It does not really matter, does it, if it is all in the past? It is not as if you can change what you did, even if it was very awful.'

He looked hopeful, for a moment, and pulled one of the straight-backed library chairs to him, and sat a respectful distance from her.

'I know it is too late to say these things. But I would do anything to take back what has happened. I never wanted anything less for you than you wanted for yourself: peace and security. That you might come to harm from behaviours of mine, things that occurred long before you knew me—it pains me more than you can imagine. And if I had known, the day we met, that I would make you unhappy, I swear I'd never have married you.'

She shrugged. 'You can have no idea what you might have done, for I dare say you had little control of yourself on that particular occasion.'

'I still cannot remember the details,' he admitted. 'Only that I was convinced you were sent by God to lead me to salvation. I'd have followed you to the ends of the earth. And still would, if you would but allow it. You have brought me more happiness than I deserve.'

'I made you happy,' she repeated numbly.

He smiled and shook his head in disbelief. 'You did not realise it? Yes, you made me happy. You are unlike any woman I have ever met. Blazingly intelligent, unfailingly honest, and a rock to which I can cling in moments of turmoil. And when we are together as man and wife?' He shook his head again. 'I never knew how it felt to join in love, until you came to me.'

'Love?' she whispered.

He nodded. 'I love you, Penelope. I cannot help myself. It is not what you wanted, of course. Not peaceful or quiet at all, for neither of those virtues are in my nature. But there it is.'

He loved her. What an amazing idea. She felt the warmth of the words against her heart, growing in her, surrounding her to keep her safe, and heating her blood in a way that was not safe at all, but just as wonderful.

'And you were faithful to me,' she said, testing.

'Strangely enough, yes. I put off my mistress, I forsook my old haunts. There has been no one but you since the day we met. What Tim saw when he spied me with Clarissa was no doing of mine.'

She stepped closer and reached out a hand to him, touching his hair, and trailing her fingers slowly down his cheek. He closed his eyes for a moment, then turned his head to press kisses into her palm, seizing her hand in his so that she could not pull away.

And she felt the familiar thrill of power at the sight of him, cradling her hand as though he feared the loss of her touch. He kissed her knuckles again, and bowed his head to her. 'My fate is yours to decide, Penny. I will do as you wish in all things. I will go tonight, if you say I must. But I beg you, do not be apart from me, for I fear I shall go mad with the loss of you.'

Fierce joy was rushing through her, and desire mingled with it. And without speaking, she touched him under the chin, urging his lips up to hers and kissing slowly into his open mouth.

His breath trembled for a moment, and then his response was eager, hungry to deepen the kiss.

She pulled away, and he looked up with hope, awaiting her answer, and she looked into his eyes, and saw only herself reflected back.

When she spoke, she was pleased that her voice sounded cool, collected and very much like the ladies of the *ton* that had once beguiled her husband and not at all like she truly was: too far gone with love of him to ever leave. 'So you love me, and wish to give me all that I might desire?'

He gave the barest nod, but his eyes sparkled with shared devilment.

She reached to his throat, and undid the knot of his cravat, tugging him up out of his chair. 'Then, we have much to discuss. But first, you must give me my garter back.'

* * * * *

THE WEDDING
GAME

To 2017.
You are still bright and unspoiled.
Please be more gentle and loving to us all
than last year was.

Chapter One

As they always were at the height of the London Season, Almack's Assembly Rooms were crowded to the point of overflowing. Amelia Summoner circled the edges of the main room, watching the marriage-minded throng unobserved. It was easy to do when one knew the place and people in it as well as she did.

She had not missed a Wednesday in the three years her family had had vouchers. In that time she had watched three crops of debutantes arrive, parade and depart on the arms of the gentlemen who married them. She had made her own come-out the first year and, after a brief splash, she had sunk through the waters of society, forgotten.

Now she moved about the place like a fish in the deep, invisible until the moment she chose to be otherwise. Unlike other unattached girls of her age, she viewed this more as a freedom than a failure. It was more relaxing to dance, speak or flirt only when one felt moved to do so, instead of obsessing on each social interaction as if it was to be a life-changing event. If one simply wished to watch others, it was much better to be *that Summoner girl.*

No. Not the pretty one. The other one. The odd one.

After her first few balls, she had known that she was not going to be a major success. She had been classified by the patronesses as an 'unconventional beauty with an excessively sharp wit'. Any other girl would have been hurt by such a damning compliment. It did not take a bit of Amy's vaunted intelligence to know that only her desirable family name kept her from being labelled 'plain and opinionated'. A connection by marriage to Lord Summoner could make a young man's future, in politics or society. But even those men were hoping for a wife who was conventional in all ways and excessively pretty, rather than excessively sharp.

But it was Amy's intention to remain just as she was. Thus far, her character had been formed without compromise and she was satisfied with the result. She'd yet to meet a man for whom she was willing to change. In the face of her stubborn refusal to aid in their ambitions by marrying them, even the most stalwart of suitors had given up wooing her ages ago. This Season, if a gentleman wished to dance with her, she knew it was out of pity.

More likely, it was because he wanted to be seen as the nice sort of fellow who bestowed his friendship evenly about the family, and was willing to stand up with her quiz of an older sister if it would make Miss Belle Summoner smile. This year, London buzzed with talk of Lord Summoner's younger daughter, the most celebrated beauty of the decade. Tonight, as she moved through the crowd, Amy had overheard more than a few men sighing that a single smile from that delicate beauty, Belle, would be worth any sacrifice up to and including being nice to Miss Amelia, the spinster.

No one had dared to try it yet and Amy had no intention of being an easy target for their cheap flattery. She moved through the crush with a purposeful step that hinted a destination in mind and no time for interruption. When she sat, it was in a corner, with her fan raised, scanning the crowd as if looking for someone other than the people in the immediate vicinity. She kept her acquaintance limited, knowing that people would not dare to speak to her without an introduction. If she did not deign to know them, then they could not use her as a conduit to meet Belle.

Since she did not have to waste her time on dancing and idle chatter, she could watch and listen. She heard dozens of conversations without being a part of any of them, while scanning the opposite side of the room to catch those that watched her sister with more than casual interest. If a gentleman in tonight's crowd was seriously interested in Belle, Amy would know his intentions almost before he did himself. Then she could prepare the proper defence against him. It would take a very special man to make a match with Arabella. No others need apply.

Tonight alone, Amy had catalogued and discounted a dozen prospective suitors. Their intentions did not matter if they lacked sufficient money, manners or station to get around Father's plans for his daughters. He expected them to marry well, if they married at all. After years of trying to find a husband for Amy, Lord Summoner had declared her too headstrong to wed a man who was not of her own choosing and agreed to let her be.

But Belle…

Amy hid a sigh behind her fan. Belle would be very easily led, by Father or anyone else. It was good that she had a sister to look out for her and keep her from harm.

And it was not as if she did not want Belle to marry and be happy. Though there were many ne'er-do-wells and fortune hunters in London, there were some promising candidates as well. As Amy found them, she scrawled their names on the back of her empty dance card for further investigation. So far, there were fully eight men who might make a good match for Belle. They were neither too young nor too old, at least passably handsome, good tempered, well born and rich, but not high flyers. A union with any of them might result in pleasant rustication for most of the year and not too much strenuous socialising.

After separating sheep from goats in tonight's field, there was but one man who fit neither category. He was the one Amy found the most worrisome. As she watched Benjamin Lovell, she did not need to hear his words to know that he was shopping for a wife.

Though Mr Lovell might pretend that he had come to London's most popular marriage mart for a few dances and a light supper, he made too great a show of uninterest to be completely sincere. He stood at the side of the room, feigning boredom to the point of turning his back to the dance floor. But he had positioned himself so that he might gaze in one of the mirrors on the wall to watch and catalogue the females in the room just as carefully as she had been watching the males.

False apathy often proved more dangerous to the hearts and minds of young ladies than active pursuit. In response to his neglect, the gentle sex worked all the harder to get his attention. It was what he sought from them, she was sure. He wished to be the prey, rather than the hunter. It was a bold strategy for a man of uncertain parentage and she admired him for it.

Apparently, the patronesses admired him as well. No amount of money was sufficient to sway them into giving vouchers to a gentleman who was not worthy to marry into the finest families in England. Illegitimacy was a stain that not all men could rise above. But rumour had it that Mr Lovell was the most exclusive sort of bastard.

His Grace the Duke of Cottsmoor had not made a formal acknowledgement of Mr Lovell, but it must have been intended. Before Cottsmoor's sudden death, Mr Lovell had often been seen in the company of the Duke and his Duchess. They had treated him as family even though they said nothing about his origins. When the Duke, the Duchess and their first born had all been taken by an influenza, Mr Lovell had withdrawn from society for a year, mourning them as lost parents and brother.

His birth and early life were shrouded in secrecy. He had been educated abroad, which raised a few eyebrows from those graduates of Oxford or Cambridge with the most school loyalty. But one could hardly blame Cottsmoor for not sending his bastard to the same school as his heir.

Mr Lovell had lost nothing by his Continental learning. His speech was flawless and no gaps had been found in his knowledge. He was thought intelligent without being didactic, witty without conceit and capable of wise counsel, but able to hold his tongue when his opinion was not required. Because of this, the new Cottsmoor, still too young for university, sometimes came to him for advice in navigating his new role as peer.

If the only flaw was that his noble father had not bothered to marry his mother? After meeting the charming Mr Lovell, society had declared it was hardly any fault at all. In fact, it might even be an advantage. The Duke had left a bequest to see that his natural son was amply provided for. According to gossip, Mr Lovell was turning his inheritance into even more money with smart investments.

But one would not have realised it, without careful observation. He did not call attention to his newly acquired wealth in his dress. His tailoring was impeccable, which made him no different than all the other gentlemen in the room. But the choices of fabric, with the richness of the black coat offsetting a white vest of expensive silk brocade, whispered that he was fashionable, but no dandy.

The buckles on his knee breeches were not overly large or brassy. But when one took the time to notice, one noted their heaviness and the dull gleam of silver.

He wore no rings or jewellery other than the fob on his watch and that was all but hidden under his coat front. It only peeped into view when he danced, revealing a heavy gold chain that ended in a shockingly large emerald that winked as if to say, *I have money, but the confidence not to flaunt it in public.*

His valet had not bothered with a complicated knot for his cravat. It was done up in an Oriental so simple he might have managed it himself. The blinding white accented the sharp, dark line of his jaw. He had the same colouring as the rest of the Cottsmoor line, distinctive dark eyes and hair, and the faint olive cast to the skin. If the young Duke grew to be half as handsome as Mr Lovell, he would not need a title to send ladies scurrying for his approval.

But tonight, it was Mr Lovell who held the attention, of all the girls in the room. Of course, Amy's fascination was purely academic. She fluttered her fan to cool the sudden heat on her face. She was not doting on the man. She merely needed to assure herself that he was no threat to Belle. If Mr Lovell was unworthy, it did not matter what Lady Jersey thought of him. He would not get so much as an introduction.

But if he was as good as he seemed?

She fanned herself again. If he was capable of being a kind and loving husband who gave as much attention to his wife as he did to his carefully crafted persona, then Amy could not hope for a better match for her sister.

She drifted in his direction, pretending to admire the line of dancers on the floor. Watching such a handsome man should have been pleasing, but there was something about this one that left her uneasy. Benjamin Lovell was too good to be true. Amy could not shake the feeling that his artless perfection was calculated more precisely than the fine watch on the other end of the emerald fob.

A part of her could not blame him. Who amongst them did not wear a mask from time to time? But it would have made more sense, were he poor. If his money was real, as it obviously was, he had no reason to be disingenuous.

With a flutter of her fan she moved closer, then past them to a chair in the corner where the candlelight from the chandeliers could not quite reach. It afforded her an excellent position to see both Mr Lovell and his friend Mr Guy Templeton in quarter-profile as they chatted.

Though the movement was almost imperceptible, Mr Templeton was shifting from foot to foot. Then, with a quick glance to check for observers that missed Amy entirely, he reached down to give his knee breeches a yank on each leg, and shifted again. 'Damn things keep riding up,' he muttered to Mr Lovell. 'It gives a new meaning to Almack's balls.'

The polite smile on Mr Lovell's face barely wavered. 'They are the price of gentility, Templeton. No lady of quality will have you if you cannot stand patiently in formal wear.'

'They are nothing more than a nuisance,' he insisted. 'I wonder, is it necessary to examine our legs before making their purchase, as if we are horseflesh?'

'Legs and wind,' Lovell agreed, with a casual gesture toward the dance floor. 'You had best prove to them you can gallop. With pins like those holding you up, you will not get a woman to take you unless you pad your calves. At the very least, we must get you a better tailor. You wear that suit like it is full of fleas.'

'Because it itches,' Templeton agreed. Then he sighed happily. 'But the girl I've got my eye on will have me even so.'

'She will need to be the most patient creature in London to put up with you,' Lovell said, 'if you will not attend to the niceties.'

Not too patient, thought Amy. With a good family, a pleasant face and a full purse, Mr Templeton was near the top of her list for prospective brothers-in-law.

'Niceties be damned,' said Templeton under his breath, offering a polite nod to a passing patroness. 'Old bats like that one insist on breeches, call tea and cake a supper, and do not allow so much as a waltz with a pretty girl. Then they make the introductions, thinking they can decide our marriages for us. Worse yet, they make us pay for the privilege.'

'It seems to work well enough,' Lovell said with a shrug.

'But if we truly love, can we not choose a more direct method to demonstrate our feelings? It is like standing on a river bank,' Templeton said, gesturing at a group of girls on the opposite side of the room. 'But instead of simply swimming across to the object of our desire, we have to pick our way across the water on slippery rocks.'

'Swim?' Lovell arched his eyebrows in mock surprise. 'The water would spoil one's knee breeches. And what makes you think romantic emotion has anything to do with the process of picking a wife?'

The words were delivered in a tone of cold calculation so at odds with the pleasantly approachable expression on Mr Lovell's strikingly handsome face that Amy almost dropped her fan in shock. She regained her grip and fluttered deliberately, staring away from them so they could not see her flush of annoyance. He was a heartless fraud, just as she'd suspected.

'Not love and desire one's future wife?' Templeton said in genuine surprise. 'Is that not half the fun of getting one?'

'Fun.' Lovell's lip twitched in revulsion, as if he had found a fly in his lemonade. 'Marriage is far too serious an undertaking to be diminished by idle pleasure.'

Then the grimace disappeared and the smile returned. But his stance, shoulders squared and one foot slightly forward, was the one her father took when on the verge of political oratory. He used the same distancing posture when encouraging her to conform to society and find a husband who would improve her weak character so her father did not have to.

To the last vertebra of his inflexible British spine, Mr Lovell was a man who knew how things should be and had no qualms in telling others the truth as he saw it. 'When one marries, one does not just make a match with the young lady, one enters into a union with her family and with society as well.'

'I should think it was unnecessary for you to think

of such things,' Templeton pointed out. 'Cottsmoor, after all—'

Lovell cut him off with a raised hand. 'For argument's sake, let us assume that I have no family at all. I am the first of my line, which makes it all the more important that I choose my attachments wisely. Picking the right father-in-law will do more for a man of ambition than choosing the right woman ever will.'

'Then you want a man with a title,' Templeton interrupted. 'The Duke of Islington is rich as Croesus and has three daughters, all of age.'

Lovell shook his head. 'Title is hereditary and lands are entailed. And I do not need his money. I am quite capable of making my own.'

'No title.' Templeton stroked an imaginary beard as if deep in thought. 'You don't need to marry for money. But of course, you will tell me the daughter of a cit is not good enough for you.'

'Nor scholars or men of law,' Lovell agreed. 'I want a proper Tory with an old fortune, distantly related to Pitts, elder and younger. Someone who dines with Wellington and has Grenville's ear.'

Amy leaned forward in alarm.

'Politics?' Templeton said with surprise.

'If one wishes to make a difference in society, where else would one be than Parliament?'

'And you are speaking of Lord Summoner, of course.'

'No other,' Lovell agreed and Amy's heart sank.

'I assume you wish to wed the lovely Arabella?' Templeton said with a bark of a laugh.

'She is the toast of the Season,' Lovell said. 'I mean to settle for nothing less than the best of the best.'

'Then you must get in line behind the rest of the men in London,' Templeton replied, shaking his head. 'Her dance card was nearly full before we even arrived. I had to fight a fellow for the last spot.'

'I did not bother. I have not yet gained an introduction to her,' Lovell said. 'There must be nothing less than respectable in our first meeting.'

Amy's mind raced to stay ahead of him. His insistence on propriety was a small consolation. It meant there was still time to stop him.

'Even when you do manage to meet her, you will find it a challenge to draw her out,' Templeton informed him. 'She is very shy. Her smile is dazzling, but she speaks hardly at all.'

'All the better,' Lovell replied. 'Who would wed a woman like that for conversation?'

The bone handle of Amy's fan snapped beneath the pressure of her fingers. This odious man was speculating over Belle as if she was nothing more than an afterthought in his plans. Even worse, she suspected the comment about a lack of conversation was a reference to something no true gentleman should speak of when referring to a lady.

Apparently, Templeton agreed. 'See here, Lovell...'

Lovell held up his hands in denial. 'I meant no slight to the lady. But one does not have to marry any woman for intellectual stimulation when one's goal is to take a seat amongst the wisest men in English society.'

Amy raised her fan to hide her smirk. Having met

some of her father's friends, Mr Lovell had a view of male superiority that was charming in its naivety.

He continued with his plans. 'I want to wed a woman who is beautiful and talented, who will do credit to my home and bear and raise my children.' He thought for a moment. 'And to win the most sought-after girl of the year will reflect well on my taste and on my abilities of persuasion. I want to be the best and I will settle for nothing less than the best from those around me. But as I said before, it is less about winning the girl and more about winning her father. He has control of two seats in the House of Commons and I mean to be in one of them by year's end. If he is here tonight, I will seek him out and find my way into his good graces. Once I have done that, the rest will follow.'

Bastard.

Another spine of her fan snapped, but Amy barely felt it. Bastard was too accurate to be an insult to his character. There were probably a great many epithets she would have used to describe him, were she a man, and Benjamin Lovell deserved every last one. He might pretend modesty in his perfect, plain suit. But the man was a trumped-up peacock, near to choking on his own pride. Without even meeting her, he'd decided he must have dear, sweet, innocent Belle, just to gain a seat in the House of Commons. He would not give a thought to her, once they were married. Worse yet, if he wished for the best from those around him, he might take out his disappointment upon her sister when he realised she was unequal to his ambitious plans.

Something must be done and it must be done immediately. Amy stood, almost bumping into a young man who was working his way along the edge of the room, balancing far too many glasses of lemonade. He muttered an apology and made to go around.

Suddenly, she had a plan.

She responded to his words with a simpering laugh. 'La, sir. It is a relief to see you. I retired to the corner for I was parched and near to fainting.'

Before he could offer or deny, she reached out and took two of his lemonades away from him, taking a sip from the first. 'Much better,' she said, giggling again and ignoring his astonishment at her rudeness.

Then, as if she was as unsteady as she claimed, she turned and staggered forward the two steps necessary to stand before Benjamin Lovell. She wavered, lurched and allowed herself a brief, triumphant smile. Then she dumped the contents of the glasses in her hand down his elegant white waistcoat.

Chapter Two

*D*amn it all to hell.

Ben Lovell was not given to outbursts of temper. Not in public, at least. Occasionally, when he was totally alone, he gave way to self-pity and cursed the strange turns his life had taken to land him where he was. Then he remembered that only a fool would complain over what must be seen by others as stunningly good luck, composed himself again, counted his blessings and ignored the rest.

In public he could allow nothing more than one brief, unspoken curse, making sure to give no indication on his face of displeasure within. Things had been going far too well for him to spoil his perfect reputation with a cross word towards the little idiot who had baptised him in lemonade.

This accident had ruined any chance for a meeting with Summoner tonight. If one wished to lay the groundwork for a political career, one could not afford to look less than one's best, or to appear out of sorts.

One certainly could not have one's mind clouded with ill will over what was an innocent mistake by a flustered debutante.

For now, he would be a gentleman and ignore the ruined coat that had cost a full thirty pounds just the previous week. He would shake off the drips of lemonade falling from the thin picot of lace at the cuffs of his linen shirt. His cravat was a sodden lump and he could feel the hair on his chest sticking to his body. How many cups had the chit been carrying to result in such havoc? Had she been actively trying to drown him?

And where had she come from? He was normally careful to avoid treading on toes or bumping elbows even in the most crowded rout. She had seemed to appear out of nowhere, as if she'd been lying in wait to attack him.

A gentleman should not be bothered with trivia and Ben did not want to be known simply as well mannered. To overcome his birth, he must be the most magnanimous man in London.

He buried his annoyance and forced his face into an expression of concern for the lady. Then he reached for his handkerchief, holding the linen out to the giggling girl. She was flapping a broken fan as if she meant to dry him off with the breeze. 'I am so sorry to have startled you, miss. Did any of it spill upon your gown?' Then he looked down into the heart-shaped face barely level with his top vest button.

He was staring. It was rude of him. To be the success he wished to be, he could not afford to be anything less than perfect. But one look into that face and he was gaping like an idiot. All common sense seemed to have fled and taken his good manners with it.

It was not that she was a striking beauty. Pretty enough, he supposed. A fine figure, though she was none too tall. In an attempt to add height, her brown hair was piled in an overly fussy style with too many braids and curls. The plumes that completed her coiffure bobbed as she nodded her head along with his apology. Judging by the giggles, he assumed her head was likely full of feathers as well.

Or perhaps not.

Her laugh was so false and inane that it might have been cultivated to put a man off. But if she meant to be repellent, her eyes spoiled the effect. They drew him in and held him captive. They were large and bright, and the warm brown of a fine sherry. Or almost totally so. The left one had a single fleck of gold in the iris that glittered like a secret joke.

The difference between the two should have been unattractive for was not beauty dependent on symmetry? Instead, it was fascinating. He was lost in that little gold speck, enthralled by it. He wanted to gaze into her eyes forever, until they revealed their mysteries. Worse yet, as she looked into his eyes he was overcome with a desire to unburden himself and share even the most carefully concealed secrets of his past.

Then the feeling dissipated. On second look, what he had taken for mystique was a glimmer of calculation. He did not have to reveal his true self to her. Somehow, she had found him out and meant to punish him for his impudence. She was merely playing the simpering wallflower to disguise a dangerous, almost masculine intelligence.

'Thank you, sir, for your concern. My dress is un-damaged. But your poor suit…' She dabbed at the liquid staining his lapels with a force guaranteed to drive the stuff deeper into the fabric.

He seized her gloved hand as gently as possible to stop the damage it was doing. 'That will not be necessary,' he said, firmly. 'But thank you for the attempt.'

'Oh, but, sir, I am so sorry.' She looked up at him with the melting gaze of a spaniel. The look appeared so suddenly that she must practise innocence in a mirror to produce it on cue. It left him all the more sure that she was not the least bit sorry. In fact, she enjoyed seeing him discommoded.

He gave her an equally practised smile. 'It is nothing. We will not speak of it again.' Because, God willing, he would never see her again. There was something far too disquieting about her. From now on, he would be on his guard and maintain a safe distance should they meet.

'Thank you.' She dropped a hurried curtsy and disappeared as suddenly as she had arrived.

Beside him, his friend laughed. 'Well done, sir.'

'Well done? I did nothing.' He wiped at the stains on his coat and then gave up, throwing the handkerchief aside.

'Apparently, you made an impression on Miss Summoner.'

Ben scanned the room for the pathway to his future. She was on the far side now, in conversation with the featherheaded chit who had doused him. Were they friends? No. There was something in the slant of their heads that spoke of a family likeness. 'Dear God, do not tell me...'

'Sisters,' Templeton said with another laugh. 'The little one is the elder. A spinster, from what people say.'

'I wonder why,' Ben said, not bothering to disguise his sarcasm.

'She claims she does not wish to marry and that she cannot be parted from her sister.'

'All women with an ounce of pride say something similar when they cannot get a husband,' Ben replied. 'It is far more likely that she behaved to others as she behaved to me and that society has taken a distaste of her.'

'It hardly matters,' Templeton said, quite reasonably. 'After several years, she is properly on the shelf. But if you want the younger, you had best get used to her. The elder Miss Summoner will likely be a member of your household after you are married.'

'She most certainly will not,' Ben said with a shudder of dread. Looking into those eyes at breakfast each morning would be no different from coming to the table naked. She would strip each defence from him, giggling all the while.

'Where else will she go?' Templeton said in the voice of reason. 'Lord Summoner will not live for ever. Then it will be up to her sister's husband to take her on.'

'Unless some unsuspecting gentlemen can be trapped into a union with her,' Ben suggested.

'What are the odds of that, after all this time on the market?'

'All this time?' Ben shot a quick look across the dance floor at her, then looked away before she could notice. 'She cannot be much more than three and twenty. That does not make her a crone, no matter what society might think. If one plucked her feathers and unbraided that hair, and perhaps chose a different dressmaker for her—' and taught her to hang on to her drinks and not to giggle so '—she would be quite pretty.'

'But the eye.' Templeton shuddered.

'Those eyes,' Ben corrected. 'She has two. And they are not unattractive. Just rather…startling.'

'What man wishes to be startled by a woman?' Templeton shuddered again. 'Perhaps you are greener than you pretend when it comes to the fair sex, Lovell. It is never good to be surprised by them.'

'Perhaps compelling is the word I am searching for. Or captivating.' Intoxicating. Fascinating. He could spend a lifetime trying to describe those eyes.

Templeton shook his head. 'Neither of those are as good as they sound, either. If you wish to be a puppet or a slave to a woman, then get yourself a mistress. Your days will be full of all the passion and melodrama you long for with no legal bonds to hold you when it grows tiresome.'

'I have no intention of living my life under the thumb of a woman, with or without marriage.'

Never again.

He continued. 'Nor do I think the elder Miss Summoner actually possesses the facility to dominate the man who marries her.' This last was not totally true. But the fact that he could imagine himself stripped bare and defenceless from a single glance might be nothing more than his own fears of the unhappy past repeating itself.

'If that is so, then there is no problem at all,' Templeton said, smiling. 'You seem to feel more than confident of controlling her. Though you do not wish to marry for love or passion, you admit you find her at least marginally attractive. If you wish a connection to Lord Summoner by marrying his daughter, Miss Amelia should be no different than Miss Arabella.'

Why not?

When presented with such a logical argument, he could not immediately think of an answer. Then he remembered the lemonade stain on his best waistcoat and the possibility of future social occasions marred by such accidents. If he wished to be thought unshakable, he could not attach himself to a woman who was constantly rattling his calm and spoiling his appearance. 'Only an idiot would pretend that the two Summoner daughters are interchangeable. Everyone in London admires the younger of the two. The elder is so far on the shelf that I did not even know of her existence. There is also the fact that I am seeking a wife who will be the picture of decorum and not an awkward wallflower. Belle Summoner glides through a room like a swan. And her sister...' He stared down at his ruined waistcoat.

Templeton laughed. 'You truly think that spill was

an accident? My dear fellow, for all your polish, you are too naïve to survive the ladies of London.'

'Whatever do you mean?'

'Simply that if you come to Almack's and hide in the corner rather than standing up for a set, an interested female will try to get your attention by any means possible.'

This horrifying thought had not occurred to him. 'You think that…'

'She is smitten with you,' Templeton finished for him.

'And she did that on purpose to win my favour.' If that was true, then women truly were mad.

'There can be no other explanation for it. She fancies you. Since she is without prospects, I am sure Summoner will be all the more grateful to you for taking her off his hands.' Templeton clapped him on the shoulder. 'Go to him now and claim your prize.'

'I cannot go to him looking like this,' Ben said absently, staring across the room towards the woman who had attacked him. Could that have been the meaning of that glint in her eye? He had been sure there was some ulterior motive in her actions. But he'd have sworn it had less to do with marriage than a desire to unravel him like a fraying tapestry. 'I do not want to marry Miss Amelia,' he said, annoyed. He should not need to say those words aloud to clarify his intentions. If she was a spinster, the room was full of men who did not want her.

Templeton gave him a pitying look. 'You want Belle, as does every other man in London. But you have lost before you've begun, dear fellow. If you break her sister's heart with your indifference, Belle will have nothing to do with you. Women are like that, you know. They love each other more than they will ever love us.'

'Break her heart? I did nothing of the sort. I gave no indication that I was interested in her.' Unless she had seen something in the look he had given her. It had been but a glance, but it had seemed overlong, as if he had become lost in her eyes and needed to fight to get free.

'Of course not, Lovell.' The smirk on Templeton's face revealed the mockery in his assuring words. 'But I suggest you let Miss Amelia down as gently as possible. Then find another man she can affix herself to. If not, when you marry Belle, you will end with Amy Summoner permanently ensconced in your home, mooning over your lost love.'

Chapter Three

The next morning, Amy came down to her father's study, her list of prospective suitors in hand. In the matter of her sister's courtship and marriage, things were moving far too fast. The Season had barely begun, and total strangers like Benjamin Lovell were already mapping out Belle's future. The *laissez-faire* attitude that their father was bringing to a match might be acceptable for some girls, but not for Belle.

She rapped on the closed door and let herself in without waiting for an answer, then seated herself in the big leather chair in front of his desk.

Her father hardly looked up from his papers. 'You wish to speak to me, Amelia?'

'I wish to discuss last night's visit to Almack's.'

'I trust you both found it enjoyable.' The statement was a courtesy, nothing more. She could sense no real interest in it. Instead, there was the unspoken feeling that, since the fate of England hung on every decision he might make, Lord Summoner had no time for trivialities.

'Belle enjoyed it,' she said. 'I found it much the same as I always do.'

He sighed. 'Meaning you only bothered with it for your sister's sake. It is no wonder that you are not married. You make no effort.'

'I am not married because I found no one I could stand to spend a lifetime with,' she said, for what felt like the hundredth time.

'It is fortunate for me that your sister is not so particular.' He signed the document he had been reading and shook sand over the wet ink before setting it aside.

'Belle loves everyone. She does not know how to be particular,' Amy said. 'It will be up to us to choose wisely for her.'

'Us?' Her father looked up, fixing her with a quelling stare that she had long since learned to ignore.

'To that end,' she said, 'I took the time to evaluate the gentlemen at last night's ball, grading them according to their suitability.' She pushed the list across the desk to the empty space his documents had occupied.

He pushed it back without looking at it. 'You are overstepping yourself if you think to choose your sister's husband instead of your own.'

She could not help an unladylike snort. 'We have made progress, then. When I was actively searching, you were under the impression that the choice was yours alone.'

He sighed. 'And so it ought to have been. When your mother died, I allowed you far too much latitude and now I must pay the price for it.'

It was the way he chose to remember the past. When

Mother died, he had not allowed or denied anything. He had simply gone to London and forgotten all about his daughters. 'It is fortunate that Arabella is more obedient,' she said.

'It is,' he agreed, taking no notice of the sarcasm in her voice.

Amy paused until she was sure that she had full control of her temper. 'I will admit that I have not been the sort of daughter you deserved. I am headstrong and wilful, but it does not mean I love you any less. Belle loves you as well. But we both know that she is not like other young ladies. It is why we must take care to protect her from those who might take advantage.'

Her father reached for another paper, nearly upsetting the inkwell in his eagerness to occupy his hands and mind with something other than the truth. 'Nonsense. If you did not coddle her so, there would be no problem. Perhaps I should have remarried. Then you would not have taken it upon yourself to mother her and she would have tried harder to catch up.'

'She tries very hard already,' Amy said, reaching out to touch her father's hand. 'And yet, there are many things she cannot manage. The doctors told you that her birth was difficult for both mother and child.'

'She was stronger than your mother,' he said stubbornly. 'Arabella survived.'

'But not unaffected,' Amy reminded him. 'She has always been slow to learn and easily confused.'

'She has as much wit as a woman needs to make a wife.'

'By that, I suppose you mean she has two arms, two legs and a smile,' she snapped.

'Her mother's smile,' he said reverently.

'She is beautiful,' Amy agreed, equally awed. It was as if God had given Belle a final blessing as he took her mother and her wits.

'And a pleasant disposition as well,' her father added. 'She is a sweet child, is she not?'

'Because we have never given her reason to be otherwise,' Amy reminded him. 'We have done all in our power to protect her. And we help her in those situations that she could not manage on her own.' The word *we* was an exaggeration. But it would gain her nothing to antagonise her father.

'Her life will not change so very much,' Lord Summoner said. 'I will find some young buck from a good family, with a decent fortune and a nice house. She will live in comfort for the rest of her life. And you will be free to do as you wish with your future, without troubling yourself over her.'

'I do not trouble myself,' Amy argued. 'Well, not exactly.' It was sometimes difficult to have someone so dependent upon her. But it was even more difficult to think of Belle struggling without her. 'I love her,' she insisted. 'I help her when she needs it, because I want her to be happy.'

'Then you must not stand in the way of the marriage I will arrange for her.' Her father reached for another letter, breaking its wax seal with a swipe of his finger. It was a definitive gesture, meant to put an end to her argument.

Amy ignored it. 'An arranged marriage might be fine for some girls. But suppose her husband looks no further than her last name and does not understand that she cannot help the way she is?'

'He will find out, in time,' her father said. 'And by then, it will be too late to do anything about it.'

'You do not mean to explain?' Now Father sounded almost as heartless as Mr Lovell.

'An intelligent man will find it out for himself before he offers,' her father replied with another warning rattle of papers. 'If he does not, he will understand that marriages are negotiated contracts, no different than all other business. No human being is perfect. Both sides must balance advantages against defects before coming to an agreement.'

In her father's mind, the Summoner name had more than enough weight to balance the heaviest of problems. It was a shame that he did not want to marry Mr Lovell himself. They were well matched, since neither of them cared a fig for the feelings of the girl they would be bargaining over. 'Suppose the husband you choose does not love her as we do?'

'Love is not necessary before marriage. It might grow in time, of course.' When he looked up from his work, his expression was distant. 'I grew to be quite fond of your mother. Her loss was a blow from which I have yet to recover.' He cleared his throat. 'Mutual respect is a satisfactory basis for a relationship and far less painful for all parties involved.'

If that was his opinion, then the odious Mr Lovell was exactly the sort of son-in-law he was seeking. But how would she explain the abstract notions of a loveless union to her sister? 'It sounds very sensible. If we were discussing my courtship, I might be swayed. Belle is different. She will be happier in a match where there is mutual affection.'

'A romance, do you mean?' he responded with a condescending smile to remind her that, in comparison to a man, both his daughters were idiots. 'The fellow you are hoping for does not exist, Amelia. You have already admitted that your sister is unusual. We love her because we are her family. Others are not likely to be so charitable. Her future husband will require the inducements I am prepared to offer to overlook her deficiencies. It will not help her or any of us if you fill her head with nonsense.'

'It is not nonsense to want to love and be loved in return,' she said, wanting with all her heart to believe that was true.

Her father sighed. 'So you told me when you refused the offers put to you in your own Season. Now you seek to make a failure of your sister's come out.' He shook his head in disappointment. 'I did not think you so selfish, Amelia.'

'I am not selfish,' she insisted. 'I want what is best for her. If she weds, she will still need looking after. If you mean to choose a husband without a care to her feelings, it will be up to me to help her adjust to her new life and to console her should it all go wrong.'

His eyes narrowed, as if her words had only confirmed his opinion. 'I suspect your coddling the girl has caused most of her problems. When she does not have you to support her, she will learn to stand on her own, quick enough.'

'She will not because she cannot.' And thus they arrived at the usual sticking point. Discussions of Belle's difficulties always ended with her father refusing to believe they could not be solved by more effort on Belle's part and less interference on Amy's. 'This has nothing to do with desire to meddle in her future. She needs someone to care for her, Father. She always has. It is why I did not marry and why I intend to live in her household, after she weds. She needs me.'

Lord Summoner passed a hand over his brow to shield himself from feminine logic. 'It is one thing to play the spinster, Amelia, and quite another to actually become one. If you seriously think to follow her into her new household, I will have to find one man willing to take responsibility for both daughters. You are making my job twice as difficult.'

'Good,' she said, raising her chin in defiance. 'It will give me time to find her a man who truly understands her.'

'If the situation is as dire as you claim, then perhaps I should find a nurse for her and a husband for you.' It was a reasonable suggestion, but his cynical smile as he spoke revealed his true feelings in the matter. 'Since you have spent years ruining all chances for your own marriage that is now quite impossible. In any case, know that I cannot die leaving two unmarried daughters to fend for themselves.'

'Since you are not near to death, we hardly need to

worry about it,' she pointed out, unwilling to respond to the bait he set for her.

'And you are not the head of the family, though you seem to think you can act thus. The final decision on Belle's future is mine and mine alone. She will be married by Season's end and your approval of my choice is not required or appreciated.'

He stood to indicate the interview was at an end, leaving her little choice but to leave the study, return to her room and plan her counter-attack.

Chapter Four

The difficult morning discussion was followed by an afternoon too beautiful to stay indoors. If Amy wished to circumvent her father's plans, there was no better place to spend it than on Rotten Row, where anyone of importance took to horse or carriage to see and be seen by the rest of the *ton*.

Belle was seated on her gentle, brown mare, looking her best in a bright blue riding habit with a tall hat dressed in lace. With hair of spun gold and eyes as blue as a summer sky, there was none to compare to her.

It was a shame.

As she did, each time the thought crossed her mind, Amy felt guilty and silently enumerated a few more of Belle's virtues. She was kind and loving. She was loyal and had a gentle heart. In comparison to all that, did her deficiencies amount to so much?

'I like to ride,' Belle said. Her hands stroked the horse's mane.

'As do I, dear,' Amy agreed and adjusted her own

grip on her sister's reins to better lead her horse. 'Did you have a nice time at Almack's last night?'

'Yes,' Belle replied. 'I like to dance.'

'Did you speak with anyone of interest?' she probed gently.

As she tried to form an answer, Belle's smile dimmed. Thoughts flitted across her face like clouds. Then she smiled again. 'I danced every dance.'

'But with no gentleman more than once, I hope.' She had kept a close watch on Belle's dance card to prevent any partner from monopolising her time. But Belle, Lord bless her, was exceptionally easy to trick.

'I danced every dance,' she repeated, still smiling.

'You did, indeed,' Amy said, sighing.

'Will there be dancing at the wedding?'

'What wedding, dear?'

'My wedding.' There was much that her little sister did not understand. But she had grasped the main purpose of the Season. It was left to Amy to help her with the details.

'Weddings are held in the morning, Belle. There will be a breakfast, not a ball.'

'Oh.'

'But we must be sure that your husband likes to dance as much as you do.'

Belle nodded, satisfied. 'Who is he?'

'Your husband?' It had been too much to hope that Belle could understand her need to participate in the process of choosing such the man. 'We do not know as yet. We cannot choose just any man. We are looking for someone whose company you enjoy. Is there anyone you particularly liked last evening?'

'I liked the dancing,' she repeated again. 'And I liked all the boys who danced with me.'

Good-hearted soul that she was, Belle liked them all equally. Amy sighed again. 'I am making a list of gentlemen who might be good husbands. I have talked to Father about them.' And enough said about that, since there was no point in spoiling this conversation with the truth. 'We will find someone who loves you as much as we do.'

'Someone who likes to dance,' Belle added.

'Most definitely,' Amy agreed.

'And who likes dogs,' Belle added.

'Definitely,' Amy agreed. In her experience, all men loved dogs. Unfortunately, it was often a matter of like being drawn to like. 'But if there is any man you meet who likes dogs and dancing, and who you favour above others, you must tell us of him, immediately.'

'Everyone was nice to me,' Belle said, her smile as bright as ever. If she had a current favourite, she gave no indication of it. On their next outing, Amy would need to watch carefully for any signs of a preference that could be guided into something more.

For now, she must pay attention to the horses. She gave a gentle pull on the reins to slow them so they did not overtake two gentlemen who were stopped on the path ahead. Instead of resuming their ride as the girls approached, the men turned their mounts to look back at them.

In front of them, blocking their way, was the person she least wanted Belle to meet. Mr Lovell rode a dapple-grey stallion every bit as perfect as he was. And as usual, he was the picture of masculine perfection. He sat the horse as if he'd been born in its saddle. His hacking jacket and breeches stretched over muscles that he had not got from leisurely rides in Hyde Park. Rich, handsome and athletic.

She must stop ogling him and remember that he had designs on her sister. That meant he was also as loathsome as the snake in Eden. Amy sighed in frustration. She could not very well cut him without risk of offending Mr Templeton, who figured prominently on her list of acceptable suitors. It was a shame that such a fine gentleman had such horrible taste in friends.

'Miss Summoner. Miss Arabella.' Mr Templeton tipped his hat and gave them a smile that was soft and welcoming.

'Mr Templeton,' Amy replied with a smile and ignored the other man.

Beside her, she could sense Belle's confusion.

'We danced la Boulanger last night at Almack's,' Templeton supplied to remind her.

'And a Scottish reel last week,' Belle said, with a surprised smile.

She could not possibly be as surprised as Amy. The single sentence was more than Belle had spoken outside the family in ages.

'You remember me because I stepped on your toe,' he said, with a proud nod.

'Both times,' she said, nodding back happily.

There was a moment of silence as the gentlemen experienced the full effect of Miss Summoner's smile and were left dazed. Then Mr Templeton regained his composure. 'Last night, you left us so quickly I did not have the opportunity to introduce my friend, Mr Lovell.'

Belle's face registered her panic as she tried to remember the name and choose an appropriate response. In the end, she simply gave the other man a puzzled nod and another smile.

Amy had hoped an introduction to this scoundrel could be delayed until her sister had been directed towards an acceptable suitor. Now, she must pray that Belle forgot Lovell, as she did so many others who'd crossed her path so far this Season. Or perhaps he would realise that he was not wanted and simply go away. Amy gave him a frosty nod of acknowledgement. 'Mr Lovell.'

'Are you ladies enjoying your ride?' Was she mistaken, or was the smile Lovell offered to Belle more intense than the one he offered her? Given the plans she'd overheard, it was not surprising. It made no sense that Amy should care one way or the other about the lack of attention directed her way.

Belle was silent, but it did not matter. Amy was accustomed to speaking for both of them. 'We like it very well, sir.'

'We must not block the path with our chat,' Templeton said, still smiling. 'Miss Arabella, would you care to ride ahead with me and allow Mr Lovell to escort your sister?'

Belle gave her a look that was half-hopeful, and half-fearful. The larger the group, the more confused she became. But it appeared that she was accustomed to speaking with Templeton. Or, at least, she did not mind listening to him. Amy gave her an encouraging nod and offered Belle's reins to him as she manoeuvred her own horse backwards.

With a triumphant smile, Templeton took control of her sister's mount and the pair trotted a few steps ahead so they might converse in private.

Did she see a flicker of annoyance on Lovell's face at being so quickly cut out of his first conversation with Belle? Or was it merely a shadow from the leaves on a nearby branch? When Amy looked again, he was all pleasantness, as if it had been his intention all along to ride at her side instead. 'Miss Summoner?' He tilted his head, indicating that they hurry to catch up.

Amy slackened her grip on the reins and let her horse proceed at a leisurely walk.

Ahead of them, things seemed to be going well. She could hear Templeton droning on about something that evoked a delighted laugh from Belle. But between her and Lovell there was a silence that would have been uncomfortable had she wanted to speak to him, which she did not.

'It is a lovely day for a ride,' he said, when he was unable to bear it any longer.

'Yes,' she agreed. 'It is.'

'And that is a very…serviceable habit you have on today.'

She smiled. Next to Belle's her costume was hardly a fashion plate. When they went on these little outings, it was usually her job to manage both horses while giving Belle an illusion of control. But it left Amy little energy to fuss over her appearance. Her current ensemble was dark green and devoid of ornament, except for a muddy footprint at the hem that had been gained when she'd ridden too close to Belle's horse and scraped against the stirrup. Despite his excellent manners, Mr Lovell could not bring himself to lie and call it pretty.

'It suits me well enough,' she replied, staring down at a loose button on the sleeve.

'If I may be so bold as to suggest it, a little lace at the cuffs might be quite flattering.'

She snapped her head up to look at him. 'Are you a dressmaker, Mr Lovell, that you question the design of my clothing?'

'Merely making an observation,' he said blandly. 'Miss Arabella is most fetchingly attired. You cannot expect gentlemen to notice you if you insist on standing in your sister's shadow.'

Now she was not just looking at him, she was staring. 'If you mean to offer me insults in the guise of friendly advice, please refrain, sir. I am quite content with both my sister's popularity and my choice of attire.'

'And your lack of escort?' he said.

'Lack of escort?' She looked around, pretending surprise. 'Correct me if I am mistaken, but are you not escorting me at this very moment? Or is this some fever dream that I've concocted featuring a man I've just met?'

'You met me yesterday,' he reminded her. 'There was no formal introduction, of course.'

She gave him a blank look, pretending to forget.

'You spilled your drink on me last night at Almack's,' he prompted.

'Of course,' she said, giving him a smile that was as overly sweet as the lemonade had been. 'I apologised. And you said we would not speak of it again.'

He gave a dismissive shrug, as if to say the circumstances had changed now that he knew her identity.

'And it was two drinks,' she prodded.

He responded with such benign sympathy that it made her wish for a pitcher of the stuff so she might pour the whole of it over his insufferable head. 'It was not necessary to do that to achieve this meeting,' he said. 'I would have been more than willing to ride with you even if you had not wasted two glasses of lemonade on my new waistcoat.'

'You think I did that on purpose?' she said, outraged. Of course, she had done it on purpose. But somehow, he had got the idiotic idea that it had been a ploy to gain his attention.

'I think there are some young ladies who take naturally to society. And the *ton* rewards them for it.' He cast a brief, longing look forward at her sister, before turning back to her. 'While others, even though they are blest with many of the same gifts, lack a certain something.' He shrugged. 'Confidence, perhaps? That natural ease amongst people. As a result, they are quite unfairly overlooked by gentlemen when it comes time to marry.'

She bit her lip before she could blurt that her sister's inability to string two sentences together was not actually feminine wisdom masking some sort of magical self-assurance. It was as she'd often suspected: though some might call Belle a fool, it was the men chasing her who were the idiots. And she was speaking to their king. 'Suppose these poor, neglected unfortunates you describe are quite happy with their lot?' Her tone rose slightly. 'Perhaps, having met the gentlemen of London society, they would much rather remain single than spend the rest of their lives pretending an unworthy man is not just their equal, but their divinely ordained superior?'

Now she definitely saw anger in his eyes, but it was stifled almost as quickly as his earlier annoyance. He sucked in his lips for a moment, biting back the words he wanted to say, burying his true feelings. He was clever enough to think before he spoke. But it proved his amiable courtesy was little more than a thin veneer that might peel away if she continued to pry at it.

'Then…' he said, pausing again, 'I would say that…' another pause '…if they were truly content with their unmarried status, they would not find it necessary to giggle unceasingly, to flap their fans like deranged parrots and orchestrate accidents to call attention to themselves.'

'Accidents like this, you mean?' She brought her riding crop down in one swift motion, slapping the tip of it against his horse's flank with a force equivalent to a wasp sting.

The enormous grey obliged with an irate whinny and reared.

His rider, who had been far too occupied with whatever condescending response he had been composing in his head, lost his grip on the reins and landed on the tan-covered trail behind his horse.

A few heads turned to stare at the man sitting in the mud. But not nearly enough of them, in Amy's opinion. This minor embarrassment might go largely unnoticed if she did not help it along. 'Mr Templeton,' she sang out in a shrieking soprano. 'Oh, dear. Mr Templeton! Mr Lovell has fallen from his horse! Someone help him, I pray.'

'I am fine.' He stood to prove the fact, one hand in the air in a self-deprecating wave to show the mildest embarrassment. But she was close enough to hear shattered pride in each of the three words. He followed them with a wry smile and an admonition. 'Really, Miss Summoner. Do not distress yourself on my account. There is nothing to worry about.'

But the look he gave her said something far different.

You have nothing to worry about, yet.

Chapter Five

Ben stared out of the window of his rooms at the busy crowds below him on Bond Street, contemplating his future. Hopefully, it would be devoid of the humiliation he had experienced on yesterday's ride in Hyde Park.

He was an expert horseman, able to handle even the most spirited cattle with ease. But after five minutes of conversation with Miss Amelia Summoner he had been displayed before all of London society as a man who could not hold his seat on a walk down a bridle path. Worst of all, her sister had turned back to see him muddied and bruised. Her laughter at his predicament was a hundred times more painful than the fall had been.

If the experience in Rotten Row had gained him anything, it was proof that his friend Templeton was only partly correct in his assessment of Miss Summoner. Ben could see no sign that she was romantically attracted to him or anyone else. But it seemed that she was, in some way, obsessed with him. Her fixation bordered almost on mania. Could it be an untreated madness, or was there something he had done to set her off? He could not think what that might be. She had seemed set against him, even before an introduction was made. Perhaps she had chosen him at random to bear the brunt of her jealousy over her sister's success. Or maybe she simply hated men.

After ten years in the thrall of one, he was more than wary of the focused attentions of overly clever women. At first he had been drawn to Cassandra's intellect and aspired to become her equal. To be worthy of such a woman, a man had to strive for constant improvement.

The day had come when he'd finally been ready for the verbal fencing matches he'd dreamed of. He'd honed his wits to a rapier point only to discover she was wielding a stiletto. She had made him suffer for his impudence in believing he could ever be her master.

Never again.

Such women might make the best mistresses. Like the mote in Miss Amelia's eye, even their flaws seemed to sparkle with a tempting vivacity. But now that he meant to marry, it would be to the quiet beauty of an Arabella. It would be like coming home to a house filled with fresh flowers, each day. Just the thought of her smile made the tensions in his soul relax. After what he had been through, he deserved peace.

It did not matter what fate Amelia Summoner planned for him. He wanted no part of it. But in one thing, his friend Templeton, had been totally right. To gain the ultimate tranquillity of a life with Belle, Ben would need to douse the conflagration that burned in her sister. If the elder of the two became a member of his household, his life would be far more difficult than he wished it to be. There must be some man in London who could take her off his hands.

First, he must find a way to charm her out of the irrational antipathy she displayed towards him. Once a truce had been declared, perhaps, he could gain some insight into her character and find an acceptable match for her where Lord Summoner had failed. He took a moment to imagine the happy gratitude of that gentleman at settling a matter that no doubt weighed heavily on his mind. It would be one more thing that would smooth the way when Ben asked for his younger daughter's hand.

And there, on the street just below him, were the two women he most wanted to impress, admiring the bonnets in the milliner's shop opposite his rooms. The older woman who accompanied them, and who he assumed was their chaperon, was swaying slightly as the terrier on the leash in her hand strained at each passer-by.

Perhaps today he might make an impression on the pair of them without Templeton swooping in to monopolise Arabella. Ben gave a brief glance in the mirror to assure himself that his cravat and coat were spotless before racing down the stairs. At the door, he took only a moment to compose himself again, so that their meeting might seem a chance encounter on London's most popular shopping thoroughfare.

But in the moments it had taken to get from sitting room to street, his future wife had disappeared along with her keeper, leaving Miss Amelia and the dog as grim sentinels prepared to thwart his plans.

The girl glanced in his direction for only a moment, before turning back to stare at the shop window in a deliberate attempt to ignore him. The terrier, however, pivoted on the line holding him to give Ben's shoes a thorough sniffing. The little beast was uncommonly ugly for a lady's pet. It seemed to be made of the parts of a variety of animals, stuck together in a haphazard fashion by someone who had no clear idea of what a dog was supposed to look like. Its long body supported an enormous head and waddled along on hardly any legs at all. The whole of it was covered with a layer of unevenly cropped white-and-tan fur. When it had completed its investigation of his shoes, it looked up at him with an air of resigned embarrassment at its own appearance. It was then he saw that its eyes were no more coordinated than the rest of it. They were large as a bug's and mismatched in colour, one blue, one brown, like a ridiculous parody of the woman who controlled it. It ambled forward and flopped down upon his foot, giving him far more notice than its owner, who was still stubbornly ignoring him.

If he meant to join her family, he could not allow her to cut him on the street. He nudged the dog gently aside and stepped forward, smiling. 'Miss Summoner.'

He was sure he had spoken loud enough to be heard, but she remained purposefully oblivious.

'Miss Summoner,' he said more loudly to prove he would not be denied. Then he took his place beside her, trying to meet her eyes in the reflection of the glass.

She did not turn, still focusing on the goods displayed. 'You are not the gentleman you claim to be, Mr Lovell.'

Her words hit so close to the truth that his smile faltered and he bit his tongue to stop the question echoing in his head.

What have you heard?

She continued with the obvious explanation for her words. 'Surely you know that when a lady does not acknowledge you, you must not persist in trying to engage her.'

It was nothing. He was safe. He let out a relieved breath and shifted his leg to detach the dog, who was now sniffing the hems of his pants. 'Have I done something to offend you?' he asked, honestly curious.

'To offend me? No, Mr Lovell, you have not. But I would hate to spoil that.'

'Do not be glib with me, Miss Summoner.'

'I was not attempting to be,' she reminded him. 'I was attempting to avoid you.'

'But why?' Now he sounded like a petulant child. He gave her reflection another disarming smile. 'Is there a reason that we cannot have a friendly conversation when we meet on a crowded street?'

She gave him a governess's sigh of disappointment. 'Let us be honest, just for a moment. You do not want to speak to me, Mr Lovell. You wish to speak to my sister.'

Did she honestly think he would be rude enough to admit the truth? He glanced around him. 'Then I will be sorely disappointed. She is not here at the moment.'

'Because she has gone to Gunter's for an ice.'

He could not help himself. His head turned in the direction of the confectioner's shop, revealing his true motive. To hide his embarrassment, he bent down to pet the dog, carefully removing the sodden fabric of his pants leg from the animal's mouth. Then he looked down at Miss Amelia, all innocence. 'There is no reason I cannot speak to both of you.'

'Now who is being glib, Mr Lovell? Your desire to be all things to all people puts me in mind of a politician. Perhaps it is my father you should be talking to instead of Belle and me.'

Was the woman really so astute as to guess his plans, or were his motives transparent? Either way, if he denied it now, she would have reason to call him a liar when the truth became clear. He gave her what he hoped was a winning smile. 'I will take that as a compliment, Miss Summoner. I would consider it an honour to serve my country by standing for office.'

She responded to this with a shudder of revulsion that surprised him.

'I would think you, of all people, would have respect for public servants,' he said.

'Because of my father?' She let out a brief sharp laugh. 'I stand corrected, Mr Lovell. You are far too naïve for politics.'

If he was being naïve, it would not be the first time. 'Perhaps I am. But that will not keep me from seeking a seat in the House of Commons. It will do more good than harm to have members willing to effect changes

to benefit the common men our government supposedly represents.'

'A reformer?' Her brows rose, making her eyes seem
even larger. 'I can hardly wait for you to meet my father, Mr Lovell. He will eat you and your ambitions
for breakfast.'

Some small part of him quailed at the thought that a
man who might be so instrumental to his future could
end it before he'd even begun. But he had come too
far to quit without so much as an attempt, based on
the word of a woman who seemed almost desperate to
thwart him. 'Then I shall work to be so palatable that he
digests my ideas and makes them his own,' he replied.

For the first time, she looked at him with what almost appeared to be admiration.

Emboldened, he went on. 'And for your information, Miss Summoner, I do not consider myself a
reformer. The modern machines found in the factories
of the north have workers in an uproar. Soldiers who
loyally served their King and country return from our
wars missing limbs and with no means of supporting
themselves beyond begging. Society changes with or
without our help. We must be ready to guide it when
it does or the country will fall to ruin.'

She clapped her gloved hands in mock admiration,
causing the dog at his feet to release his leg and retreat
behind her skirts. 'Bravo, Mr Lovell. What a stirring
speech. But it was hardly necessary to give it to me.
The elections for the position you seek are, for the most
part, forgone conclusions.'

'The votes are controlled by men like your father,'

he agreed. 'But that does not mean I do not belong in government, nor will it stop me from trying to win your favour. Were you able to vote, perhaps you might agree with some of my positions.'

'Perhaps I would. I at least agree with your position that our country should be concerned with the welfare of the weak as well as the strong.' She shrugged dismissively. 'If I have grown cynical over the likelihood of that happening, it is the world and my father that have made me so.'

There was something in the unwavering and intelligent gaze she returned that made him wonder if he might be better off if Amelia Summoner could vote. Perhaps, if her quick wits were acknowledged and put to use, she would not be using them to bedevil the men in her life.

'Let us call a truce, then,' he said. 'I acknowledge that my behaviour has been abominable, demanding that you speak to me when you clearly did not want to. I should not have done so.'

At this, she turned to look at him and he saw the faintest shift in the fleck of her eye, as if deep waters had been stirred to give a glimpse of what rested beneath. 'And I had no right to mock your ambitions. They are noble ones, though I suspect they are doomed to failure.' Then the vulnerability was gone and she was just as hard and brittle as she always was. 'But that does not mean I will allow you access to my sister. You can want only two things in gaining an introduction to her.'

'Really?' he said, his apology forgotten and sarcasm coming to the fore again. 'Enlighten me.'

'You either seek a dishonourable liaison...'

'Dishonourable?' He blew his breath out in a great puff that would have been a curse if he had not been in the company of a lady. The terrier reappeared and gave a low growl to remind him of his manners. 'I can assure you I would never intend such a thing.'

'Then you are thinking of marriage,' Miss Amelia said, tipping her head to the side as she looked at him, as if observing some exotic creature. 'Since that is not to be, it hardly seems necessary for you to seek her out for a deeper acquaintance.'

'I have barely spoken to her yet. How, exactly, would you know that there is no hope?' he asked. Then he studied her just as closely as she did him. 'Are the lady's affections fixed upon another?'

'To the best of my knowledge, they are not,' she said. 'But the lack of a rival does not automatically make you a good candidate for husband.'

'Nor should it exclude me,' he replied, doing his best to be perfectly reasonable. 'I ask again, have I done something to make you set against a possible match?'

Again, he saw the movement in the depths. And again, it resulted in nothing. 'I know her. And I know you.'

'You hardly know me at all,' he reminded her. 'We have just met.'

'I know you well enough to see that you will not suit,' she countered.

He swallowed his denial. Could she really see past the façade so easily and know that he was unworthy?

'I know that you are exactly like all the other gentlemen of the *ton*,' she finished.

So it was nothing about him that she specifically disliked. 'Then you have a problem with males in general,' he said.

'Not at all.' She gave a slow, cat-like blink of her mismatched eyes. 'I merely think that you are ordinary. My sister will require the extraordinary.'

The last word touched him like a finger drawn down his spine. His mind argued that she was right. There was nothing the least bit exceptional about him. If she learned the truth, she would think him common as muck and far beneath her notice. But then, he remembered just how far a man could rise with diligence and the help of a beautiful woman. He leaned in to her, offering his most seductive smile. 'Then I shall simply have to be extraordinary for you.'

For Arabella.

That was what he had meant to say. He was supposed to be winning the princess, not flirting with the gatekeeper. But he had looked into those eyes again and had lost his way.

She showed no sign of noticing his mistake. Or had her cheeks gone pink? It was not much of a blush, just the barest hint of colour to imply that she might wish him to be as wonderful as he claimed.

In turn, he felt a growing need to impress her, to see the glow kindle into warm approval. Would her eyes soften when she smiled, or would they sparkle? And what would they do if he kissed her?

He blinked. It did not matter. His words had been a simple mistake and such thoughts were an even bigger one. They had not been discussing her at all. And now her dog was tugging on his pants again, as if to remind him that he should not, even for an instant, forget the prize he had fixed his sights on from the first.

She shook her head, as if she, too, needed to remember the object of the conversation. 'If you must try to be extraordinary, Mr Lovell, then you have failed already. You either are, or you aren't.'

He gave another shake of his leg, trying to dislodge the animal, and glared down at her. 'So you think a man who is not born as pure as Galahad is not worthy to marry into your family.'

'That is not what I meant and you know it.'

Then she had heard the lie everyone believed about his parentage, judged him by it and found him wanting. If illegitimacy shocked her, how distasteful would she find the truth? 'Is your view of the world really so narrow that you cannot acknowledge a man might rise above his birth and endeavour to improve his character when he sees deficiency in it?'

She glanced away from him, down the street towards the confectioner's shop where her sister must have gone. 'My view is not the least bit narrow. But I know for a fact that there are some obstacles that cannot be overcome by wanting, Mr Lovell. You are not the right man for my sister and that is that.'

He had been foolish enough to speak of his ambitions and she'd seemed to agree. But apparently he was still not good enough. Not for her or her precious sister. He gave her a pitying smile. 'While it is kind of you to want the best for her, perhaps you should let Miss Arabella choose her own husband and tend to your own future. If she is just down the street, there is no reason I cannot meet with her now and see what she thinks of me.'

'Don't you dare.' Amelia glared back at him, like a five-foot three-inch pillar of fire. 'Your fine and idealistic talk is nothing more than that, Mr Lovell. Nothing but words. And I will not have you making sheep's eyes at Arabella, only to abandon her when your conquest has been successful. Leave her alone or I shall set the dog upon you.'

The animal in question was still tugging at him, as if to emphasise his mistress's words. Ben gave a yank and heard cloth rip as his pants leg tore. When he looked down, her dog was holding a piece of his best pantaloons between its crooked teeth, tail wagging furiously as if he expected a reward.

For a moment, his temper got the better of him and he grabbed the scrap of cloth from its mouth, glaring at the girl who held the leash. 'Miss Summoner, if you cannot control this miserable cur, then you should not bring him out in public to trouble the rest of us.'

Miss Amelia looked down at the dog with a triumphant smile. 'Good dog, Mellie. You see him for what he is, don't you? A man who does not care one bit for our Belle. If he did, he would know that you are not a miserable cur. You are Belle's best friend in the world.'

Then she looked back at him, her smile disappearing. 'Belle has very few requirements of the men who court her, Mr Lovell. She has requested someone who likes both dancing and dogs. When you were at Almack's, a place where there is little else to do but stand up for a set, you did nothing but stand at the side of the room and speculate on others.'

'You cannot mean to judge me on a single evening,' he countered.

She gave no quarter. 'It is plain from your opinion of Mellie that you have failed in the second requirement as well.'

'I like dogs,' he argued. Perhaps not this one. But it was hardly the standard bearer of its kind. 'I like them as well as any man.'

'But they do not like you,' she said. 'And neither do I.' She gave a sharp tug on the leash and abandoned him to find her sister.

Chapter Six

Amy sat with her sister in the parlour of the Summoner town house, waiting for the maid to bring their tea. Their shopping trip that afternoon had been, for want of a better word, illuminating. To his credit, Mr Lovell had made no effort to hide his ambitions and his views did him credit. He would make an admirable politician and, perhaps, if he was not ground down by bitter reality, he would do the world some good.

The earnestness of his manner as he had talked of the future had come close to breaching the barricades she had created between herself and the masculine sex. Here was a man she might like to talk to and who was willing to treat her like something more than a silly girl who was Summoner's daughter.

And when he had looked into her eyes…

It was an autonomic reaction on her part, more biological than rational. He was pleasant to look at and quick witted. When he turned his full attention on her, it was only logical that she became flustered. If his plans had involved her and not her sister, Amy might even have liked him.

But they did not. He wanted Belle. And Amy had only to look at their father to know that a politician would be the worst type of husband for Arabella. The eyes of such men were ever on the horizon and their minds were fixed on the future. It left no time or interest for the problems in their own homes, right under their very noses.

To his credit, he was persistent. She doubted he was ready to concede. In another man, such unwavering devotion would have been a virtue. But his cold-blooded approach to courtship ruined everything. Her attempts thus far had done nothing to put him off. She must have a better plan in place before their next meeting.

She glanced over at her sister and smiled. 'How is your needlework coming?'

'It is done.' Belle handed her the handkerchief she had been hemming, picked up Mellie from his place on the floor at her feet and scratched his ears.

Amy glanced at the row of uneven stitches, then moved it over to her pile to rip and redo.

'I tried,' Belle said, more to the dog than to anyone else. Then she gave Amy the worried, frustrated look that she sometimes got when forced to do a thing that was beyond her ability. 'Is it good?'

'You did your best.' Amy gave her an encouraging smile in return and watched as her sister's brow unfurrowed. She had tried. But years of watching had taught Amy her sister's limitations. It did no good to try and push her past them.

'I don't like sewing,' Belle said, gathering the terrier in a hug and being rewarded by a lick on the nose.

Amy nodded sympathetically. 'You must try, for Father's sake. He says it is important that young ladies know such things.'

'Maybe my husband will know how to sew,' Belle said, using her embroidery scissors to trim the stray locks of hair that were obscuring Mellie's mismatched eyes.

Amy sighed. It would be far easier to find a man in London capable of sewing a button that did not immediately fall off than to teach Belle to do it. 'Instead, we will find you a husband who does not care who does the mending.' Then a thought struck her. 'And, in case he should ask, I do not think you should marry Mr Lovell. When I saw him on Bond Street, he had holes in his trousers that needed fixing.'

'I do not know how to do that,' Belle said, frowning.

'Neither do I,' Amy assured her. Short of turning them into knee breeches, she suspected the aforementioned garments were a total loss. In gratitude, she took a biscuit from the plate on the table between them, tossed it to Mellie and added, 'Also, he did not like dogs.'

'Then I do not like him.' Belle frowned. 'Which one is Mr Lovell?'

The fact that he had already been forgotten made Amy regret introducing him into the conversation. 'The man who fell off his horse in Hyde Park.'

Belle smiled. 'He looked very funny.'

Amy toyed, for a moment, with the idea of reminding her sister that it was not kind to laugh at the unfortunate. Then she answered, 'Yes, he did. And you must trust me to know what is best for you. You would not be happy married to a man like that, even if he is funny.'

Now her sister's lips pursed, ever so slightly, as she tried to imagine what it might be like to be unhappy. All the more reason that Amy must care for her. While she might have no trouble imagining circumstances that were less than ideal, Belle really had no idea what that would be like.

After a long pause, Belle spoke. 'I think I would like to marry Mr Templeton.'

The words came as such a surprise that Amy stabbed her finger with the needle. She jammed the injured digit into her mouth, to forestall a response until she had chosen the correct words.

Belle took advantage of the silence to tell her more. 'Mr Templeton has no holes in his clothes and has promised to bring a ball for Mellie when I take him to the park.'

Amy pulled her finger out of her mouth and shook the sting from it. 'Mr Templeton is a fine gentleman. He seems very pleasant.' He was also near the top of her list of candidates and seemed to enjoy her sister's company even though he must have some clue by now as to her difficulties.

Belle smiled and patted her dog. 'The next time I see him, I will ask him to marry me.'

This resulted in another missed stitch and poked finger. 'You will do no such thing.'

'Why?' Belle was staring at her with wide, guileless eyes, probably fearing that she was to be scolded for yet another thing she did not understand.

Amy took care to moderate her tone and smile, as she delivered her explanation. 'Ladies do not do the asking.'

'I am better at talking than at sewing,' Belle reminded her.

'Yes, you are. All the same, you must wait for Mr Templeton to decide that he wants to marry you. If he does, he will ask you. Then he will talk to Father about it. And then...'

Her sister's eyes were beginning to glaze, lost in the many steps between her and an absolutely perfect solution.

Amy reached out and patted her hand. 'Your way would be easier, but it is just not done. Do not worry. I will help you discover his intentions and it will be settled in no time at all. Perhaps we will see him tonight, at the Middletons' musicale.'

Lord and Lady Middleton's entertainments were a favourite of Belle, who loved anything to do with music. But since they were usually concerts with no dancing, the crowds tended to be smaller, older and more sedate than those at Almack's. Guests sat for the majority of the evening in rigidly arranged gilt chairs listening to the musicians before partaking of the cold supper at midnight. If the Summoner girls left early, there was little time for conversation, which worked to Belle's advantage. And by careful selection of seating, Amy was able to control her companions.

Tonight she seated Belle on the aisle and near the front. From there, her sister would have a clear view of the soprano performing and no gentleman would dare drag a chair to sit on her opposite side without calling undue attention to his actions and blocking the way for others. Amy took the seat on her other side, watching the door for the appearance of Mr Templeton. She meant to hold the place until he arrived. Then she would find an excuse to go to the ladies' retiring room, yielding the chair to him so he might spend the rest of the evening beside her sister. It would be far easier to encourage the right man than to battle a slew of wrong ones.

The performance was almost ready to begin. Lady Middleton was talking to the accompanist and Belle was facing front, printed programme clutched in eager hands, ready for the first song. But despite Lord Middleton's assurance that he was expected, there had been no sign of Mr Templeton.

Amy was almost ready to give up when she heard a commotion in the hall and the sound of a man's voice, apologising for his lateness. It was him! She touched her sister's shoulder in apology and was out of her seat and halfway down the aisle before she realised the truth.

Mr Lovell stood in the doorway to the room, scanning the crowd for an empty chair. By leaving hers, she had played directly into his hands, all but saving the perfect seat for him. Past him, she heard the sound of another latecomer. Certainly, that was Mr Templeton. If it was not, any other man would be a better companion than the one she had been trying to discourage. What was she to do?

She continued forward blindly, pretending she did not notice him, though she could see through the lashes of her downcast eyes that his mouth was open, ready to greet her. When she was barely an arm's length away, she feigned a swoon.

His fingers closed around her upper arm in support catching her before she collapsed. 'Amelia.' His urgent whisper of concern sounded surprisingly sincere.

'Please,' she whispered back. 'Help me from the room. The air is so close. The heat…' It was neither warm nor stuffy in the music room. If anything, she was glad of her shawl. But he had not been there long enough to notice, nor did he show any signs of questioning her distress.

Instead, he maintained his grip on her arm, turning to add a gentlemanly hand at the centre of her back as he escorted her from the room. A footman who was dealing with Mr Templeton's hat and stick leaned in, ready to help.

Amy waved him away with a gloved hand and then gestured to the other late arrival. 'Please, Mr Templeton,' she said, fluttering her lashes as though struggling to remain conscious. 'See to my sister. She is alone at the front of the room.'

Mr Templeton hesitated, ready to help her instead.

She shook her head and, as they passed him, she gave a sharp jerk of her head to indicate that he go immediately to the place he really wanted to be. Then she followed it with an annoyed roll of her eyes to the man at her side.

Mr Lovell was too busy ushering her forward to notice this silent communication. But clearly, Mr Templeton understood. He responded with a slow smile and a nod of thanks before turning towards the music room so he might take her unoccupied chair.

Now that he was settled, she must figure out how to free herself from the situation she had created with Mr Lovell. It was a large house. Large enough to hide a body in, she thought with a grim smile. She need do nothing as dire as that. She just had to find an empty room with a key still in the door, or a chair that might be propped under a handle to detain this troublemaker.

'I will find someone to help you.' He looked around. 'A maid, perhaps.'

'The ladies' retiring room,' she said faintly. 'If you could escort me there, I am sure I will be fine.' She raised a limp hand and pointed down a corridor that the servants had not bothered to light.

'Are you sure?' he asked, confused. 'I would have thought…upstairs, perhaps…'

'I have been here before,' she assured him. 'I know the way.'

He did not question further, but shepherded her in the direction she had suggested, towards the perfect spot.

When they drew abreast of it, she reached across his body and gripped the handle, turning it and giving a sharp, sudden tug to open the door beside him. At the same time, she staggered into him, pushing him off balance and through the darkened opening.

He had time for one brief, surprised curse as he realised what was happening. Then he grabbed her by the shoulder and carried her body along with his. They lurched together over the threshold, as the door slammed shut behind them.

Chapter Seven

It had been a grave miscalculation.

Amy had had a vague recollection of the Middleton house, from previous visits. The door she'd thought she was choosing opened on to a small card room. It was well away from the rest of the house, but hardly uncomfortable.

Perhaps she should have turned right instead of left. The door she'd actually opened was for a cupboard. Now she was wedged chest to breast with Benjamin Lovell, in a space that was never meant to hold one person, much less two.

There was a moment of silence in the darkness punctuated by the sounds of their laboured breathing. Then he said in a low voice, so near to her ear that she could feel his breath moving her hair, 'Why, Miss Summoner, I had no idea you cared.'

Her own breath hissed out between her teeth as she stifled a dozen possible responses, all of them caustic. But it was her fault that they were here. It would only make things worse to snap at him.

Carefully, she fumbled for the door handle behind her, preparing to back out into the hall. Then, if possible, she would find a way to pretend this never happened. Her fingers closed not on metal but on his hand, which was wrapped around the handle and holding the door shut. She jerked her hand away. Even through her gloves, the nearness of his skin was dangerously exciting.

Amy unclenched her jaw, forcing herself to breathe slowly through her nose instead of her mouth. That did no good at all, for it flooded her senses with the intoxicating scent of the man beside her. She had not noticed his cologne when they had been in public, for it was subtle. Now she was drifting on a cloud of lime and laurel that was as soothing as it was intriguing.

She took another breath, through her mouth this time, and did her best to ignore it. 'Do not flatter yourself, Mr Lovell. You know my reason for trapping us here.'

'Really, I have no idea,' he said in a dry voice. 'Enlighten me.'

There was nothing to do but be honest. 'I did not wish you to sit beside Belle. The place was saved for someone else.'

'And rather than allow her to tell me so, you took it upon yourself to lock me in a closet,' he said, making her plan sound all the more illogical.

'We are both in the closet,' she reminded him. 'And the door is not locked.'

Behind her, the door rattled but did not open. 'On the contrary.'

'It cannot be,' she whispered, praying that he was wrong.

'Why not? That was the fate you planned for me, I'm sure. You planned to lock me in here. Then I would have to hammer on the door, interrupting a performance and embarrassing myself in front of my friends, all because you did not wish me to sit next to your sister.'

'I did not intend…' It was a lie. That was exactly what she had meant to have happen. Even if the man was a puffed-up bounder, she should have found a way to put him off that did not involve his total humiliation.

'I'm sorry,' she said at last. 'Not that it will do any good in the current situation.'

He sighed. 'Too true. I suppose we will both have to call for help. If we are loud enough, they will hear us over that canary they have screeching in the main room. Someone will come and open the door. It will cause the devil of a scandal when they find us together. But I am afraid it cannot be helped.'

'Please, do not.' She raised a hand to cover his mouth. This was far worse than letting him speak to Belle. What had she been thinking to allow herself to be trapped by him?

He took advantage of the opportunity to nip her fingers. Rather than painful, the pressure of his teeth through the white kid leather was shockingly pleasant. Hurriedly, she pulled her hand away again. 'Stop that.'

'Do not do this. Do not do that.' He tsked. 'Did you not wish to ruin my chances with Arabella? Being caught playing hunt the squirrel with her sister would most assuredly do so.' In the darkness, she imagined his mocking smile.

'I did not mean to do it by ruining myself as well.'

'Are you sure? If you wish to trap a husband, there is no quicker way to do it than to force him into such a compromising position.' The hand that had been holding her arm was stroking the bare skin between sleeve and glove. Suddenly, she felt as light-headed as she had pretended to be a few moments ago.

'For the last time, I do not wish to wed anyone. Most especially not you.'

'Then perhaps this is the sort of dishonourable liaison you spoke of on Bond Street. Maybe I am the one in need of rescue,' he said, his voice hoarse. 'It would be better for both of us if we were discovered immediately.' His hand stroked down her arm until her glove pooled at her wrist. Then he continued to her fingertips to pull it away, leaving her hand bare.

'What are you doing?' she whispered, though she was sure she knew. Even worse, she did not mind.

'Taking a forfeit,' he said, raising her hand to his lips again. 'You might think it amusing to play childish tricks with me, Amelia. But I am not some green boy put on this earth to be the butt of your joke. If you play games with a man, you must prepare for what will happen when you lose.'

He was right. It had been foolish of her to push this man to the point of anger. Even more foolish to become trapped with him in a situation that could lead to ruin for both of them. Suddenly, she was all too aware of the size of him and the feel of his body, hard against hers. She should at least have the sense to be frightened. Instead, she held her breath, eager to know what came next.

He pressed his mouth to her palm and she felt the tip of his tongue following the lines on her skin. She had once been to a gypsy who claimed to read one's future there. It had been nonsense, of course. The old woman had proclaimed her destined to a long and lasting love based on an unbroken wrinkle of skin.

But now, Mr Lovell was running his tongue along that very line, his lips creating a gentle suction. His teeth were teasing the flesh that the fortune teller had called the mound of Venus. She had hinted at a carnality that Amy and her school friends could not understand, though they had giggled over it at the time.

But today, she was sure she knew what had been meant. The pressure of those straight white teeth made her bite her own lip to keep from crying out.

She should do the sensible thing and pull her hand away, with some cutting remark about his unwilling attention. But she made no effort to move. It must be shock. Nothing more than that. She should not be enjoying this.

He took her inaction as permission to take more liberties. His other hand came up to cradle hers to his mouth and he bit down hard enough to make her jump. Then he turned it slightly, settling his lips over the web of skin between thumb and forefinger.

She gasped and yanked her hand away. 'What was the meaning of that?'

'I should think the meaning plain enough,' he said,

in a voice that was annoyingly calm. 'As long as we are trapped in a cupboard together, we might as well find a pleasant way to pass the time.'

'You flatter yourself if you think I am enjoying this,' she said, though her breath came in gasps that proclaimed she lied.

'Then I must be doing it wrong.' The hand that had been on the door handle was now cupping her bottom. 'Is this better?'

Infinitely so. But Lord knew what would happen if she admitted the truth. 'If·you need a woman to correct your technique, there are houses full of them in Covent Garden. I suggest you go there and leave proper young ladies alone.'

'I am not normally prone to such assignations. I certainly do not indulge in them at public gatherings. I am very conscious of my reputation.' He sounded puzzled by the statement, as though he needed to make the sort of maidenly assertion she could not think to make. 'Apparently, I'm more conscious of my rep than you are of yours.' This was followed with a pinch that made her jump forward, pressing herself even tighter to his body.

'I know perfectly well that this is improper,' she said. She put her hands flat on his chest, meaning to push him away. Instead, the fingers of her ungloved hand found the opening of his shirt, dragging a nail along the bare skin. 'It was never my intention to be in here with you.'

He sighed. 'I suppose that is as close as I will get to an apology. You must give over these attempts to separate me from your sister. I will meet her eventually, you know. And speak to your father as well.' Their lips were separated by a bare whisper of air. She could feel the imminent kiss, like the flutter of a moth's wing against her face.

'I only mean to forestall you until a worthy gentleman makes his move,' she reminded him. Perhaps, once he knew he had lost, things might be different between them. Or perhaps they would change right now. She opened her mouth, ready to yield.

But no kiss came. 'A worthy gentleman?' The air around him seemed to chill with a dangerous silence. 'What, exactly, is it about me that you find objectionable? Is it my character? I make sure that it is exemplary. Is it my birth? Because that does not seem to bother the rest of London.'

It was because she had thought him cold and demanding, when she'd overheard him at Almack's. He had been anything but cold, a moment ago. And under certain circumstances, demanding could be quite nice. 'It is more than that,' she said, searching for an explanation that did not insult. 'A match between you would be disastrous for all concerned.'

'You mean it would be a disaster for you,' he said. 'Since you are so free with your opinions of my character, let me enlighten you as to yours. When she marries, you intend to hang on your sister's skirts and burrow into whatever home she makes like a tick on a dog's back. Since you know I will not allow it, you cannot abide me.'

He thought of her as a parasite on her sister's happiness? And just now, she had been ready to... 'How dare you.'

'How dare I?' he said in a tone of mock outrage. 'With complete confidence, Miss Summoner. It is the common view of society that you are nothing more than a frustrated spinster. You had a horrible Season and no man would have you. Now you mean to spoil your sister's come out as well.'

'I am not frustrated,' she retorted, before she could stop herself. She owed this man no explanation. 'My Season was not horrible.' It had been a sometimes delightful lesson in what men expected from women. She had survived it informed but unscathed. But her sister had a desirable body, a docile temperament and no understanding of the consequences of flirtation. If they were not very careful, she would not be so lucky. 'And Belle should not be out at all.' She bit her lip, for she was dangerously close to speaking the truth.

'Jealousy,' he said, satisfied.

'I am not jealous.' At least, she hoped she wasn't. It was not as if she had sought out Ben Lovell's attention. But why did life seem so much more exciting when she had it, and so disappointing now that she knew what he really thought?

'That is a shame.' He rested a finger on her cheek like a Judas kiss. 'If it is not that, then I must assume that, based on what you have heard of my past, your problem is nothing more than snobbery. In my opinion, pride is an even greater sin than envy.'

'You are too quick to assume the worst in me, Mr Lovell. It is not conceit that keeps me from helping you. It is that…' How could she explain without ruining her sister's chances with another? 'Belle is a special.'

'And I am not,' he finished for her, wilfully misunderstanding. 'You think I am all right for a tussle in the dark, of course. But not good enough to marry your sister.'

'We are not…tussling,' she said. Not yet, at least.

'Well, let me inform you of the truth, Miss Amelia, since you are so quick to assume you understand me. Despite what people might think, my birth was as legitimate as yours. Perhaps my pedigree would not be to your liking. But I have come far in life and mean to go further still. I will do it with or without the help of your family. At the very least…'

He reached behind her and she heard the click of a door handle that had apparently been unlocked all along. 'I have the sense to discover facts for myself and not assume the worst, just because I was told something by another. Good evening, Miss Summoner.'

And with that, he was gone, leaving her to retrieve her fallen glove and slink off to the retiring room to regain her composure.

Chapter Eight

In the carriage on the way home, Ben stretched his feet in front of him, staring at the toes of his boots as Templeton yammered on about the evening from the seat opposite.

'Normally, I prefer lighter fare. A sprightly tune on a decent pianoforte. Something that one can hum the next day. But tonight's soloist wasn't half bad.'

Ben grunted in response. When he'd finally made his way to the music room, he had been too wrapped in his own thoughts to notice the entertainment.

'It is a shame you missed the first few songs. There was an absolute cracker with high notes that rattled the windows. It was in Italian, I think. I had no idea what she was saying. But still…'

He doubted Templeton had heard a word of what was sung, being far too preoccupied by the lovely lady at his side during the performance. From his seat in the last row, Ben had watched the pair of them, heads tipped towards each other, bobbing in time to the music.

The only saving grace of the evening was that there had been no repeat meeting with Amy Summoner. Miss Arabella had needed to depart immediately after the concert because Miss Amelia had taken ill at the beginning of the evening and stayed in the retiring room so as not to spoil her sister's enjoyment of the music.

Ha! When he'd heard the excuse, he'd wanted to shout to the whole room that, unless being green with envy was a debilitating condition, Amy Summoner was as right as the rest of them. She was simply hiding in the retiring room, waiting for the best time to reappear and ruin her sister's evening.

And his as well. His sole purpose in going to the event was to court the sweet and innocent Miss Belle. Instead, he'd spent the whole evening brooding over a woman who was as tempting as Circe and twice as dangerous. What had he been thinking to shut himself up in a cupboard with her? He'd have been safer climbing into the tiger cage at the royal menagerie.

'Of course, if I had spent the evening making my own music, I doubt I'd have missed it.' He looked up to find Templeton staring at him with a knowing smile.

'What the devil are you talking about?' he said, daring the man to answer.

'You were absent from the room for several minutes after we arrived. I assumed it was because of a clandestine meeting with a member of the fair sex.'

'Do not talk rot.' Under his bluster, he felt the beginnings of panic. Who else had noticed his absence? What conclusions had been drawn?

Templeton took a deep breath. 'So the lingering scent of cologne I detect means nothing?'

Ben gave him what he hoped was a quelling glare. 'If you smell something, it is probably that bay concoction I picked up from Floris.'

Templeton gave another sniff. 'Definitely not. And it is not the lavender scent that Miss Arabella wears. I think what I smell is called Florida Water. Imported. Light, but exotic.'

Ben deepened his glare. 'Since when have you become an authority on ladies' colognes?'

Templeton raised his hands in denial. 'Not an authority, dear fellow. The scent is distinctive. Few wear it. In fact, only one woman I can think of.'

It was a warning then. If he walked about London reeking of Amy Summoner's cologne, no one would believe his sincerity in courting her sister. 'If you are speaking of Miss Amelia, she most likely spilled it on me during one of her many assaults upon my person.'

'I am sure that is it,' Templeton agreed with a smirk. 'But would it be such a bad thing if it were else? She is Lord Summoner's daughter and you are intent on marrying into the family. Your affections are not still fixed upon Miss Arabella, are they?'

'Have I given you reason to think otherwise?'

Templeton shook his head in amazement. 'I should think the fact that you have spent no time with the girl, in public or private, is an indication.'

'It is not for want of trying. Her perfume-spilling sister is doing her best to prevent it,' he said. 'Once I have got her out of the way, it is only a matter of time before I win Belle's favour.'

'I see.' If Templeton saw anything, his tone implied that what he saw was something quite different from Ben's vision of the future. 'As long as you are not wasting time with flirtation. It would reflect poorly on you if you were romancing one girl while seeking to marry another.' It would be even worse if the girls were sisters. Templeton did not have to say it for his meaning was plain.

'I know better than to do that,' he said, wishing it was true. Perhaps a peer could risk playing such dangerous games. But a man with no real rank and a dubious past might destroy his future trading kisses in closets.

Templeton nodded. 'Men have *known better* since Eve tempted Adam and the results are always the same.'

'Miss Amelia is not tempting me,' he insisted. At least, she was not trying to. As far as he could tell, his response to her presence was his own fault. 'And she is not fascinated by me as you suggested at first. She loathes me.' If she hadn't before, she most certainly did after he called her a frustrated spinster.

'That is a shame,' Templeton said, with a sympathetic nod. 'The pair of you seem to be very well suited.'

Ben laughed. 'She is proud, obstinate, domineering and far too clever for her own good.'

The silence in response implied that he had proved his friend's point.

'It does not matter what you think,' Ben said, ignoring the insult. 'My plans have not changed, nor has my opinion of Amy Summoner. She is a curse upon humanity.' Though she'd shown every sign of wanting to dally with him in private, she did not think him good enough for anything more than that. He'd had a lifetime's bitter experience with women who adored in the dark what they would not acknowledge in daylight. He did not need more of it from her.

More importantly, he did not need to tell her any more secrets. He could not even blame the hypnotic effect of her eyes. She had goaded him to revelation with a few choice words. 'No,' he said firmly. 'I want no part of Amy. But Belle Summoner is a different matter entirely.'

'She is, indeed, very different,' Templeton agreed. 'And yet, the pair of them are inseparable. Have you decided where Miss Amelia will sleep when she moves into your home after the marriage? As I recall, there is a blue bedroom at the end of the hall with a lovely view of the garden.'

And there was a cupboard for linens just around the corner from it. At the thought, Ben could feel the tips of his ears flushing pink with embarrassment. 'She will be in her own home, with her own husband by then.' Even if he did not succumb to another mad impulse and kiss her, the brief interlude they'd already shared would make his life hell.

'You have plans for her future?' Templeton leaned forward, surprised.

Unbidden, his mind returned to the brief encounter in the cupboard and the feel of her hand against his mouth. How would her lips have tasted? Would she have even wanted him had they been discovered and scandal forced their hand? And what would happen between them if another opportunity for privacy presented itself?

And none of that had been what Templeton had meant by plans. 'She will be married before her sister,' Ben said, vowing that it would be true. 'I do not know to whom. But I will find the man and make the match if I have to drive them to Gretna myself.'

Then, perhaps, he could have some peace. Amy Summoner was, by turns, irritating, intriguing and enchanting. It was unnatural that such a woman should be alone. For her sake, and the preservation of his sanity, a match must be made.

Now they were home and getting ready for bed, it should be possible to relax. Although Amy had seen very little of it, tonight had been a success. Belle had spent the whole evening with Mr Templeton. Ben Lovell had been thwarted yet again in his desire to meet with her.

But she must be more careful in the future. After the few minutes spent with Mr Lovell, her nerves had been frayed to the point where she had been ready to forfeit her own reputation. It was fortunate that he had taken her dismissal of his suit so personally. Because they had begun talking about Belle, he had left angry and far sooner than he might have.

But when it had been just the two of them, alone in

the dark and talking of nothing, things had been moving quickly towards a point where they would not have been talking at all. The feel of his kiss on her hand and his touch on her body would be her companions in bed for many nights to come.

Perhaps, when Belle was properly married to Mr Templeton, Ben Lovell might notice that there were other women worthy of his attention. There might even be one in the family he sought to join.

And if pigs flew it would not make them birds. Delightful as it was to be alone with him, she would never be anything more than his second choice. If she decided to marry at all, it should be to a man who loved her above all others. But feelings might change, with time. And it was not as if Ben Lovell had ever really loved Belle.

Then the familiar feelings of guilt rushed in to settle the matter for her. She should not even consider the possibility of her own marriage until she was sure that Belle's future was assured. There were some things more important than personal happiness. Married or unmarried, her sister was unable to manage without help and it was Amy's responsibility to care for her.

'Did you enjoy the music tonight?' Amy set aside the handful of pins she'd removed from Belle's hair and reached for the comb, dragging it through her blonde curls.

'It was pretty,' Belle said, smiling at her in the mirror.

Amy smiled back and uttered a silent prayer that

the risk she had taken was not in vain. 'Did you enjoy the company?'

Her sister's face went blank.

'Did you like sitting next to Mr Templeton?' Amy said.

'He said I should call him Guy.'

This was progress. 'What did you say to him?'

'I told him he had a funny name.'

Amy winced. 'And what did he say to that?'

'He said it was a funny name. And he said my name meant pretty.'

This was much more encouraging. 'He is calling you Belle, now?'

'That's my name,' her sister agreed, unaware that such familiarity had meaning.

'Did he say anything else?' Amy held her breath.

'We were listening to the singer.' Belle gave her an impatient look to remind her that a concert was no place for conversation.

'Of course.' It was probably too soon to hope for a proposal, but Amy could not help it. She did not know how many more meetings with Mr Lovell she could stand. The man was both unbearable and irresistible.

'Did you have a nice time with Ben?'

Amy fumbled the comb, nearly dropping it. 'What makes you think I was with Mr Lovell?'

'You were not with him,' Belle said, smiling in surprise that her sister could not understand a simple question. 'Guy said I was not to worry about you because you were with Ben.'

'Of course.' Mr Templeton had seen them in the hall. She must hope that no one else had.

'Who is Ben?' Belle fixed her with a bright-eyed stare.

'He is not who I thought he was,' Amy said absently. He might seem cold, but he was not without passion. He was ambitious, but if he meant to better the world, it was a virtue, not a vice. And he was not illegitimate. Had he ever claimed to be a duke's bastard, or did the world jump to a conclusion that he did not correct?

But if he was not Cottsmoor's son, then who was he?

Chapter Nine

To say that Ben did not like the hubbub of Vauxhall Gardens did not do justice to his feelings on the place. More accurately, he did not want to like it. It was enjoyable, in a plebeian sort of way. If he wished to be seen as the sensible sort of politician who could lead a nation, he suspected a pleasure garden should be beneath notice.

But somewhere beneath the polished façade he'd cultivated, the simple youth he had been before meeting Cassandra was near to fainting with excitement at the prospect of a visit. There was music and dancing. Madame Saqui walked on a wire far overhead as balloons rose and fireworks lit the night sky. Try as he might to be aloof and sophisticated, how could he resist?

It was also a place where pretty, young girls wandered about, loosely chaperoned and eager to test boundaries that could not be breached under the watchful eye of Almack's patronesses. It was a perfect place to separate Arabella Summoner from her overprotective sister and persuade her that, despite what she might have heard about him, he was the answer to a maiden's prayers.

But, as usual, the younger of the two Summoner girls was eluding him and the elder was all too easy to find. As he moved through the crowd and conversed with friends and acquaintances, he asked discreet questions about Belle's location. It seemed everyone had seen her just a moment ago. He remained perpetually one step behind.

And each time he stopped to reconnoitre Amelia was there, smiling in triumph. He would not be surprised to find that she was herding her sister around the grounds specifically to keep them apart. Amy Summoner had far too much time to meddle in the business of others. She needed some occupation other than arranging her sister's life.

And after the interlude at the Middletons' house, he had an excellent suggestion for her. He closed his eyes for a moment, reminding himself that she was the last person in the world he dare dally with. She could ruin his future with a single word to her father. But closed eyes only reminded him of discovering her secrets by touch when they had been shut up together in the dark.

If it been anyone else in the world, he'd have allowed himself to explore the depths of this fascination. Like the boy who longed to see fireworks, there was a part of him that could not seem to resist her. And though she might be too ladylike to admit to it, she was as eager as he was to see where another meeting might lead them.

All the more reason that he should find her a husband. He opened his eyes again, keen to dispel the fantasy with cold, hard truth. She was far too volatile for his tastes. She took far too much pleasure in tormenting him. And judging by her comments about his insufficiency, she would destroy him as a matter of principal, should she find out the truth about his past.

But a woman so warm and vibrant should not remain single. It was not just a nuisance, it was a waste. He could not abide wastefulness. How hard could it be to change her future? Her wits were quick enough and she was not unattractive. In fact, it was her exotic beauty that had first attracted his attention. If others did not see it, then her family name should have been enough to attract suitors like flies to a honey pot.

And yet, she had none. If he applied masculine logic to the situation, she would be married in no time. He would likely win the favour of Lord Summoner for taking the girl off his hands. And once she belonged to another, maybe he could stop thinking about her and return his focus to the more agreeable of the two sisters.

It was simply a matter of finding the right candidate to partner her. He glanced around the crowd, searching for a match, and found one almost immediately. Stanton Haines was walking towards him, balancing a stack of paper-wrapped ham sandwiches in his folded arms.

Ben calculated silently. Haines had a new phaeton and matched bays and a coat cut by the finest Bond street tailors. His apartments in Jermyn Street were decorated in the height of fashion. His winters were spent at his family estate, which was at least equal to the Summoner home. Ben suspected he must have close to ten thousand a year and more to come upon the death of his father.

Best of all, he was still single and claimed to be looking for a wife. In Ben's opinion, if the search had gone on for several years, Haines was not looking hard enough. The man was clearly in need of help. He put on a welcoming smile and raised a hand in greeting. 'Haines, old fellow.'

'Lovell,' his friend responded with a smile. 'Care for a sandwich?'

'They are all yours?'

'There is hardly enough meat in them to make a decent meal. I thought to combine it and throw the bread to the ducks. But I could spare one.' He eyed Ben suspiciously. 'You always have a hungry look about you.'

If this was meant as a jibe at his ambition, Ben would let it pass. 'Why not share with a young lady instead? Surely there is one here who would be better company than a duck.'

At this, Haines laughed and Ben put a guiding hand on his shoulder, pushing gently in the direction of the prey. 'You are already acquainted with Miss Summoner, I suppose.'

The other man's eyes took on the glazed expression that Ben often saw when conversation was turning to Miss Arabella. 'I have not. She is dashed hard to meet, you know. Her family guards her like a princess in a tower.'

'Surely not,' Ben answered, deliberately misunderstanding. 'I was riding with her myself, just the other day.' He paused, waiting for the good-natured ribbing that would follow had Haines been aware of his very public fall in the mud, but it did not come.

Instead, he said, 'You rode with her?' There was a proper amount of awe in his companion's voice at the achievement.

'I will introduce you, if you like.' He added a generous smile. 'Perhaps she would like a sandwich.'

'Yes. By all means, let us see if she is peckish.' Now Haines was not so much being led as pulling in his harness, eager to go forward.

Ben shepherded him towards the pavilion where he had last seen Amelia. 'There she is now. Miss Summoner,' he called out, and the girl turned slowly to face him.

'Damn.' The legs of the man next to him locked and he dug in his heels like a stubborn mule. 'I thought you meant… Damn.'

But it was too late for him to change direction without being unspeakably rude. Ben pressed on, forcing the man the last few feet. 'Miss Summoner, how nice to see you again. Are you enjoying your evening?'

'Mr Lovell,' she said. The knowing smile she directed to him suddenly disappeared. 'I had been enjoying it.' The words left the clear implication that her pleasure had come to a sudden end upon seeing his companion.

'Have you met my friend, Mr Haines?'

'Yes.' If her greeting to him had been chilly, her acknowledgement of the other man was positively glacial.

'Miss Summoner,' Haines answered, with a shallow bow, never taking his eyes from hers, like a man facing down a wild animal.

'Mr Haines was wondering if you would care for refreshment.' He jabbed a sharp elbow in the other man's ribs, causing him to drop the top sandwich from the stack.

She looked down at it as if it was poison, then back up to stare at the two of them. 'No, thank you.'

'Well, then,' Haines said, with a sudden, relieved smile. 'I must go and ask someone else.' He shook Ben's hand from his shoulder, turned and left the two of them to an awkward silence.

She was staring at him now, and Ben wondered if it was her basilisk gaze that had put Haines off his game. Guy Templeton had claimed to be disturbed by it as well. Though it was threatening, he could not see what they found so troubling in it. Perhaps they felt the same desire he did, to stare back and study her as closely as she seemed to be studying him.

It was rude to stare, he reminded himself. And after their last meeting, showing this woman any interest at all sent a message he did not want to give. He did his best to change the stare into a surprised blink. 'Well, that did not go as well as I'd hoped.'

She responded with a raised eyebrow. 'What, precisely, were you hoping for, Mr Lovell?'

'Merely to broaden your acquaintance. I think it is a shame that such a pretty girl should have so few male friends.'

'Suitors, you mean,' she said, still not smiling.

'Perhaps no one wants to spend time with a frustrated spinster.'

There was no point in pretending their last meeting had not happened, if she meant to throw his hasty words back in his face. 'I apologise. I should not have said such a thing.'

'Even if it is true?' she said, finishing his thought.

'As I told you before, it is not.'

'But it surprises me that your sister receives so much attention, while you receive none at all.'

Instead of drawing her into a wistful admission of disappointment, she laughed. 'Do you talk this way to all the girls, Mr Lovell? You truly are new to the marriage mart, to say such things.' She added a coquettish flutter of her fan, as if to cement her disguise as just another silly girl.

He knew her too well for it to work. Her actions were as calculated as his were. 'I was merely matching my statement to your behaviour, Miss Summoner. You are a surprisingly blunt young woman.'

She nodded. 'Then let me use that candour to enlighten you. First of all, I am not moved by your obvious flattery. I will not apply false modesty and deny that I am passably pretty. But neither will I pretend that Belle is not my superior. I might be pretty, Mr Lovell, but my younger sister is a goddess.'

It was true. And said without a trace of the envy he expected to hear in such a statement. 'But some men do not want to worship at the feet of perfection. A goddess can be haughty and distant, not the warm flesh-and-blood woman who makes for a good…helpmeet.' What was he saying? He had been about to suggest something totally inappropriate for a conversation with a lady. Even worse, he had forgotten his purpose in talking to her was to gain the hand of that same goddess he was now denying.

If she had noticed the pause, she did not acknowledge it. 'If you knew Belle, you would discover that she is not the least bit distant. She is as human as the rest of us and as sweet tempered a creature as God ever put on this earth.' She gave him another arch look. 'That is why we are so careful in her company. I would not see her taken advantage of.'

'Of course not,' he agreed hurriedly. 'But though concern for your sister is admirable, it is a shame that she overshadows you.'

'I do not find it so,' she said. 'Because it is not true. Last night you assumed my Season was a failure. But you were not in London for my come out, Mr Lovell. I assure you, I received more than enough attention. In fact, I entertained the suit of your Mr Haines for several weeks.'

'You knew him?' By Haines's shocked reaction, it had been obvious that he knew of her. But Ben had assumed that it had been the same mock-shuddering response Templeton had given him and not based on actual familiarity.

Then he noticed the glint of nostalgia in her eye.

'What did you do to the poor fellow?'

'No more than he deserved.' The glimmer had become a twinkle of amusement.

'Let me be the judge of that. What did you do to him?'

'Would it not be better to ask what he did to me?' she said, now smiling with evil glee.

'Probably not. I did nothing at all to you at Almack's. We had not even been introduced. Your assault on me was unprovoked.'

The look in response to that was pointed and the fleck in her eye no longer seemed to dance. It glowed amber with accusation. 'You did nothing? Think again, sir.'

Had he done something to upset her? She seemed to think so. But what could it have been? He could not remember even hearing her name before the moment she dumped her lemonade on him. 'We were not speaking of me,' he said cautiously. 'But if you insist on it, I will ask the question in a way that is most likely to get me an answer. What did Haines do to you that caused you to respond in a way that left him so wary of you?'

She nodded in approval, as though he were a particularly smart pupil and she the tutor. 'I made my come out two years ago and he was one of the more promising suitors.'

'You had more than one?' It was rude of him to doubt the fact. Had he not just acclaimed her exceptionally pretty?

She responded with the sort of coy pout he'd have expected on any of the playful misses flirting by the pavilion. 'More than two, as well. I will make you a list, if you wish. It will save us both the trouble of you making introductions to people I already know all too well.'

'That will not be necessary,' he said, suddenly afraid to ask how many men had tried and failed to win her.

'But as I said, at one time, Mr Haines was a favourite.'

'Of yours?'

'Simply a favourite. But on an evening much like this, he lured me to the dark walks and attempted to take liberties.'

'He tried to kiss you.' This was quite at odds with the awkward spinster he had been imagining.

She gave him a disappointed look. 'You tried to kiss me, Mr Lovell. Mr Haines tried to take liberties,' she repeated in a flat tone that made it quite clear she set her bounds of personal propriety well past a simple peck upon the cheek.

He was not sure if he was horrified or impressed. 'And I assume you were discovered. Was there was a scandal?'

She laughed. 'No on both counts. You should know that after our rendezvous at the Middletons' I have no intention of being forced by scandal to marry a man I do not respect.'

He was not sure which stung worse, her glib dismissal of their last meeting or the slight on his character. Did the woman have no heart at all? Then he remembered that it did not matter if she cared for him. She was not the woman he wanted.

She snapped her fingers in his face. 'Really, Mr Lovell, contain yourself. You are gaping at me like a beached cod.'

He gave a brief shake of his head to regain his senses. 'I apologise, Miss Summoner. I was shocked because I thought, for a moment, I was speaking with a normal young lady. Do go on.'

There was a brief flash of those exceptional eyes to tell him that his answering shot had struck home. Then she continued. 'As I was saying, I had no desire to marry Mr Haines and he had no desire to explain to all of London that the bruise he received did not come from Gentleman Jackson.' She laid a finger on her cheek beside her nose.

'You blacked his eye?' His shock changed to awe. 'I should consider myself lucky to have escaped from the cupboard unscathed.'

'You only kissed my hand,' she said.

But what a kiss it had been...

'And a simple *no* did not dissuade Mr Haines,' she continued. 'He was most ardent. Should he claim to you that I broke his heart, it is an exaggeration. His feelings were no more engaged than mine were.'

At this, he hardly knew what to think. 'Were you in the habit of trifling with men's affections, Miss Summoner?'

She gave another flutter of her fan. 'Some mutual trifling might have occurred. I was poorly chaperoned and had no mother to warn me against flirting. Since my father left me to the care of servants when Mother passed, it was most foolish of him to think he could reappear when I was old enough to marry and put strictures on my behaviour.' While he saw no bitterness in her when she spoke of her sister, her feelings for her father were far more readable. At the mention of him, her lips thinned, her jaw tightened and the spark in her eye went so dark as to almost disappear.

'He was fortunate that you did not ruin yourself to spite him,' Ben said.

'Perhaps so. But that was long ago, Mr Lovell, and no real harm was done.' Mischief returned to the eyes peering at him from over her fan. 'Now, I am older and wiser and have charged myself to be sure no one takes similar advantage of my sister.'

Was it meant as a warning? It certainly seemed so. 'Once again, I assure you, Miss Summoner, that my intentions in that direction are nothing but honourable.'

'Honourable?' She lowered her fan to show there would be no dissembling between them. 'At Almack's, I heard you give high praise to my father and hardly a word for my sister. You had decided, since she was the prize of the Season, she would increase your stature. If that is all you care for, then you are not worthy of her.'

And that explained the lemonade. 'You should not have eavesdropped,' he said, though it was far too late to scold her on it.

'And you should not have said things you didn't want heard.' The fan returned and there was another flutter. 'It does not speak well of your judgement, Mr Lovell. Nor does it make you a suitable husband for Belle.'

Amy's opinion of him had been ruined before he'd even gained an introduction. But that did not mean his plans were hopeless. 'You should let Miss Arabella be the judge of her own heart.'

'Or my father?' The fluttering stopped again. 'Because my father is the person you really wish to please, is it not, Mr Lovell? Since he left the raising of Belle to me, it should not surprise you that I claim the right to approve her husband. I have been both mother and sister to her for the whole of her life.'

He had been wrong about her from their first meeting, flattering himself that she pined for him or assuming that she needed help to correct her character and find a husband. She was totally in control of her heart and her future and had set both aside for the sake of her sister. And from the first moment they'd met, his behaviour had been a textbook example of what not to do to gain her approval.

He held his hands up in a gesture of surrender. 'I have no choice but to apologise again for my behaviour. You are correct. It was reprehensible. I should not have spoken of my plans regarding a lady, especially not in a public place. But I hold firm in my belief that I would make a fine husband for your sister, despite what you might think of me. No man is perfect, Miss Summoner.'

She lowered her fan and studied him carefully, as if trying to decide whether to change her opinion. Then she shook her head. 'I am not seeking a perfect man for Belle, Mr Lovell. I am seeking one with the correct set of flaws.'

The conversation grew more curious the longer it continued. 'Tell me what you seek that I may mould myself into that man.'

Her eyes widened in surprise. 'Your character sounds exceedingly malleable.'

And once again, he was nagged by the desire for confession that sometimes took hold of him as he looked into her eyes. Did she really deserve to know just how changeable he was? He shook off the urge. 'Any man's character must be changeable for the better. But my heart remains constant.'

'Oh, I believe that, Mr Lovell. Your heart, if you have one at all, remains fixed on your own needs and desires. Since you have barely met Arabella, do not try to convince me that it is set on her.'

His needs and desires were synonymous with Arabella, since she was a means to an end. Put thus, even he could see how cold it was and how unworthy it would be in the protean eyes of the woman in front of him. Perhaps it was the straightest path to gain the power and admiration he wanted. But was it the right way?

Easiest was not always best. He knew from experience that what seemed pleasant often came with a price. It was one thing if he suffered. But suppose Amelia was right and her sister's future would be better with someone else in it? At the very least, the situation deserved more thought than he had given it.

'Miss Summoner! Miss Summoner!' The stout older woman who had been with the girls in Bond Street was hurrying down the path towards them, a look of panic on her reddened features.

'Miss Watson?' Amelia turned to her, instantly alert.

'Miss Belle is missing.'

Chapter Ten

Belle was lost.

Amy struggled to take her next breath. It felt as if she'd been holding it for a lifetime. But that could not be. Everything had been normal, only a few seconds ago. Then, suddenly, her lungs had turned to iron and her throat had become a narrow glass tube that would shatter at the first gulp of air.

It had been her job to care for her sister. Her only, her most important job. And just as she had known some day she would, she had failed. Had Belle wandered away? Had someone taken her by force? Or had she been coerced?

It would take little more than a smile and the promise of a dance to lure her away from her chaperon. On a starry night, in a pleasure garden full of secret grottos and dark paths, anything might happen to her. Amy knew from experience that not all men who claimed to be were gentlemen and protected herself accordingly. But Belle was as innocent as a babe.

And Amy had wasted the evening sparring with Benjamin Lovell. It was a mere pretence that talking to the man had been about protecting her sister and not the pleasure she felt in a battle of wits. If she had truly been thinking of Belle, she'd have been at her sister's side and not indulging in distractions. Then she would not have disappeared.

What was she to do now? Miss Watson was frantic and she herself could barely manage to speak, much less to act. She turned to scan the crowd, eyes darting so fast between faces that she could not tell one from another. So many people and so many places to look. What was she to do?

'We must find her. Before…'

A hundred possibilities flashed through her mind, each more awful than the last. Before she could stop herself, a whimper of desperation escaped her lips.

'Really, Miss Summoner. We are in Vauxhall Gardens, not Whitechapel. A few moments' absence is not the end of the world.'

'But Belle is my responsibility,' she whispered. 'If anything happens to her…'

Mr Lovell held up a hand. 'Say no more.' He turned to the chaperon, his voice calm but commanding. 'Where was she when last you saw her?'

'By the trained dogs.'

'And where have you been so far this evening? Was there any spot she was loathe to leave that she might have returned to alone?'

'She likes dancing,' Amy managed at last.

'Then, Miss…' Mr Lovell gave a pointed look to the chaperon.

'Watson,' Amy supplied.

'Then, Miss Watson, please return to the pavilion to check the dancers. If you do not find her there, proceed systematically towards the east. We will search west and enlist any friends we find along the way to help us. We will find her in no time, I am sure.'

His voice was like a soothing balm on Amy's nerves. On some level, she had always enjoyed the rumbling bass sound of it, as he had argued with her over every small thing. But now it was even and calm. With each word it loosened the grip of the panic that had taken her.

He reached out to take her arm. 'Come, Miss Summoner. Do not distress yourself. Let us locate your sister and set your mind at rest.'

For a moment, she hesitated. If she accepted his help and they found Belle in some unfortunate or compromising situation, would he use it to his advantage?

He sensed her misgivings and answered the question she hadn't asked. 'Let us worry over our previous conversation at a later time. For now, we must locate Miss Arabella. It is probably nothing, you know. In any case, I am the soul of discretion and you are in need of a friend.'

'Thank you.' She felt the last of her fear dissipate, replaced by confusion. She had always longed for a friend to share some of the burden of caring for Belle. But she'd never have thought such aid would come from Benjamin Lovell. Now he was leading her deeper into the park, stopping at each attraction to search the people assembled there.

'How old were you?'

'I beg your pardon?' He was looking ahead of them into the crowd and his question had seemed to come from nowhere.

'How old were you when your mother died?'

'Five,' she said, equally distant. She had been so small. But Belle had been even smaller. From the first moment she'd seen her, Amy had known that the tiny baby with the blue-tinged skin was in need of protection.

'Ten,' he muttered in response.

She tightened her hand on his arm, waiting for explanation.

'I was ten when my father died. Old enough to remember what it was like before I was forced to become man of the house.'

'I am sorry,' she said, in response to the familiar pain of loss she recognised in the words.

'But you were not much more than a babe yourself. Where was your father in all this?'

'At first, he was lost in grief for our mother. But when Parliament was in session he had the business of governance. We were too young to come to London for the Season. We were left in the country.'

'And you took it upon yourself to be sure that things ran properly while he was gone,' he finished. 'You cried yourself to sleep at night, didn't you? And woke each morning afraid to leave your bed, lest this be the day you failed in your mission and everything fell apart.'

'How did you know?' she whispered.

He answered with the sad smile of someone who had spoken from experience. 'I slept better after I went to live at Cottsmoor. In time, there were new things to disturb my dreams. But when I was removed from their cause, the old fears subsided.'

'Are you are suggesting that I let her go?' Amy said slowly. 'I do not know how.' Though she wanted to resist, the idea of gaining her own freedom was more seductive than any man had been.

'When she marries, you will have to,' he said.

But that had not been the plan. She was not going to abandon her sister. She just needed someone to share the duties. If there was a man she could talk honestly to, who understood Belle's difficulties and was clear-headed in crises, her life would be much easier. After talking to him tonight, it seemed that Benjamin Lovell might be just the husband she had been looking for.

The husband for Belle, she reminded herself. For a moment, she had lost sight of the goal altogether. Mr Lovell wanted to marry Belle and had just won her approval. But now that she had remembered it, why did the future feel so empty? Had she grown so used to defining her existence around the care of her sister that she could not imagine how to live life for herself?

Or was it because she took personal pleasure in leaning on Ben Lovell's arm as they searched the park? She did not wish to marry him or anyone else. He was not the first man who had flirted with her. Whispers in darkened cupboards meant nothing to either of them. And though admirable, his help and concern tonight was no more than she'd have expected from any honourable gentleman.

But in her heart, she wanted it to be more. It was likely proof that she was becoming the frustrated spinster he'd accused her of being. None of this mattered if Belle was lost. She must not be wasting energy speculating when there were more pressing matters to attend to. She scanned the crowd, searching for a familiar face. 'We have been to the acrobats, the supper rooms and down the colonnade, but no one has seen her. Where could she have gone?'

'I think it is time that we look in the areas that are not so well lighted,' he said, in an offhand manner.

It was exactly the place she most feared to find her sister. With their dim, winding pathways, the dark walks of Vauxhall were a notorious meeting place for young lovers. More than one gentleman had suggested the place to her during her first year out. Some had even succeeded in taking her there. But even then she had been far more worldly than Belle and knew when to call a halt to straying hands and lips.

She swallowed her dread. 'Let us go, then. Quickly.'

He patted the hand in the crook of his arm. 'Are you not afraid of what people will say, should they see us there together?'

'They will probably assume you are taking your life in your hands,' she snapped. 'But I do not care what they think, as long as they do not suspect the truth.'

Despite the seriousness of the situation, he chuckled. 'Take heart, Amelia. If you have the presence of mind to be sarcastic, things cannot be too dire.' Then he led her forward, out of the light.

It was just as she remembered it. The hundreds of lanterns that hung in the trees over the rest of the park became a distant glow that disappeared once they passed the first curve in the path. The only light remaining was the glimmer of moonlight filtered through the trees above them. They paused for a moment so that their eyes could adjust to the darkness. But now he was the one who hesitated and she was the one to tug his arm to lead him forward.

'A moment, please,' he said, still rooted to the spot, 'while I decide how best to go on.'

She snorted. 'You act as if you have never been here before.'

There was a profound silence from the man at her side.

'Really, sir? Do not tell me...'

'If one wishes to kiss a pretty girl, it is not necessary to drag her into the bushes,' he said, irritably.

'Nor is it necessary to drag her into a closet,' she replied.

'You instigated that encounter,' he reminded her. 'You have more experience here, as well. Do not try to claim I was a bad influence upon your character. From my standpoint, the opposite appears to be true.'

Before she could frame a retort, she heard her sister's voice, calling her name, far too loudly.

'Amy?' Belle appeared around the next bend in the

path, smiling broadly and oblivious to the impropriety of discovering or being discovered.

'Shh.' Amy held a cautioning finger to her lips.

By her sister's puzzled expression, Amy was about to be peppered with loud questions about the need for silence.

Amy touched her lightly on the arm to reassure herself that all was well. 'The birds are asleep in the trees. We do not want to wake them.'

Belle nodded in agreement.

'Why did you leave Miss Watson?'

'It is easier to see the fireworks in the dark,' Belle replied.

There was more than a little logic to that. But agreeing with her would not get Belle to safety. 'It might be hard to see them through the trees. You will miss the balloon launch as well.'

Belle blinked. 'I would not want to miss that.'

'Perhaps I might be of assistance.' And now Mr Templeton was there, polite as always, offering his arm to Belle. 'May I escort you to the fireworks grounds, Miss Arabella?'

'That would be most helpful,' Amy supplied, not giving her sister a chance to refuse. Then she paused. When Templeton appeared, had he come from the lighted park behind them or from further up the dark path? She puzzled over it for only an instant before deciding that it was a matter that could be discussed at home, if it was discussed at all. 'But please, Belle, first you must go and find Miss Watson and tell her you are all right. She is at her wits' end.'

Belle looked distraught at the thought that she had caused trouble.

Mr Templeton gave her a brief, encouraging smile and then replied, 'We will find her this instant and set everything to rights. Come, Miss Summoner.' And then they were gone and Amy was alone in the dark walks of Vauxhall, with Benjamin Lovell.

For a moment, they stood silent, listening to the rustling of the wind in the leaves and the occasional whispers and sighs of couples alone in the dark. When she gathered the nerve to speak it was to state the obvious. 'Well, we have found her.'

'Safe and sound, just as I promised.' In the dim light, she could see his supremely confident smile.

Belle had not been alone. But it did not seem to bother him. 'Will you keep our secret?'

He touched her shoulder. 'I saw nothing out of the ordinary tonight.'

'Thank you. And thank you for your kind words as we walked.' Perhaps relief made her foolish. Perhaps it was the moonlight. Or perhaps it was simply that she wanted to do it. But before she could stop herself, she was up on her tiptoes and leaning forward to press a kiss on his cheek.

He responded without hesitation, turning his head so their lips met. There was an instant where she might have withdrawn, pretending shock where she felt none and ending the kiss. Instead, their mouths opened on one another's and their tongues tangled in a frenzied caress. It was everything she'd hoped it would be.

His hands took hers and lifted them, wrapping

them around his neck. Then he clasped her around the waist and pulled her off the path, deeper into the undergrowth. Despite the darkness, the worry of a few moments before burned away like morning mist in the first rays of sunlight. She wanted to strip herself bare and bask in the heat of that sun until it had touched every part of her body.

His hand rose again to touch her cheek. Then it stroked down to grasp a breast and squeeze it possessively.

She whimpered with desire and writhed against him, eager to follow the moment where it led.

He answered with a shaky sigh. 'From the first moment we met, you have been a hazard to my peace of mind, Miss Summoner.'

'Amy,' she whispered back.

'Amy,' he said and touched her lips with his again.

'And do you value your peace?' she asked as he rained desperate kisses down her throat.

'I am learning to do without it,' he said. Then he pulled away, setting her gently back on her feet. 'But I had best not lose my common sense as well. If we are gone any longer, someone will miss us.'

She doubted the truth of that. When she had been younger and trying to shock, no one had noticed what scandal she was courting. Now, if she was gone, anyone who might care would assume she was doing some sensible thing that needed doing. No one would guess she was trading kisses in the dark with Ben Lovell. She sighed and straightened her gown. If she meant to lecture her sister on propriety, she had best not flout it herself. 'Very well. Take me back to the pavilion, Mr Lovell.'

She paused, waiting for the invitation to use his given name.

None came.

Chapter Eleven

The next morning found Ben in the receiving room of the Summoner town house. Even though he was unobserved, he forced himself to stand at the window, facing the street as if admiring the view. Despite the purpose of the room, it was doubtful that Lord Summoner would come to him. More likely a footman would come to lead him to an office or study. In either case, he would not be caught pacing about the room like a caged animal. No hint of nervousness must spoil his first introduction with the one man in London he most wished to meet.

Assuming that it had not been spoiled all ready. The invitation had arrived with his first morning post, written by the great man himself and not some secretary or underling. But there was nothing in the brief note to indicate a purpose for the meeting.

So here he stood, resolutely still, trying not to focus on the most likely scenario. If someone had seen him leaving the dark walks with Amelia, word might have got back to her father. If so, he had been summoned to give an account of himself. Either he was about to be warned off or Summoner would expect him to make the offer that a gentleman should.

On reflection, he was surprised to realise that little pressure would be necessary to bring him to accounts. Though Templeton had suggested that one daughter was much like another, marrying Amelia had never been a secondary course of action, should he fail to attain the primary goal of Arabella's hand. Though his reasons for marrying were rational and analytical, it seemed too callous to swap sisters like cravats, when the first knot failed.

But now? When he thought of Amy, he was dangerously close to an involvement of the heart. Even worse, his body clamoured for a more intimate match and the sooner the better. When they were alone together, he was possessed by an earthy, primal attraction that he did not feel when looking at the ethereal Arabella.

Even now, when he should be in terror of the meeting about to occur, he could imagine torn and scattered clothing, and frenzied thrusts while staring down into passion-drugged, mismatched eyes.

It was settled, then. Her father's permission, one simple question to the lady, three weeks to read the banns and he could begin acting on that passion with vigour and frequency.

At the thought, he reached for a handkerchief to mop a drop of cold sweat from his brow. He had but to look at his own past to remember why one did not trust heart and groin to make important decisions. Though it all might end well, the path to success was lined with tumult and heartache. Ranked in a lifetime of female acquaintance, Amy Summoner scored a close second in the administration of pain and suffering.

It had taken years for Cassandra to break his heart. Last night, after one kiss from Amy, he'd been ready to let it shatter all over again. If he took her to bed, it would be the death of reason and free will.

But what a glorious, hero's death it would be. Despite what one promised at the altar, it was not really necessary to love when one married. He respected her and he wanted her. That was more than enough. He would give anything else she required of him, but he would keep possession of his heart.

A footman interrupted his thoughts and led him down a long hall. It ended in a heavy oak door that stood open, ready to receive him. He passed through it to find Lord Geoffrey Summoner seated at an enormous desk in front of the window. He was sifting through the stack of letters before him, deliberately oblivious to the man he had invited for a meeting.

Ben refused to let himself be fazed by it. Instead, he stood before the desk, waiting patiently to be acknowledged.

After a few seconds, he looked up and Ben bowed. 'Lord Summoner.'

Summoner responded with a smile that was both warm and genuine, as if he had actually been looking forward to the visit. 'Mr Lovell. Please, sit down.'

He indicated the chair before the desk and Ben sat. 'How good to see you. Does the day find you well?'

'Indeed, my lord.'

Summoner steepled his fingers. 'And I suppose you are wondering at the purpose for the meeting.'

Ben gave a brief nod and smiled back at him. 'If there is something you require of me I am at your service.'

'Require of you...' Summoner smiled again, drumming his fingers against each other as if he had a surprise that he was not ready to reveal. 'I am merely interested in seeing if you are half the man my friends seem to think you. At White's they speak well of you.'

'I am glad to hear it, my lord.' He was far more than glad if it meant that his indiscretion with Amy had not been discovered.

'You are thought to be moderate in all things, intelligent, well spoken and wealthy enough to be your own master.'

Ben gave another nod of modest acknowledgement.

'And you are in search of a wife,' Summoner finished.

Ben blinked in surprise and prepared to revise his previous assumption, then gave another, hesitant nod.

Summoner cleared his throat. 'I have a daughter...' He paused. 'Two daughters, actually. Both unmarried.'

Ben blinked again. There was still no indication of censure in the man's tone that might hint at knowledge of how well he already knew Amy. Instead, it sounded rather like Summoner meant to arrange a match himself. Finally, he nodded. 'I have met them both. They are lovely girls and do you credit, my lord.'

Summoner let out a relieved breath. 'Thank you,

Mr Lovell. It does a father's heart good to know they are admired. But as I said earlier, I want to see one of them in particular settled with a man I can respect.' He gave Ben a long appraising look. 'Everyone I know speaks well of you. You have the means to care for her and the ambition to make a bright future from what you have already been given.'

Fraud. Upstart.

Ben silenced his doubts and responded as a man of his position would be expected to. 'That is my goal, sir.'

'Then I see no reason why we shall not both have what we wish.'

At this, Ben blinked twice. Of all the scenarios he had imagined for his future with the Summoner family, being approached by the father and solicited to court the daughter was not one of them. Was the man really so doubtful as to Amy's chances of success that he was willing to barter her away? 'Your blessing on my suit sets my mind at rest,' Ben said cautiously.

'On your suit?' Summoner gave a short laugh. 'You have my consent to a marriage, Mr Lovell.'

Even though it had been his plan to ally with the family through marriage, things were moving too fast for comfort. 'I have not yet spoken to the lady on the matter,' Ben reminded him. 'There is no guarantee that she will have me.' It was far more likely that she would hand him his head for settling matters with her father before proposing.

Summoner gave a dismissive wave of his hand. 'When you do, you will find her in agreement. Young girls are far too flighty to make such decisions based on their hearts. And she truly is the most obedient of children. When I tell her that you are my choice, she will agree without argument.'

For a moment, Ben could not manage to respond at all. It had been his plan to take only the first step. But it appeared that he had all but completed his journey to the altar. And after that—

The older man interrupted his reverie. 'There is also the matter of a settlement. As I understand it, you do not need my money. I have little land, other than the house in the country, which is entailed. But I control two seats in the House of Commons. They cannot very well be given to my girls.'

He paused to laugh at the idea of women in office. But Ben saw it for what it was: a carefully structured pause to build drama for the offer he was about to extend.

'You seem like a bright young fellow. Have you considered standing for office?'

Though he had seen it coming, it still took effort to hide his amazement. He had gone to bed dreaming of the future and woken to find his future was made. He answered with as much composure as he could manage, 'Indeed, my lord. It is my fondest wish to serve.'

Summoner nodded. 'A noble ambition, to be sure. Then we are in agreement. Welcome to the family, Mr Lovell.' The man stood and offered his hand.

Ben rose as well, giving it a firm shake. 'Thank you again, my lord. I will endeavour to exceed your expectations of me. And I will do my utmost to make your daughter as happy in the future as you have made me today.'

'Excellent.' Summoner stepped from behind the desk. 'I am so glad to have the matter settled and so early in the Season. Social events are tiresome for Belle and I had no wish to put her through more than was necessary to secure a match.'

'Belle?' Had they discussed the identity of the bride to be? Or had he just assumed he knew it?

'We call her that at home,' the other man said, misunderstanding his confusion. 'Arabella is a beautiful name, but so formal.'

'Of course,' Ben answered, his mind still racing to catch up.

'We call her elder sister Amy for the same reason,' he said. 'Sometimes I worry that there is power in the names we give. Amelia always struck me as an excellent name for a spinster. And my Amy has grown adamant that she will never marry. Many men have tried, but there is no changing her mind.'

How many men? And just how hard had they tried to persuade her? It would be naïve of him to think that a woman with a passionate nature and the sense to be discreet would deny herself pleasure if it was offered. It was obvious, after their discussion last night, that he was not the first man to have kissed her. It was unlikely that he would be the last.

'You are certain she will never marry?'

'She's refused more than one offer,' Summoner assured him, 'and has been most adamantly opposed to men I've suggested for her. I suppose I should be thankful that she has not run off with a dancing master, or some such foolishness. If she means to spite me, remaining respectably unmarried pales in comparison to actively courting disgrace.'

Her devotion to her sister outweighed any desire to elope to spite her father. Once Belle had married, perhaps she would consider it. Or would she return to one of the suitors she had already rejected? In either case, Ben doubted she would want him once she knew he had Lord Summoner's approval. And if he truly did not want to involve his heart in his marriage, it might be wise to take the perfectly lovely daughter being offered to him and not the one who raised such conflicting and uncontrollable emotions in him. 'I have heard that Amelia intends to follow her sister to her husband's house,' he said, cautiously.

'Perhaps that is her intention,' Summoner replied. 'But I have no plan to indulge it and neither should you. My daughter can refuse to marry if she wishes, but it does not entitle her to live off her sister's husband under the guise of sisterly devotion.'

'I am glad to hear you say it, my lord.' If he meant to wed Belle, he could not be staring at those disquieting eyes and luscious lips for the rest of his married life. Even a wife who did not expect total fidelity from her husband would not stand for an affair inside the family. Nor did he want to give himself up to a woman who might be tempting him now, just to spite her father.

'And if I am honest, Belle is far too influenced by her sister,' Summoner said with a worried frown.

That might explain why she had been in need of

rescue the previous evening. She had only followed the bad example of her sister. 'I am sure Miss Amelia regrets any harm she might have done,' he said. This, at least, was true. Amy had been genuinely distraught at her sister's absence and unwavering in her devotion.

'Once we have separated the pair of them, you must be Belle's guide in all things. It is your duty, as husband. I trust that you will have a care for her, sir. Simply have a care.' There was a slight tremor in the older man's voice that spoke of barely controlled emotion.

'Of course, I will care for her. With all my heart,' Ben added. Or some of his heart, at least. The poor man was feeling the loss of his daughter already. It could do no harm to hint at more affection than he felt for the girl. He would generate it easily enough, after he actually spent some time with Belle and they'd discussed the wedding between them without Amy or her father there to organise the matter for them.

'See that you do, my son.' Summoner paused again, his face becoming suddenly grave. 'After you leave this room, there will be no turning back from the matter.'

'I have no intention of it,' Ben assured him.

'No intention? That is hardly enough assurance for me. Men intend many things. But how many actually follow through?'

Was Summoner now having second thoughts? It did not matter. With the ultimate goal in sight, Ben would not allow himself to fail. 'I cannot speak for other men, Lord Summoner. But when I intend to do a thing, it is as good as done.' If he could tell the man just how far he had come on intention alone, he might actually be impressed. Then he would throw Ben from the house for being an upstart imposter.

'Would you be so kind as to swear to the matter?' Summoner turned away and walked to the nearest bookshelf. When he turned back, he was holding what appeared to be the family Bible. He set it down on the desk between them.

'Of course. But...' Was it truly necessary?

'I would not normally be so demanding. But Belle is...special.' There was the choke in his voice again, as if he could not bear to be parted from her.

Even so, if a man gave his word, an oath should not be required. But if a man's life was based on lies, then did he truly have honour to swear on? It was a question that he'd asked himself many times over the years. But today was not the day to search for the answer.

Summoner sensed his doubts and pushed the book towards him. 'Swear to me, that, from the time you leave this room until the end of your life, there will be no second thoughts and no regrets at your haste. Swear you will do nothing, no matter how small you might think it, to hurt my daughter.'

'As you wish,' Ben said and laid his hand down on the leather cover. 'I swear before God that I will care for your daughter and do only what is best for her.'

Summoner nodded. 'Very good.' He laid his hand down as well to cover Ben's. 'For I swear, if you break this oath, so shall I break you. You have a bright future in front of you, Boy. But if you hurt my child, embarrass her, disgrace her, or do anything to sully her reputation, there will not be a scrap of hope left in you, once I have finished with you.'

The threat was made with such conviction that Ben wanted to snatch his hand away in denial. But it did not matter what he wanted to do. It was already too late to change his mind. The man had said no retreat and he had promised.

Since the prize was Belle Summoner, it would not be a hard promise to keep, as long as he stayed far away from Amelia. And once she realised she was free of her responsibility for Belle, she would not be a spinster for long.

It would take a particularly brave man to stand up to both her strong will and her protective father. But he should not be brooding on it. That woman's future was no longer his concern. She could kiss as many men as she liked, in Vauxhall or a cupboard. Since she was not to be a member of his household, he need never know of it.

Considering how much the prospect of Amelia kissing other men annoyed him, the less he knew about it, the better.

Chapter Twelve

❧❧❧❧

When Amy awoke the morning after Vauxhall, the sun was surprisingly bright and the sky an unusually clear shade of blue. Her breakfast chocolate was delicious as well. The song of the sparrows on her window sill was so delightful that she raised the sash and rewarded them with the last of the crumbs from her toast. Fortunately, she was too practical to mistake the reason for her euphoria.

Benjamin Lovell had kissed her.

It had been almost three years since the last time she'd been kissed. Was that long enough to forget how it had felt? She remembered those early kisses as awkward, wet and messy. When her beaus had felt confident enough to risk a caress, she had been more annoyed by it than aroused. They always seemed to be holding her too tight, or not tightly enough.

And to a man, they had seemed to enjoy the whole thing more than she had. They'd sighed and moaned, and swore that they would not eat or sleep until next they held her in their arms.

In return, she'd felt nothing in particular. She had grown good at dissembling, for it hardly seemed polite to tell them she felt no matching ardour. If she was doing it wrong, she had no intention of admitting her ignorance. But in the end, she had come to the conclusion that when it came to love, men were actually the more flighty and fanciful of the sexes. To spare their masculine pride, women pretended to have the more sensitive feelings and the delicate and easily broken hearts. It certainly seemed that the men who courted her were genuinely disappointed when she refused their offers.

But what else could she do? She had found no real favourite amongst them and she did not think she could abide an entire life pretending to more than she felt for any of them. And there was always Belle and her future to consider.

Then she had kissed and been kissed by Benjamin Lovell. Had she been overly vulnerable because she was so used to handling all problems herself that she had forgotten what it was like to lean on anyone? Was it because he was a much more handsome rescuer than her previous suitors had been? Was it the masterful way he had come to her aid when Belle had disappeared, stunning her to reticence and taking control? For the first few minutes she could do little more than allow him to lead her about the park, searching crowds and questioning strangers. Sensing how frightened she was, he had teased her until she regained her nerve. Then, when they had found Belle in a compromising situation, he had sworn to keep her secret. She had needed a hero. And when she had turned to him, she'd found no sign of the unfeeling social climber she had overheard at Almack's.

Was it the combination of all those things that had made their need so immediate and mutual when, at last, they were alone together in the dark? As they had been in the cupboard at the musicale, his kisses had been so rapturous, his so touch possessive, her body had tingled, even in the places he was not kissing.

With other men, she'd always ended things before they got out of hand and demanded a return to the lights of the pavilion. But last night, if Mr Lovell had asked her to lay down in the grass and submit that instant, she'd have done it without a thought. She'd had to depend on his clear head to rescue her from disaster. He had been the perfect blend of gentleman and rogue. In the space of an hour, she was undone and happy to be so.

What was he thinking today? She doubted he was dancing around his rooms as she had done earlier and laughing over nothing. But she hoped that he was thinking of her and smiling as he did. Perhaps he was contemplating their next meeting. And maybe, just maybe, he was planning to call on her, to take her driving, or for a walk in Kensington Gardens.

She was infatuated. She had been so before, when she was a silly young girl. It would pass, in time, like a cold or a mild influenza. Passionate arousal was an unfamiliar and possibly new symptom. But as long as she did not explore any more dark, secluded spaces with him, she would survive it as well.

But suppose it was something more?

It was probably not. She did not have the time or the desire to fall in love. Nor had Mr Lovell given her reason to hope. He had not even offered the use of his first name. She absolutely refused to fall in love and allow her heart to be broken by his uninterest.

If anyone was going to fall in love first, it should be him. Then, if she felt so inclined, she would love him in return.

To that end, she dressed with exceptional care in her favourite morning gown of gold-striped muslin that suited the amber cross Father had given her on her last birthday. Admiring herself in the mirror, she'd never have claimed to be as beautiful as Belle. All the same, she looked exceptionally pretty this morning. One might even call her adorable. She had only to find her disciple to test the effect.

Even though she had prepared for company, she didn't actually expect it. The last person she expected to find when she descended the stairs to the ground floor was Mr Lovell, already standing in the hall with a puzzled expression on his face, staring down the hall towards her father's study.

'What are you doing here?' she demanded. There were no trace of society manners in the question. She stopped to remind herself that, even though he was used to her treating him with brusque uninterest, things had changed between them. As an afterthought, she softened her words with a smile and a toss of her head and prepared to start again.

'I just spoke with your father,' he said. The response

was delivered in a monotone that proved his usual town bronze had abandoned him. Neither did he answer with the smile he'd worn last night, when they had parted.

'Is something the matter?' If Father had got wind of what had occurred at Vauxhall he might have summoned Ben to account for it. Since her father had done nothing about her previous trips into the dark walks, it was surprising that he should take an interest now.

'No,' Ben said slowly. 'Nothing is the matter. We have been discussing your sister's future.'

After what they had done last night, he had come to talk about Belle. Her mind flooded with responses, but the one she most wanted to give was the one pride would not let her say aloud.

How could you?

Instead, she answered in the distant tone she'd used with him when she was trying to put him off. 'Really? You obviously did not consult her in the matter, since she is still abed. What did you two men decide between you about Belle's life and happiness?'

'I am on my way to arrange for a licence,' he said, his voice still flat. 'The banns will be read for the first time this Sunday.'

'And at what point do you mean to speak to the bride?' she said, horrified. She had known his plan. Why did she think a few kisses would change it? 'And when you do, will you tell her what happened last night, after we found her?'

'Last night was a mistake,' he said. Though he stood a few feet from her, it was as if he was delivering a line in a play, speaking in her direction, but not to her. He looked at her, but not into her eyes.

'A mistake? Yes, I believe it was.' It was the biggest mistake she had made in years. The sort of error a green girl would make before she learned to protect her heart as carefully as her reputation. She had lost her head and kissed him, and encouraged him to kiss her in return. Then she'd allowed herself to believe that it might be more than a typical male response to her wanton behaviour. Now he was about to tell her that any further contact between them would be impossible, since he was going to marry Belle, just as he had meant to, all along.

She spoke before he could. 'Do not worry. My curiosity is satisfied. There was nothing about the experience that I wish to repeat.'

His gaze snapped to meet hers. She could see by the sudden flash of anger there that he wanted to insist that she was lying. The kiss had been phenomenal. It was the sort of passion that came along once in a lifetime. How dare she deny it?

Then he remembered that, for all their sakes, the kiss had to mean nothing. The light in his eyes died and he responded in the same unemotional voice. 'I am glad we are in agreement.'

'On that, perhaps,' she said. 'But my opinion of your marriage to my sister is the same as it ever was. You will not suit.'

He raised an eyebrow. Some of his original Almack's hauteur was returning. 'Lord Summoner approves of me and has sanctioned the match. You do not have a say in it.'

'The fact that you do not value my opinion makes it no less valid,' she said. 'You will know soon enough that I am right. Then perhaps you will find the decency to withdraw your offer.'

'Disabuse yourself of the notion, Miss Summoner,' he said, finally showing his annoyance. 'I gave my word that the wedding would go on, no matter what happens. Your father is happy with it, I am happy with it and your sister will be happy as well, because I promised that I would make her so.'

'If you are happy, then why are you shouting?' she asked triumphantly.

'I *am* happy! And I am not...' he lowered his voice and finished '...shouting.' He took a deep breath and returned to the impassive man whom she'd found at the bottom of the stairs. 'The only one not satisfied with the situation is you. But there is no pleasing a person who makes such a concerted effort to be contrary. Now, if you will excuse me? I have a marriage to arrange.' With that, he turned and left her.

She waited only a moment before turning down the hall in the opposite direction and hurrying to her father's office. She did not bother knocking or waiting for permission to enter, but barged into the room and threw herself into the chair in front of the desk.

'Amelia?' Her father looked up, not even trying to pretend that he was too busy to give her his full attention.

'What have you done?'

'If you are here, then you already know. I assume you spoke to Mr Lovell in the hall.'

'He said you sanctioned the match.'

'He is the perfect choice,' her father said with a nod of satisfaction.

'He is not the man for her. Guy Templeton...'

'Is not the equal of Lovell,' her father finished. 'Lovell is known as the quickest wit in London, just as his father was. Cottsmoor was a genius.'

'The Duke of Cottsmoor.' When they had been alone in the cupboard, Lovell had denied a connection. But how could it be possible to embarrass a man by accusing him of legitimacy?

'His ambitions mesh well with his intelligence. After they have married, I assured him there will be a place for him in government.'

'You had to bribe him to marry Belle?' It was all that Ben Lovell had wanted from the first. How had she allowed herself to forget it?

Her father gave her a surprisingly disarming smile. 'It was not a bribe. It is perfectly natural that I would want to assure my daughter's husband will be successful.'

'And did you assure that Mr Lovell was aware of her difficulties before he agreed to wed her?'

'Belle is a trifle foolish, but no more so than other young girls,' her father argued.

'And I suppose later, when he returns to you and argues he has been tricked, you will tell him to lower his opinion of the female gender to the abysmal level you set for it,' Amy snapped.

'On the contrary, I have nothing but respect for the fair sex,' he argued. 'But there is a reason that you are not allowed to make decisions for yourself, your children or your country. Women are far too emotional to be trusted with the future.'

'So says a member of the gender that has got us into two wars while the factory workers riot in the North,' she said.

'We are not discussing the Luddites,' he said, turning back to the papers on his desk. 'We are discussing Arabella. If Lovell finds some reason to be dissatisfied by the match he has made, then he should have taken the time to know her before accepting my offer.'

'Then you admit you tricked him.'

'I admit nothing of the kind,' he said, reaching for a pen and taking out his knife to sharpen the nib. 'Only a fool thinks all the advantages will be on one side of a bargain. If Mr Lovell was naïve in his expectations about the ease and tranquillity of marriage to Belle or anyone else, then he is no different than all other men his age. Now run along, Amelia. I have business to attend to.'

'And I have needlework,' she said, even more annoyed by the dismissive nod that proved her sarcasm was lost upon him.

Chapter Thirteen

'Lovell!'

Ben quickened his step down Bond Street, in no mood to stop and chat with anyone. His mind was still in an uproar over the turns his life had taken in one short day. He needed peace, quiet and solitude before he could calculate his next step.

Or perhaps he simply needed time to accept the fact that his entire future had been organised by another and done so quickly that he could no longer separate his decisions from Summoner's.

Such a thing had happened to him before, first with Cassandra, then with Cottsmoor. In the end, most things had worked out for the best. He told himself often that the gains outweighed the losses. But he had vowed that, from now on, his life would be his own to plan. And then he'd met Lord Geoffrey Summoner.

'Lovell! Hallo, sir.' Templeton was coming across the street towards him, impossible to avoid.

It took but a second to affix a confident expression

that reflected what he should probably be feeling on such a momentous day. 'Hello to you, Templeton. You must be the first to offer me congratulations.'

His friend looked at him with a surprised smile. 'Good news? And I surmise it involves a young lady.'

'You are correct, sir.' He forced an answering smile. He had no reason not to. His fondest dreams were about to be realised. Therefore, he was a happy, happy man. He had but to remind himself of the fact and act accordingly.

'Does the engagement involve a member of the Summoner family?' Templeton responded with playful encouragement.

Ben nodded. 'It hasn't been announced yet, of course.'

'But it is only a matter of time, I'm sure. Special licences are all the rage.'

'I am a conventional man,' Ben countered. A regular licence would take three weeks minimum to read the banns. But if this marriage was what he had wanted, why stall?

'More time to prepare the guest list. It will be the event of the Season, I'm sure.'

'I want nothing less.' Though the prospect of notoriety had appealed to him at the beginning of the Season, now he wanted nothing more than to get the marriage over with as quickly as possible.

Eventually. In a month or so. Maybe two.

'Good for you, my friend.' Templeton was clasping him by the hand, pumping vigorously. 'And congratulations to Miss Amelia.'

'Amelia?' Ben shook his head. 'I am sure she would as soon spit in your hand as shake it. She was none too happy, when she heard the news.'

'But I thought…' The handshaking stopped, as Templeton understood the truth.

'I am engaged to Miss Arabella,' Ben said, fighting back a panicked laugh. It was easy enough to confuse the sisters. He had made that mistake himself while swearing away his future in Summoner's office.

For a moment, Templeton said nothing at all. Was the idea that he'd done as he planned really so shocking? Then the man stuttered, 'B-but you barely know the woman.'

'I spoke to her father,' Ben replied. 'He spoke to me, rather. He summoned me to his house and suggested the match himself.' He still could not decide whether to be flattered or suspicious. 'He had heard of me and wished to further my career. It is only natural that we strengthen the bond with a family alliance. It was exactly as I had planned.'

And yet it did not feel like his plan at all.

'Natural. Yes. I see.' Apparently, Templeton did not see the sense in it either. Though arranged marriages were not the least bit uncommon, he looked as if he had never heard of such a thing, much less seen it happen. 'Lord Summoner called you to his home and gave you his daughter. And now you are seeking congratulations, before you have spoken to the lady.'

'Not as of yet,' Ben hedged. 'I was just down to Phillips to pick up a ring. I will arrange for the licence and talk to Belle directly.'

Templeton withdrew his hand. 'Your cart is not just before the horse. It is miles ahead of it.'

It was true and he knew it. But he could not help but protest. 'Summoner said there would be no problems with the offer.'

'Of course there won't be. When you finally take the time to speak to your fiancée on the matter, you will know why.' Templeton's smile had disappeared. In a few scant moments, he had gone from a picture of *bon ami* to distant reserve.

An unpleasant thought occurred to him. 'Is there some reason that she might be willing to make a match with the first man who asks?'

'You want to know if she is pregnant.' Templeton followed the inappropriate question with an oath before realising that they were on a public street and discussing a lady. His next words were dangerously quiet. 'I do not know whether to laugh, or punch you in the mouth for even considering such a thing. I would call you out, but apparently, it is to be none of my business.'

The last words made no sense at all, but the threat was clear enough. 'I apologise for the assumption. But it was you who led me to it with your vague hints of trouble. If there is nothing to fear, than why have you not answered the question?'

'Because it is beneath dignity,' Templeton replied. 'Arabella Summoner is as sweet and pure as any girl in London. Her only faults are that she is too innocent, too trusting and far too obedient. She will do what her father tells her without thinking of the consequences to her happiness.'

'She will be happy,' Ben insisted. 'I will give her no reason to be else.'

'Because you are supremely confident that you can be all things to all people.' Templeton made no effort to hide the sarcasm in his voice.

'I made no such claim,' Ben argued. 'I only know that my intentions towards the young lady are honest.'

Intentions. Summoner had called him to account for using the word. Why did people find it so unlikely that he could do what he meant to do?

Templeton seemed equally sceptical. His eyes narrowed and his expression changed from aloof to actively antagonistic. 'Very well, then. You mean to do well by her. Perhaps there is nothing I can do to save the girl from all the people who are sure they know what is best for her, but never take the time to ask what she wants. But know that, if I hear you are treating her with anything less than the respect and tenderness she deserves, you shall answer to me. And now, good day.'

But something in his words sounded less like a parting comment than a permanent end to their friendship.

It was afternoon by the time Ben had arranged for a licence. Nearly four o'clock seemed far too late to propose marriage. There was evening, of course. But the Summoners likely had plans and he had anticipated a quiet evening at his club. It seemed a shame to disrupt everything for a formality that could be handled just as easily in the morning.

As he wrote the note of his intentions to call at ten the following day, he could not help imagining Templeton's stern expression on learning of the engagement. Ben had never planned for a love match and nothing had changed his mind on the subject. But the total lack of interest he had in meeting the girl and going through the motions of the offer did not bode well for the future. It was probably Amy's fault. Her continual harping on his unsuitability for her sister must have shaken his confidence.

Or perhaps she was to blame in another way. Last night, his dreams had been of brown eyes flecked with gold. She had claimed that the kiss in Vauxhall was nothing more than curiosity. For her, perhaps it was. From his side, it was nothing less than compulsion. He'd wanted to kiss her. He wanted to do it again. And despite the engagement, he wanted still more.

If his mind had not been clouded by thoughts of Amy as he'd spoken to Summoner, things might have turned out quite differently. He'd have offered for her. And, since it was clear that she did not care for him, she'd have crushed his heart without a second thought as she had all the other men who'd crossed her path. He must not forget the fact. Those few moments in the dark were not heaven. They were a mistake, just as she'd said.

It was with a pleasant smile and a stoic attitude that he arrived at the Summoner home the next morning to take Miss Arabella for a drive in Hyde Park. And, as had been the case every other time he'd tried to meet with her, he came face to face with Amy. Today, she was dressed for a ride, as if she intended to come along with them.

'Miss Summoner,' he said with a slight incline of his head. 'Do not let me stop you, if you are going out.'

She smiled sweetly. 'You are not likely to, since I will be accompanying you and my sister.'

'I do not recall inviting you,' he said.

'Nor would a gentleman assume that Belle could go out without a chaperon,' she countered.

'In this case, it is entirely appropriate,' he said. 'There are things I wish to say to Miss Arabella that are not for another's ears.'

'If another man said it, I might demur,' she whispered back at him. 'But I know from experience how you behave when you are alone with a lady.'

'Was that all some sort of a test, then?' he whispered back. 'If that is the case, then I was not in the presence of a lady at all.'

'You insufferable cad. Are you always so quick to place the blame on another? If so, look no further when wondering why I do not trust you with my sister. Lord knows what will happen when the two of you are together. But I now know exactly what you will say if it is discovered.'

'Amelia!' Lord Summoner was standing in the doorway of his office. The tone of voice he used was harsh enough to quell even his older daughter.

'Father,' she answered meekly.

'You are not making our guest feel welcome.'

'We were just leaving, Father,' she said.

'On the contrary. They are leaving. You are not

going anywhere. I wish to see you in my study immediately. Leave Mr Lovell to his business with your sister.'

'But propriety,' she argued.

'Do not worry, Amy. I will take Mellie. He will protect me.' His intended was standing at the top of the stairs. It took but one glance to remember why it was he'd wanted her in the first place. Her golden hair glowed in a beam of morning sunlight, but it was no match for the brilliance of her smile.

Ben gritted his teeth and smiled. 'By all means, let us bring the dog. The fresh air will do him good.' At least it was unlikely to do him harm. Mellie had one of his owner's hair ribbons tied around his scrawny neck, but it did nothing to improve his looks. He ambled down the stairs at Belle's side, tail wagging slowly, watching Ben's pants leg as though he'd just recognised an old friend.

Ben dragged his eyes away from the animal and back to the beautiful woman in front of him. 'Miss Arabella?' He bowed low over her hand.

There was no immediate response to his greeting. Then he heard Amy's hissed whisper. 'Mr Lovell.'

'Mr Lovell,' Belle repeated, like an actor in need of prompting. When he rose from the bow, she made an answering curtsy and gave him a smile that more than compensated for a moment's confusion over his name.

'Might you do me the honour of taking a turn about the park with me in my carriage?' From somewhere behind him, he could feel the eyes of the elder Summoner girl boring into his back. Let her stare. She had tried to prevent both the meeting and the engagement, and failed on both counts.

'I like to take rides,' Belle said, still smiling.

'Then you will like my phaeton,' he replied. 'It is quite high, but you need not worry. I have a very steady hand and the team is well matched.'

'Let us go, then.'

She let him guide her out of the house and to the carriage, as docile as a lamb. She was the very opposite of her sister. When he'd escorted Amy about Vauxhall, he'd had the sense that she'd much rather lead than follow. There was a fierce independence in her, yearning to break free.

This was safer. He smiled at Arabella as he lifted her into the carriage. There was no sense that she was scheming behind that pleasant face, or secretly plotting against him. He would not end the day covered in mud or locked in a closet. Today's outing would be utterly predictable.

There was no logical reason to be disappointed at the prospect of success. Why did he need to keep reminding himself of that fact?

The little dog at his feet was gathering its miserably short legs to jump for the running board and follow its mistress. The attempt was destined for failure, so Ben scooped up the dog and dropped it into the footwell before climbing in after.

The mismatched eyes responded with a look of disapproval that was oddly familiar. He blinked to dismiss it. If he meant to retain his sanity and Lord Summoner's good grace, he must stop thinking of Amelia and measuring one sister against the other. The decision had been made and that was that.

He gave a gentle pull on the reins and manoeuvred them out into traffic, relieved that she was not one of those women who felt the need to talk every moment they were together. Instead, she was unusually silent, staring in wonder at the passing streets as if she had never seen them before. 'It is a lovely day, is it not?' he said to fill the void between them.

She tilted her head towards the sky like a flower leaning towards the sun. A pretty flower. The prettiest flower in London. As he pulled the carriage into the park, he could feel a wave of envy from the people around him and faint whispers of excitement from both men and women. An introduction had finally been made between the two greatest catches of the Season.

The world thought them a handsome couple. As well they should. One had but to look at them to see they were destined for each other.

But the woman at his side seemed unaware of the people around her, still staring up into the sky as though not quite realising that there was nothing left to see. He reached out and touched the tip of her nose. 'If you are not careful of the sun, you will spoil your complexion.'

She giggled. 'That's what Mellie says.'

'Mellie?' He stared down at the dog drooling on his Hessians.

She giggled again. 'You are silly. Dogs don't talk.'

'But…' He looked into the eyes of the dog again. 'Do you mean Amelia?'

Belle smiled. 'Mellie. Amy. My sister.'

'I see.' It was not unusual to have childhood nick-names, he supposed. But he wondered what Amy thought of sharing hers with the benighted beast rest-ing on his shoes. 'And did Amelia tell you why I wished to ride with you?'

'Because you like driving?' she said, giving no clue that she understood.

'Because I like you,' he said, smiling.

She smiled back. 'Then I like you, too.'

He could imagine the caustic response he'd have got from Amy had he begun a proposal with a comment as banal as that. She had likely rejected as many men for insufficient ardour as she had for being too forward.

But he must remember, her sister was different. 'Do you like me well enough to marry me?' he said with a wink.

He waited for her to laugh at his impudence. Even the greenest girl would take such a comment as a joke meant to soften her for a serious discussion.

But this one frowned at him. 'I will have to ask Mellie.'

The last thing he needed was the involvement of the sister who had been trying to sabotage this union since that first night at Almack's. 'On a matter as important as this, I think you need to make up your own mind.'

To this, she said nothing. Then her frown deepened and her breathing quickened as if the act of giving an opinion was pushing her near to panic. After nearly a minute of silence, she closed her eyes and clutched his hand, her grip desperately tight. 'What does Papa want me to do?'

He slowed the vehicle and transferred the reins to one hand so he could use the other to clasp her hand in reassurance. 'I think your father would like you to marry me.'

'Then that must be the right thing to do.' Her eyes flew open. 'But...'

He waited. If she had a doubt in her mind, she had but to say so. She could ask for time to think. She could use any number of delaying tactics and he would happily wait until she was ready. She could even say no if she wanted to.

Then he would be free.

For a moment, he felt just as panicked as she did, waiting for the answer. Then she turned back to him, her face clear but vacant. Her smile was as brilliant as ever, though her eyes still held a hint of worry. 'If Papa wants me to marry you, then that is what I should do.' Then she fell silent again, looking out at the people riding by, as beautiful and distant as a swan in the middle of a lake.

Suddenly, his new fiancée turned to him, smile bright but worried. 'Can I bring Mellie?'

He started. 'Bring Mellie where?' And did she mean the dog or the sister? He was afraid to ask for clarification.

'When we get married and I go to my new house. Everyone says I will have to go to a new house, but no one has told me where it will be. If I bring Mellie, than I shall not be lonely.'

This time he listened, really and truly listened to her words, searching out the meaning of them. She did not say *his* house, nor did she describe it as a home. Listening to her question, his mind imagined a child's drawing of a house, no more detailed than a box with windows and perhaps a chimney or two.

'What else do they tell you about getting married?' he asked cautiously.

'We will go to the church and then have cake for breakfast.' She smiled as if this was quite the nicest thing that she could imagine. 'And then I will go to the new house and have servants and babies and a husband.' Her tone seemed to imply that all things on the list needed no particular order because they were all of equal importance.

Since the beginning of the Season, he and every other man in London had taken her silence as a ploy to attract. But could it be less an attempt to allure than a disguise for something else? Suppose the bright smile on that pretty face existed like an elegant cloth over a plain table, hiding the rickety intellect beneath.

Suddenly, he understood Summoner's demand for an oath and Amy's continual insistence that this marriage would not work. It was not his past that concerned them. It was Miss Arabella. Since she barely understood the engagement, it was unlikely that she would cry off it and give him an easy escape. To break the offer himself would tarnish her reputation and risk revealing to all of London what her family already knew: Arabella Summoner was as simple as a child.

'Well?' She tugged on his sleeve. 'Can I bring Mellie?'

'Of course,' he said absently. 'Bring them both.' Then he turned the phaeton back towards her town house.

When they arrived at the front door, Belle hopped down to the street before he could come round to help her. Mellie, the dog, was still coiling for the jump, looking down at the cobbles with the dread of one who had too often leapt into situations only to be totally out of his depth.

Today, Ben sympathised. He scooped the dog up again and set him down on the ground so he could scramble into the house after his mistress. Ben followed a step or two behind. He wanted to say his farewell to Arabella and perhaps a few choice words to Lord Summoner on the nature of honesty.

But once he left the house, he would never be able to speak on the subject again. Nor did he expect society to recognise her disability. As long as her looks held, gossip amongst women would be seen as jealousy. And men would likely claim that wits in a woman paled in comparison to the attributes that she already had. There might be rumours that Mrs Lovell was not quite right, but no one would hear them from her husband.

And there, standing just inside the door, was Amy, helping her sister untie her bonnet. Why had he not spotted the real difference between them, from the first? Belle's beauty came from her innocence. Her heart and mind were unaffected by care. It was the simple bloom of an untouched child.

But Amy's beauty glowed from within. It was a

complex, difficult, prickly sort of loveliness, more like a wild flower than a rose. But once seen, it could not be unseen. Even as they stood together, his eyes, his mind, his heart, were all drawn to the elder sister and he could not pull them back.

'Belle, darling, do not dally too long in changing out of your walking gown.'

Now Amy was shaking the wrinkles from her sister's coat before handing it to a maid. As she turned, he saw her hair, loose and cascading down her back in a smooth wave. He had thought it an unremarkable brown, when first he'd seen it. But today it shone with the same gold that he saw in her eye. Why did she bother with curls and braids? Did she know that the sight of her undressed hair would render a man speechless with the urge to touch it?

'It is almost time for tea. We are having your favourite.'

Their conversation was mundane, but to Ben it was like music. He had accused her of jealousy and his father proclaimed her a bad influence. But the love Amy felt for her sister wove through the words.

His fiancée turned to her sister, her smile blindingly brilliant as if she heard it as well. 'Jam tarts.'

'Yes, dear.'

'May we have them for supper as well?'

'No, dear. At supper, we need something more sub… stantial.'

He could tell the exact moment she noticed they were not alone by the hitch in her words. She glanced in his direction and favoured him with a smile that was polite, but cool. 'Mr Lovell, will you be joining us?'

Had her father lectured her on her behaviour towards a future brother-in-law? The animosity that had seemed to sizzle between them was gone. And surprisingly, he missed it. What if the passion was gone as well? Suppose there was nothing left but this benign courtesy? 'I can stay but a few moments,' he responded, just as polite. 'But if it would be possible to speak with your father...'

'Unfortunately, he is away from the house. But I can answer any questions you might have. If you care to wait in the salon, I will be there directly.'

He nodded his thanks and made his way to the room he'd waited in on the previous day, before making his devil's bargain with Summoner.

She came to him a few moments later, closing and locking the door behind her. Then, without asking, she went to a cabinet in the far wall and removed a brandy decanter and two glasses. She poured both and handed one glass to him, before taking a sip from her own. 'It is unladylike to admit it, but there are times when a delicate restorative is not enough.'

This was definitely such a time. He drank deeply before speaking. 'You were right.'

She laughed bitterly and took another sip. 'It is a day too late to tell me so.'

'And I swore to your father, on the Bible, no less, that I would not withdraw my offer.'

'There is a reason my father is respected as a master politician,' she said with a grim smile. 'It would take a smarter man than you to outwit him.'

He knew he should be insulted by her assessment.

But since it had been proven true there was no point in arguing. 'What am I to do now?' he said, more to himself than to her.

'I suggest you do exactly as you planned to do from the first. Marry my sister and take the seat in the Commons that is offered you. Perhaps she is not as you assumed she'd be, but she is not beyond hope. She is quite good with some things and hopeless at others, of course. But her temperament is pleasant and she is very, very pretty.'

And she had a sister who knew her strengths and weaknesses better than anyone on the planet. She had learned to display her to best advantage and guard her against peril. It was the reason Belle's entry into society had been such a success. 'You have been keeping her secret, for all this time?'

'For as long as I can remember,' Amy replied. 'In the classroom, I did her work as well as my own so our tutors did not punish her. And it is not really so necessary that a woman be as learned as a man.' She glanced in the direction of her father's office as if she'd got those words from him. 'Men expect very little of us, save that we be lovely.'

'And Arabella is that,' he agreed.

'As are you,' she said, giving him a look that said she had no patience left for handsome but foolish men. 'Marry my sister, retire to the country and raise a mob of perfectly beautiful offspring between you.'

'But, I cannot…' He should have known that a simple life with a quiet woman was an illusion. Nothing with women was ever as it appeared. And in this case, it was not just difficult, it was impossible. Arabella had proven today that it was not a simple matter of obedience that led her to this marriage. She had hesitated when he'd proposed, because she had been searching for the words to refuse him. When she had not found them, she'd been as trapped as he was.

Now they would be wed and she would feel nothing for him other than what she had been told to feel. And when he looked at her, he would feel nothing but obligation.

'There will be nothing wrong with those children, if that is your concern,' Amy said, interrupting his introspection. 'What happened to Belle occurred at the moment of her birth. When she was finally delivered she was blue from lack of air.' Amy tapped her forehead. 'It was not good for her mind. But the rest of her is as perfect as she appears.'

'It is not the children I am concerned with,' he said, horrified. 'Does she even know what is expected of her?' He had never lain with a virgin. He had been told that their first time was painful. No passionate reward could induce him to hurt her. He would never forgive himself.

'Do not worry on that account. I will take it upon myself to explain to her. She will be prepared to do her duty.' Now Amy looked as burdened with obligation as he was.

'And how much do you know of such things?' he said, not sure he wanted the answer.

'There are books on the subject,' she said primly.

'Does your father know you've read them?' He could

not decide whether to be shocked or impressed. But for propriety's sake, he was sure he should not be feeling as aroused as he was at the idea of her puzzling over pictures of copulation.

'For the smartest man in London, my father can be woefully obtuse when he chooses to be,' she replied. 'He has no idea what his daughters have got up to, nor does he fully recognise Belle's incapacity. But in the matter of her future, someone had to provide her with the details of her womanly duties.'

'And you took that upon yourself,' he said.

'Among other things.' She shrugged. 'Father means to see her married, whether I think it is a good idea or not.' She paused. 'The plan is not impossible. She could make the right man very happy, and he could make her happy in turn. But the final decision did not rest with me. So, I have been planning accordingly. I did not want to risk her being totally ignorant of the process and terrified by an equally ignorant man who did not care for anything but his own needs.' She gave him a long, searching look, as if trying to decide if he fit that description.

'I can assure you, I am quite capable of putting a woman's pleasure before my own.' He'd had years of experience doing just that, his own needs and desires subsumed by a demanding woman. He'd thought that when he married, he might finally be lord and master. Instead he would be more caregiver than husband.

And worse yet, he was discussing the intimacies of marriage with the woman who he should be treating as a sister. No matter how sophisticated she might pretend to be, her understanding of love making was based on purloined books and a few vague fumblings in Vauxhall. Her cheeks had gone so crimson at his last response that the blush must have extended all the way to her toes.

Which meant that it had spread to all the interesting places in between. He cleared his throat. 'Enough about Belle. What plans did you make for yourself?' But his thoughts of the immediate future had him imagining her skirts around her head as he gave her a practical demonstration of the subject she meant to teach. He shook his head, trying to dislodge the image, and set down the glass, cursing the brandy in his hand for clouding his judgement. 'I mean, what do you mean to do once your sister is settled?'

She cast her eyes down, her face still pink from their previous conversation. 'I decided that it would be best if only one of us married.' She paused. 'It would not be so unusual if Belle took in her spinster sister when she found a husband. Then I would be there to help her with the running of her household.' There was an entreaty hidden in the words, though she tried her best to make them hypothetically innocent.

'No.'

Her eyes flew up to meet his, surprised at the vehemence of his response. 'She is not as feeble minded as you might think, after conversing with her. But neither can she manage alone.'

'I did not claim that she could,' he agreed. 'But that does not mean I want you in my house.' Although he was still not sure that he hadn't agreed to it when talking to Belle in the carriage.

The colour was draining from her face now from the shock of what she must assume was an insult. 'We have had our differences,' she admitted. 'But please, let them end immediately. You are to marry Belle and I will not stand in the way of it. All I want is that she has a kind and gentle husband who will take the time to understand her. You can be that man. I can help with everything else.'

'No.' She was near to trembling with mortification. He wanted to go to her, offer comfort and assure her that it was nothing she had done to make him reject her. But he did not dare, for the same reason he could not have her in his house. 'You are the last person in the world who can help with my marriage to your sister.'

'But why?' She reached out a hand in petition.

He stared at it for a moment, fascinated by the graceful curve of fingers and the way it cut through the space between them. His skin prickled in awareness, as if she was actually touching him. Every nerve came alive to fight against reason for possession of his soul.

Then he looked up, into her eyes. The lashes were spiked with unshed tears. The dark centres were huge, the gold in the left one balanced like treasure at the edge of a bottomless pit. If he claimed it, he would fall. And nothing would ever be the same.

'This,' he said at last and gave in as the pounding tide in his blood battered the last of his resistance to rubble. As he seized her, the empty brandy glass fell from her hand, shattering on a mahogany side table.

Then he was kissing her. She tasted sweet and heady like the liquor she'd been drinking. He wanted to drink her in and get drunk on her, as if he was not already intoxicated just by sharing a room with her.

Apparently, she felt the same for she made no effort to fight against him as he loosened the string at the neckline of her gown and let the bodice gape so he could touch her bare breasts. 'Did your books tell you of this?' he asked, tugging her chemise out of the way and taking a tight pink nipple into his mouth, sucking hard.

The answering groan told him what he already knew. Reality was better than any book. Her back arched and he looked up to see the delicate curve of her throat begging to be kissed. He obliged, stroking her breasts with his hands. Then he used them to push her backwards and down on to the divan behind them.

He stopped for a moment to admire the perfection of her, effortlessly wanton and waiting. Brown hair was wild about her face and her head was cradled on one arm. The muscles of it tugged at one breast so it rode higher than the other, nipple pointed toward the heavens.

If she was painted, just like this, it would result in the sort of masterwork that drove artists mad and made collectors kill to possess it. But he alone would have the flesh behind the canvas. There was no way he could live innocently as a brother to a woman like this.

Perhaps she would learn her lesson, after today. But he feared he never would. It sometimes seemed, the more unattainable a woman was, the sweeter she tasted.

To test the theory he went to her, resting one knee on the cushion between her legs, and pushed her skirts to her waist.

'What are you doing?' She tried and failed to make the words sound like a scold, but there was too much eager curiosity in them to warn him away.

'If you don't know, then you've been reading the wrong books.' He ran his hands up the naked thighs above her stockings, then wrapped his arms about them and lifted her to his mouth for the most intimate kiss.

Her body gave one brief jerk of shock before she relaxed and opened herself to his mouth, letting him take her, sweet and salty, musky and wonderful. He eased his fingers into her and took her in easy thrusts as his tongue pushed her to heaven and beyond. And now she was shaking in the throes of orgasm.

Was it her first? he wondered. The first given to her in this way, he was sure. In a few moments, he would be her first in the only way that really mattered. First, last and only. His erection gave an eager twitch at the thought of entering the tight channel that his fingers had found.

Her spasms of pleasure were subsiding. Her eyes were closed tight. Straight white teeth bit her full lower lip. Strands of that glossy brown hair clung to her face. Her gown pooled at her waist, where he'd pushed it, her perfect breasts still tight with desire.

He eased her legs down from where they had been resting on his shoulders, covering her mound with his palm. She opened her eyes again, watching, silent. And once again he balanced on the brink of disaster, unable to pull himself away. 'I do not want you in my house,' he whispered. 'I want you in my bed. I want you in my life. I want you to fill every moment of my future.'

She sighed. The hand that had reached for him before touched his face and he felt it tremble as her knuckles grazed his cheek.

He reached to undo the flap of his trousers.

And then, without warning, the hand that had just caressed him pulled back and struck his cheek, hard, as if to knock sense back into him.

He reeled back, suddenly aware of what he'd been about to do. Then he scanned the room, staring at the windows that faced a busy London street. The curtains were partly drawn, the divan obscured by a corner of the fireplace. Thank God she had locked the door when she had entered. But what if a servant had overheard what was happening? He thought they had been quiet, but it had been minutes since he'd been able to hear anything over the pounding of his own heart and the music of her ragged breathing.

Apparently, she'd come to her senses as well for she'd pulled away from him to sit up, pushing her skirts down and her bodice up and trying to return to decency. 'You've made your point,' she said, focusing on the arrangement of her clothing, unwilling to meet his eyes. 'I agree. It will be unwise of me to stay in your house, once you have married my sister.'

'If I marry her,' he corrected. Surely after what had just happened, she did not think he would carry through on the farce that they were playing.

'Once you marry her,' Amy said, still not looking

up. 'What just happened between us does not change a thing.'

'And why shouldn't it?' At the very least, it had turned his future from difficult to impossible. He could not marry Arabella. Though he had vowed to himself that he would never love anyone again, what he felt for Amy Summoner was not something that could be ignored.

'You made the bargain with my father,' she said, finally looking up and shaking her head in what looked like pity. 'One does not simply walk away from Lord Geoffrey Summoner, after a deal has been struck. You will understand soon enough, I am sure. But for now, you must excuse me, Mr Lovell. I need to attend to my sister's tea. Please, take a moment to compose yourself before you leave.'

Chapter Fourteen

Two years earlier, when Amy had decided that she would never marry, one of the reasons had been to avoid situations just like the one she was in. It had been clear that a future with any of her suitors was likely to end in disappointment.

They all began with the same fine words: compliments, protestations of devotion and promises of future happiness. If she encouraged them, they followed with smouldering gazes, lingering kisses and furtive touches in dark corners. But no matter how ardent they were, their heads turned should another young lady walk past. Only a fool would expect fidelity from them, since many kept mistresses, even as they looked for wives.

If pressed on the subject, they would deny it, of course. They would claim to live and die on her every breath. But when questioned in detail there was no indication that their affection was anything more than physical attraction. They did not seem to *know* her, nor did they show an inclination to learn. The impression they gave was that courtship was a man's game. But once a marriage had taken place, it was the wife's job to learn the husband's likes and dislikes and cater to them accordingly.

If she was to be forced to live her life for another, she'd decided it would be better to live for Belle than for someone who was likely to forget all about her once the thrill of the chase had faded. There was no subterfuge in her sister. Belle loved without condition and without end. If she ever caused pain, she had the sense to regret it and apologise. She was worthy of Amy's devotion.

Ben Lovell was not. He did not even bother to pretend that his ultimate interest lay with the woman he courted. He had kissed Amy one night and offered for Belle a few hours later. Then he had gone back to seducing Amy immediately after he'd got his acceptance.

Even worse, she had wanted him to do it. The steady heart that she had devoted to caring for her beloved sister was beating quicker at thoughts of the worst man possible. Even knowing that he was engaged to the one person in the world she had vowed to protect, she had allowed him to raise her skirts and prove to her how little she knew about what really went on between men and women. Worst of all, she regretted that she'd sent him away before they had finished what they'd begun.

'Amy!'

She looked up to see her sister holding out her needlework for inspection with the same hopeful smile she wore every day. Perhaps this time her work would be satisfactory. 'Did I do it right?'

'Let us see.' Amy kept her focus on the fabric, unable to look her sister in the eye. 'This bit is all right, but the last will have to be undone.'

'Better, then,' Belle said and put her sewing aside to scratch Mellie's ears.

'Better,' Amy lied and began to rip out the stitches. It was not as if Belle would notice the change, any more than she would notice that Amy was too ashamed to meet her gaze.

I want to lie with your fiancé.

There was no way to make her feelings honourable. Neither was there a way to make Belle understand how horrible it was. Even thinking about what had happened in this very room made her want to melt back into the cushions and touch herself. How was she to explain the details of married life to Belle without thinking of her sister's future husband and imagining herself as the recipient of the skills he had demonstrated on her just a few hours ago?

She returned to her own needlework, staring towards the window instead of at Belle. 'Did you enjoy your ride with Mr Lovell this morning?'

Belle nodded. 'The carriage was very high, but he said not to worry about it.'

'I am sure you were very safe,' Amy said. 'What did you talk about, as you drove?'

'He said he liked me,' Belle said, smoothing Mellie's hair.

'And what did you say to that?'

'I said I liked him, too.' Belle looked up with a confused frown. 'You said before that I should not like Mr

Lovell because his pants had holes and he did not like dogs. But I did not see any holes and he let Mellie ride in the carriage with us.'

'I was wrong,' Amy said. 'What I should have said was…' And just what was it she should have said? 'You should be sure that the man you like has your best interests at heart.' It was a good lesson and one that she should learn for herself before lecturing her sister.

'Mr Lovell was nice to me. But I like Mr Templeton better,' Belle said with a definitive nod.

And where was he, now that he was needed? 'Perhaps Mr Templeton was not as nice as he seemed.' If he had lured Belle into the dark walks as she suspected, he had taken advantage of her trusting nature. If he'd meant to do anything more, he should have spoken up when he'd had the chance. Silently, Amy damned the man for his leisurely wooing.

'He was very nice when we were in the Gardens.' Perhaps Father had been right, after all. The secretive smile on her sister's face hinted that it was none too soon to accept an offer, if only to keep her safe from the predatory nature of supposed gentlemen.

'In the end, it does not matter who you like best. Mr Templeton did not offer for you,' Amy snapped. 'Mr Lovell did.' Almost immediately, she regretted her harsh tone. Even if the marriage had been arranged without consulting her, Belle deserved to know that her feelings were important. She asked the next question more gently. 'But I assume he proposed on your ride this morning. What answer did you give him?'

Belle stared down at Mellie, nervously petting his

head. 'He said Papa wanted me to marry him. And Papa said I must always obey, because he knows what is best for me.'

And not all syllogisms were true. It was unlikely that she would ever get Belle to understand the finer points of reasoning. It was best not to confuse her with them now. 'So you said yes,' Amy finished for her.

Belle nodded and gave her the same hopeful look she used after crooked stitching. 'Did I do all right?'

Amy nodded. 'I think, this time, you did as well as any of us could have.'

'Good,' Belle said and relaxed a little. Then she held her dog up, its short legs dangling, and offered him her cheek for a kiss. 'It is all very confusing. But you will help me to understand when I get married and we go to live with Mr Lovell.'

This was even worse than before. 'I know that it was our plan, that I should come to live with you when you married. But now I do not know if that will be possible.'

Belle dropped Mellie on the cushion beside her and stared at her sister in shock. 'But you promised.'

And she had. In all her life, she had never broken a promise to Belle. Why did she have to begin with the one that would most affect her future? 'That was before I realised you would be marrying Mr Lovell.'

'But you said I did the right thing.' Belle's lip trembled with confusion as she tried to reconcile the two ideas.

'You did,' Amy assured her. 'He is a nice man. He will make a good husband.' At least, he would be no worse than the man who had lured her sister towards ruin without honourable intent. 'I just think Mr Lovell will want some time alone with you, after you have married.'

'Why?'

She was nowhere near ready to give the explanation that question deserved. Especially not while she was still blushing from the demonstration of what Ben Lovell did when he got a woman alone. 'I will explain it all to you at another time.' She reached out to pat her sister's hand. 'For now, do not worry your head about the future. You will talk to Mr Lovell many more times before you are married. In no time at all, you will come to like him so well that you will not even need me.'

And perhaps, some day, Amy would not need him, either.

It had been less than twenty-four hours and Ben was back in the same room that had been the location of his emotional undoing. To stand there, even alone, and pretend that he was not thinking of what he had nearly done with Amy was the greatest challenge to composure that he had faced all Season.

In the hours between dusk and dawn, he had replayed their meeting, over and over, under the pretence of discovering the moment when things had gone wrong. Once he understood it, he could be sure it would not be repeated. Eventually, he'd been forced to admit to himself that the obsession was nothing to do with remorse. It was only an excuse to imagine more and more lurid scenarios where she was willing and he was free to do as he liked with her.

When he tried transferring the fantasy to its correct object, the woman he was going to marry, he could manage nothing more than brotherly affection. She was beautiful, of course. And so quiet and simple that he never need worry about a domineering woman sucking the marrow from his bones, even as he took pleasure in her body. That was what he had wanted, wasn't it?

He'd wanted it before he'd found Amy. Each meeting between them had been a battle of wits. Even when she'd bested him, he'd left eager for the next contest. Her intelligence was as desirable as her body.

Thank God, she was not here to distract him from what he must do. He had seen both Summoner girls turning their horses into Hyde Park as he had driven by it that morning. He'd offered a polite greeting to the pair of them. Amy had ignored him and Belle had smiled and waved, but he saw no evidence that she favoured him over any of the other people she acknowledged, nor remembered that they were to be married in less than a month.

It was just as well. He meant to put a stop to the engagement immediately. The announcement had not yet reached *The Times.* If he cried off now, the whole thing might end with very little embarrassment on either side. Then he had but to explain it to Amy.

She would most likely be angry. She would not want her sister to be jilted, even by a man she wanted for herself. And she did want him. After the incident on the divan, she could not deny there was a mutual attraction. But did she love him?

It did not matter. It would not be the first time he'd

developed feelings for a woman who had no heart. Perhaps, this time, passion would be enough. It made no sense at all to fight against something that they could happily succumb to once he had ended his engagement to Belle and offered for Amy instead. It was unorthodox, but it was the only course of action that made sense.

'Lord Summoner will see you now.' The same footman who had led him to the office two days ago was back again to take him on the same short journey down the hall. The great man had the same stack of diversionary papers in front of him to put guests in their place. But Ben had no intention of being put off so easily.

Summoner glanced up with a polite smile. 'Lovell, I did not expect to see you again so soon.' He made a vague gesture to the chair by the desk.

'My lord.' Ben gave him a shallow bow and took the offered seat.

'You have not come to pester me about your future, I trust. The election is not for some time, you know. We can settle the details after the wedding.' His smile, which had seemed wise before, now seemed merely sly.

'It is the wedding that I have come to talk to you about,' Ben replied, his tone and smile free of hesitation or apology.

'You wish a special licence? It can be easily arranged, you know. I have friends at the Inns of Court. We can have the whole matter settled by evening.' To prove its importance, Lord Summoner put down his papers, as if ready to handle the matter immediately.

Why had he not wondered at the man's haste, when

last he'd been here? It had been stupid of him to be flattered by the man's attention and sure of his own merit. The boy he had once been would have known that there was nothing more dangerous to a common man than a smiling and helpful lord.

'I am not here to seek a special licence,' he said. 'I saw no need to rush a matter as important as marriage and do not wish to do so now.' He took a deep breath and said what he had come to say. 'In fact, I wish to call a halt to the engagement.'

The smile on Summoner's face disappeared. 'And I assume I can guess the reason for it.'

'I do not think...'

'You have met my daughter and realise that she is simple minded.'

Ben held his hands up in protest. 'That is not my reason.'

Summoner's eyes narrowed. 'What other reason can there possibly be?'

'The best reason that there is. I do not love her.'

At this, Summoner laughed. 'You are telling me you cannot marry because you do not love? It did not bother you when last we spoke, nor should it have. Do me the credit of finding a better lie than your sudden need for a love match.'

A week ago, Ben would have agreed with the man that love was the last thing to consider when choosing a mate. He had been in love before, or so he'd thought. It had been a disaster from start to finish and an emotion he had hoped he would never feel again.

Then he'd met Amy. And now he was not sure what he felt. He only knew it could not be ignored.

'It is not a lie,' he said, embarrassed by his own earnestness. 'It is the truth. My heart belongs to another. I thought it was still my own when I agreed to offer for Arabella. But…things changed.' It would gain him nothing to explain his confusion on the day he'd sworn, or where he'd been when he had made his decision. 'It would be unfair of me to give myself in marriage if I cannot commit my whole person to the woman I wed. And as a gentleman…'

'If you were truly a gentleman,' Summoner interrupted, 'you would know that marriage in the upper classes rarely has anything to do with love.'

'If I were a gentleman?' If he was a gentleman, he'd have been angry at the slight and not feeling the tangle of emotions that rose at those words.

'We both know who your father is,' Summoner said.

So it was just the matter of his supposed illegitimacy. He opened his mouth to give the usual equivocations that stopped just short of an outright lie.

'We know who he is not, as well,' Summoner finished before he could answer, his smile becoming a sneer. 'I give you credit for being sensible enough not to claim aloud that it is Cottsmoor. You allow people to assume it, but I find no evidence that the story can be traced back to you.'

In the face of such potentially damning evidence, Ben offered a guarded nod.

Summoner continued. 'However, if one bothers to send a man to the village on the Cottsmoor property, one finds Andrew Lovell. From there, it is not all that difficult to discover the truth.'

It was finally over. Though people claimed that hope was necessary to live, the destruction of hope was better than living in dread that it would happen. His future might be in tatters, but Ben felt a tranquillity he had not known in years. 'So you know my past. What do you mean to do with the information?'

Summoner pushed his papers aside to give his full attention to Ben. 'What I do depends on what you do.'

'Knowing what you know, you cannot seriously want me to marry your daughter,' he said. Now that Summoner had the truth, it was unlikely that he could marry either of them.

Summoner smiled again. 'On the contrary. I chose you for Arabella specifically because of what I knew. Men with no secrets are much more difficult to control.'

'Blackmail?' Ben said in surprise.

'Hardly,' Summoner said, with an expression of distaste. 'It is not unusual that I should want to know the particulars of my prospective son-in-law. And as I said before, I had no problems with them when we agreed on the marriage. But I also told you there would be no turning back from an offer, once it was made. You must have known that I had the power to enforce the agreement.'

'I assumed that would not be necessary. My word of honour...'

'Is worthless,' he finished. 'You demonstrate the fact by coming here today.'

'As is yours, sir, if you think you need to use lies and blackmail to catch a husband for Belle. Had I known the whole truth, I never would have agreed to the engagement.'

'Nor should you have considered another, when you were already affianced,' Summoner countered, making no effort to deny his duplicity. 'The previous commitment outweighs the latter.'

'Normally, that would be true. But the heart is not so easily managed as the head. If I cannot treat your daughter with the respect she deserves...'

'You can and you will,' Summoner said in a tone that brooked no further argument. 'You will go ahead with the marriage as planned. What happens after is between you and your wife. If you insist on following your heart?' He gave a cynical shake of his head. 'There is nothing stopping you. If you have not already realised it, Belle will hardly notice should you stray.'

Now it was Ben's turn to be incredulous. 'You are suggesting I be unfaithful?'

'I am suggesting nothing. I am telling you that what happens between a husband and wife is no one else's affair.' His manner gentled. 'All I wish is what I requested from the first. When she leaves this house, she must be secure and happy. You have money enough to keep her safe and she is surprisingly easy to please. Let her keep the damned dog. Buy her dresses. Take her to places where she can dance and eat cake. That is all that matters to her. In exchange, you will have a seat in Parliament and all the advantages I can offer.'

'And if I tear up the licence and end this before it begins?'

Summoner was smiling again. 'Then I will ruin you. Like a Biblical judgement, no stone of your life shall rest on stone. Hurt my daughter and I will make you, your lover and anyone else I can find pay for your perfidy.'

If he took Summoner's advice, he could have them both. But eventually, someone would realise the truth and the scandal would be even worse. Nor could he live with himself if all he had to offer Amy was a clandestine affair with her sister's husband. A woman with such wit and beauty deserved more than just a pitifully secret slice of his life.

It did not really matter if Summoner destroyed him. In fact, the thought was liberating. He would still have the Duke's bequest. It was more than enough to start again. But without Summoner's support, there would still be a scandal. He might be destroying one sister in an attempt to have the other. In the end, he would lose them both and gain nothing.

'Very well, then,' he said, bowing his head and recognising his defeat. 'I will say no more about it. I will abide by my promise to your daughter. She shall want for nothing.'

Summoner's smile returned to the good-natured beam it had been when he entered the room. 'I am glad you have come to your senses. And, of course, I will keep my half of the bargain as well.'

'On the contrary,' Ben said, raising his head to stare, unsmiling, into the eyes of his future father-in-law. 'I will take nothing from you, no matter how willingly it is given. It will not be said that the decisions I've made are based on the bribes of a powerful man. I might lose my heart over this. But I mean to keep my honour as my own.'

With that, he turned and left before Summoner could say another word.

Chapter Fifteen

Ben had visited her father. When she and Belle had
returned from their morning ride, he had been at the
door, collecting his hat and stick from the footman in
preparation of leaving. He had greeted them with per-
functory courtesy, a hollow smile and the standard
lament that he could not stay longer to have tea with
them.

But there was something in the stiffness of his bow
that announced he would rather be anywhere than
where he was. Though he probably considered himself trapped in a marriage he no longer wanted, there
was no sign that he held the bait responsible for his predicament. The smile he gave to Belle in their brief conversation was as near to genuine as he could make it.

In Amy's opinion, it spoke well of him. No matter
what he thought about his future, he would take good
care of her sister. But his feelings for her father were
clear enough, if one bothered to look. Before he'd left,
he'd cast a brief look of undisguised loathing down the

hall towards the office. Whatever had been said between them, it had not gone as Ben Lovell had hoped.

Amy was not surprised by the fact. She had warned him on the day before that if the deal had been done, there would be no escape from it. Like all men, everywhere, he had not been willing to take the word of a mere woman on something that would have been painfully obvious had he known Lord Geoffrey Summoner as well as she did.

Now he understood. He hated her father. And though he did not love her, he harboured no ill will towards Belle. But for Amy he seemed to have no feelings at all. He had hardly looked at her, though they'd been standing scant feet apart. Words and his smiles had been tossed in her direction as if he wanted her to think nothing had changed between them. But when she'd tried to catch his eye, he had looked past her, through her, or at anything else but her.

Perhaps yesterday's torrid interlude had meant nothing to him. Maybe he was embarrassed that it had happened at all. But if she'd been expecting some acknowledgement that it had been more than a moment's diversion, she was to be disappointed. It was over and they would never speak of it again.

It proved that she had been right all along about men. They thought no further than their own needs, unless forced to do otherwise, as Ben had been by her father. It was all the more annoying that a part of her would always wonder if Ben's response to her today might have been different had she had allowed him to finish what they'd started.

It was a sign of weak character that she was thinking about that at all. If she had any regrets, they should be that she had not put a stop to things much sooner than she had. What had happened was unchaste, undignified, unladylike…

And wonderful. She sighed.

At the sound Mellie, who had been dozing on the hearth rug of the parlour, looked up and growled at no one in particular.

'Silly dog,' said Belle, tossing the last bit of her biscuit to him and setting her tea cup aside.

'Do not spoil him,' Amy said, stretching out her foot so she could rub his exposed belly with the toe of her slipper.

'I still have not taken him to the park to play ball with Guy,' Belle said, staring out the window as if hoping that the gentleman would appear.

Amy frowned. And there was another fine example of manhood. They must consider themselves fortunate that they had stopped him before he had irretrievably compromised her sister. Though he had been all but underfoot for the entire Season, they had seen no trace of Guy Templeton since the incident at Vauxhall, four days ago. Hopefully, the formal announcement of the engagement would be enough to scare him away permanently.

But none of that made it any easier to explain his absence to Belle. 'Now that you are to marry Mr Lovell, you will not be able to socialise with other men as you used to.'

'We are not going to socialise,' Belle said, looking

at her as if Amy was the one who did not understand. 'We will be playing with Mellie. And it is not other men. It is just with Guy.'

And there was another problem to be corrected. 'Now that you are engaged, you must go back to calling him Mr Templeton.'

'But he said I should call him Guy,' Belle said, clearly confused.

'Things have changed between you since then,' Amy said, as gently as possible. 'Mr Lovell would not like you being so informal with another man.'

'But Mr Lovell is Mr Templeton's friend,' she offered hopefully, sure that this would make a difference.

'No one's friendship is that strong,' Amy replied.

'When I see Mr Lovell, I will ask him if it is all right.' Belle was clearly not convinced.

Just then, a footman entered with the afternoon post. At the top of the stack was a letter from Mr Benjamin Lovell. It was addressed to The Misses Summoner. Amy stared at it for a moment, afraid to break the seal.

If the contents were in any way personal, he would not have addressed it to both of them. But that did not keep her from wishing that it was a *billet doux.* When she had been actively courting, no man would have had the nerve to send such a thing to Lord Summoner's daughter. But if she was to spend her life alone, without even Belle for company, it might be nice to have a stack of ribbon-bound letters to remind herself of what might have been.

It would be even better if they were written in Ben Lovell's elegantly masculine hand. She stared down at the folded paper in front of her, memorising each line and loop of the address, focusing on the sight of her surname. Without thinking, she ran a fingertip across the words, imagining the forceful pressure of his pen to the paper.

In response, she felt a rush of heat, sudden as a lightning strike. It coursed through her body to settle in the wet place between her legs. If this was all it took to make her want him, than he had been right. There was no way they could reside under the same roof. Even if nothing happened between them, ever again, people would have but to look at her to know what she wanted from him.

Now he'd sent a letter. It was better that it go directly to his intended, if only to teach Belle that future communications between them did not have to be shared. Amy took one last look at it, then handed it to her sister. 'Mr Lovell has written you. Open it and see what he has to say.'

Belle cracked the wax that held the paper closed and looked at it only a moment before handing it back with a confused shrug. 'Help me, Amy.'

No wonder she needed help. The tidy script on the outside degenerated into a confusion of crossed writing inside. Why had he bothered to turn the paper on its side to write the second half of the missive? There was no need for economy. They could more than afford the postage for a second sheet of paper.

She looked across at her baffled sister. Belle sometimes had trouble deciphering a regular letter, if the writer did not have a clear hand. Separating one direction of writing from another was far too difficult for her to manage. To send such a letter, Ben might as well have been writing in Latin.

Or in code.

There could be no more innocent way to get a private message to her than this.

'What does it say?' Belle was eagerly awaiting her half of the letter.

'Let us see.' Amy smiled at her sister as if the paper in her hand was just ordinary social correspondence and not the most important message she had ever received. Then she looked down, forcing herself to focus only on the first part of the letter, making no effort to let her eyes dart to the left to read the sideways writing crawling in and out between the words. 'It seems we are invited to a house party at Mr Lovell's estate in Surrey.'

'A house party,' Belle said, her worry over Guy Templeton forgotten. 'I have never been to one of those.'

'No, you have not,' Amy agreed, glanced down at the letter again and then tucked it into her pocket so as not to be distracted by it.

'What will it be like?'

Extremely difficult for all concerned, thought Amy. But she continued to smile. 'This one is to celebrate your engagement to Mr Lovell. I suspect there will be fine dinners, parlour games and perhaps a ball where you can meet his friends.' Belle would be under the scrutiny of everyone there for several days. Since she was the guest of honour, they could hardly creep away home if things got too difficult. Amy grew tense just thinking about it.

'Dancing and games,' Belle said happily.

'It will also be a chance to see your new home,' Amy said with as much enthusiasm as she could muster.

'And I will get to see Guy again,' she said. Then she remembered she was not to be familiar and added, 'Mr Templeton.'

'Perhaps,' Amy said, hoping that, after Vauxhall, Ben would know better than to trust him.

'And it will be your new home, too,' Belle finished, smiling as though relieved that it was all settled.

Amy wet her lips. 'After you are married, things might be quite different than you expected. Still good,' she added hurriedly. 'But different.'

'I like things the way they are,' Belle said, with a surprising show of independence.

'I know, dear. But we cannot always have things the way we want them.'

Belle frowned, trying to understand.

'For one thing, even if Mr Templeton is there, you must not go off alone with him, as you did at Vauxhall. You must not go off into the dark with any gentlemen. It is not a polite thing to do.'

'It was bad to go off with Guy?'

That answered the question of what had happened when she had disappeared. Belle had been alone in the Dark Walks with a man. And despite what she'd hoped of him, Guy Templeton had not stepped forward to make an offer or done anything else to prove that his intentions toward her had been serious. 'You did nothing wrong. It was my fault for encouraging you to spend so much time with him.' She had been so sure that a proposal was imminent that she had thought there would be no harm done.

'It was all Mr Templeton's fault,' Amy said, firmly, knowing it was her own fault as well. 'And I am sure Mr Lovell would agree with me.' He would not like it any more than she liked to think of Ben kissing Belle. 'But you must not let it happen again.'

Belle gave her a doubtful look. 'When we see Guy at the house party, I will ask him if we did wrong.'

Amy looked back in surprise. It sounded almost as if her sister had disagreed with her. If that was true, it was the first time in ages she had heard anything like rebellion. 'You should not even speak to Mr Templeton,' she said, in a firm tone. 'And in no case should you listen, if he tells you to do something. From now on, you must let Mr Lovell make these decisions for you.'

'But what if I do not want to do as he says?' It was a legitimate question and one Amy had asked herself many times, when forced to follow one of the many rules that men expected women to abide by. Men were not always right. And when they were wrong, it was stupid to follow them.

But it was a very different matter when Belle was the one who wanted freedom. 'Mr Lovell is to be your husband. It will be his duty to decide what is best for you in all things.'

'Papa makes decisions for me,' Belle said slowly. 'And so do you.'

Amy nodded.

'And now Mr Lovell will.'

Amy smiled, relieved that she was beginning to understand.

'When do I get to decide things?' Belle asked.

It was a question Amy had hoped that she'd never hear, for she did not have a good answer to it. 'We all want what's best for you,' she began cautiously. 'And on some things…the very important things like marriage…what is best is that you let the people who love you make the decisions.'

'Then why does Mr Lovell get to do it?' Belle's smile had disappeared. Her lower lip jutted out in a pout that would have been unattractive on any other face. 'He likes me. But that is not the same as love.'

For someone thought to be simple, her sister had an excellent grasp of the current situation. 'He is a good man,' Amy said, still not sure if that was true. 'He will take good care of you.'

'But he does not love me,' Belle insisted. The lip that had pouted now gave a warning tremble.

'Love is not really all that important.' Even as she said it, she knew she did not believe it. Love was the most important thing there was. If it was not, then why did it hurt so much when one did not have it?

Belle recognised the lie as well. And for the first time in ages, she dissolved into tears. 'Liar.' She pointed a finger at Amy. 'Guy says love is all that matters.'

'And where is your precious Guy, now that you need him?' Amy snapped, tired of hearing his name. 'If love was so important to him, he would have been the one to offer for you. But he did not. It was a mistake to let him anywhere near you.'

'It was not!' Belle wiped the tears from her face with the back of her sleeve. 'Mr Lovell is the mistake. And so are you.' She gave a loud sniff, trying to clear her running nose. 'He does not love me. And I do not love him. You cannot make me marry him.' With that, she was out of her chair and running towards her room.

'Belle!' It took only an instant for Amy to drop her needlework to follow. But Belle had outdistanced her easily, taking the stairs two at a time. By the time Amy had gained the landing, she heard the slam of the bedroom door.

'Belle!' She knocked and then pounded, trying the door to find that it was locked. She gave it a futile rattle, as though wanting would be enough to make it open. She had the key in her own room. It would take only a moment or two to run down the hall and get it.

But that had never been necessary before. The door had never been locked. Nor had it been slammed. Even when it was closed, she was seldom on the wrong side of it. She had kept the room key safe and untouched, just as she'd kept Belle safe for eighteen years. And now everything was falling apart.

She knocked on the door again, harder this time. 'Do not be a child, Belle. Let me in.'

But Belle was not being childish at all. She was acting like an adult. She had been all but sold to a man she'd never met. And when she'd had the audacity to question the decision, the person who loved her most in the whole world had lied to her and dismissed her feelings as unimportant.

'I am sorry that I did not listen to you,' Amy said, running her fingers over the panel of the locked door. 'Come out and we will talk.' Then she could explain again, but better, this time. And then everything could go back to the way it had been and they would be happy.

But that was not true, either. No amount of explaining could take them back to a time before Ben Lovell. Nor could it make Guy Templeton into the sort of man who was worthy of her sister.

'I know this is hard to understand,' she began again. It was hard to explain as well. 'But this marriage is for the best. You cannot simply lock yourself in your room to avoid it.' Nor could they drag her down the aisle and force her to marry a man she did not want. All the plans she'd made for the pair of them had been based on a willing and agreeable Belle. She had sacrificed her own life to that end, knowing that, even if she had no one else, Belle would always love and need her. What was she to do, if Belle no longer wanted her help?

She stroked the door again, as if it were possible to transmit the comfort through the wood to the person who needed it. 'Have a good cry. Later, when you are feeling better, come to my room and we will talk.'

Then she walked slowly down the hall to her own room, near to tears herself. What was she to say or do that would make any of this better? It had always been her job to take care of Belle. She was always there to make sure things did not go wrong and to fix them if they did. But how could she fix something that was just the way it had to be?

Perhaps Ben Lovell had an answer. It was his ambition that had brought them to this point. He should take some responsibility for the misery he was causing. He had been so kind, when they had been together in Vauxhall. If only he were here to help her.

Then she remembered the letter in her pocket. As Belle had done, she locked her door, wanting to savour the moment of reading, whether it brought pleasure or pain. She unfolded the paper again and turned it on its side to read the second half.

Amy, dearest,

I have no right to call you such. And yet I cannot help myself. No matter what you feel in return, to me you are and always will be dearest.

I have been trying to find the words to explain my behaviour towards you. But there is no justification for what I have done and what I would do in the future if the opportunity presents itself. I cannot see you without wanting you.

Please accept my apology for the liberties I took. I know how you responded to another who overstepped himself. And I have earned far more from you than the blackened eye you gave to Haines.

She stopped to smile and touched the letter to her lips before reading more.

I am promised to another and bound by oath to the current course of action. The engagement is unbreakable as you warned me it would be. But when I am with you, I forget all that. Hon-

*our has no value. The future has no meaning. I
only see the moment. I only see you.*

*Though you might not want me, if I could find
a way to free myself, I would run to you. Perhaps
you would cast me off as you did the other men
who courted you. Even if it cannot be, you will
always have my heart.*

*But the rest of me is promised to another.
Please, for the sake of your sister, accept the invitation to my home. As I made clear on our last
meeting, sharing a household would be disastrous. But we must find some way to be sure that
your sister has the help she needs in her new life.*

*It will not be easy for either of us, but we must
both do what is best for Arabella. I swear, I will
not trouble you, as I have in the past. It will be
best if we try, as we should have from the first,
to abide by the constraints of society and make
use of a chaperon, for the sake of your reputation and my peace of mind.*

She smiled again. Once, he had said he did not need
peace. Now that it was gone, he had changed his mind.
One could almost feel sorry for him.

*I eagerly await your answer to my invitation
and your attendance at my home.
With love,
Ben*

She held the letter for a moment, unwilling to admit
that she had reached the end. It was everything she

could have hoped for. He burned for her, as she did for him. He had called her his dearest and offered his heart.

He had offered his love in the closing, but that was hardly an uncommon way to end a letter. There was no point in either of them saying that particular word too often. With things as they were, it could mean nothing but pain. It was far better that the feeling they shared was something far less permanent, a flame that would burn itself out once they stopped feeding it.

But for now all he needed from her was an answer to his invitation.

She read it through again. Then one more time so she would not forget the words. And then she went to the fireplace, searching for one remaining ember from the previous night's fire. She dropped the paper upon it, watching the edges blacken and curl. From any other man, it would have been the perfect keepsake of a brief, romantic interlude. But such words from her sister's future husband should not exist in anything more concrete than memory. In a moment, there would be nothing left to prove they had ever existed.

When the paper had all but disappeared, she seized the poker and dragged the last scrap away from the flames, picking it up and patting the glowing edges until her fingers singed. The bit that remained had an L, an O and part of a V. The E that would have finished the word was little more than a shadow of ash.

She went immediately to her jewel case and found a locket to hide it in. Once she had closed it up, she gave it a brief kiss before clasping the chain around her neck.

Only then did she sit down at her writing table to write a response to Mr Lovell's brilliant suggestion of a house party. The words were polite, prosaic and completely unsatisfying.

Chapter Sixteen

The journey to Ben Lovell's country house was largely uneventful. With Parliament in session, their father politely declined the trip, citing too much work in town to take even a few days away.

After her brief excitement at the thought of a party, Belle continued to brood about the impending marriage and her lack of control over her own future. It took almost a full day after their argument before she was willing to leave her room and even longer before she spoke to Amy. She complained of pains in her stomach and insisted that Miss Watson bring her meals upstairs, and replied in monosyllables, even if Amy avoided the subject of marriage.

When Amy reminded her of their need to pack for the house party, so they might set off on the morrow, Belle flatly refused. Though the thought had excited her as they'd read the invitation, she now declared she was far too sick to leave the house. When all of her usual tricks to manage Belle had failed, she was forced to appeal to their father to convince her.

He had called Belle to the office and closed the door before Amy could follow her in. There followed almost an hour of ominous silence. Then the door had opened and Belle had emerged, white faced and teary, but prepared to go to Surrey the next morning.

Amy breathed a sigh of relief at this partial return to normal. But while there was no more talk of stomach aches and wanting independence, there were fewer smiles as well. Belle was still answering most questions put to her with a shrug and announced that it did not matter what she wore and that they should simply pick the first dress in the cupboard and be done.

The final straw had been when Miss Watson had declared herself a victim of Belle's imaginary illness and taken to her bed, unable to accompany them. This left Amy to organise both of them, their maids and enough luggage for a week's worth of parties in Belle's new home. She could have left it to the servants. But the more she thought about the letter she had thrown into the fire and the man who had written it, the more anxious she became.

While Belle had decided to do nothing, Amy found it was much easier to occupy herself matching hair ribbons to gowns and deciding if it might be necessary to take the large trunk and not the small one. Then they would have room for their habits, in case there was an opportunity to ride.

She would make sure everything was perfect, just as she always did. Then, perhaps, Belle would be happy again. The time was fast approaching when she would have to abandon Belle to her new life. And what would become of either of them, after that?

For now, she imagined a dozen ways to keep herself busy that did not involve talking with the master of the house. She hoped that Belle's new home had grounds to explore. Perhaps there would be a chance to visit the nearby Royal Botanic Gardens. She could leave one of the maids to watch over her sister and escape for a while.

There might be a library that held books she had not yet read. If there was a music room and sheet music, she might attempt to teach herself a new tune on the pianoforte. Her skills were little better than adequate, but that was probably reason to seek improvement. Beyond that, there were cards, games, needlework…

But suppose the house was small and ill suited to entertain? Suppose, wherever she went, she saw Ben? It would be hard enough being in his home and learning the intimate details of it. If she was near him, there would be a constant threat of intimacy. She never should have agreed to the trip.

But then she reminded herself of the perfectly reasonable request in the letter. They were doing this for Belle's sake. She must learn to love her new husband and the man she was to marry. No amount of talking had put an end to her rebellion. But if this brief and painful trip was needed to convince her, then Amy would make the best of it. There was nothing she could not attempt, if it meant that Belle would be happy again.

* * *

The roads were dry and they had made fair time, pulling up the sweeping drive to the house less than an hour and a half after leaving the Summoner town house. She had not meant to be impressed by his home. But if Amy's only concern had been to place her sister in the nicest house, it would have been impossible to deny Ben Lovell her hand.

The structure was new and had been designed by no less than the great John Nash, himself. The majestic symmetry of the white limestone walls was framed by terraced gardens and carefully trimmed boxwood hedges.

The well-ordered building was tended by an equally efficient staff. Footmen and butler greeted them with warmth and were spiriting their luggage above stairs before they had even come down from the carriage.

The tall front door opened on to a breathtaking hall with spotless marble floors and ivory walls rising to a vaulted ceiling trimmed with gilded rosettes and wreaths.

But while Amy viewed it with wide-eyed admiration, Belle reached out for Amy's hand, clutching it in fear. 'Mr Lovell lives here?'

Amy patted her hand to comfort her. 'Yes, dear. And soon, you will live here too. Is it not beautiful?'

Belle shook her head. 'I do not like it. It is too big. Too big and too white.'

'That is not such a bad thing,' Amy whispered. 'But if you tell Mr Lovell it does not please you, he will let you repaint it, I am sure.'

'It will still be white underneath,' Belle said, not moving.

Amy took her hand, tugging her forward over the threshold. 'It is bigger than our house, to be sure. But that does not mean that it is not a nice place. And I doubt you will live here all year.'

'There will be more?' Now Belle looked truly help-less, unable to comprehend how her small, secure world had become so large and strange.

'He has rooms in the city and will likely get a town house once you are married. And if he means to stand for Parliament, perhaps he will have a house near our land in Dorset.'

While Amy felt a perfectly reasonable envy at the idea of three fine homes, Belle could manage to do nothing but shake her head in denial.

'Welcome, ladies. Please come in.' Ben was coming down the stairs towards them, his midnight-blue coat a perfect foil for the austere design of his home. As his eyes met hers, the flame of envy in Amy's heart turned into a raging covetous fire. It did not matter that he was to marry Belle. He was hers and always would be. Without thinking, she stroked the chain of the locket and the scrap of love that it contained.

When he took the last steps down to their level and came towards them, his eyes were focused upon her sister. At her hesitant smile, he got the same stunned expression that all men wore when confronted with Belle's full attention.

Then he bowed low and took her hand, kissing the

knuckles. 'Welcome, Arabella. Please, treat my home as your own, for thus it will be.'

For the first time in days, Belle's foul mood improved and she smiled back.

'Let me show you about the house, while your rooms are being prepared. Then, after you have refreshed yourselves, I will introduce you to my friends. They are all eager to meet you.'

Ben offered his arm to Belle and after a brief hesitation she took it and let him lead her out of the hall. Amy followed a pace or two behind, regretting each step. It had been a mistake to accompany Belle here. She should have forced Miss Watson out of bed and sent her instead. She might have stayed in London for the Season's festivities.

Perhaps it would have looked odd when she did not attend her sister's engagement ball. But society was used to thinking her odd. It did no harm to her reputation to reinforce that opinion with her actions.

Anything would be better than spending the next few days feigning approval as Ben escorted Belle about the grounds, rode with her, danced with her and fostered the intimacy necessary to make a happy union. Even the affection she felt for her sister was not without bounds. It was one thing to sacrifice the man she loved and quite another to pretend to be happy as she did it.

Ben escorted the Summoner sisters on a tour of what was to be the home of one of them. The wrong one, of course. It was too much to hope that it might be home to the pair of them, just as Amy had always planned.

He had told her it was impossible. He knew in his heart that it would be. But he could not help hoping that she would ignore him and come anyway. If she did, he would not be able to send her away.

Maybe this week they could find the restraint that had been lacking in their previous encounters. If they could aspire to a platonic relationship, he would be spared the terrible emptiness he'd felt as he'd written the letter. Even if he could not have her, he could still see her. It was something, at least.

At the moment, Belle was on his arm, following with less spirit than Mellie the dog. If she was impressed by the size and modernity of his home, he saw no sign of it. If anything, she looked frightened.

One step behind them, Amy kept up a running commentary on his tour, pointing out the smoothness with which the kitchen ran with no help from the master, the spacious bedrooms and the pleasant view of the gardens where Mellie could chase rabbits while his owner sat in the shade of the oaks.

Did she actually like the place, or was she only encouraging her sister? Damn his pride, but it was important that she be impressed. But she sounded no more attached to it than an agent hired to rent the house.

'If you like dancing,' he reminded Belle, 'you will find the ballroom delightful.' He opened a door and brought them out on to the little balcony that had been designed to hold the musicians. The sound of their voices echoed through the room below.

'Think of the lovely parties you will have here,

Belle,' her sister said coaxingly. 'And you will dance every set.'

It was likely not true. As hostess, she would have to attend to the happiness of her guests before her own. But the idea that she might dance here brought back the sparkle that had disappeared from her smile. 'We will dance here tonight,' he agreed, 'After the rest of the guests have arrived.'

'I would like that,' Belle agreed hesitantly.

Now that he knew her better, her beauty did not have the same, devastating effect on him that it had. Was it really so easy to become jaded with perfection? Or was it simply that she was not the one who had been meant for him?

When had he begun to crave a love match? He had learned when he was much younger that love was a dangerous business. Life was better when one was not caught and suffering like a fly in a web, about to be devoured by the teeth of one's own passion.

He had come to London well aware that love was not necessary for a successful marriage. He wanted tranquillity. And he might still have it, if he learned to take satisfaction in the smiles of the pretty but simple girl.

There were likely many tricks to making her at ease. He would need Amy to teach them to him for it might take years to learn them on his own. If he could have her here, just to talk to…to explain…

And there he was again, standing on the edge of a cliff and wanting to jump just to feel the wind in his hair as he fell. If he could not even turn around to look her in the eye without being near to overcome by lust, his future was not likely to be full of innocent conversations about her sister's happiness.

'Ben?' The young voice came from the doorway, directly under the balcony they were standing on. Belle stepped forward to peer cautiously over the edge, wondering at the source.

'In the gallery, above you,' he called, then turned to the girls, leading them to the steps down to the main floor. 'I have been looking forward to this moment for some time. I would like to introduce you to a special friend of mine.'

It was hardly fair to the boy who stood at the foot of the steps, watching their approach. Even travel-weary, the Summoner girls were intimidatingly beautiful. Despite his recently acquired *sangfroid*, John was still, underneath it all, a fourteen-year-old boy, struggling with the same feelings that showed no more mercy to kings than they did to bootblacks.

'Your Grace.' Ben bowed. 'May I introduce my fiancée, Arabella Summoner, and her sister, Amelia? Ladies, his Grace the Duke of Cottsmoor.'

For a moment, he was caught between mutual expressions of owl-eyed wonder on the faces of John and Amy. Belle seemed to understand that she should be in awe. But from her expression, she could not get past the fact that the person who should demand her respect was also barely out of leading strings.

Amy regained control after only a second or two and executed a perfect curtsy. 'Your Grace.'

A single glance to her side demonstrated to Belle

what was expected of her and Belle duplicated her sister's greeting.

John was the slowest to regain his wits. He looked from one to the other, then managed a clumsy bow, 'Miss Summoner,' he said, turning to Belle. 'Miss Arabella.' The second bow had a hitch in it, as though someone had punched him in the stomach to make him bend.

But it was far better than he'd have managed at that age. Ben smiled at the boy, unable to disguise his pride at the success. Then he rescued them all from awkward silence. 'Cottsmoor has agreed to take a few days from his studies to celebrate with us.'

'We are honoured, Your Grace,' Amy said, with a smile almost as charming as her sister's.

'It is I who am honoured,' John said, looking from one to the other. Then he looked back to Ben in an incredulous aside. 'This is your fiancée?'

'Try not to sound so surprised,' he said, smiling. 'But indeed, I have been very fortunate.'

'We just met,' announced Belle. 'But now we are engaged.'

Inserting the unvarnished truth into a polite conversation was always a hazardous thing. This one brought the exchange to a dead halt.

It took only a moment for Amy to recover, and give the John another one of her brightest smiles. 'We consider ourselves fortunate as well, Your Grace. Mr Lovell is quite well known and well thought of. He does credit to your—'

He could tell by the panicked look in her eye that

she had been about to say family before she remembered that the common rumour that they were brothers was both rude and untrue. It took less than an eye blink, for her to finish with '—patronage.'

John had not noticed the hesitation. He had been too busy staring at the gold light in her eye that so fascinated Ben. Proof that the boy had excellent taste in women. Then he pulled himself free of her influence long enough to answer, 'I have known Ben my whole life. I consider myself just as fortunate to have his counsel.'

They were headed towards the usual awkward pause, as Amy realised that she could think of no conversational topic worthy of a peer. It was a shame. Though John longed for ordinary human interaction, he had already learned that a few moments of Cottsmoor was all the average person could stand.

For a moment, he shifted from foot to foot, displaying a child's eagerness to hold the attention of adults. Then he steadied himself and the Duke reappeared. 'We must talk further, this evening,' he said, with a surprisingly adult smile. 'I look forward to dancing with you both, since, clearly, you will be the loveliest ladies present. And now, if you will excuse me?'

'Of course, Your Grace,' Ben said. And, after a brief exchange of bows and curtsies, he was gone.

If and when she ever got Benjamin Lovell alone, Amy would give him her opinion on surprise visits from the peerage. It had not been the most mortifying conversation of her life, but it had been one of the most difficult.

When the boy was properly out of earshot, she turned and pulled her sister aside for a whispered scolding. 'Belle, in the future, you must not speak so candidly about the circumstances of your engagement, especially not in the presence of Mr Lovell's friends.' By the innocent expression on her sister's face, there had been no malice intended. But that did not make it right.

'It was the truth,' Belle said, quite reasonably. 'Miss Watson says we should tell the truth and shame the devil.'

'In this case, telling the truth shames Mr Lovell.' Of course, when they were alone together, he was the devil. It made Belle's logic irrefutable.

'You did not shame me,' he said softly from behind them, making Amy cringe in embarrassment.

'You were not supposed to hear that,' she said. She'd assumed there was enough distance between them for her comments to pass unnoticed.

He gave her an innocent smile. 'As I said before, the acoustics in the ballroom are excellent.' Then he looked to Belle. 'Do not concern yourself. Cottsmoor found you both quite charming.'

'He was a nice boy,' Belle agreed.

'But in the future, you must remember that he is a very important man,' Amy reminded her.

'And, since he is male, he is just as susceptible to your charms as the rest of us,' Ben said, with a tone of finality. 'Do not trouble yourself, Amy. If you smile at him, he will forgive you anything.'

If Belle knew nothing else, it was how to smile on command. To end the conversation she did exactly that. Ben smiled back at her and held out his arm. 'Let us continue our tour.'

Now that she had seen most of it, it was apparent that her initial assessment had been accurate. The house was perfect. Annoyingly so. Just like its owner. It was also impossible for Belle to manage without help, just as its owner would be.

It was a shame that looks were not enough, for they made the most handsome couple imaginable, walking arm in arm, in front of her. And Ben was doing his best to be the man who was required. He was solicitous of her sister, trying to interest her in the many advantages to the place and tempting her with jam tarts and dancing. He even pointed out a window seat in the library that would be a perfect spot for Mellie to nap.

But if he meant to have a seat in Parliament, he could not also be at home helping his wife to navigate the complexities of married life. Mere good intentions would not be enough. But it was unfair to suggest that he stay away from his own house and allow her to resume her place as Belle's right hand.

And though she was pleasant for the Duke, no matter what Ben did to please her Belle moped from room to room to room, not saying a word. It was not until they passed through the front hall again that her mood improved.

'Guy!' At the sound of his voice in the entryway,

Belle pulled free of her fiancé's hand and galloped down the hall toward the open door.

'Miss Summoner.' Guy Templeton turned at the sight of her, bowing deeply.

She ignored the formal greeting and took both of his hands in hers. 'It has been forever since I've seen you.'

'Only a few days,' he replied, laughing.

Amy came into the room at a slower pace, not wanting to show the alarm she felt at the sight of Belle's enthusiastic greeting. 'Mr Templeton,' she said, catching his eye to give him a warning glare. 'What are you doing here?'

The smile he returned was as innocuous as ever. 'I was invited. I have a house not a mile from here and I am a good friend of our host. It is hardly a surprise.' He gestured toward Ben, who was still standing in the doorway.

'You are a good friend of my sister, as well,' she said, watching carefully for his reaction.

'That I am,' he agreed.

'And this is still my house,' Ben said quietly beside her. 'I will invite who I choose to visit me. And Templeton is not just a good friend. He is my best friend.' He stepped forward then and offered Mr Templeton his hand, which forced him to release Belle to accept it. 'So good to see you. We will have far too many unpartnered ladies tonight. I cannot be expected to dance with all of them.'

'Guy is a good dancer,' Belle announced. Apparently, the recent lecture on discretion had gone unheeded.

'You flatter me, my dear.' Templeton smiled at her and held her gaze for longer than was necessary.

'I am sure Mr Lovell is a good dancer as well,' Amy said, trying to get her sister's attention.

But Belle did not turn away from Mr Templeton. 'I do not know. I have never danced with him before.'

In a lifetime of caring for her sister, Amy had learned to think of her disposition as placid, docile and agreeable. But never before had she been so consistently contrary for such a long period of time. She looked helplessly at Ben, readying another apology.

He warned her off with a slight shake of his head and then said, 'That is true, Belle. But we will dance tonight and you will be able to judge for yourself.'

Then he turned to his friend. 'It is clear that my fiancée is eager to speak with you, after so much time apart.' He continued to smile as if there was nothing untoward in Belle's reaction. If there was irony in the statement, it was very well concealed. 'Perhaps you can be the one to escort her about my gardens. You know them almost as well as you do your own.'

'I would be honoured.' Templeton responded with a bow that was a trifle too formal to be given to a close friend. 'Miss Arabella?' He held out his arm to her.

Her sister embarrassed herself yet again by responding with such a relieved sigh that he might well have been rescuing her from a dungeon and not her own future home.

When they were gone, she turned to confront their host. 'Are you sure that was wise?'

'Allowing my best friend to escort my fiancée on a tour of the grounds?'

'Some might say you are too good a friend in return,' Amy said. 'He was your rival before the engagement.'

'As was every other man in London,' Ben responded.

'But none of the other men were such particular favourites of my sister,' she reminded him.

'Perhaps so. But I have faith that he will honour her commitment to me,' Ben said.

It was surprising that a man who seemed so worldly could be so naïve. Amy rolled her eyes. 'You trust him. Very well. But now that she is engaged, Belle should not be cultivating the attentions of other men.'

'You make your sister sound quite calculating, Amy. We both know that she is not.'

'It is not a matter of subtlety,' she said. 'It is quite the opposite. She barely understands the effect she has on men, much less knows how to use it. It is why I have been guarding her so closely.'

'And now it will be up to me to protect her,' he said with a sigh.

Which meant that her job was ending. What would Belle do without her help? And what was left for her, if there was no Belle to give meaning to her life? She could imagine nothing ahead but emptiness. 'I do not think she is ready to be married,' she said. 'Many things have changed for her in the last week.'

'For all of us,' Ben agreed.

As far as Amy could tell, the biggest change was that they were all less happy than they had been. 'I have been trying to explain things to her,' she said. 'I must make her understand that you will be good to her and that what is happening is for the best. But until she is used to the idea of your marriage, it is best not to give her false hope.'

'Is marrying me really such a repellent prospect?' For a moment, he sounded genuinely hurt.

'You know it is not that,' she said softly.

He nodded and turned toward the stairs. 'Let me show you to your rooms. Then you may go and retrieve your sister from the dangerous Mr Templeton.'

He was treating the situation as a joke. She opened her mouth to tell him so and to make him understand the risks involved with leaving Belle alone, even for a moment, with a man who could no longer be trusted.

And then she reminded herself that it was no longer her business. Belle did not want her help, nor did Ben. They would have each other, for better or worse, just as the ceremony said. And she would become the spinster everyone thought she already was. With time, her opinions would hold even less value than they did now. In time, they might forget her altogether.

She took a deep breath to banish the self-pity and followed Ben up the stairs to the bedrooms. Her room he called the blue room. It was charmingly decorated and looked out over the garden. She glanced down to see her sister and Mr Templeton in animated discussion next to a plot of rosemary.

'See? They are perfectly safe together.' Ben was standing behind her, looking out as well. He was close enough that his breath stirred her hair as he spoke.

They were together, alone. And her bed was only inches away. She stepped away from the window and went quickly toward the door. 'They are safe together, but we are not.'

He followed her out into the hall, shutting the door behind them. 'I am sorry, Miss Summoner, I meant no offence.'

Of course, he had not. Neither had she. And yet they had been about to forget themselves, just as they did each time they were together. She nodded an acceptance of the apology. 'Show me Belle's room so I might go to the garden and fetch her.'

Before something terrible happens.

At this point, she was no longer sure whose virtue most needed guarding. But it might be best if she stayed at Belle's side for the rest of the visit.

Ben was standing before the next door and removed a key to unlock it. It opened on a room far larger than the blue room beside it, decorated in a cream and gold scheme very like the entryway below. By the size of the large canopied bed and the connecting door on the far wall, it appeared that Belle had been given the room reserved for the lady of the house.

Ben saw her raised eyebrow at the nearness to his bedroom. 'I thought it best that she be given the same room she will inhabit when she comes here after the wedding. I do not want it to seem strange when we...' He faltered as if unwilling to think the next words much less speak them aloud.

When you share a bed.

She did not want to think about it either. The time

was growing near when she would have to explain it all to Belle. And just the thought of that conversation made tears trickle down the back of her throat.

Without another word, Ben removed another key from a ring in his pocket and handed both to her. 'In case you are concerned about the connection to the master suite, here is the only key to it.'

She responded with a solemn nod. 'Thank you, for your thoughtfulness.' She slipped the keys into her pocket. As she felt the weight of them dragging at her skirts, she could not help wondering if either of them opened the door to his room as well.

Chapter Seventeen

The evening was as perfect as he'd promised it would be. Despite the fact that there was no lady of the house to see to the menu and the decorations, the ballroom was charmingly arranged and the supper delicious. He had hired musicians from London who performed in all of the best households.

The guest list included half a dozen couples along with John, Templeton and the Summoners. It was almost too intimate to be called a ball. But for Belle's first visit to his home, it would be better to start small.

He had done well.

And beside him, staring at the room in wonder, was his reward. Arabella Summoner wore a gown the colour of a maiden's blush. The sheer muslin was bound by gold cords that crossed between her breasts. A matching gold cord wound through her fair hair. She was a goddess come to earth, so beautiful it hurt to look at her.

Her sister was a much more cerebral deity, an

Athena to her sister's Aphrodite. She'd dressed in warm brown silk, a colour that hardly seemed festive enough for such an occasion. But when she turned to look at him, he saw that it matched her eyes. The gold of the locket at her throat echoed the light shining in them. Tonight, there were no plumes or braids to spoil the long, tawny hair and no fan to hide her lovely face. He could stare into that face for ever.

He did not dare to. He dragged his eyes away from her and turned to smile at Belle. 'Is it to your liking?' He waited, breath held, for her answer.

After what seemed like weeks of trying and failing to catch Arabella Summoner, now that he had her, he approached her warily. It was as if she was an untamed cat and he expected to be scratched. It was nonsense. There was not a tamer creature in the room than the woman he was about to marry.

But cats sometimes scratched because of fear. That was what he sensed from her now. At his words, her beautiful head dipped and, though her eyes darted nervously about the room, her smile was as bright as ever. But it was ruined now that he knew how little there was behind the artifice. 'The ball,' he prompted. 'Do you like it?'

'Yes, thank you,' she said, automatically.

'We will be expected to dance the first waltz,' he said, offering her his arm.

Her head tipped to the side.

'You have not waltzed?' Of course she hadn't. She was young and it was still too improper for the likes of Almack's. He gave her an encouraging smile. 'I will teach you. It is a very simple dance.'

'I like to dance,' she said. He had begun to think it was as much a ruse to hide a lack of conversation as a statement of truth. But at least she was not as blunt as she had been that afternoon. Perhaps she was growing accustomed to him.

'So your sister says.'

Belle gave him another worried look. 'She says I must obey you in all things.'

'That is the way marriages usually work,' he said, surprised that he would have to explain it. 'If Amy marries, she will obey her husband, just as you should.'

'She will not like that,' Belle said. 'Amy likes to give orders, but she does not take them well.'

He could not help himself. He laughed. 'You are wiser than they give you credit for, Arabella.'

'Thank you,' she said automatically.

'And you must try not to worry too much about our future together.' He would do all the worrying for both of them, just as Amy had done. 'For now, all I require of you is a dance.' He took her hand to lead her to the centre of the room. 'Here. Let me show you how to waltz.' He lifted her hand in his and put his other hand on her waist.

She stared down at it as if trying to decide whether this was an actual dance, or a trick to make her behave improperly.

'Now you put your hand on my shoulder.'

Her touch was tentative as she rested it there, but at least they were positioned correctly.

'Watch my feet. Step, step, step. Step, two, three. Do as I do. But with the other foot. My right, your left.'

They managed a few tentative steps in harmony with each other and he gave her another smile. 'Very good.'

She smiled back at him with a relieved sigh, then tried to detach her hand from his.

He shook his head. 'Now we will dance around the floor in a circle.' He nodded to the musicians, and they struck up the first notes of the Sussex Waltz. When she did not immediately follow his lead, he set them off with a rocking first step that would have been more appropriate in a polonaise than a waltz.

She succumbed to the momentum of it, only to falter again as he made the first part of a turn. Though he had thought it instinctive, apparently the process was more confusing than he'd assumed. Or perhaps he was not a very good teacher. She was pressing back against his hand instead of yielding to its direction and they faltered on another step before finding the rhythm again.

They managed quite well for a few measures and he was beginning to hope that the worst was over. But then, other couples came to the dance floor to join them. Her head tipped again, a posture he was beginning to recognise as confusion, rather than flirtation.

It should not have surprised him that the new pattern was baffling to her. When one was accustomed to dancing in matched lines and staying with the set, a jumble of bodies making lopsided circles within circles must seem like nonsense.

She was fighting against his lead again, trying to see what was happening around her rather than letting him do the watching. The ribs beneath his hand felt as immovable as corset bones, though he was sure under her delicate gown there could be but the most cursory of stays.

It was all the more annoying to see Templeton pass them in a graceful spiral with Amy in his arms. They danced so naturally they might have been created as partners like Meissen figurines come to life. The sight should not have annoyed him. They were nothing more than close friends enjoying the hospitality of his home. Their smiles were a sign of his success. And success was what mattered after all. It was why he was going to marry a woman he did not love who did not want to follow his simplest instructions.

You must be patient with her.

It was Amy's voice in his head, reminding him that this was to be his life, from now on: one part husband, one part father, one part teacher. He had no right to be frustrated if Belle could not keep up. He would need to slow down and help her.

Templeton was about to pass them again. Instead, he paused with a smile. 'Might we change partners, Lovell? It seems forever since I've spoken to Miss Arabella, and I have not had the opportunity to congratulate her on the nuptials.'

'You spoke with her just this afternoon,' Amy said, eyes narrowed. 'You had ample opportunity for felicitations then. Besides, I do not think changing partners in the middle of a dance is allowed.'

Which was better: a woman who had trouble following instructions or one who refused to do so? He had told Amy not to fuss over Templeton and Belle, but she could not seem to let it alone.

It was either that, or she preferred to partner with Guy instead of him. Were both of the Summoner girls so afraid of him that they could not dance him? It was one thing to keep a safe distance and quite another for Amy to be appalled at the idea of his touch. He smiled stubbornly at her. 'As host and hostess, the rules are what we wish them to be. And I say we should switch partners.'

Apparently, his fiancée wanted to obey him, after all. By the time he looked to Belle for her opinion, she was already stepping clear of his embrace and holding out her arms to Templeton. In a show of propriety, he held her more loosely than Ben had done. Perhaps that had been all that was necessary. The pair of them set out together as gracefully as Guy had danced with Amy.

Ben stared after them for a moment, annoyed. Then he heard the sound of a clearing throat about the level of his first waistcoat button.

When he looked back, Amy was staring at him expectantly. 'Are we going to dance? Or are you going to wait until they come round again so you might trade back and be rid of me?'

'I apologise.' He scooped up her hand and they set off, spinning easily about the room. 'I was just noticing that Templeton is a better dancer than I am.'

'As someone who has danced with you both, I beg to differ,' she said. 'But if it improves your mood to have me abuse you on the subject, I will be happy to accommodate you.'

'That will not be necessary,' he assured her, irritated that she might be right about Templeton and Belle.

It was some comfort to find he had no trouble at all dancing with Amy. She responded effortlessly to his guidance, matching him step for step. 'You are an excellent dancer,' he said, trying to focus on the steps and not the nearness of her.

'A better dancer than my sister?' she said in a dry tone.

'She was unfamiliar with the waltz,' he replied.

'She does well enough with your friend,' Amy goaded. 'In the future, perhaps you will take my advice and be less eager to push her into his arms.'

'Don't be so dramatic,' he said, glancing across the floor to see Belle laughing in the arms of his best friend. 'One last dance is hardly a reason for concern.'

'Are you sure it will be the last?' she said. 'You are neighbours, after all. She will see him again.'

Of course she would. Templeton dined here once a week, at least. If Ben stood for office, with or without Summoner's help, he would not have the time to guard his wife.

'You are beginning to see the problem,' Amy said, nodding in satisfaction. 'You heard her today. She views you as a stranger. As such, she feels no real loyalty to you. But after Vauxhall, we both have reason to distrust Mr Templeton.'

'I am sure they are guilty of nothing more serious than a few kisses,' he said.

'Some might say the same of us,' she reminded him.

It took nothing more than the mention of what they had done to send a rush of blood through his body, stirring the desire that had lain dormant. The woman he wanted was already in his arms. It would take nothing more than a tightening of arms to pin her body against his.

And Summoner's horrible suggestion whispered at the back of his mind. He could keep them both. One for his mind, his heart and his body, and the other for the illusion of perfection that his future demanded.

Belle would not expect fidelity. Neither should he. What did it matter whose arms his wife slept in, while he was lying with another? If they could not all be happy, there was no reason that they might not at least be physically satisfied.

It might not have been the marriage Miss Arabella imagined for herself. But that was because she was a naïve child and her sister was not much better. But it would not take so very much to kill their innocence and bring them both to their senses, so the four of them could live comfortably.

Most importantly, a man could not let his life be ruled by romantic nonsense, if one intended to do great things. Humans, both the male and the female, were nothing more than animals. They had an animal's desire to rut and breed. Only when that biology was appeased could the mind be free for higher thoughts.

He stopped, dead in the middle of the dance floor, disgusted by his own thoughts. But they were not *his* thoughts at all. *He* knew that humans were imbued with divine virtues: reason, honour and temperance. They were what separated a man from a beast.

Ben knew that. But old Cottsmoor hadn't. He had spent half his life trying to escape the worst of that man's teachings. Tonight they had all come back at once, ready to claim his soul.

'Mr Lovell?' Amy was staring up at him in confusion, waiting for him to move. When he did not she whispered more urgently, 'Ben?'

'Excuse me.' He dropped her hand and released her, walking from the room without another word.

Chapter Eighteen

Amy stared at the canopy over her bed, trying to forget the evening she had just endured. The days leading up to the trip had been difficult enough, what with Belle's sudden change of disposition. Relocating her and presenting her with this *fait accompli* of a marriage complete with house, servants and friends in the peerage had only made it more complicated.

When Amy added the feelings she held for the host, her troubles multiplied exponentially. But really, it had been going quite well, all things considered. Other than that brief moment of temptation while looking out the bedroom window, she'd been the picture of decorum. For a moment, while they'd been dancing, she had actually convinced herself that something like a normal friendship might be possible.

They had been talking. It had been their usual, squabbling banter. Then, with no explanation, Benjamin Lovell had gone mad. There was no other way to explain it. He had stopped dancing. Instead of laughing away the pause, he'd stood stock still for almost a minute and grown so distant that she feared she might be witnessing the beginning of an apoplexy.

With even less warning, he had come back to himself, offered the briefest apology and abandoned her on the dance floor. His behaviour had been so bizarre that it took a moment for her to notice her own humiliation.

She was standing alone in the centre of a crowded room, staring after him. It did not take long before the other dances stopped as well. And then the music stopped and the whispering began.

Lovell had been dancing, not with his fiancée, but with her sister. The first dance was not even finished. What had he said? What had she said? What could possibly have happened to bring about such a bizarre turn of events?

When Mr Templeton noticed what had occurred, he went to search out his friend and demand that he attend to his guests. He returned a short time later to whisper that Mr Lovell had shut himself up in the library with the brandy bottle and would not be returning.

Showing surprising presence of mind for one so young, Cottsmoor announced that the host's indisposition was no reason that the rest of them could not still enjoy themselves. He demanded that the musicians begin again and partnered Belle at the head of the set for Brown's Reel.

Her sister was delighted. She was also the only one who did not seem at all concerned by her fiancé's absence. But her renewed vivacity was enough to keep the male guests on the dance floor and the evening was salvaged.

Tomorrow, perhaps Amy could find Ben and scold him for acting the fool. He'd got exactly what he'd wanted, after all. Though it gave her no real pleasure to be proven right, she had told him from the first that it would never work. If he had refused to listen, he had no right to complain.

Belle would learn to adjust. Despite her nonsensical worries about the whiteness of the walls, she could be happy here. It was a beautiful house, modern and well attended. The servants seemed nice, as well. Perhaps they would recognise the deficiencies in their new lady and fill the gaps themselves. In a place like this, Belle could find a way to manage without her.

The thought brought another swirl of emotions. After a lifetime together, she was about to be parted from the sister she loved. She should not be feeling relief that someone else would be taking over the burden of care. Belle could not help how she was. And what good did it do Amy to be set free when no one was left who wanted her?

She should be happy that Belle was to be married and not jealous. This was no different than those childish tears she'd shed when her baby sister had got a toy that she desired, even though it was clear that Belle lacked the ability to appreciate it. It had been unworthy.

But, no. This was worse. They were both full grown and the man she wanted for herself had been handed over to her sister. Amy was left to help them start a life together, before stepping demurely out of the way.

There was a limit beyond which sisterly devotion could not pass. She had always imagined that it would be death. That their final parting should be because of a man was something she had never suspected.

In the darkness, she heard the hall door open and close again. She did not know whether to pray it was him, or pray it wasn't. She held her breath until his silhouette hovered over the bed.

'What are you doing here?' she whispered, even though they both knew.

'I came to apologise,' he said.

'Then you may do it in the morning,' she said primly, pulling the covers up to her neck. 'When you do not reek of spirits.'

'In the morning, I will not have the nerve to say what needs to be said.'

'Your cowardice is not my concern,' she said.

'So says the woman who used to hide behind her fan each time I spoke to her,' he said and sat down on the edge of her bed.

'What good would a few ivory sticks do me, if my closed bedroom door did not stop you?'

'It was not locked,' he said.

To this, she had no glib riposte. She had not locked it because, in her heart, she had hoped he would come to her, just as he had. 'Then state your business and leave,' she said.

'First, I must tell you that, on the day your father sent for me—'

'And what day was that, precisely?' she said, in no mood to hear about men and their plans.

'The day after Vauxhall,' he said, with a trace of impatience. 'I—'

'He sent for you?' She sat up in bed, trying to see his face in the dim light.

'He invited me to your house,' Ben said. 'I assumed he had heard what we had been up to, the night before. I was prepared to offer. But—'

'Offer? For me?' All this time, she'd assumed he had come to carry out his original plan without a thought to the kiss they'd shared.

'If you insist on interrupting, I will never be able to finish,' he reminded her.

'Very well, then.' She gestured to cede him the conversation, then bit her lip to keep from interrupting again.

'I came to your father, ready to make amends. And when he began talking of a betrothal, I assumed…' Now he was the one to pause. 'We were talking at cross-purposes. He kept insisting that you had no interest in marriage, especially not one he might sanction. And before I knew it, I was engaged to Belle.'

No matter what his original plans had been, he had not been the instigator of the sudden and bloodless engagement. Why had she not recognised her father's hand in it, from the first?

'And now you must think me an idiot,' he said with a sigh. 'But you must believe me when I say, it was you. It has always been you. I did not want it to be. But it has been you from the first moment I looked into your eyes at Almack's.'

And even though she knew she should send him

away, she held out her arms and he came into them, burying his face against the side of her neck to kiss her pulse. 'I had plans,' he said, with a shaky laugh. 'But they are a handful of dust, compared to how I feel, when you are in my arms.'

'How clever of you to notice now that it is too late.' She wanted to be as sharp and cutting as she had been in their first meetings. But what was the point? There was no fight left. She had lost. She ran her fingers through his dark hair, urging him on, even as she knew she should push him away.

'It is not too late,' he argued. 'Tonight, as we danced, I realised that I cannot go through with a loveless marriage to your sister. It is not fair to her, any more than it is to us.'

To us.

Only two words, and yet they were even more seductive than his kisses. She must ignore them.

'And what will become of her, if you cry off? The scandal will be on her head more than yours.'

'She will not be hurt,' he whispered as his fingers twined in her hair. 'I promised your father that and I promise you the same.'

'How will you accomplish it? And even if you can, what am I to do about Belle? Someone must care for her, no matter what happens. She is my baby sister and she needs my help.' Should they decide to marry, if that was what he intended for her, taking Belle into their house would be just as awkward as if Amy had tried to live with them. Even if he cried off, there was no way that they could all be free to start again.

Finally, after so many years of being strong, she broke. She had not cried in ages. But suddenly tears were spilling down her cheeks faster than she could wipe them away. She took a breath to gain control of herself and it emerged in a sob.

He needed to go. If he would just leave her alone, perhaps she could still pretend that there was nothing between them. And tomorrow, when the brandy wore off, he would rethink his words and the wedding would go on as planned, with her standing at her sister's side as witness.

But he must not do what he was doing now.

He had climbed into her bed and was holding her racked body to his, kissing her hair and running his hands over her shoulders, trying to soothe the sobs that were coming faster and faster as she finally allowed herself to cry. 'Let it out, my love. It's all right.' He pressed his lips into her jawline and she felt her muscles working against them as she tried to swallow the tears.

'It's not all right.' And she was not his love. She could not be without hurting Belle. She shook her head to dislodge his kiss. 'It has never been all right. Father refused to believe there was anything wrong. I tried to make it seem so, for his sake. For both their sakes. But it has been so difficult. And now?' She gave a helpless flap of her hand. 'This.'

'You are not alone anymore.'

She felt a strange shift deep inside as if, with a few words, he had managed to lift the heavy load that had been weighing on her soul.

'I promised to take care of her,' he said. 'And I will do so to the best of my abilities, no matter what happens.'

Her tears were slowing now and she raised the sheet to dry her eyes. She felt him reach into the pocket of his dressing gown to get the handkerchief he was pressing into her hand. Then he shrugged out of the garment and lay naked beside her.

No matter what happens.

The words sounded ominous. If there was a new plan forming, she suspected she would not like it. But she did not want to think about the future as he rolled to cover her body with his. 'This is wrong.' She made a last, half-hearted effort to push him away, but he held her fast.

'It is not prudent. But it is not wrong,' he said. 'In fact, it is the only right thing in the world.'

'You are only telling me what I want to hear,' she said. And doing what she wanted him to do. Beneath the hem of her nightgown, his bare legs tangled with hers. Warm arms were wrapped around her body and she could feel every muscle. Her cheek rested against the smooth skin of his shoulder. The feel of so much flesh pressed to flesh made her dizzy with desire.

'Do you want to hear that I love you?' he said. 'Because I do. And I never wished to love anyone, ever again, because it hurts.'

He was right. It did. Though her body rejoiced, her still heart ached.

'Please,' he said softly. 'Let me know you, even if it is only for one night.' The words sounded like goodbye. And if they were, this could be their last chance to be together.

Without another thought, she turned her face to his and kissed him, open mouthed and hungry, letting passion burn the pain away. When they broke, minutes later, they were both panting, eager to be as one.

'I was lost from the first moment I saw you,' he said, reaching down her body and stripping away her nightgown to leave her as naked as he was. 'Those incredible eyes. One look and I was yours. I will never be free of them.'

That was good. She did not want him to be free. She wanted him to be hers. Though they were in darkness, she saw into his heart and was not afraid. His hands were stroking her breasts and she could not keep from moaning at the pressure of his fingers. The eager sound came from an untouched place, deep within her.

He reached between their legs, rubbing her until she was wet for him. His hands on her were rough and hurried, but she did not mind. She ached with wanting him. The punishment of being without him could only be relieved by an equally punishing joining.

She raked her fingers down his sides, scraping her nails down his flanks until she could reach no lower. Then she brought them back up again to the crease at the back of his legs, clutching the tight muscles of his buttocks as they tightened for the first thrust.

And then he was inside her and she would never be alone again. He was hard as stone, stretching her body to the point of pain, but it did not matter. As he pounded into her, she sank her teeth into his shoulder to muffle the cries of desire. She wanted to mark him, to claim him as he was claiming her so that no other woman could have him without knowing that he belonged to someone else.

Perhaps it had been too much. He withdrew suddenly, leaving her empty and longing. Then he grabbed her again, rolling her, arranging her body as if she was a puppet and he her master. He pushed her up on to hands and knees, then grabbed her waist to steady her and took her from behind, like an animal.

He hunched over her and one hand wrapped around to stroke her in time with the short, sharp pumps of his hips. A final touch and she surrendered to him, totally and completely, her overwhelmed senses making her shudder with relief as he surrendered in return.

She collapsed forward on to the bed and he followed her down, on top of her, inside of her, part of her. Then slowly, they rolled to the side, skin to skin, his arms wrapped around her and a leg slung over her hip. Thus, they drifted towards exhausted slumber, nestled together, tight as spoons in a silver drawer.

Chapter Nineteen

$\mathcal{B}$en lay in bed watching for a change in the darkness of the room. Soon, it would go from pitch black to coal. Then the beginnings of grey would creep in at the edges of the curtains. Before that happened, he would need to be gone. He could not be seen leaving her room when the first servants woke to begin their duties.

It was as good a day as any to destroy a man's reputation. But the woman involved…the women, he corrected…must remain as near to untouched by scandal as he could manage.

Amy was beginning to stir as well. They had made love once more during the night, slowly, quietly, each knowing that this might be the last time. When they slept again it was side by side. The distance between their bodies was slight, no more than an inch. But to Ben it already felt oceans wide.

He could feel her beside him, pretending that she was still asleep. But her tiny hand rested against his chest with too much weight to do it unconsciously. She was trying to bind him to her not with strength, but with the weight of her longing.

It was an interesting feeling. Women had held him in bed with tears, both of sadness and rage. He'd been seduced, threatened, begged and, on one particularly memorable occasion, restrained by ropes. But he had never felt such hesitant need. It was like a flower trying to hold on to the sun. To know that such a fragile creature depended on him for happiness made him feel strong, invincible to an almost godlike degree.

He wished it could never end.

Her head rested in the hollow of his arm. He could see her eyes were open now. There was a glitter of wetness on the lashes, as the first hint of daylight touched them. She reached up to stroke his cheek. 'You love me, do you not?'

He could see the lines of her face now, so classically pure in form that he could barely stand to look at them. She was beautiful. Not the equal of Belle, but her superior. Why had he not noticed before, when there had been more time?

It was the eyes, he suspected. He'd been so caught up in their appearance that he'd never looked past them to the woman within. While Belle might have a sweet soul, it was childlike and untouched. But Amy had seen things and known them and been marked by them. She was ageing, like wine, and he longed to drown himself in her.

'If you do not love me,' she whispered, 'then lie to save my feelings. I will not feel so foolish, then.

I will tell myself it could not be helped because we were in love.'

Light or dark, perfect or ugly, she had not changed from the first day he met her. He laughed. 'You are not supposed to suggest such things. It is unfeminine.'

'To request that you lie, or to pretend to believe you when you do?' she asked.

'Either, I think,' he said. 'And I am finished with lying, for all the good the truth is likely to do me. I love you, Amelia Summoner.'

'Says a man who has no heart.' She sighed.

'It must have grown back, but it is beating as if it might break.' He covered her hand with his and moved it so she could feel the thumping in his chest. 'I love you,' he said again, enjoying the sound of the words.

'And I love you,' she said, nestling closer to him. 'Why does this not make everything easy?'

'If we were the last people on Earth, it would.' He laid a hand on her bare hip, wishing that there were more time so that he might love her again before they had to part.

'Go to my father and tell him you cannot marry Belle. You must—' She stopped suddenly, as if realising that she could not be the one to demand a proposal, she could only agree to it.

He thought of the destruction it would bring to his reputation and to Belle's should he cry off. The idea fascinated him. To be able to stand in the ruins of his old life and start again. 'If I left her, would you be there, waiting for me?'

'I could not love a man who hurt her,' she said without hesitation.

'So, your answer is no.' He felt another part of him break. 'You do not have to worry. There will be nothing left of me to marry. If I break the engagement, your father swears he'll ruin me.'

The sweet woman in his arms let loose with a most unladylike curse.

He laughed, in spite of himself. 'He wanted to protect your sister. He was afraid, once I knew about her, I would abandon her.' The oath to Summoner was a growing weight in his gut, crushing the air from his body and ruining the moment. But, at least, now he understood the need for it.

Swear that you will never hurt my daughter.

Amy could fend for herself, but Belle needed protection.

'If either of you had listened to me in the first place...'

'You were right, all along,' he agreed.

'It would be better to be happy than right,' she said.

It was true, but it did no good to think about it. 'I swore,' he repeated. 'And it would be better if my word had any value. But it does not. No matter what I swore, I cannot follow through on it.'

'If you jilt her, she will be ruined as well.' Amy's voice was bleak as she realised the truth.

'It would be even worse should I cast her off to marry you,' he agreed. 'But there is a way out.'

For some of us, at least.

'Let us take it, whatever it is,' she said hurriedly.

'First, I must tell you a story.' And he had best do it quickly. The room was getting lighter by the minute. 'Once upon a time, there was a foolish young man…'

'Do I know him?' she asked playfully.

She still had hope that the ending was a happy one. He swallowed the shame that welled in his throat and went on. 'He was the son of a cabinet maker. His father died leaving him without money or prospects and a widowed mother to care for.'

She made no answer in response. It made him wonder if a horror of such an ordinary birth had stunned her to silence.

'Then, one day, a beautiful and powerful woman caught sight of this young man…who was little more than a boy, really…' Seventeen had been old enough for some things. Wisdom was not one of them. 'And they entered into an arrangement.'

'Who was the lady?' It was barely a whisper.

'You will know the truth soon enough.' He tightened his hold on her hip, waiting to see if she shrank from his touch.

She did not pull away.

'And you and she…'

'I came to help with the apple harvest,' he said, 'hoping to be paid in windfalls.' His mind wandered back to the distant autumn day he'd first seen Cassandra. 'She was taking an afternoon ride, when she saw me.' And he had seen her, golden in the slanting sunlight. The memory of it still made his body quicken after fifteen years.

'You must have been very handsome,' Amy murmured, as if she could picture the scene herself.

'And she was very beautiful. I loved her,' he said. It had been true, at first. 'I could not help it. She was magnificent. Charming and witty and not too many years older than I. And there were advantages to the arrangement.' Other than one that his loins had noticed from the first.

'You were not educated abroad,' she said, her voice flat.

He laughed in surprise. 'If that is what you take from my confession, you are very innocent indeed. No, I was not formally educated, in this country or another. But it is amazing what can be accomplished when one wishes to impress a woman and has access to a library.' He could still remember those early days, alone with all those books and the feeling, almost like hunger, for all the things he did not know.

'I read,' he said, simply. 'And I questioned. And then I read some more. But there are still so many questions left unanswered. Why are some men dukes, and others common? Why do some men make the laws when others can only be punished by them? The system is not ordered by their innate wisdom or lack of it. I have seen that it takes little more than a decent tailor and a set of proper manners to pass amongst the upper classes unnoticed.'

'But people think you are Cottsmoor's son,' she said, obviously still stunned.

For a moment, he wondered if she meant to cry out the truth and see him cast down into the depths that had been his future, to work with his hands and keep his eyes and mouth tightly shut so that he might not upset a divinely ordained system. 'It began as a joke between the Duke and his wife,' he said. 'He said I was there so much, I might as well be family. To spite him, she told someone I was his son. To spite her in return, he agreed and encouraged me in my studies.'

'He knew about you and...'

'...his wife,' Ben finished for her. 'He did not care. They loathed each other. Cottsmoor and I became quite good friends. But the better he liked me, the more she hated us both. And yet, she did not want to let me go.' And then it had been too late for him to get away. 'My love for her died, long before she did.' He had stared down into the grave and felt nothing but relief.

'By then the world was convinced that you were a duke's son. You acted like one, at least.'

He shrugged the shoulder that supported her head. 'I am sorry to disappoint. But it is better to be thought a bastard than known as a paid satyr to a lady of importance.'

'And the resemblance between you and the Duke?'

'Purely coincidental,' he replied. 'But my family has lived on the Cottsmoor lands for generations. It is possible that a previous duke hid a natural son close by and there is some distant blood connection.'

'And he encouraged you to exploit it,' she said and then fell into silence.

'If he'd thought I could carry it so far, he'd have been just as likely to see me swing at Tyburn. But he is not here and I am.'

'And planning to stand for office,' she finished.

'After a long acquaintance with a member of the House of Lords, is it so surprising that I might want to use the education I gained to see that men like him are not the only ones making the laws?'

To this, she had no response. If this had been enough to shock her, he did not dare tell her the rest of the truth. But he did not want her to be disgusted with him. He wanted to hear her reassurance that it did not matter who he truly was. Could she still love a man who had gained his current life by taking money for the use of his body?

At last, she spoke. 'You said before that there was a way out of our current predicament,' she said, as if his past did not matter to her. 'What did it have to do with what you just told me?'

'I thought it would be obvious,' he said. 'I have given you all you need to betray me. If you go to Cottsmoor village, you will find someone who can corroborate what I have told you and give you some parts of the story I am honour bound not to divulge. I promise, they are more than enough to shock even the most jaded gossip.'

'And what am I to do with this information once I get it?'

He carefully disengaged himself from her caress, threw back the sheet and swung his legs out of the bed. 'Get the whole truth and bring it back to London. Share the news and ruin me. Your father will be forced to break the engagement immediately and Belle will be free.'

'But what about us?' There was a plaintive note in her voice that told him she had still hoped for a future. But when she sat up, it was on the opposite side of the bed, far from him.

He shook his head, wondering if she could see the denial in the dim light. 'The truth will out and I will not have to break my oath to your father.'

Or to Cottsmoor's family.

The thought actually cheered him for a moment. 'And if I am not worthy of Belle, then I am certainly not worthy of her sister. There is no hope for us, my love.'

'But Belle will be free,' she said hesitantly.

'I will marry her, if that is what you think best. And I will care for her, just as I promised. But you have seen her with me. She does not want this.'

'She does not,' Amy agreed.

'If we truly want what is best for her, we should not force her to accept it. Help me to end this farce of an engagement. Ruin me. But what we have…' He shook his head again. 'It is over, my love. Do what is right, I beg you, no matter how much it hurts.'

Then he left her and walked down the hall to his room.

Chapter Twenty

Amy was gone before breakfast had finished, making mock apologies about a sick aunt. She must have explained to her sister, for Belle nodded along with the news as if it was the most natural thing to be left behind in the middle of a family crisis with the man who had walked out on their engagement ball.

He gave her a reassuring smile across the table. 'She will be back soon.'

'Because we do not have an aunt,' Belle said quietly. 'Once she remembers that, she will come back for me.'

'You are probably right. In the meantime, please, make yourself comfortable in my home.' He tried to think of something that might interest her. 'There is a fresh litter of pups in the stables. I am sure none of them is as nice as Mellie, but they might welcome a visit.'

She smiled and rose from the table. 'I will go see them directly.'

Now there was nothing left for him but the waiting. Amy would find the truth and form her own opinions of it. Then, if she was wise, she would do what he hoped and spread the news about London, bringing a halt to this foolishness.

If she broke the scandal, she would be seen as the brave rescuer of her sister. Belle would have survived a narrow escape from a duplicitous villain and not become the cast-off goods of a gentleman. The result would be the same. But in society, appearances were everything. At the end of the day, Arabella must be blameless.

When he looked up, young Cottsmoor was standing in the doorway of the breakfast room, hands closed into fists and held out before him. Slowly he opened them, revealing the black and white kings of the library chess set. His expression turned hopeful.

Ben pointed to black, as he always did, and smiled back. Then he led the way to the library.

'You will regret giving me the advantage of the first move,' the boy said with a grin, once the door was closed. 'I have been practising since the last time we were together.'

'I am glad to hear it, Your Grace,' he replied. 'If only for the sake of the country. We need clever men to lead us.'

'Thank you, Mr Lovell,' he said and broke out in snorts of laughter. 'Can you not call me John, like you used to?'

Ben smiled. 'It would be a great insult for me to be so informal, Your Grace.'

'I promise not to chop off your head, or whatever I

am supposed to do to people who do not behave.' He moved a pawn tentatively forward.

'Ask your uncle. I am sure he will have the answer,' Ben said.

'He would say you should be whipped,' the boy said, sounding slightly worried.

'Because he does not like me,' Ben agreed.

Stay away from the boy. Now that Cassandra is dead, you have no business with the family, you worthless cicisbeo.

Ben's lips thinned in a bitter smile. Dislike was too mild a word to describe what old Cottsmoor's brother felt for him. But it did not matter. They were only words, after all. He'd heard worse than that from Cassandra, towards the end.

He stared down at the board. It was clear that what had seemed a hesitant beginning had been a ruse to draw his knight. He countered and took a pawn.

'Then I will not tell Uncle when I visit with you. And I insist, as Cottsmoor, that when we are alone, I will be John and you will be Ben, just like it used to be.' The boyish laughter had disappeared and the Duke stared coldly into his eyes, demanding obedience.

'Very well, John,' said Ben with an impressed nod. 'You are becoming quite intimidating.' Though still a cub, he was definitely a lion in the making. And the cub had just taken his bishop.

'In a few years, I will care for nothing and no one,' John answered in a surprisingly adult tone. 'I will think no further than my own pleasure, just like the last Cottsmoor.'

'You will not,' Ben said, in a tone just as imperious as the boy's had been. 'You will think of your King, your country and the needs of its people. The Dukedom is a reward for the honourable service of the first Cottsmoor. His successors should prove themselves worthy by their actions.'

'That is not what the last Cottsmoor would have said,' John said. 'Not to me, at least. He was too busy doting on the heir.' Anger made John reckless. He had exposed his queen.

Unfortunately, what the boy said was true. The Duke had doted on his first son to the exclusion of everyone else. Though John had been born into the most privileged of lives, the loneliness of his years was still sharp in both their memories. 'Cottsmoor had his reasons.'

John responded with a grim smile, 'And if he can see me now, he regrets them.'

'As do I,' Ben said softly. 'I know how difficult it can be to have no father.' And yet he did not know at all what it must have been like for John. When Ben's own father had died, the loss had nearly crushed him. But it was very different to share a house with one man who refused to acknowledge you existed and another who knew but was forced by circumstances to deny it.

'There was nothing you could have done,' John reminded him.

'I should have found a way,' Ben said. The regret lingered like a bitter aftertaste.

'It was not as if you were allowed in the nursery.'

'It would not have been appropriate,' Ben agreed.

Even Cottsmoor's extreme generosity had its limits. They stopped well short of his wife's paramour dandling infants and playing at peekaboo.

'And you did not leave me,' John reminded him.

He had been young and stupid. But he had known in less than a year that his love for Cassandra was a poisonous thing. As more years passed, even his lust had died. And yet he had stayed with her, serviced her, taken her money and hated himself for it. 'I did not leave you,' he said.

John sensed the moment of sentimental weakness and took advantage, moving his bishop to attack. 'Check.'

Ben laughed and gave him a nod of approval before moving a knight to protect his king. 'But you will be a better duke than he was, because of it. Hardship makes you stronger.'

John sighed. 'Sometimes, I wish I did not have to be quite so strong.' Then he moved his queen and smiled again. 'Check.'

Ben moved a rook. 'You might have to be stronger yet. There is something we must discuss.'

'You mean there is something you wish to say that has not been said,' John corrected, taking the rook. 'Check.'

This time, Ben moved his king. 'Sometimes, you are too smart for your own good. In the near future, you will hear unpleasant rumours about me.'

'And I am not to believe them?' the boy said, contemplating the next move.

'On the contrary, they will all be true,' Ben said.

John's eyes widened in surprise. 'What have you done?'

'Nothing recently,' Ben assured him. 'But Summoner knows I am not your brother. He has threatened to reveal it. Miss Amelia Summoner is on her way to Cottsmoor to talk to my mother.'

'I will make them stop,' John said, falling easily into the role of autocrat again. 'Check.'

'Do not bother yourself.' Ben rescued his king yet again. 'I have decided it is better for all concerned if I call his bluff. One cannot blackmail a man who has no secrets.'

'You will be disgraced,' John said, obviously worried. His attention wavered and Ben took his queen on the next move.

'When I am, you must distance yourself from me,' Ben said, though his heart ached at the thought. They'd had precious little time together before Cottsmoor died. Now he would lose the future he had hoped for and any chance to make amends for the past. But there was no alternative. 'I want no stain on your reputation, because of my past behaviour.'

'Do not worry about me,' John said, taking a bishop. 'If Cottsmoor taught me anything, it is that I am far above scandal, even when I am at the centre of it. Pay attention to the game, Ben. Check.'

Ben laughed in surprise and searched the board for his next move. 'I do not know why I worry about you. You have obviously learned to take care of yourself without my help.'

'But I appreciate that you do,' the boy said quietly.

'And I will not allow you to keep your distance to protect me. I have few friends. I cannot afford to lose you.'

'Thank you, John.' He smiled and tipped over his king. 'I see mate in three. An excellent game.'

Pleased, the young Duke nodded. 'Another?'

Ben began to set up the board again. 'You must give me a chance to recover my pride.' As if that was necessary. When he was with the boy, pride seemed to swell inside him like a lump in his throat that sometimes made it difficult to speak. He coughed to clear the roughness from the next words. 'This time, I will take white, since you are near to my equal. But that is no surprise. Your father was an excellent chess player as well.'

'Yes, he is,' John said. 'Yes, he is.'

Chapter Twenty-One

The trip to Cottsmoor took most of the day, what with stops for changes of horses and refreshment. The maid she had brought with her dozed silently in the seat opposite for most of the journey, for she knew well enough not to question the purpose of the trip.

Before she'd left, Amy had gone to her sister's room, shaking her awake. 'Belle. There is something I must tell you.'

The sleepy blonde head rose from the pillow to look at her.

'I need to go somewhere, just for a day or two.'

'You are leaving me alone?' She was instantly awake, staring at Amy in terror.

'Not alone, dear. Your maid will still be with you. And, of course, you can trust Mr Lovell.'

Belle shook her head at this, as though she'd rather do anything in the world other than that.

Amy squeezed her hand. 'Do not be afraid of him. I am going on this journey because he and I discussed your future and how unhappy you are.'

'You told him?' At this, Belle looked even more frightened.

'He understands. And we have found something that will help.'

Belle's eyes went wide. 'Are you going to tell Father? He will be angry.'

'Not yet. When I get back from my trip, in a day, or perhaps two, I will go to him and explain. In the meantime, you must stay here. You must keep my secret until then.'

'A secret?' Belle smiled.

'A good secret.' Amy did her best to smile. 'Now go back to sleep. I will see you again, very soon.'

It had been a lie. There was nothing good about the truths she was going to uncover. What she knew so far was sordid enough. If, as he had hinted, the rest was worse, she did not know if she wanted to hear it.

But the story was fascinating as well. There had been no pride in taking money to do what he had done. But it explained why his current credo was excellence in all things. He had made himself into the man he'd wanted to be and had never looked back.

Now she was entering the sleepy village of Cottsmoor, a place as far as she could imagine from the life that Benjamin Lovell aspired to. It took only a single enquiry at the local inn to learn that Mrs Lovell still lived in a small, rose-covered cottage on the edge of town.

Amy stared out of the carriage window at it, amazed. It was a pleasant little house with a nicely kept garden and a fresh coat of paint on the green front door.

Compared to the house she had just left, it seemed so tiny. Though Ben did not spend lavishly, he certainly had the money to spare something for the woman who birthed him.

But neither did it appear that she lived in the poverty he'd hinted at. Perhaps there had been discreet gifts so that she could live in comfort and safety, even though he was not there to care for her.

She got out of the carriage and went up the neatly swept path, then rang the bell and waited.

A maid opened for her, who took only one curious glance at the Summoner carriage before offering refreshment and directing her to sit in the parlour to await the lady of the house.

When she entered the room, Amy had no doubt that she'd found the woman she sought. Though her hair was silver grey, Mrs Lovell had the same high cheekbones and piercing, dark eyes as her son. But there was also the faint cloud of sadness that she sometimes saw when Ben bothered to lower his guard. There was a wistfulness about this woman that spoke to a lost time that could never be regained.

'Miss Summoner?' Mrs Lovell greeted her with courtesy, but was obviously surprised by an unannounced visit from a total stranger.

'Mrs Lovell.' What was one supposed to say at a time like this? And would his mother even welcome the visit? 'I am a friend of your son.' It was not quite true, but it was ever so much easier than the truth.

But it was enough. Before she could say another word, the woman rushed to her side, reaching to take her hands. 'You know my Benjamin? Do you have word from him? Was there a message?'

The look in response to the slight negative shake of Amy's head was more desperate than she could have imagined.

'It has been so long,' she whispered, closing her eyes, as if in prayer. 'Is he well?'

'He is fine,' Amy added quickly. By the sudden, relieved slump of the older woman's shoulders, it appeared she had been worried that Amy had come to deliver news of his death.

'He is a great man in London. He is welcome in the best homes and has many friends.'

Mrs Lovell squeezed her hands in gratitude, so moved that she could hardly speak. Then she whispered, 'Tell me of him. Tell me everything. When did you see him? How did he look?' She was clearly hungry for any scrap of information.

'I saw him just last night,' she admitted, hoping that her face did not reveal how it had been when they parted. 'It was at a house party in his home in Kew. He is in excellent health, wealthy, well mannered and well respected. He is the most handsome man in London.' And now she had been too effusive in her praise. She wet her lips, embarrassed to go on. 'He is engaged to my sister.'

'Oh.' Mrs Lovell gave her a slow, probing look, as though reassessing everything she had suspected about the visit and Amy's reason for making it. 'But more importantly, is he happy?'

'He's not.' It was the one question she was sure she knew the answer to.

'Oh, dear,' the other woman murmured. 'Oh, dear. I knew, from the first moment that the Duke and his lascivious young wife got their claws in him that it would end in tears.' Mrs Lovell shook her head.

Amy held her hands and led her to sit on the sofa by the fire. 'He has told me only the most basic facts. But he sent me to you to learn the rest.'

'He was a beautiful boy.' She shook her head again. 'He was not even eighteen, when that she-devil first saw him. The Duke was away in London, with friends of his own.' She wrinkled her nose. 'He was no better than his wife and some might say worse.'

'He had mistresses?' Amy said, eyes wide.

The woman nodded. 'And no interest in his duchess after the first boy was born.'

'So she took a lover.'

Mrs Lovell shook her head in regret. 'At first, he would come home from the manor with gold in his pocket and a smile on his face.' Her face contorted with the shame of the memory. 'I took the money he offered. His father died before Ben could learn a trade and left us with nothing. What was I to do?'

'You had no choice,' Amy agreed.

'But then the visits became longer and longer. And when the Duke returned, rather than putting a stop to it, he encouraged it.'

'He befriended him,' Amy said.

'He called him son.' Mrs Lovell's eyes narrowed in loathing. 'Andrew Lovell was a good man. An honest man. When I heard that Ben was claiming that old reprobate as father, I gave him the lecture he deserved. And rather than beg forgiveness for his proud ways, he moved to the great house and did not come back.' By the time she had finished, tears of regret were running down the older woman's face.

'And the Duke allowed him to live there, with his family.' She offered the woman her handkerchief.

'They kept my son like a pet. And when I saw him after that, he was riding through the village in the Duke's carriage, dressed like a gentleman. Or side by side on horseback with that red-headed succubus of a duchess, talking French and laughing at her jokes.' She gave a shudder of distaste. 'No matter how hard he laughed, I could see he was not happy. But when he saw me…' She flinched again. 'He looked right through me.'

'And he did not come home, even after the old Duke died?' He must have known how he'd hurt her. How could he have left his mother to suffer?

She shook her head. 'By then, it was too late. After what they gave him, he was too good to come home to me.'

'I am sure it was not that,' Amy said and paused, remembering the bleakness in his voice as he had told her his story. 'I think he was ashamed.'

'I would have forgiven him for what he had done,' Mrs Lovell said, her lip trembling. 'And I did not care what people might say, when they saw us together.'

'What did they say to you?'

'If they thought he was Cottsmoor's son, then I must have been his whore.'

It was true. While society might forgive a man his natural birth, it was seldom so charitable to the women who bore the bastards. 'Surely, after all this time, the scandal is old news,' she said. Perhaps in this village. But when she told it in London, it would be a nine-days' wonder.

'It has been more than fifteen years.' Mrs Lovell nodded. 'Both the Duke and Duchess are gone to judgement and cannot hurt him, or anyone else, ever again.'

'And their son,' Amy agreed. Then she paused, adding the years in her head. 'You say it has been fifteen years?'

'Or more,' Mrs Lovell replied. 'Would you like to see a picture of my boy? The Duchess had a miniature painted of him shortly after he went to her.' She made a face at the mention of the other woman, but smiled as she reached for the chain around her neck to unfasten it.

'When she died, he mailed it to me.' Now the woman who had raised him lifted her head in defiance. 'He sent me money as well. More than I would ever need. I do not spend it. I do not want money. All I want is to see him once more and to hear from his own lips that he is well.' She shook her head and released a watery sigh as she handed Amy the locket.

She opened it to see just what she had known would be there. At first glance, she would have assumed it was a painting of the young Duke of Cottsmoor. But a closer look proved the young man in the miniature was three or four years older than the Duke. The painter had managed to capture the distant look in the eyes of this boy that she saw in her own beloved Ben.

He had said there were secrets that he was bound by honour not to tell. This was surely what he meant. But was it a secret if the world knew but refused to believe? It did not matter who Cottsmoor's true father might be. The acknowledged son of a duke was the Duke's son, and therefore also a duke. But the embarrassment of rumour might be enough to separate Ben from his young friend for good.

If he lost a son because of her, he could regain a mother. 'He is still just as handsome as this.' Amy handed her the locket back. 'Would you like to see him?'

The older woman stared hungrily down at the picture in her hand as if wishing would bring him live to her doorstep. 'There would be no sweeter gift than to have my boy back,' Mrs Lovell murmured. 'Even if it is only for a little while.'

'Suppose I could give you that?' Amy said, feeling half-hopeful, half-guilty. 'I will take you to him, this very day, if that is what you wish.'

'Please,' the woman said, squeezing the locket tight in her hand.

'We will go as soon as you are ready. But you must do me one favour in return.' Amy held her breath, hating what she was about to do.

'Anything.' Mrs Lovell leaned forward in her chair as if ready to leave with just the clothes on her back.

'When we arrive in London, you must tell my father the story you have just told me. Immediately after, I

will take you to Ben. And then he will take you home.'
He would have to, for it would be too humiliating to
remain in London. Would the woman beside her still
be so eager to go if she knew that their visit might be
the first step in ruining her son's life?

Chapter Twenty-Two

Now that there was nothing to do but wait for his plan to come to fruition, the hours seemed to drag so slowly that the clock might have been standing still. Although what he was waiting for, he was not sure.

It was unlikely that he would hear anything at all until he returned to London at the end of the week. It would take a day for Amy to reach Cottsmoor and another to return to London. Once there, she would learn that her father knew the truth and was not planning to use it. She would have to find another way.

She was sensible enough to take the story to the person who could do the most damage with it. A patroness at Almack's would be an excellent choice. Soon, there would be one of those horrible stories in the papers about Mr L., the late Duchess of C. and the broken heart of the beautiful Miss S. In no time at all, the Summoner family would close ranks against him, and the rest of the *ton* would cast him out.

Was it really so wrong of him to hope that, once she

had learned the whole sordid story, Amy would love him enough to follow him into exile? It was doubtful that she would come back to the man who had supposedly broken Belle's heart. Her first concern had always been for her sister.

No matter what might transpire, he would be the one to hurt her. He was doing the best thing for Belle, just as he had promised. There was nothing left to do but wait for the inevitable.

Thank God, there were no activities planned for the guests today. After his spectacular failure as host on the previous evening, he was at a loss as to how he might recover the goodwill of his friends. In fact, all of them save John could go to the devil. Since John had gone riding after beating him three times at the chessboard, Ben wanted nothing more than an afternoon of solitude.

Perhaps there was a book in the library that was not too melancholy and could fill the last few hours before dinner.

As he opened the door to the room there was a sudden rustling, as though it had taken a flurry of activity to change whatever had been going on into a scene acceptable to prying eyes. Which made him wonder just what he had interrupted, for Guy Templeton was seated on the leather sofa far too close to his fiancée, holding both of her hands in his. The tails of his cravat hung loose down the front of his waistcoat.

Belle's gown and hair were dishevelled and her cheeks were flushed, but it was hard to tell if it was from passion, or simply because she was weeping, openly, loudly and in a most unattractive and un-ladylike way.

'Templeton? Explain yourself.' Ben squared his shoulders, hoping he would not have to challenge his friend because of an unsatisfactory answer. It was even more annoying that his own anger at this scene was little more than a gentlemanly reflex and had nothing to do with any possessive affection for Belle.

'What have *I* done?' Guy looked at him with a frown and raised eyebrow, as if it was possible to lay the tragedy, whatever it was, at Ben's doorstep.

'He wants to go away,' Belle said, with another sob.

Templeton put a consoling hand on her shoulder and glared defiantly back at Ben as if daring him to demand its removal.

'Back home?' Ben said, surprised by her reaction. 'It is hardly the end of the world. He lives less than a mile from here. When you come to live with me, we will visit him often.' Not that it was likely she would be here, once Amy had finished with him.

'Actually, I was thinking of something a bit further away,' Templeton said calmly. 'I have been trying to explain to Belle that Virginia is not something that one can come and go from like taking the mail coach to Bath.'

Now it was Ben who was shocked. 'Are you mad? We are at war.'

'And they are likely in need of soldiers for it,' Templeton said with finality.

'You mean to buy a commission?'

'If that is what is necessary. The alternative is that

she comes away with me to Gretna Green, immediately. But we have not got that far in the discussion because I made her cry with my other plan.' Templeton seemed more frustrated with his own ineptitude than the girl's lack of understanding.

But Belle brightened immediately at being presented with an alternative. 'Then I will go to the Green place with you. Why are we going there?'

'So he can marry you,' Ben said, calmly.

She smiled in relief. 'I would rather marry you than Mr Lovell. Let us go right now, before Amy comes back to stop me.' It did not seem to occur to her that Ben might have reason to stop the elopement, as well.

'I do not know if you can marry me, now that Ben has heard our plans,' Templeton explained gently. 'Our going to Gretna was to be a surprise for him.'

'I'm sorry if I spoiled it,' Belle said, looking truly contrite.

'Do not worry,' Ben assured her. 'I am definitely surprised.' He looked back at Templeton. 'How well do you know Miss Arabella?'

'Well enough that she should not marry anyone but me,' Templeton said, not the least bit contrite. 'We were alone at Vauxhall for quite some time.'

'You did not…'

'I was on my way to offer for her when you delivered your good news on Bond Street.' His friend gave a disgusted shake of his head.

'You should have said something,' Ben replied.

'And you could have noticed the obvious,' Templeton retorted. 'I've spent every spare minute with her since the beginning of the Season. I did not want to state my intentions until I was sure she understood the implications of them. I love her with my whole heart, but I did not wish to rush her into something she did not want.'

'As I did,' Ben said, ashamed.

'But then, when we were alone…'

'Things got out of hand,' Ben finished for him. 'I can understand how that might have happened.'

Templeton nodded. 'I suspect, by your lack of anger with me, that Miss Amelia was in the vicinity when you learned the lesson.'

'We are not talking of me and Amy. This conversation is about you and my fiancée.'

'That is correct,' Templeton replied. 'With her sister gone from the house, I meant to act quickly and convince Miss Summoner to run away with me.'

'I suppose I should be trying to stop you,' Ben said. 'And I will, if the lady is not willing.' He sat down in the chair opposite them. 'Now it is your turn to talk, Belle. Your father wants you to marry me. But he and I should not be the ones to decide. Who would you like to marry?'

Belle bit her lip, as if the mention of her father made her afraid to answer.

'It is all right,' Ben assured her. 'I promised your father on the Bible that I would take care of you and make sure you were always happy. Who makes you happiest?'

She looked immediately to Templeton. 'I told Amy that I did not want to marry you. I wanted to marry

Guy. She said I could not, because he had not asked.' She gave him a hesitant smile. 'And I do not want him to go away. I would be very unhappy if I could not see him any more.'

He looked to Templeton. 'You understand her difficulties and are not concerned with them?'

'She needs patience. Nothing more than that.' Templeton shrugged. 'And I do not claim to be the cleverest man in London as you do. I am happy with her, just as she is.'

Guy smiled at Belle and touched the tip of her nose, making her giggle. 'More than content, actually. I am hopelessly in love with you.'

Ben cleared his throat to remind them that they were not alone. 'I think what I am supposed to do at this juncture is to call you out and put a sword through you.'

'You can try,' Templeton replied. 'But I would rather you didn't.'

Belle reached out to grab his hand and put her body in front of his, to shield him. Then she gave Ben a militant glare that was every bit as pretty as her smile.

He sighed. 'It is a good thing for all of us that I swore to Summoner that I would do what was best and make his daughter happy. I cannot do either of those things by marrying her.' He raised his hands in surrender.

'We have your blessing, then?' Templeton put his hands on Belle's shoulders and pulled her back to his side.

'You do if you go quickly,' Ben said. 'I will give you several hours' head start before I find the note you will be leaving me. I will be too distraught to go immediately to Summoner and will search without success. But her father will have to be told, eventually.'

'There will be a scandal, of course,' Templeton said.

'Surprisingly, not as big a scandal as I was expecting,' Ben said, trying not to smile. 'But the important thing is that Miss Arabella has the husband she really wants.'

Belle smiled at him with the mind-melting brilliance that had attracted all the men in London. 'Mellie is right. You are a nice man. But I am glad I do not have to marry you.'

'And I am glad I do not have to marry you,' Ben admitted. Then he leaned forward to kiss her on the cheek. 'We can be neighbours instead,' he said.

'That will be nice,' she said.

Templeton rose and offered her his hand, pulling her after. 'It is all settled then. Give my apologies to Miss Amelia when you see her next.'

'I will do that,' he said, wondering if, after Summoner heard the news, he would be allowed to see either of the girls ever again.

Chapter Twenty-Three

Pushing the horses to their limit and travelling through the night, Amy and Mrs Lovell arrived back in London little more than a day from the time she had left Ben's house. If the older woman had questions about the need to speak to Amy's father before visiting Ben, she did not ask them. To her, it was but a small obstacle on the trip she had been longing to make.

Only Amy questioned the wisdom of the trip. Suppose her father humiliated the woman with questions about her virtue or tried to pay her to make the truth go away?

As if sensing her worries, Mrs Lovell laid a hand on hers. 'This must be awful for you, my dear. When scandal rears its head, it is difficult to look the beast in the eye. But you must trust me. No matter what is about to happen, it will be better for all involved than doing nothing. Our secrets have been bottled up for far too long.' She finished with an encouraging smile.

Amy took a deep breath and answered with a smile

of her own. Then she ushered the woman into the Summoner town house and made her comfortable in the receiving room before she went to seek out her father.

As usual, he was in his office when she rushed in without introduction, fearing that delay might make her lose her nerve. 'Father—' she leaned over the desk to confront him '—you must end Belle's engagement immediately! I have discovered the unfortunate truth about Mr Lovell. It is all quite shocking. There is a woman here you must speak to, who can verify all I have learned.'

Her father stared across the desk at her, simmering with annoyance. 'Whatever this woman has to say should remain between her and Mr Lovell, Amelia. It is no longer any concern of ours.'

'No concern of ours? Of course it concerns us. He is to marry Belle. She will be ruined.'

'She is ruined already and by her own hand,' Lord Summoner said with a disgusted sigh. 'And nothing would have happened if you had not failed in the one task you were entrusted with. Instead of watching over her, you left your sister alone to go chasing stories that I knew long before I spoke to Mr Lovell.'

'You knew?' It explained why Ben had been unwilling to break the engagement himself. Her father had been using his past against him.

'What I knew is immaterial. What I *did not know* was that your sister would take your unplanned absence as an excuse to elope.'

Amy sat down hard in the chair in front of the desk,

suddenly at a loss. When she could manage to speak, she asked, 'With whom?'

'Guy Templeton. The very man whose case you were pleading the day I promised Belle to Lovell.' Her father's eyes narrowed. 'Did you orchestrate this disobedience? Because if you knew and arranged this trip simply so you would not be blamed...'

'What utter nonsense. You know, Father, that if I meant to disobey you, there would have been no subterfuge involved.'

'I suppose that is true,' he said, after a moment's thought. 'You really are the most contrary creature.'

'And I did know that Templeton was fond of her,' Amy admitted. 'But since the engagement, I have been doing my best to warn her off him. I had no idea that things had progressed so far.'

But she had. Belle had all but admitted the truth to her, and argued for her right to think independently and marry the man she loved. In return she had scolded her and told her the exact thing that everyone else did: that she was not smart enough to know her own mind on the most important decision of her life.

And now Amy did not know whether to be hopeful for Belle or horrified. But she definitely felt ashamed of her own behaviour. 'Is there no chance we can get her to come back?'

Her father shook his head. 'Their absence was not noted for some time. Lovell found a note, explaining their intentions. I suppose we must console ourselves that he means to marry her.'

'Oh.' In either case, Belle had likely spent more than

one night as a woman with no feminine instruction and with only Guy Templeton for company. Surprisingly, the thought did not panic her as it should have. Instead, it seemed more than right. She had a gentle and caring husband to teach her what she needed to know.

Most of her recent advice to her sister had been totally wrong, anyway. Perhaps in this, it would be better to let Belle make her own way. 'I am sure Mr Templeton loves her, Father. And she is very fond of him as well. It will be all right.' Having seen the look in Mr Templeton's eyes as they'd danced, it was obvious that they belonged together, no matter what others might think. Wherever they were now, they were probably quite happy.

'But I do not want Guy Templeton as a son,' her father shouted. 'The man is a ninny. Even worse than that, he is a Whig.' At this, he held his head in his hands, clearly beyond consolation. 'Lovell sent a search party after them, as soon as he knew, but they were too quick. He blames himself, since he was the one who invited that damned interloper into his home. But really, it was all your fault.' He glared at Amy again. 'If you had left well enough alone and watched your sister instead of abandoning her to search for things that did not concern you, this never would have happened.'

Leaving Kew was far from her greatest sin of the week. But if it made her father feel better to blame her, she would allow it, if only so she didn't have to explain herself. 'I am sure Mr Lovell will recover,' she said, trying not to smile.

'Thank you so much for your opinion, Amelia,' he

said, sarcastically. 'But suppose he doesn't? What am I to do to make amends? I promised the man a future in government and the hand of my daughter. I have no idea what to say to him, now.'

'You still have the seats to offer,' she reminded him. 'And you have two daughters.' She regretted the words as soon as they were out of her mouth.

'It is not as if I need to be reminded of the fact. You are standing right in front of me.' By the look on his face, the information was currently an unpleasant truth. 'But we live in modern England and not the Book of Genesis. I cannot exactly throw a veil over you and trade one girl for another like Leban tricked Jacob.'

'You are probably right,' she said with a moue of feigned disappointment. 'Especially since it was your trickery over Belle's engagement that has brought us to this point. I doubt he will trust anything you say, should you try to hand him me as a substitute.'

'Do not be flippant with me, girl.'

In the past, she might have let the comment pass unremarked. Today, she was in no mood to be bullied. 'Do not be flippant. Is that what you said to Belle that left her crying on the day we departed for Kew? She told us both that she did not want to marry him. We have got what we deserved for ignoring her.'

'All I wanted was for her to be safely married,' he snapped back. 'It was my perfectly reasonable hope that one of my daughters would obey me.'

'I will go to him immediately and offer apologies,' she said. And congratulations as well. His reputation had not suffered the blow they'd both expected. 'Where might I find him?'

Her father laughed. 'Am I his keeper? He is not here, if that is what you are wondering. Why would he be? I suspect he has gone back to his rooms to drown his sorrows. The loss of a fiancée to a man who claimed to be his friend was terribly embarrassing, no matter how gracious he pretended to be about it.'

When she collected Mrs Lovell from the receiving room, she could but hope that their raised voices had not carried down the hall from the office. If the older woman guessed any of what had transpired, she gave no sign of it. Nor was she particularly bothered by the fact that they were to go immediately back to the carriage.

When Amy informed her that their next stop was to be the address on Bond Street where her son might be found, she tensed slightly, as if suddenly afraid to do the very thing she had wanted all along. 'Does he expect us?' she asked in a quiet voice.

Amy shook her head. 'But we will not be the first unexpected thing to happen to him this week.' And, even after her father's dire rant on the subject, there was no reason to expect that they would be unwelcome.

They arrived at the building and climbed the stairs to his rooms. There, they were greeted at the door by a manservant who directed them to a small parlour overlooking the street. Mrs Lovell was so fascinated by the crowds of people on the street below them that she did not notice the arrival of her son.

Ben stood in the doorway, staring at the woman on the sofa as if he could not quite believe what he was seeing. Amy waited in silence to see his reaction. Though he had given her the facts she needed to bring this reunion about, he had not requested that she return with his mother and risk tarring her with the brush of scandal.

The lady shifted in her seat, turning to face the door at the sound of his gasp.

'Mother.' For a moment, the reserved façade disappeared and he looked like the young Cottsmoor. He had become a boy again, his desire for independence at war with the urge to return to the comfort of his mother's embrace. Then the Benjamin Lovell she knew returned and he strode forward, pulling the woman out of her chair and enveloping her in his arms, pressing his dry cheek to her wet one, offering comfort instead of taking it.

As he hugged her, his features contorted in pain. Then the expression faded and he was at peace, his eyes closed tight, as if trying to freeze the moment and keep it for ever in memory.

'Benjamin,' his mother sobbed. 'It has been so long.'

'I am so sorry,' he whispered back. 'Sorry for what I said, when we argued. When I left you, I did not think it would be forever. But there was a reason I could not leave.'

'The Duchess,' she said, making a face.

'No.' He leaned close to whisper in his mother's ear.

Her face relaxed in an understanding smile. 'It is hard for a boy to become a man without a father to teach him.'

'A boy needs both his parents,' he said, in a ragged voice. 'A mother and a father. I never should have left you.'

'It is all right,' she said, patting his hand. 'And look at you now.' She held him away from her to admire him. 'Tall and handsome. Wealthy and educated. That is what a mother wants for her son, to see him do well.'

'But I left you behind,' he said, sounding again like the boy she had lost. 'And the things I did to make my future… I am no longer worthy to be your son.'

Amy bit her lip to keep from speaking. He had become so much more than he had been. But, even though he had reconciled with his mother, there were still so many things he could never admit to the world.

'It is all in the past,' Mrs Lovell said in a soothing voice. 'If there is a penance, by now you have paid it tenfold. Forgive yourself as I forgave you, years ago.' Then she kissed him upon the forehead as one might when putting a child to sleep.

His shoulders slumped, but it was in acceptance, not defeat. Then he straightened again, and he seemed even taller than he had been, as if the shame that had weighted him down was gone. When he turned back to Amy, he looked different, as well. The grim determination behind his smile was gone, replaced by a lightness of spirit that she had not seen in him before.

She wanted to go to him, to have him hold her and tell her that his mind was as free as his heart. She wanted to know that he loved her and wanted her, just as he had claimed to before. But now he needed to be with the woman he loved, but hadn't seen in years.

Amy rose to excuse herself. 'You must have much to talk about.' As she turned to go, she kept her eyes downcast, not wanting him to see her longing for reassurance.

'Wait.' He leaned forward to whisper into his mother's ear again and Amy saw her smile. Then he rose. 'Let me escort you out, Miss Summoner.'

She responded with a nod of thanks and an attempt at a smile to hide her disappointment. Was she to be Miss Summoner again?

He laid a hand on her shoulder, shepherding her to the door. 'Thank you.' His voice was warm, friendly. But there was no trace of the passion she had heard in it when last they'd parted.

'I didn't do it to help you,' she reminded him.

'I know. But the reason does not matter. It is the good that that has come from your actions. I, of all people, must believe that. All that has happened has happened for the best.'

'But your son,' she whispered. 'Without knowing, my father might have announced the truth to the world.'

'I have no son,' Ben said, the regret returning to his eyes. 'Cottsmoor did. When he claimed him, I lost all right.'

'But to live a lie...' she said, shaking her head.

'As you did for your sister,' he reminded her. 'It was shared guilt that drew us together.'

'I have no regret,' she insisted.

'But perhaps you should,' he whispered. 'You know now who I really am.' He shook his head in amazement. 'I am sorry for the burden of secrecy I have placed on you, even if it is to one other person. I cannot explain what a gift that it is to have told the truth.'

Words of gratitude were sweet. But they were not what she was seeking from him. Where was the love he'd whispered about in the dark?

Perhaps, as she had always thought, the word meant something different to a man. Perhaps she had misunderstood. Or perhaps she had given him something today that he wanted more than he could ever want her: confession, forgiveness and absolution.

'If it has made you happy, then I am happy,' she said. She loved him. And she had learned from loving Belle that sometimes love meant you wanted the best for your beloved, even if it destroyed your own dreams.

They were at the door now. Only a few more steps until he allowed her to walk away. He paused and she held her breath, waiting for the word that would make her stay.

Instead, he said nothing, and looked both ways to make sure they were not seen before he leaned forward to kiss her on the forehead in a way that was more brotherly than passionate. 'We will see each other soon. Until then, thank you.' He pressed her hand with his to emphasise the depths of his emotion. And then he waited for her to pass through the door so he could close it behind her.

Chapter Twenty-Four

It was another painfully ordinary afternoon in the Summoner home, but with a few major changes. Belle Templeton was visiting her sister and had settled in her usual seat beside the window to make a hash of a lace-trimmed pillow slip. Amy was in her usual seat on the opposite side of the window, ready to rip out the stitches again when it all went horribly wrong.

'I like sewing now,' Belle said with a ladylike nod.

'You do?' Amy looked up in surprise.

'It is a thing that married ladies should like to do,' Belle said. 'So I like it now.' She handed the project to Amy for inspection.

Marriage had not improved her technique in the least. But at least she enjoyed the attempt more than she had in the past. Amy gave her a nod of approval. 'You are trying very hard to be a good wife, aren't you?'

'Guy says I am doing a wonderful job.' Belle leaned forward and whispered, 'There are things that married ladies do that are much easier than sewing and much more fun.'

'That's nice,' said Amy, faintly. 'But I am sure your husband would not want you talking about them.'

'He said I was not to tell you about that time in Vauxhall Gardens,' she said. 'But I am sure, now that I am married it is all right.'

Amy blinked in shock and focused on the needlework in her lap like the proper spinster she'd always claimed she wanted to be. At the back of her mind, she must have known that one day, Belle would outstrip her in knowledge of some subject. Since Belle was to be the one to marry, it was only logical that it would be this one.

There was something deeply consoling about needlework. If one did not care about the results, one did not even have to think while doing the task. At some point, she would look back on today's stitching and notice the unevenness of it. Then she could pull it out and do it again.

But it was no longer necessary to care so much about her work, or Belle's. From the besotted look on Mr Templeton's face when he came to collect her after her visits with Amy, the last thing in the world he cared about was whether his wife could stitch a straight seam.

When she had hinted to him about Belle's need for assistance in the running of the house, he had politely but firmly refused her offer of help. Worse yet, Belle, who had been so dependent on her before, showed no interest in opening her home to Amelia the spinster. Apparently, the happy couple had not forgotten her efforts to keep them apart and no longer required her assistance.

Her sister was happy. That was what she'd wanted, all along. But she had never imagined a future where her own life had passed by unlived while she managed Belle's. And now, without her quiet sister in it, the house was emptier than she could have imagined.

When she glanced up from her work to check on her sister, Belle was staring back at her. 'Are you sad?' She put aside her work basket and leaned forward to lay a hand on Amy's cheek.

Amy forced a smile. 'Do not worry yourself. I am fine.' Belle was happy. She reminded herself of that fact several times a day. She had always told herself that this would be enough. And now to pretend that it was so made her throat tighten.

'Do you want to come with Mary and me to pick curtains for my new house? I think I like blue. Guy says I can have any colour I want.'

'But not white,' Amy said, smiling. 'You are very lucky to have found a man as good to you as Guy.' Then she paused, repeating her sister's last words in her mind. 'Who is Mary?'

'Mary is my new friend. Mr Lovell says she is coming to live with us and help me with the things I do not know about running a house and being a wife. That way, you do not have to.'

'But…' She wanted to live with Belle. It was not a burden. And what else was she to do?

Belle's smile had not dimmed. 'I like Mary. She is very nice.'

'You've met her?'

Belle nodded happily. 'She likes me, too.'

She had been replaced. Amy took a moment to control her temper before speaking. There was no point in being angry with Belle. She could not have known what the news would mean, if Amy had not known it herself until just that moment. 'Of course she likes you,' she said, not losing the smile. 'And I am glad you are happy. Truly, I am.'

'At first, when you said I had to get married and leave home, I was frightened,' Belle said. 'But it is very nice. I like being married. You should do it, too.'

Amy swallowed until she could breathe around the lump in her throat. She had not seen Ben at all since the day she had brought his mother to him. It had been almost a week and there had been no visit, no letter, nor any sign of him at the parties she'd attended. If he felt any of the things he'd claimed to, what had become of him?

It took almost a minute to remember that she had decided years ago that she did not want to get married and was happy with things just the way they were. 'I am far too old to marry,' she said, forcing her smile to be as bright as Belle's. 'And Father still needs me. I shall remain here and take care of him.' Not that Geoffrey Summoner needed caring for. She had never met a more independent man in her life. 'Perhaps I will get a cottage near Mr Templeton's home so I can come to your house in the afternoons, as you do to mine. Then I might help with the mending and other things you do not like.' But the thought of a lifetime spent re-stitching Belle's spoiled hems made her want to weep.

Her plans had not been as noble and selfless as she

had thought them. She had assumed that she would simply follow Belle in marriage. She had wanted to arrange a future that would suit her own needs as much as her sister's. But she had forgotten that even a man as gentle and kind as Guy Templeton might not want to share his life with a sister-in-law who could not be bothered to find a husband.

'I will have Mary and Guy for things like that.' Belle was glancing out the window of the sitting room towards the street in front of the house. Then she leaned forward in her chair, too excited to be still. 'He is here! He has come to take me home.' Now her face lit with a smile that was different from the one she used to wear. There was a warmth and depth to it that had been missing from her childlike joy for parties and dancing.

Belle was in love.

Before she could stifle it, a sob escaped from Amy's lips. It was just as Ben had always claimed. She was jealous of her sister. And she was angry at the fact that she had given so much and, in the end, there was nothing left for her. She had no love of her own and her sister did not need her.

'Don't be sad.' Belle's hand was on her cheek again, her husband's arrival forgotten. 'Guy promises that he will take good care of me.'

Who will take care of me?

Of course, she did not need anyone to take care of her. She was quite capable of making her own decisions and managing her own life. But at a moment like this, she could not help but wonder if it might be nicer not to be so completely independent.

'I will miss you,' she whispered, cupping Belle's face in her palms.

'You do not have to miss me. We can be neighbours.' Belle beamed at her again. 'You must marry Mr Lovell. Guy says he lives so close we can walk there.'

'But…' Was it really necessary to explain, again, that a woman had no power in this? 'I cannot just decide to marry Mr Lovell. He must ask me. And there is no reason for him to do so.' None that she could admit to, anyway. Without thinking, she touched the locket that hung at her throat.

'I know something you don't know.' Belle was trying to look smug as a kitten in the cream. But since she could not manage to stop giggling, the effect was spoiled.

'Not about this, I'm afraid.' Amy pulled Belle's hand from her face, clasping it in her own.

'I know that you like Mr Lovell, even though you pretend that you do not.'

What point was there to lie about it now? 'Yes, I do.'

'And he likes you, too. That is why he's talking to Papa.'

'He's talking…' She paused in confusion. 'When did he talk to Father?'

'He is talking to him right now,' Belle said. 'I saw him come in.'

'You saw him?'

'I have been watching out the window for Guy,' she said. 'And when I saw him on the street…' she pointed towards the front door '…he saw me in the window, and he…' She held her finger up to her lips to indicate silence.

Amy shook her head. Belle was not making much sense. But then, she often got more confusing when there was something important to convey. 'Mr Lovell wanted you to keep his visit a secret?'

Belle frowned. 'Did I do wrong?'

'No,' Amy assured her. 'I am sure he just wished to surprise me.' It was far more likely that he had business with her father and hoped to save them both the embarrassment of a meeting. If he left the house as quietly as he arrived she need never know he had been there.

Belle had no intention of allowing discretion. She stood and tugged on Amy's hand to pull her to her feet. 'You should go to him.'

'No, Belle,' she said quietly. 'I am sure, if he wants to see me, he will come.'

'She is right, Belle. Ben must come to her.' Guy Templeton was standing in the doorway, with Mellie the terrier pulling on the leash in his hand. He dropped the leather strap and the dog ran past his mistress to throw himself on to his favourite spot on the sofa.

'Guy.' Belle dropped her sister's hands and went to her husband, pulling him into the room.

'My angel,' he said, giving her a kiss on the cheek. 'How was your afternoon?'

'I made a pillowslip,' she said. 'It is very bad.'

He looked down at it. 'It is.' Then he whispered something in her ear that made her laugh.

'Templeton.' Their father was standing in the doorway Guy had vacated. He was glaring at his new son-in-law with an expression of thinly veiled contempt.

'Lord Summoner.' Guy looked back at him with a serene smile devoid of offence. He took a step closer to Belle in a subtle display of possession. 'I have come to collect my wife.'

At the last word, Father gave a visible wince of displeasure. 'Then do so and be gone.' He looked at Belle, his gaze softening. 'And if you need to return home, for any reason, you are not to hesitate. I will send a carriage immediately.'

At this, Belle laughed. 'Do not be silly, Papa. If I wish to come here, Guy will drive me in his own carriage. And then he will come to bring me home, just as he is doing now.'

For a moment, their father had the same perplexed look on his face that summed up what she felt about her sister's new-found independence. He gave one more cold glance in Guy's direction and said, 'Very well, then.'

'Very well,' Belle agreed. 'Come, Mellie. We are leaving now.' Guy offered her his arm and escorted her towards the door. But as she passed her father in the doorway, she stopped to kiss him on the cheek.

For a moment, he softened and his hand rose, as if to beckon her back. Then it dropped again and he sighed in defeat.

Mellie sighed as well, hopping to the floor and giving one last, longing look at his cushion before wagging his tail and following his mistress out of the house.

Her father cleared his throat, as if coughing away

the inconveniently soft emotions. 'Amelia. I wish to see you in my study.'

She gathered up her sewing. 'I will be with you momentarily.'

'Now, Amelia. We do not want to keep our guest waiting.'

Ben.

She had assumed he must be gone. But he was in this very house with her, waiting. She stood up so quickly she dropped her workbasket and smoothed her skirts and hair, wishing for a mirror. Then she did her best to walk at a ladylike pace one step behind her father.

But she touched the locket for luck as she did so.

As she entered the room, he rose, turned and bowed. But his face remained expressionless, giving no hint of what was to come. He waited until she had taken the chair on the opposite end of the desk before resuming his seat.

She looked from one to the other, but neither man spoke. The silence drew her nerves to the breaking point, so, she broke it. 'Good afternoon, Mr Lovell. What business did you have with me?'

He showed no mercy and did not answer the question she had asked. 'I came to assure myself that your sister was well and offer my apologies again for what happened in my home.'

'No apologies are necessary,' her father said hurriedly.

Ben held up a hand to demur. 'Despite my efforts to do just as your father wished, my engagement to your sister ended badly. I promised that she would not be hurt and wished to assure myself that all was well with her.'

'I assume you know it to be so,' Amy said, growing impatient. 'For it appears you helped her husband to engage a companion for her.'

'How gracious of you,' her father said, smiling.

'So kind,' she added, 'to make it unnecessary for me to follow her to her new home.'

'It was the least I could do,' Ben said, ignoring the warning glare her father shot her and responding with a modest nod. 'I wanted to be sure my oath to you was properly discharged.'

'Of course, my dear fellow. Any obligation is fulfilled. You have done all you could.'

'But that still leaves the matter of the seat in the Commons we discussed,' Ben added. 'And certain threats that you made against my character.'

'They were not meant as threats, per se,' her father hedged.

'I spoke to Cottsmoor about them. He found them to be most ominous.'

'Cottsmoor?' her father said weakly.

'I believe you said something about biblical retribution, if I failed in my duty,' Ben said quietly.

'Father is a great fan of the Bible,' Amy supplied. 'Especially Genesis. Jacob and Esau. Leban and Rachel...' She gave him a significant look and pretended to veil her face.

'And you did not fail, Mr Lovell,' her father said, ignoring her. 'I have no reason to seek retribution.'

'But that does not reduce the power you have over

me,' Ben reminded him, turning to her. 'And you as well, Miss Summoner. For you took the time to find my mother and verify the truth about my past.'

At your request.

She wanted to shout it at him and end this pointless charade.

'I am sure she meant no harm,' her father wheedled.

'On the contrary, she has been trying to harm me since the first day we met,' Ben said with a laugh of incredulity. 'Spilling drinks. Knocking me off a horse. And locking me in a closet at the Middletons' musicale.'

'That door was not locked,' she insisted, before remembering where she was.

'Amelia!' her father said, obviously appalled.

'In short, I have no reason to trust the pair of you,' Ben finished.

'No more than I trust you,' she said, growing tired of waiting for him to make good on his words.

'But there is no need to involve a peer,' her father said hastily. 'I am sure we can come to a mutually agreeable resolution.'

'I would have more faith in your words if you had as much to lose as I,' Ben reminded him. 'If we were related, by a bond of marriage, as planned? Then the last thing you would want was to see me disgraced.'

The room fell silent and both men looked to her.

'It was never my intention to marry,' she said to her father, trying not to smile at his suffering.

'And I promised that I would not force a husband

upon you,' he replied. 'But for all that is holy, just once would you consider doing what is best for both of us?'

She sighed. 'This is not much of a proposal. You did better by my sister, I think. She at least got a carriage ride.'

'After the preliminaries were settled in this office,' Ben responded. 'And I have not, as yet, proposed to you. You cannot complain about my technique until after.'

'You have my permission and she has not rejected you on principal,' her father said, throwing up his hands. 'You have already got further with her than any other man.'

Ben's next comment was lost in an embarrassed cough. He cleared his throat again and her father reached for the brandy, pouring them both a glass and ignoring Amy's outstretched hand.

'As I was about to say...' Ben glanced in her direction with a polite smile and drained his glass. 'If the lady and I can speak privately for a time, perhaps we can come to an understanding.'

'By all means,' her father said. 'Go to the sitting room and talk for as long as you like.'

Ben rose and preceded her.

When he was out of earshot, her father said in an angry whisper, 'And do not come out of that room until you have said yes. I will lock you in together, if I must. But there will be a marriage and the matter will be settled.'

'I will consider his offer,' she said, trying not to laugh. Then she swept out of the office with the imperious glare of a disapproving spinster. She walked down the hall to the room where her lover waited and shut the door behind them, turning the key in the lock.

He glanced at the handle. 'Are you sure that is wise?'

'It was recommended to me,' she assured him. 'Either we lock it, or he will do it for us.'

'It is always a comfort to have the support of the father when making an offer,' he said, drily.

'It is also necessary to have the support of the woman you wish to marry,' she reminded him.

He hesitated. 'Once, not long ago, I thought I had it. But if, after you know the truth about me, you have changed your mind, tell me now. I will go immediately and speak no more about this.'

'Do not be foolish,' she said, stepping into his arms. 'As your mother said, it was very long ago.'

'And I was very young,' he said, by way of explanation. 'And I thought I was in love.'

'Did she love you in return?'

He rested his chin on the top of her head, holding her close. 'For a time, perhaps. But neither she nor her husband were capable of really loving anyone but themselves.'

'But what of your son?' she pressed, and felt him still.

The look in his eyes grew distant. 'I am honoured to be a friend of the Duke of Cottsmoor,' he said. 'He is a fine boy and will be a fine man.'

'Who will always be welcome in our home,' she finished.

'He is alone now. He needs my...' He paused. 'He needs our help.'

She nodded. 'And we both know how hard it can be to lose a parent.' Then she frowned. 'I have but one question left.' She poked him sharply in the ribs. 'Who is Mary and why is she taking my place as my sister's friend?'

'Mary?' He laughed.

'Mary,' she repeated, not bothering to contain her jealousy of the interloper.

'Mrs Mary Lovell,' he replied.

'Your...?'

'Aunt,' he finished. 'Let us say, for convenience's sake, that she is my aunt. As long as there are people who believe the story about my father the Duke, I would not want my mother to be the subject of speculation. As Belle's caregiver, she will be living a scant mile from my home.'

'Where you can see her whenever you like,' she said, smiling and snuggling back against his chest.

He nodded. 'It is time that I made amends. It will be good as well for Belle to have a new friend. And it will leave you free to marry. You would be living as near to your sister as I am to my mother.'

The arrangement was almost too perfect and she thanked him for it with a kiss that left them both breathless. When they parted, she asked, 'Is the scandal of your changing sisters greater or less than that of my sister's elopement?'

'At this point, there are so many secrets between us, I cannot rank them,' he said. 'I have already procured a special licence. But if you wish to rival your sister, my carriage stands waiting and we can set off for Scotland immediately.'

She thought for a moment, then ran a hand down his chest to press against his heart. 'I think the sooner the better. But choose what you wish. I have strict instructions to say yes to you, no matter what you request of me.'

He froze and she felt the beat against her hand increase. Then his hands on her back strayed lower, well past the bounds of propriety. 'Anything?'

'Anything,' as he pressed her body tight against him.

And now he was walking slowly forward, pushing her towards the sofa in the corner and down until the weight of his body had sunk hers deep into the cushions. 'Then, my dearest Amy, if you don't mind, I think I shall rephrase the question.'

* * * * *

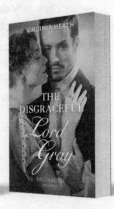